PER WAHLÖÖ

The Generals

Born in 1926, Per Wahlöö was a Swedish writer and journalist who, alongside his own novels, collaborated with his partner, Maj Sjöwall, on the bestselling Martin Beck crime series, credited as inspiration for writers as varied as Agatha Christie, Henning Mankell, and Jonathan Franzen. In 1971 the fourth novel in the series, *The Laughing Policeman*, won an Edgar Award from the Mystery Writers of America. Per Wahlöö died in 1975.

JOAN TATE

Joan Tate was born in 1922 of English and Irish extraction. She traveled widely and worked as a teacher, a rehabilitation worker at a center for injured miners, a broadcaster, a reviewer, and a columnist. She was a prolific writer and translator, well known for translating many leading Swedish-language writers, including Astrid Lindgren, Ingmar Bergman, Kerstin Ekman, P. C. Jersild, Sven Lindqvist, and Agneta Pleijel. She died in 2000.

Also by Per Wahlöö

With Maj Sjöwall

PER WAHLÖÖ

The Generals

A NOVEL

Translated from the Swedish
by Joan Tate

VINTAGE CRIME/BLACK LIZARD
Vintage Books
A Division of Random House, Inc.
New York

FIRST VINTAGE CRIME/BLACK LIZARD EDITION, JUNE 2013

Translation copyright © 1974 by Michael Joseph Ltd. and Random House, Inc.

Library of Congress Cataloging-in-Publication Data for this edition has been applied for.

Vintage ISBN: 978-0-307-74478-4

www.vintagebooks.com

Printed in the United States of America
10 9 8 7 6 5 4 3 2 1

To MAJ

THE GENERALS

On a small island in the temperate zone a court-martial has assembled. Corporal Erwin Velder is on trial for his life. Some of his 127 alleged crimes are military, but others are civil and moral: bigamy, rape and sacrilege. Per Wahlöö's new novel takes the form of the proceedings of the trial, stretching over three months.

It emerges that this trial is of great political importance to the régime. The result is a foregone conclusion: Velder has been prepared in prison by 'specialists' for three years. He is a physical and mental wreck and confesses to all but one of the charges. In reality the court-martial is an elaborate rehearsal of the events of the last eight years. The past and the dead are on trial.

A group of civilised, intelligent men took over the island, we learn, and began to build an ideal state. There were no politics, religion, laws, bureaucracy or taxes. The country was carefully developed and enjoyed great prosperity and general happiness under the loosely exercised authority of the state's founders. After five years the first cracks appeared with a disagreement in the ruling council. Slow disintegration set in: a secret armed force was built up by one of the rulers and eventually civil war broke out. The rout of the liberal party was followed by full-scale fighting between the 'fascists' and the 'reds'.

At the time the action of the book takes place the country has enjoyed, officially, three years of peace after the cease-fire, but in fact the Generals, who rule with an iron grip, are ceaselessly struggling for power with one another. As the inevitable verdict is pronounced on the innocent, unprotesting Velder, the latest coup takes place.

Record of proceedings at sessions of the
extra-ordinary court martial
opened at Air Force Headquarters
on 26th February

Those present:
President of the Court: Colonel Mateo Orbal, Army
Members of the Court Martial: Major Carl von Peters, Army
                         Colonel Nicola Pigafetta, Air Force
                         Commander Arnold Kampenmann, Navy
                         Major Tetz Niblack, Air Force
Prosecuting Officer:
  Judge-Advocate: Captain Wilfred Schmidt, Navy
  Assistant: Lieutenant Mihail Bratianu, Army
Defending Officer: Captain Roger Endicott, Air Force
Officer Presenting Case: Lieutenant Arie Brown, Air Force
Civil Law Observer: Justice Tadeusz Haller
Witnesses: Max Gerthoffer, Laboratory Technologist
            Emil Roth, Farmer
Accused: Corporal Erwin Velder

First Day

Lieutenant Brown: Are the members of the court prepared to proceed with the internal section of the session?

Colonel Orbal: Of course.

Lieutenant Brown: Present at the internal section of today's proceedings are the President of the Court, Colonel Orbal, Major von Peters, Army, Colonel Pigafetta, representing the Air Force, Commander Kampenmann, Navy, and Justice Haller, co-opted to this extra-ordinary court martial as civil law observer and representative of the Ministry of Justice.

Major von Peters: You've forgotten yourself.

Lieutenant Brown: Case presented by Lieutenant Brown, Air Force, appointed to General Staff Operations Division.

Major von Peters: Excellent. Continue.

Lieutenant Brown: At non-internal sections of the sessions, Captain Schmidt from the General Staff Judicial Section will act as Prosecuting Officer.

Major von Peters: He's too soft.

Lieutenant Brown: Assistant Prosecuting Officer is Lieutenant Bratianu.

Major von Peters: Bratianu, he's a good man.

Lieutenant Brown: The accused will be defended by Captain Endicott from the Air Force.

Major von Peters: Who chose that particular man?

Colonel Pigafetta: I did. He's under orders, after drawing lots.

Major von Peters: Well, Bratianu's a good man.

Lieutenant Brown: Justice Haller has asked to be allowed to make a statement.

Tadeusz Haller: May I speak?

Colonel Orbal: What?

Tadeusz Haller: I requested to be allowed to speak.

Colonel Orbal: Of course. Request granted.

Tadeusz Haller: As representative of the Ministry of Justice, I should like to point out that the government attaches great importance to this session. I need only point out that for more than three years this case has been prepared in different stages.

Commander Kampenmann: Why?

Tadeusz Haller: I'll be coming to that point shortly. Counsel for the Prosecution will submit one hundred and twenty-seven charges and the documents of the case already amount to ten thousand pages.

Major von Peters: Prosecuting Officer.

Tadeusz Haller: Pardon?

Major von Peters: Prosecuting Officer, I said. Not Counsel for the Prosecution. This is a court martial.

Tadeusz Haller: I beg your pardon. Well, to continue, the considerable care which has been devoted to the preliminary work on this session naturally has a definite purpose behind it. The conclusions and verdict of this court, together with the already existing proceedings and documents, will form the basis of work to be carried out by the civil-military legislature, that is, the Legislative Assembly.

Major von Peters: Don't talk to us as if we were idiots.

Tadeusz Haller: I beg your pardon. That was indeed not my intention. Well, to continue, although it may seem somewhat superfluous, I should like therefore on behalf of the Ministry of Justice and the Legislature to emphasise with extreme urgency that the case be completed in minutest detail and investigated thoroughly in all its moral, judicial, pardon, military-judicial and psychological aspects.

Colonel Orbal: Who's treating us like idiots?

Commander Kampenmann: I still don't understand this exaggerated interest in this particular individual.

Tadeusz Haller: The man whose case is now to be tried has acted as representative for two separate régimes, and, in addition, been a member of two separately organised revolutionary movements. He has served in the armed forces of all of them and has betrayed them all.

Major von Peters: But you can't betray armies that don't exist. You ought to express yourself more precisely.

Tadeusz Haller: I ... understand your viewpoint. A slip of the tongue. It will not be repeated.

Major von Peters: Excellent. Have you ever been a soldier, Mr Haller?

Tadeusz Haller: With all due respect to this court martial, I feel that that is a matter of irrelevance. More important, perhaps, is that this court has the opportunity to reveal the mental mechanism of an individual who has committed treason against the State, and who both before and during the relatively limited time of the duration of the war ...

Major von Peters: What war? You mean the disturbances. You really ought to express yourself more precisely.

Tadeusz Haller: ... and both before and during the attempts to overthrow the government, broke more or less every essential moral law fundamental to our ideology, our way of life, and our constitution. That is why the Chief of State has expressed the definite wish that the case be handled with the greatest care and that the motives, impulses and errors of the accused which led to the deeds be investigated and accounted for in the minutest detail. It is also the Chief of State's intention at the completion of the session to hand over the assembled material to the legislature for closer analysis. The Chief of State has emphasised that point very strongly.

Major von Peters: Why didn't you say that in the first place?

Commander Kampenmann: I still don't understand why the sections of this case that lie outside military jurisdiction can't be dealt with by a civil court.

Tadeusz Haller: As the honourable members of the court are no doubt aware, we are still very much in arrears with the task of legislation. It would have created great difficulties to have had this case tried by a civil court. In addition ...

Major von Peters: In addition what?

Tadeusz Haller: In addition, the Chief of State is of the opinion that this task is of too great importance to be entrusted to the representatives of any other authority than the armed forces.

3

Major von Peters: Well, that's obvious.

Tadeusz Haller: Especially as other authorities hardly exist. Be that as it may, apart from the psychological analyses for the protection of the moral and spiritual welfare of the people, which can be based on the record of the proceedings of this court martial, the verdict and sentence for each charge on which the court finds the accused guilty, are to be regarded as a precedent and a foundation for civil-military legislation.

Major von Peters: I see. Have you finished now?

Tadeusz Haller: Yes, that is all I have to say.

Colonel Pigafetta: If I've understood you correctly, the whole court martial procedure is to be regarded as a military emergency.

Tadeusz Haller: Yes, formally.

Colonel Pigafetta: And your authority at this court martial does not embrace the sections of the case which concern military matters?

Tadeusz Haller: My assignment is to act as judicial adviser and function as an observer.

Colonel Pigafetta: For the government?

Tadeusz Haller: And for the Chief of State.

Colonel Pigafetta: I see ... well, no doubt we can come to some agreement.

Tadeusz Haller: I'm sure we can. I beg your pardon, Mr President, I didn't quite catch what you said.

Colonel Orbal: What?

Tadeusz Haller: I didn't hear what you said.

Colonel Orbal: I didn't say anything. I was yawning. Lieutenant Brown, you may continue.

Lieutenant Brown: The procedure of the case includes one closed and one open section. The sessions will be introduced with the open section, to which the general public and representatives of the press, radio and television have access. Is the court prepared to conclude the internal deliberations and proceed to the open section of the session?

Major von Peters: The press? Foreigners, too?

Lieutenant Brown: To some extent, sir. Three foreign news agencies have been granted an audience.

Major von Peters: From friendly nations?

Lieutenant Brown: Naturally.

4

Major von Peters: You should say 'naturally, sir'.

Lieutenant Brown: Yes, sir.

Major von Peters: Good.

Lieutenant Brown: In addition, the foreign news agencies are represented by the same journalist as our own mass media are.

Major von Peters: Have any of the general public come?

Lieutenant Brown: No, sir.

Colonel Orbal: It's dreadfully cold in here.

Tadeusz Haller: It wouldn't do any harm if a few representatives of the general public were present. Looks better.

Colonel Pigafetta: Arrange that, will you, Brown. There's bound to be a few people in the messes.

Lieutenant Brown: Yes, sir.

Colonel Orbal: Does it have to be like this? So damned cold, I mean?

Colonel Pigafetta: I'll try to get something done about it.

Colonel Orbal: This mineral water just makes you colder than ever. And it tastes of sulphur. Can't you arrange things so that we get something hot to drink? Coffee or tea, or something?

Colonel Pigafetta: Of course. I suggest we go upstairs, to my quarters.

Major von Peters: Switch off the tape-recorder.

Lieutenant Brown: I have no authority to interrupt the proceedings until the members adjourn the court.

Major von Peters: Adjourn the court, Mateo.

Colonel Orbal: The internal proceedings are herewith concluded. The court is adjourned for an hour and a quarter.

Lieutenant Brown: Is this extra-ordinary court martial prepared to proceed to the open section of the session?

Colonel Orbal: Of course.

Major von Peters: Are the general public organised?

Lieutenant Brown: Yes, sir.

Major von Peters: Then you can open the doors and summon the parties.

Lieutenant Brown: This extra-ordinary court martial herewith proclaims the case of the Armed Forces versus Erwin Velder open. Will the parties concerned please take their places. No, you may remain seated until the press and the general public are ready.

Major von Peters: Who's the journalist?

Tadeusz Haller: Doctor Brandt from the Ministry of Information.

Colonel Pigafetta: Brown, for God's sake get those men to stop rattling the chairs about.

Lieutenant Brown: May I request the public to maintain silence and order.

Major von Peters: The Air Force. No discipline.

Colonel Orbal: What did you say?

Lieutenant Brown: This extra-ordinary court martial herewith presents the case of the Armed Forces versus Erwin Velder. I call on all parties to rise. You too, Lieutenant Bratianu, please.

Major von Peters: I told you discipline's always bad in the Air Force.

Colonel Orbal: What? Yes ... of course.

Lieutenant Brown: The presidium of this extra-ordinary court martial has for dealing with this case been constituted as follows: President of the Court, Colonel Mateo Orbal. Members of the court martial and representatives of the armed forces, Major von Peters, Army, Colonel Nicola Pigafetta, Air Force, and Commander Arnold Kampenmann, Navy. In the event of non-appearance of members of the court during sessions, they will be replaced by personal substitutes. The case for the prosecution will be submitted by Captain Wilfred Schmidt, with Lieutenant Mihail Bratianu to assist him. The accused is defended by Captain Roger Endicott. The President of the Court Martial will now declare the public section of the session open.

Colonel Orbal: The public section of the session is herewith declared open.

Lieutenant Brown: The parties may now be seated.

Major von Peters: Your name is Erwin Velder?

Velder: Yes.

Major von Peters: Stand up, man. That's right. Well, what's your military rank?

Velder: Lieutenant-Colonel.

Major von Peters: For God's sake, man. Are you standing there insulting the court?

6

Colonel Orbal: Nice start.

Major von Peters: Captain Endicott. I presume you're familiar with the documents?

Captain Endicott: As far as has been possible. During the three days in which I have held this appointment ...

Major von Peters: That's nothing to do with it. What's the accused's rank in the armed forces?

Captain Endicott: Velder was what was called Senior Guard in the militia of the time. When it was reorganised, he was designated corporal.

Major von Peters: So he's a corporal in the army?

Captain Endicott: Yes.

Major von Peters: What are you looking for, Mateo? The instructions? They're there, look.

Colonel Orbal: Corporal Velder, I would like to remind you of the importance of your answering all questions as truthfully and exhaustively as possible and of elucidating the questions which the Prosecuting Officer, the President of the Court and other members of the court martial will ask or submit to you.

Velder: I'm prepared to answer everything.

Colonel Orbal: May I ask the Prosecuting Officer briefly to summarise the case for the Armed Forces.

Captain Schmidt: Mr President, officers and gentlemen before this extra-ordinary court martial, I intend to show with the help of fully substantiated evidence that the accused Corporal Velder has committed the grossest offence in one hundred and twenty-seven different instances. In the case of eighty-six of these offences, which come under military law, among others murder, desertion and high treason, I submit that he is declared to have forfeited his right to all military honours and decorations ...

Major von Peters: Decorations, ha ha.

Captain Schmidt: ... and that his military rank as a non-commissioned officer in the Army be stripped from him and that he be demoted to a private in the same service. Moreover I submit that for these eighty-six offences, *as well as* the remaining forty-one offences which cannot be regarded as coming under regulations arising from the military state of emergency, the accused shall be sentenced to lose his national citizenship. Also that for the one hundred and twenty-

7

seven specified charges, which on account of the far-reaching nature of this case I intend to develop and account for more closely during the course of the session, on each separate count Velder be sentenced to punishment to be executed in such a way as the presidium of this extra-ordinary court martial deems suitable.

Colonel Orbal: We have now heard the Prosecuting Officer's preparatory summary. Has the Defending Officer anything to add at this stage ... yes, what the hell is it, Endicott?

Captain Endicott: The accused requests that the charges which do not concern his military service shall be transferred to a civil court.

Major von Peters: That's absurd. Refused.

Colonel Orbal: Request refused. Where was I now? Oh, yes, here. Has the Defending Officer anything to add at this stage of the session?

Commander Kampenmann: Briefly, Velder, do you admit the charges?

Velder: What?

Major von Peters: For Christ's sake, man. It's 'What, *sir*'. Stand up. Do you admit to committing an offence, let's see, in one hundred and twenty-seven different instances?

Velder: No, sir.

Colonel Orbal: Do the parties now wish to report, summon or register any witnesses?

Captain Schmidt: I request to be allowed to call witnesses as the need arises throughout the session.

Major von Peters: Request granted.

Colonel Orbal: Granted.

Captain Schmidt: On account of the inhuman, and morally deeply reprehensible and in certain cases grossly depraved nature of the offences, I submit that future sessions are not open to the press and general public. Apart from stated motives, I would cite Military Secrets Regulations, paragraphs eight to twenty-four, and elementary and general consideration of the reputation and security of the State.

Major von Peters: Submission granted.

Colonel Orbal: Of course. Quite right. Granted.

Lieutenant Brown: May I ask the members of the press and of the general public present to leave the premises.

Major von Peters: Air Force. Sloppy lot of men.

Lieutenant Brown: Is the court martial prepared to proceed to the closed section of the session?

Colonal Orbal: Of course. We now proceed to the closed section of the proceedings.

Major von Peters: What's the time?

Commander Kampenmann: Half-past five.

Major von Peters: We lay off now, Mateo.

Colonel Orbal: What?

Major von Peters: We go on tomorrow.

Colonel Orbal: This extra-ordinary court martial will be resumed tomorrow at eleven o'clock. Remove the accused. It's still just as cold. Will it be any better tomorrow?

Colonel Pigafetta: I'll do what I can.

Major von Peters: Adjourn the session now, Mateo.

Colonel Orbal: Of course, yes. The session is adjourned.

Second Day

Lieutenant Brown: Present: Colonel Orbal, Major von Peters, Colonel Pigafetta, Commander Kampenmann and Justice Tadeusz Haller.

Major von Peters: You've forgotten yourself.

Lieutenant Brown: Officer presenting the case, Lieutenant Brown.

Colonel Orbal: I still think it's damned cold in here.

Colonel Pigafetta: As you know, domestic oil is rationed. And the central heating system doesn't function well. We've had a lot of trouble with it.

Colonel Orbal: That's odd.

Colonel Pigafetta: It was installed by army engineers. They come here every week and try to repair it.

Colonel Orbal: Oh, Christ.

Major von Peters: Stop that now, Mateo. Listen, Mr Haller, there's one question you haven't thought of and which, if I've got it right now, must be sorted out first of all.

Tadeusz Haller: What would that be?

Major von Peters: How the hell did this wretch ever become a soldier in the first place.

Colonel Pigafetta: That would undoubtedly seem to be a logical start.

Colonel Orbal: Of course. Agreed.

Major von Peters: Brown, call the Prosecuting Officer.

Major von Peters: It is the court's view that we must unravel this skein from the right end, that is, with the question: How could that swine become a soldier and be appointed a Senior Guard?

Captain Schmidt: That question is gone into at great length in the preliminary investigation material.

Major von Peters: My dear Schmidt, you don't really mean that the members of this court should sit down and read right through that enormous tome, do you?

Tadeusz Haller: Otherwise I don't see what use the presidium can find for the documents and records of proceedings.

Major von Peters: This is a court martial, not a reading circle. What we have to decide about will be said within these four walls, and it will be said clearly and concisely and in a loud clear voice. Anyhow, I'm not going to waste my time sitting here reading all that rubbish.

Tadeusz Haller: With all due respect to this court, it is perhaps not quite in keeping to call the results of three years' investigation rubbish.

Colonel Orbal: Now, now.

Tadeusz Haller: I must repeat that the Chief of State demands all possible care in this investigation. We may not avoid any truths or facts. Neither must we forget that Velder as a phenomenon is unique. He is now the only living person who has survived all the phases in our national development from anarchy to model state. He is also the only living person who was close to those three people who at the time were referred to as 'The Three Generals'.

Major von Peters: I never expected to hear that filthy expression coming from your mouth.

Tadeusz Haller: I beg your pardon.

Colonel Pigafetta: The idea of reading all that stuff doesn't really appeal to me either.

Colonel Orbal: No, God forbid.

Major von Peters: So that's that. Anyhow, Schmidt, it is also our view that you must do something about the tone of this case. We won't tolerate any form of meekness towards that filthy swine. I noticed even yesterday that you show certain tendencies to be much too kindly disposed.

Captain Schmidt: Really?

Major von Peters: Yes. Now let's start.

Colonel Orbal: Bring in the accused.

Major von Peters: Why isn't Bratianu here today?

Lieutenant Brown: According to court martial regulations, only one of the Prosecuting Officers need be present. Captain Schmidt himself decides whether he requires his assistant.

Major von Peters: Oh.

Captain Schmidt: I should now like to draw the presidium's attention to the complex of charges which comprises Velder's criminal activities during the time when he was enrolled as what is called a Senior Guard in the militia. That is for us more than a decade ago, in fact at the moment of birth of the republic as an independent national unit. As the gentlemen of the presidium have asked for verbal submission of all material, I suggest that the officer presenting the case should read suitable extracts from the records of the preliminary investigation. I should warn the court that parts of the records are quite comprehensive.

Major von Peters: Why does it all have to be so bloody long-winded? Corporal Velder, why did you become a soldier?

Velder: You might say...

Major von Peters: Stand to attention, man. Captain Endicott.

Captain Endicott: Yes?

Major von Peters: You're responsible for the accused's appearance and personal behaviour. This is a court martial, not a pub.

Captain Endicott: Velder, I should like to draw your attention to the fact that technically you're still a soldier and you should behave according to military regulations.

Major von Peters: I asked: Why did you become a soldier?

Colonel Orbal: Damned odd.

Colonel Pigafetta: What d'you mean?

Colonel Orbal: What? Oh, that he became a soldier.

Major von Peters: Well, Velder, it would help if you would deign to answer.

Velder: You might say that it was due to an unfortunate matter of chance. I've never really had much aptitude for soldiering.

Colonel Pigafetta: There's scarcely any need for you to point that out.

Velder: There weren't many who voluntarily went into the militia at the time. Perhaps I thought it was my duty. I was one of those who had the physical qualifications.

Major von Peters: With your bearing? I find that very hard to believe. You look like a scarecrow.

Captain Endicott: Corporal Velder was wounded during ... the

12

disturbances. In addition to that, he has spent three years in prison . . .

Velder: To be more precise, fourteen months under interrogation at the Military Police's Special Department and two years at an interrogation centre. The interrogations . . .

Major von Peters: This is not a conversation salon, Captain Endicott. See to it that the accused confines himself to answering the question.

Colonel Pigafetta: I don't consider that the question has been exhaustively answered.

Tadeusz Haller: May I make an interjection?

Colonel Orbal: Interjection? Yes, by all means.

Tadeusz Haller: Major von Peters' question touches on events and circumstances that are of the greatest significance to later developments. Apart from the accused, I think there is only one person in this room who was in the country at the actual time, that is, the time of national liberation.

Commander Kampenmann: Yourself, in fact?

Tadeusz Haller: Quite correct. On the other hand, none of the members of the court, as far as I know, had yet come to live here.

Colonel Orbal: Thank God for that.

Tadeusz Haller: In accordance with the general directive for this investigation and with the central objective of this session in mind, I find that an account of the so-called philosophy—naturally, it is deeply reprehensible—that led to the national liberation . . . well, briefly, I consider that such an account is motivated. Not to say necessary.

Captain Schmidt: These details are dealt with in the appendices to the preliminary investigation. On page three hundred and twelve in the first volume.

Major von Peters: You're not going to suggest that we should start reading again now, are you?

Colonel Orbal: No. No. Refused.

Captain Schmidt: I didn't mean that at all. May I suggest to the presidium that the officer presenting the case reads out aloud the extracts I indicate?

Colonel Orbal: Reads out aloud? That's not a bad idea.

Captain Schmidt: First of all I'd like to draw your attention to Appendix V 1/33. This consists of a summary of the reported survey,

13

drawn up by the National Historical Department of the General Staff. Both the summary and the publication are marked Top Secret. The same applies to most of the other documents and records I will be referring to during the session. Have you found the place, Lieutenant Brown?

Major von Peters: Loud and clear, now, Brown.

Lieutenant Brown: Yes, sir.

Major von Peters: Just a moment. This is directly relevant to my question on the reason for the accused enrolling in the Army, isn't it?

Captain Schmidt: Yes, in my view.

Major von Peters: Then there's no real reason why the accused should not stand to attention during the report.

Colonel Orbal: Exactly. Yes. Stand to attention, Velder.

Lieutenant Brown: Appendix V 1/33. Reference to National Liberation. Compiled from Volume Six, prepared by National Historical Department, General Staff. Marked Secret according to paragraphs ...

Major von Peters: We've heard all that before. Get to the point.

Lieutenant Brown: ... paragraphs eight, eleven and twenty-two. National Liberation was an historical necessity, which over the centuries was delayed by the systematic oppression and exploitation of the extant colonial power. In an account from the period of time shortly before the liberation, the island was described as 'a calm and idyllic out-of-the-way spot, forgotten and thinly populated'. It lacked industries and modern buildings almost completely, and the few communities that existed were what might be best described as villages. Despite the favourable climate, especially during the six summer months, the tourist trade was not developed, mainly due to lack of good roads, poor communications with the mainland and lack of initiative on the part of the local government—the political majority was moderate socialist.

The principle activity of the island was agriculture and—in the coastal communities—fishing. The arable land, which consisted of more than ninety per cent of the island's total area, was divided into large farming units. These were well mechanised and gave good crops; the result was a marked over-production of food, which was then transported to the mainland in barges. The neglect of industrialisation and consequent lack of employment opportunities led to con-

14

siderable emigration to the colonial power or—as the terminology of the day stated—the mother country. This emigration caused an increasing decline in population, which at the time of national liberation had gone so far that the number of inhabitants had fallen to a fiftieth of the population figure considered to be reasonably relative to the area of the island.

Military installations on the island consisted of a chain of unmanned coastal defence installations, and military stores of arms and ammunition in eight underground concrete casemates. For protection and maintaining guard over these, there was a minor force, mainly composed of national servicemen whose homes were on the island. Maintenance of law and order was in the hands of the local police organisation. This was built up on the principle of one policeman per six hundred inhabitants, and both its personnel and material resources were extremely limited. Such was the situation immediately prior to the action which finally led to the country's autonomy.

Round the great thought that lay hidden in the concept of national liberation gathered people of all kinds; the fact that by no means all of them—not even the leaders—had sufficient moral and spiritual qualities to be able to take the responsibility of liberators was soon apparent. The plans for the take-over of power were worked out with the greatest care and during the last two-year period of time, they entered, as far as can be established, into an intensive stage. The leaders of the operation, which went under the cover name of the Project, included men of the noblest elevation and moral qualities, as well as people less well qualified for national leadership. These people were united by two powerful motives: the will to throw off the yoke and give the island independence, and a feeling of repugnance and contempt for the circumstances in the mother country. For these reasons they sought each other's support, a fact which later on certain historians found hard to explain. Through skilful and thorough preparations on diplomatic and financial levels, the Liberation Committee—on which, besides Paul Oswald and Tadeusz Haller, were also the notorious herofied traitors Joakim Ludolf and Janos Edner and a woman called Aranca Peterson—was, however, without causing suspicion, quickly able to achieve a favourable psychological and economic starting point.

Military preparations, however, were far less satisfactory—the majority of committee members were wholly ignorant of technical defence matters—and the organising genius and tactical brilliance of a General Oswald was needed to lead the revolution to victory. The majority of the Liberation Committee had opposed the creation of a regular armed force, which undoubtedly would have given the only possible guarantee that the liberation would not be frustrated at the last moment. In this position, General Oswald had no other choice, and that was a compromise. He created the national militia and made it effective with the help of available resources.

But the economic part of the preparations was dealt with in quite a different manner. Via diplomatic by-ways, amongst others through secret discussions with several of the nation's natural arch-enemies, and agreements with capitalist private interests, they succeeded in procuring sums in millions. By eighteen months before the liberation, through proxy purchases, they had acquired more than eighty per cent of the island's properties and nearly two-thirds of its arable land for the so-called Project. In this way they could render innocuous long beforehand several possible enemies, resident inhabitants who might join those in opposition to the liberation idea, sabotage its realisation, or, at a critical military stage, disturb calm and internal order. This humane way of achieving peaceful national consolidation can also be ascribed to General Oswald's foresight and genius.

Unfortunately, his ideas were corrupted almost immediately. After the take-over of power, it appeared that the majority of members of the committee had by no means been guided by idealistic and national motives, but had acted from motives of private profit and had been poisoned by confused and deeply reprehensible thoughts, based on immorality, ungodliness and anarchy. This naïve but dangerous philosophy was soon to lead to tragic national complications which were hard to overcome. One of the earliest and most grotesque expressions of this was in a preposterous doctrine, according to information prepared by Janos Edner and Aranca Peterson several years before the national liberation. This was the so-called Method, a phenomenon which was cynical and against all human values, which led not only its originators but also the whole nation into self-debasement and defeat. I will now go over to ...

Major von Peters: Are you going to stand there and read the whole blasted volume to us, Brown?

16

Colonel Orbal: Books are the devil. It's no better when someone else does the reading.

Captain Schmidt: I would now like to draw the President's attention to Appendices V 1/24 and V 1/42xx, page three hundred and eighty-six in the first volume.

Colonel Orbal: Do we have to take them now?

Captain Schmidt: I have been asked to answer the question of how the accused came to be a soldier and the circumstances surrounding the formation of the militia. As I understand it, this material I am referring to from the preliminary investigation is of vital importance, in this case, the matter of recruitment.

Major von Peters: Mr Haller here was in on all that himself. Wouldn't it be better if he told us? Just let him testify.

Captain Schmidt: Do you wish to testify now or later, Justice Haller?

Tadeusz Haller: I would prefer to make any comment I have to make and testify on these matters some time further on during the session.

Captain Schmidt: The appendix I am now referring to is of a unique character. It consists of a fragment of Janos Edner's memoirs, which were found and confiscated and which he clearly never completed. The fragment consists of two parts, of which the first is a short description written with something which seems to be an attempt at a more literary flavour. It reflects the atmosphere in which Janos Edner found himself exactly a week before the day of national liberation. It is manifestly a reconstruction, written many years later somewhere abroad. The other part of the appendix consists of several pages from a notebook. Originally the text was in code and there seems to be no doubt that it was written before the liberation, that is, over ten years ago. Presumably it is an extract from some kind of diary. The document was found fastened with a paperclip to the typed sheets which made up the original of the first part of the appendix. It is probable that Edner used these notes to assist his memory and for source material for writing his memoirs.

Colonel Orbal: God, how involved.

Captain Schmidt: It has been definitely ascertained that Janos Edner wrote this in his own hand. The decoding has been carried out by the cipher department of the General Staff. The original documents have been kept for about a year in the archives of the secret police. They are marked Secret.

Major von Peters: Read loudly and clearly, now, Brown. In an even voice. As if you were on duty on the barrack square, but slower.

Lieutenant Brown: Appendices V 1/42 and V 1/42xx. Reference to National Liberation. Confiscated documentation written by the traitor, Janos Edner. Marked Secret according to paragraphs eight, nine, eleven and fourteen to twenty-two. The text is as follows:

The plane is an Ilyushin 18 turbo-prop from CSA. It is flying at four thousand metres height and the air in the cabin is dry and smells of cloth and leather. You are sitting leaning forward with the brown brief-case on your lap and you have placed your right arm over it so that no one shall see the chain between your wrist and the handle.

You turn your head to the left and look at the woman in the seat beside you. She has short dark hair and is wearing a red costume with blue lapels. She is sitting slightly hunched, her left elbow on the foam-rubber padded arm-rest, her head resting on her hand. On her lap lies an open notebook and a page of stencilled tables and she is smoking as she reads. When she pokes a flake of tobacco off her mouth with her little finger, you can see that her nails are bitten to the quick and that she has no make-up on and there is a thin downy shadow on her upper lip, and you think that most women see to such details with a little razor or electrolysis. There's nothing remarkable about her. She would remain anonymous in the crowd on any European city street and if she had been sitting a few yards farther away, it is not likely that you would have noticed her. But although you have never met her before and have not even had time to find out what her name is, you know her, and you know that she would not be sitting there if she hadn't qualities which you appreciate and understand. She is one of the two thousand five hundred on which everything depends, later, and above all in a week's time. When she turns her head and looks at you with her light grey-blue eyes, you know you are right. She smiles, faintly and tranquilly.

You look at your watch and turn away, leaning your forehead against the window-pane and staring down. You don't want to miss this opportunity, which should be the last.

The island lies below you. Although it's late in the year, the air is clean and bright and you see everything very clearly, as if on a large-scale map.

It's ninety-eight miles long and thirty-five miles across and you're just flying over it, from west to east.

You see its abrupt coastline with the continuous sandy shore below, like a trimmed edge or an imaginary borderline between sea and land, and you see the chequered pattern of fields and occasional farms and small white churches.

You see all this and at the same time everything that no one else can see. The towns, the hotels, the airports, the grey ribbons of roads and the three harbours with their white hovercraft. And you feel for the first time: all this is mine. This is my country.

The plane's vibrations are transmitted from the window-pane through your forehead and . . .

This part of the appendix ends in the middle of a sentence.

Major von Peters: Funny bastard calling himself 'you'.

Lieutenant Brown: I will now go over to the second part, the one marked V 1/42xx. The text is as follows:

We agreed on the following. To gain power is meaningless if the only aim in gaining power is to gain power. It's just as futile to gain power in the belief that one would be able to create an ideal state—after the words ideal state there is a question mark in brackets—with the help of something from existing so-called political systems, for they are all essentially based on the same type of society. All forms of state have the same fundamental structure and not one of them can be said to be successful. When we in our foolishness occupy ourselves with comparisons and appraisements, it is suggested that we are operating with a scale which simply consists of symbols for different grades of failure. Ergo: It is also meaningless to gain power and apply some newly constructed system or apply some previously unknown or misinterpreted ideology, because so long as the structure of society, that is, the circumstances of the individual, is not radically changed at the same time, the result will in all certainty become more or less identical with what one was opposing in the first place. If we take over the island—none of us really doubts that we can and will do so—and if we manage to build the society we want, then never-theless, this progress cannot make the basis for any norm-forming reasoning. We would know in that case precisely as much as we knew before: that this was possible to achieve—and in addition right —for us in particular in that place at that particular time. Ergo: a handful of people create for themselves, and on behalf of a relatively speaking small number of like-minded others, a society according to a certain very simple method, which in this particular connection has the advantage of being infallible. The Project is totally dependent on the Method and the Method is worthless without the Project. On the one side the Project is built on complete internal unity and understanding, and on the other naturally on an equally destructive cynicism and egoism in all external matters of cohabitation. And— and this is the most important—on radical simplifications of the conventional but never thoroughly tested rules for living and structure of society. We have—*pro primo*—the object, that is, the island. True, it is not yet at our disposal, but we know the ways in which it can and will be taken over. Against this O, astonishingly enough, suddenly protests that on the mainland they can mobilise an army of three hundred thousand men plus planes and ships. How many? He quoted figures, but I forgot them at once. We talked about this for a while. Uninteresting.

On the other hand we have not yet completed the human initial capital. We are still agreed that two thousand five hundred is definitely the minimum figure. A and I discussed the Method again a few days ago—despite her optimism, she is just as ready to raise objections. Good. It is—A said—certainly true that with our international contacts we can easily together make a network of two thousand five hundred people, who even if they don't know each other, are still alike in principle—each other and us—and move them to a certain place at a certain time without previously having to account for where and why, and there we have our human initial capital.

Anyhow—A went on—we could just as well let the chain reaction continue and go on and get hold of twenty-five thousand or two hundred and fifty thousand at once. A said: Why not a hand-picked élite consisting of less than a quarter per thousand of the population of the world?

Where would she get the élite from? A's main objection is however still the same. Can't we even rely on each other? Answer: Naturally, first and foremost as we've gone into this for years and know that it's only a matter of agreeing on a few main points; once we've started, our successes and mutual respect will mean that the rest will come by itself.

A: Of course we can rely on each other today, but what will it look like in a few years' time. Even I don't know that I will be the same then as I am now; our cells are said to be renewed every seven years and then one's character perhaps will suddenly be different? Answer: Shit. And also it wouldn't matter. See above.

A: L is drinking even more than before, but that doesn't matter. Answer: Perfectly correct observations, both of them. This about A.

Discussed with H and O again the in itself insignificant matter of why we feel more repugnance and distaste for this well-behaved country in which we happen to have landed, than if it had been a Catholic Fascist feudal state or a pure dictatorship, on the lines of Stalin's in the thirties. The answers were the same old ones; but happily we now say *it* instead of *we*: it is collapsing from well-being and galloping democracy. It understands everything except for the fact that human individuals do not necessarily have to be looked after and treated as if they were leek plants. It maintains continuously and in all connections that it is best and everyone likes it very much there, despite the fact that everyone knows that everyone dislikes it, to a degree of deadly boredom. Exhausted by its own futility, it lulls itself to sleep by boasting about order and numbing welfare. In its nightmares it boasts about abolishing war two hundred years ago and, in the same snore, about its powerful and extremely expensive armed forces, élite defences with warships and tanks, which naturally are also the best in the world, not to mention the soldiers. Then it wakes up with a belch and lies there with its suicidal thoughts, with its simulated socialism, on its home-made bed of nails of mindless laws and meaningless regulations, regretting that the rest of humanity cannot enjoy the fruits of the same rich life. It is the kind of state which can be bluffed and caught unawares by anyone who wants to. It will be a pleasure to do it.

H has once again taken up the question of the militia and arming it. The thought is abominably objectionable. I don't want to have anything to do with it. But I see that he is right. So does A.

L and O seldom talk about this. Who will look after it? Who

21

could do it? A suggested a kind of guard service for everyone; it would only mean a day a month for each person. A bit like organising a rota. Something for the future?

Lieutenant Brown: The notes end there.

Colonel Orbal: What in the world was all that about? I didn't understand a thing.

Major von Peters: There's just one small point I'd like to know about. What are those incomprehensible letters and figures in front of each paper?

Captain Schmidt: That's easy to explain. V 1/42xx means, for instance, Velder Investigation/Volume 1/forty-second item/second appendix.

Major von Peters: Easy to explain? Is that supposed to be an insinuation that I ought to have understood such a simple thing by myself?

Captain Schmidt: Not at all. I apologise for expressing myself so badly.

Captain Endicott: Does the accused still have to stand to attention?

Colonel Orbal: What? Of course. We shall be adjourning shortly, anyhow.

Major von Peters: Well, Kampenmann, you're just coming to, are you? Presumably you like all this literary stuff just about as much as I do. Bet you didn't hear much of Brown's reading exercises.

Commander Kampenmann: Yes, I was listening, as a matter of fact. But it wasn't really necessary for me to do so. Actually, I've already read through my copy of the preliminary investigation.

Major von Peters: All of it?

Commander Kampenmann: Yes.

Major von Peters: That says a lot for service in the Navy. Must be tremendously busy.

Colonel Orbal: I was just wondering about one thing.

Major von Peters: Captain Schmidt, you're in the Navy, aren't you?

Captain Schmidt: Yes, but for the moment I am posted to the General Staff Judicial Department.

Major von Peters: Why aren't you in uniform?

Captain Schmidt: There is no such instruction in the regulations.

Major von Peters: That's possible. All the same, we would appreciate it very much if you would do so.

Colonel Orbal: Yes, there was something that interested me. The woman with a moustache who was mentioned at the beginning. Who's that? Do you know?

Captain Schmidt: Yes, she has been identified. She was called Rodriguez and was Janos Edner's secretary and closest personal collaborator. Most of the journey that fragment deals with is also known about. It took place on the day a week before national liberation. Janos Edner was on his way to Prague to hasten the ratification of a secret agreement on arms deliveries to the militia.

Colonel Orbal: Did she really have a moustache?

Captain Schmidt: I don't know, but I can investigate the matter. In the decoded diary notes, in all likelihood L stands for Joakim Ludolf, A for Aranca Peterson and H for Justice Tadeusz Haller, who is present. O is presumably General Oswald.

Captain Endicott: Excuse me, but ... Brown, give me a hand here, will you ...

Colonel Orbal: What now? Has he died? That mustn't happen.

Captain Endicott: Unconscious, probably fainted from the strain of standing upright for so long. Better call in the guard.

Major von Peters: The parties may leave the room. You stay, Lieutenant Brown, but see to getting the men with the stretcher out first. This extra-ordinary court martial will now deliberate in private.

Colonel Orbal: What a day!

Major von Peters: Yes, and we're not a step further on, either. This will go on for months. I'm also very dissatisfied, very dissatisfied, with Schmidt and his way of presenting the prosecution. Too bloody soft.

Colonel Pigafetta: On that point, I'm prepared to agree with you.

Major von Peters: We'll have to do something about it. It wasn't exactly the interrogation that made that swine pass out ... if he fainted at all.

Commander Kampenmann: I'm sorry if I openly question the method, but is there really any point in making the accused stand to attention for so long?

Colonel Orbal: Damn it all, standing to attention never hurt anyone, did it? On the contrary, good for a man's bearing.

Commander Kampenmann: Considering the man's physical condition...

Major von Peters: Aren't there any malingerers in the Navy?

Commander Kampenmann: This is like an old joke. Yes, there are malingerers in the Navy, but they don't pretend that their left eyes have been removed, or that their kneecaps have been smashed or that all the fingers on their right hands have been amputated.

Colonel Orbal: Oh, yes, the man was wounded, wasn't he?

Commander Kampenmann: Yes, in the neck. That's why he finds it difficult to hold his head up. The rest are of a more recent date.

Colonel Pigafetta: Don't start getting soft now, Kampenmann.

Commander Kampenmann: I'm not. I'm just telling you a few facts.

Major von Peters: May I ask one thing? How the hell do you know all this?

Commander Kampenmann: I told you. I've read the record of the preliminary investigation.

Colonel Orbal: I'm getting tired of all this now. Am I the only one who wants to have a pee? Where's that instruction thing, Carl? Good. This extra-ordinary court martial is herewith adjourned until eleven o'clock on Monday. Thank you, gentlemen.

Third Day

Lieutenant Brown: Present: Colonel Orbal, Major von Peters, Colonel Pigafetta, Commander Kampenmann. And Lieutenant Brown presenting the case.

Colonel Orbal: Isn't Haller here?

Lieutenant Brown: Justice Haller has been prevented from appearing. He's at a meeting of the government.

Colonel Orbal: You seem to have got some life into the central heating, anyhow.

Colonel Pigafetta: I'm afraid that's due to the weather rather than the heating system. It's considerably warmer out today.

Colonel Orbal: Spring's coming.

Commander Kampenmann: Didn't Haller's behaviour seem a bit peculiar on Saturday? Why didn't he want to testify until later?

Colonel Orbal: Are you asking me? How would I know?

Major von Peters: Who is Prosecuting Officer today?

Lieutenant Brown: Captain Schmidt.

Major von Peters: Alone?

Lieutenant Brown: Yes.

Major von Peters: It's getting tiresome having to repeat it, Brown, but it should be 'Yes, sir'. Is Schmidt in uniform?

Lieutenant Brown: Yes, sir.

Major von Peters: Well, that's something.

Colonel Orbal: Then let's start, shall we? Summon the parties.

Captain Schmidt: At Saturday's session matters prior to national liberation were dealt with. Does the presidium consider that that part of the commission calls for further study?

Colonel Orbal: No, no.

Captain Schmidt: We come then to the time of the formation of

25

the militia before the liberation; this moment—perhaps I needn't point this out especially—has considerable judicial significance, as this extra-ordinary court martial is not bound to pronounce sentence in cases which arose prior to it.

Major von Peters: You needn't point out so bloody much, Captain Schmidt. It'd be better if you kept to points of prosecution.

Colonel Orbal: Yes, so that we get somewhere.

Captain Schmidt: I shall proceed with the case for the prosecution itself in a moment. At first I should just like to be rid of one more formality. I hereby submit that the militia began to function as a military unit the moment the independent State was proclaimed and that Velder from that moment in time, that is 0530 hours on Independence Day, was subject to military law.

Major von Peters: That seems absolutely obvious. Get to the point.

Captain Schmidt: The first section of the case for the prosecution covers the period of the first thirteen months of Velder's service in the militia. During this period he committed offences on thirty-two occasions. All these fall within the framework of military penal regulations, and they must be judged all the more seriously in consideration of the fact that the tense and critical situation during the nation's first year made the position comparable to a state of emergency. In all these thirty-two cases, the main evidence consists of Velder's own confessions. To avoid any unnecessary waste of time, I do not intend to call upon the accused for each separate charge.

Major von Peters: Why not?

Captain Schmidt: Mostly because in that case the session would probably go on for years.

Colonel Pigafetta: That would undoubtedly be highly undesirable.

Captain Schmidt: There are also some practical reasons. The preliminary investigations have not taken over three years for nothing. Concerning each and every one of these thirty-two charges, Velder has confessed and rendered full accounts of them. These he has sworn on oath, they are witnessed by interrogators from the General Staff Judicial Department and have been perused by experienced psychologists. The completeness and truthfulness of these confessions are beyond doubt.

26

Commander Kampenmann: I seem to remember that the accused pleaded not guilty to the first charge.

Captain Schmidt: That did not concern this part of the case. Of the separate offences in this series of crimes, some are more or less of the same kind. They concern various kinds of insubordination and more serious breaches of duty. I here present the material to the presidium of the court with the recommendation that the accused be given the opportunity of pleading guilty to these offences all in one go, so to speak.

Colonel Orbal: Aha. I see. Do you plead guilty to these thirty-two offences?

Velder: Yes, sir.

Colonel Orbal: Then that's that.

Major von Peters: One moment, this is quite a list of sins, I must say. Velder!

Velder: Yes, sir.

Major von Peters: The fact that you simulated a fainting fit on Saturday does not mean that you needn't observe elementary discipline. Stand to attention.

Velder: Yes, sir.

Major von Peters: So you've been guilty of absence without leave seven times by just not turning up on duty. In most cases you've quoted various personal reasons for your behaviour.

Velder: Yes, sir.

Major von Peters: Four times, you were so drunk on duty that your fellow-soldiers were forced to lock you up so that you wouldn't do yourself any harm, it says here.

Velder: Yes, sir.

Major von Peters: You've fallen asleep while on guard-duty a number of times, I see, and sat fishing during guard-duty. On eleven occasions when on guard-duty, which no doubt you remember, you've brought women with you into military areas and...

Velder: Only one, sir. I mean, it was the same woman each time.

Major von Peters: Don't interrupt me, man. Are you insane? And you've had intimate relations with them in guard-posts and ammunition depôts and various other places. On one of these occasions you were surprised by your Section Leader. You had on that occasion undressed and left your own and the woman's clothes lying in the

27

guard-post alongside arms, ammunition and map-holders, while you had sexual intercourse with each other on the beach three hundred yards away.

Colonel Orbal: I say, I haven't read all that. Hand over those papers.

Major von Peters: On this occasion you seem to have excused yourself by saying it was a warm night and you felt like a bathe.

Velder: Yes, sir, that's correct.

Major von Peters: We have been given an admittedly confused answer, but at least an answer to the question of how it came about that Velder became a soldier. But can anyone tell me why the hell this man wasn't executed there and then? Or at least dismissed the service?

Captain Schmidt: To enlighten you on that matter, and on a number of other relevant questions, I request to be allowed to call a witness.

Major von Peters: Who?

Captain Schmidt: A person called Roth, who was the accused's leader in the militia during the first thirteen months after the liberation.

Major von Peters: Have this witness called, Mateo.

Colonel Orbal: What? What did you say? What's this all about?

Colonel Pigafetta: A witness, who is to be summoned.

Colonel Orbal: Oh, yes, of course. Call him in.

Lieutenant Brown: Mr Roth, you are now to bear witness. Do you swear by Almighty God to tell the truth, the whole truth, and nothing but the truth?

Roth: I do.

Lieutenant Brown: I should remind you that this is a court martial and perjury is a punishable offence.

Roth: Hullo, Velder. It's been a long time, indeed it has. Hardly recognised you.

Major von Peters: No fraternising with the accused, please.

Captain Schmidt: You're no longer in military service, are you?

Roth: No, I left the militia after thirteen months, when the danger was over, so to speak, and became a farmer again, just as I was before. I had a farm quite near here, fourteen miles west of

28

Oswaldsburg, and still have. Great big place. Now of course, it's mostly army supplies.

Major von Peters: Is there anything wrong with army supplies?

Roth: Well—wrong—you know—as things are, one can't grumble.

Captain Schmidt: How did it come about that you became Section Leader in the militia?

Roth: Group Leader it was called. Now did that come about? Well, someone has to do these things, don't they? I was an experienced hunter and a good shot, and that was enough.

Captain Schmidt: Can you, in your own words, tell us about the formation of the militia and the circumstances within the force?

Commander Kampenmann: Especially in connection with your relations to Velder.

Roth: The militia came about more or less ... well, if not exactly at random—but anyhow very hastily and in a strange way. The whole idea of liberation, and all that, was said to be pacifist and—yes, sorry—anti-militaristic. We were short of arms and had no trained men, and there was never any question of being able to offer any resistance if the mainland lot decided to start bombing and landing troops from the sea. We simply had to rely on them being completely foxed over there, at least for a few days. Then our proclamations and international pressure would do the trick, and that's what happened, too. We relied on the armed forces not daring to do anything until they'd got clearance from the politicians and that that would take at least a couple of days before the politicians had had time to realise what had happened. We'd reckoned all that out, and we were right, too.

Captain Schmidt: You keep saying 'we' all the time—I suppose you mean the Liberation Committee.

Roth: Well, at that time, we all felt very much welded together as a group, all of us. What I said just now about not offering resistance was only in reference to the Army, of course. There was one thing we were much more scared of, and that was the police. There were several towns on the mainland only a few hours away from here, and we could almost certainly reckon on the police there not standing about with their hands in their pockets while we annexed a bit of the country for ourselves. In some way or other, we had to repulse purely police actions—otherwise a hundred or two hundred policemen could just come ashore and arrest us and put an end to the revolution within a few hours. So the only answer was to form a militia. They say that the members of the Council—or the Liberation Committee as it was called right at the beginning—drew lots out of a hat for who should be chief of the militia. The woman, Aranca Peterson, was there too, but it was Oswald who won ... so to speak.

Major von Peters: General Oswald, if you don't mind. And listen to me ...

Colonel Pigafetta: Calm down, von Peters, and let the witness tell his story in his own way.

Roth: He wasn't in fact a general then. About half of the soldiers that were here on the island joined us, about fifty men, and some of the policemen. Then we started at about midnight, opening the stores and arming ourselves. The division into groups had been done beforehand roughly. Most of the two thousand five hundred, who belonged to the so-called inner section, had dropped in during the week. At about three in the morning, we'd managed to get hold of members of the resident population who were considered to be directly in opposition and dangerous, and collected them up into a temporary camp. That was easy, as there weren't many of them, and the lists had been ready ages beforehand. No one offered any resistance. Not a shot was fired.

Commander Kampenmann: Was the accused already under your command at the time?

Roth: Command—oh—well. Velder was in my group. He had volunteered because he was big and strong and could handle a machine-gun. In the morning at half-past five, the declaration of independence and our appeal to the United Nations for a peaceful settlement went out over our own and a lot of foreign radio stations —our own, incidentally, was extremely temporary. The militia was to be in place by then, and it was, too. But it didn't look up to much. We probably had altogether about four hundred men, pretty well armed, they were, ten machine-guns and four or five artillery pieces which had been brought ashore during the night. I still don't know who gave them to us, for that matter.

Colonel Pigafetta: We know. That's enough.

Roth: Oh, do you? Wherever that boat came from, it had laid

30

a whole lot of mines too, but they weren't much use. Not then, anyhow. But they were afterwards, of course, when they tried to blockade us and we mined the coast. Anyhow, the militia were sort of divided up amongst the three harbours, the largest lot placed in and around Ludolfsport, as it was called then. It was only a little fishing village, then, of course, but boats of up to five or six hundred tons could tie up at the quays. We had about two hundred men and two guns there—ordinary 12.5 centimetre howitzers. Two fishing trawlers, each with a machine-gun mounted on the foredeck sailed out of the harbour and anchored there as guard-ships. Oswald, that is General Oswald as he has become, was there and directed the whole thing as well as was possible. There weren't many orders as such given, anyhow I didn't hear any, but that didn't matter because everyone knew what they were supposed to do. At about ten, just what we'd expected to happen happened. A tug and two big motorboats came in towards the harbour, all of them packed with uniformed police. The trawlers, which had the new national flag flying, hailed them, but they went on all the same, and so they opened fire from the trawlers with their machine-guns. One of the police-boats seized up almost at once and stopped, and then the guns began to shoot at the tug. We had a good gunner—and the second shot scored a hit in the stern. The tug began to sink at once, but thank God it swerved out of the channel and got stuck on one of the sandbanks with its stack and bridge above the water, so we could pick up most of those who'd been on board. The motor-boat that was still untouched began to pull away with the other, but it was a slow business, it was, and after a bit of chitchat, Oswald sent off one of the trawlers and took all the policemen prisoner. After an hour or so, he changed his mind and let the motor-boats go again, after we'd taken the police's arms off them, of course. They only had pistols and tear-gas grenades, anyhow. They'd shot at the trawlers from one of the motor-boats and a fisherman had got a bullet in his shoulder, but that was all. And the police didn't do too badly anyhow. Five or six copped it, perhaps, when we sank the tug. We got it up again, as a matter of fact, a few weeks later, and it wasn't badly damaged.

Captain Schmidt: And then?

Roth: Then there wasn't any more fighting. Their planes flew backwards and forwards above us, but quite high up, and we didn't shoot at them, because we'd appealed to all the international organisations and all the great powers to find a peaceful solution, as it's called. And they didn't shoot at us, either. After a few weeks, when they were still at the height of the jawing at the United Nations, they stopped flying over, too.

Commander Kampenmann: To what extent did Velder take part in all these events?

Roth: He was in my group. We lay protected behind sandbags on the pier, covering the harbour entrance. That wasn't actually necessary any longer, as no one ever got that far. But two or three years later, he and I both got a medal. Everyone who'd been at Ludolfsport at the time got one.

Captain Schmidt: What were the circumstances within the militia during the period that followed.

Roth: The only important task we had was passport and immigration control. My group did mostly guard-duty, event-free mostly. The militia was also responsible for internal order and other purely police matters. That was even more uninteresting, because all that happened was an accident or two, usually in connection with the big building projects.

Captain Schmidt: What was your opinion of Velder as a soldier?

Roth: We didn't regard ourselves as soldiers.

Captain Schmidt: How did he behave? Did he obey orders? Was he reliable?

Roth: Don't know what to say, really. He didn't exactly obey orders, but he would have done so if it'd been necessary. I think.

Colonel Pigafetta: That last comment was an important addition.

Captain Schmidt: Did Velder seem to you more undisciplined than the others in the group?

Roth: We—ell, he was full of life. Perhaps more so than the others; than me, for instance. But he was ... I mean, I thought he was a good guy.

Colonel Pigafetta: Why did you leave the militia?

Roth: I wanted to do something useful. More useful, I mean. At the time, it looked as if the militia had done its job once and for all and could be dissolved, which was what was intended in the first place—except the personnel who saw to immigration control, of course. The development work was in full swing. Oswaldsburg and Ludolfsport were being built up into large cities by our standards, and hotels and restaurants and casinos were springing up like mushrooms out of the ground round Marbella.

Commander Kampenmann: And the brothels. You forgot them.

Roth: Yes ... but we didn't see anything wrong with that then. Anyhow, all labour was wanted for production, for development. I was a farmer, and liked farming too. I could be most use there, I thought. At that time, the population was increasing at a rate of between eighty and a hundred people a day.

Colonel Orbal: Were you the person who caught Velder naked on the ground with a naked woman when he should have been on guard-duty.

Roth: Yes ... but how ...

Colonel Orbal: What do you mean ... how?

Roth: I mean, I've never told anyone about that ...

Colonel Orbal: What were Velder and that woman up to?

Captain Schmidt: Answer the colonel's question.

Roth: Well, you know ... the usual.

Colonel Pigafetta: Have you ever been in prison yourself?

Roth: Yes, I was interned for three months during the war ... the disturbances, I mean. Then they wanted to send me to a political rehabilitation camp, but I managed to persuade them that I only minded about my farm and could be most use there. That was true, too. Farming here certainly isn't what it used to be, and then it was even worse. Lots of mouths to feed and with all those half-finished factories ...

Colonel Orbal: About that business on the beach ...

Major von Peters: Cool off, for God's sake, Mateo.

Colonel Orbal: What? Why do you sound so strange?

Captain Schmidt: No more questions.

Lieutenant Brown: Has the Defending Officer any questions?

Captain Endicott: Yes. My first question is: were there any service regulations for the militia?

Roth: No.

Captain Endicott: Did it often happen that other militiamen behaved in the same irresponsible manner, so to speak, as the accused?

Roth: Yes.

Captain Endicott: Were you punished?

Roth: No.

Captain Endicott: No more questions.

Lieutenant Brown: The witness may leave.

Roth: Goodbye.

Colonel Pigafetta: Endicott, I know you're under orders to defend this man, but that doesn't mean that you have to behave like some film or television hero. Be careful not to exaggerate.

Major von Peters: Thank God we've got rid of that swine. Christ, what an affair! How can such people be allowed to go free? In our country? I had to keep myself well in check. Hardly dared say a thing. If he'd answered me in that insolent way, I'd have shot the wretch on the spot.

Captain Schmidt: The question of how Velder became a soldier can now be considered to have been investigated. I am prepared to submit the first part of the case, which consists of thirty-two charges, to the court.

Colonel Orbal: That's all right.

Captain Schmidt: No objections?

Commander Kampenmann: I have no objections to this part of the case being submitted to the court, but on the other hand there is just one detail I would like cleared up.

Major von Peters: You're hellish on the spot today, Kampenmann. What is it now?

Commander Kampenmann: I have gone very thoroughly into the accused's confessions to these thirty-two offences. What I want to know is, in what way was Velder induced to give these detailed accounts of his crimes? So that we shall be able to judge the value and truthfulness of the accused's already approved and recorded evidence during the rest of the session, we must at least know something about the methods used during the investigation. I presume torture has been used, but do not know to what extent.

Colonel Pigafetta: Agreed. We ought to have that cleared up. It will facilitate judgement.

Captain Schmidt: I had considered the point that the presidium would sooner or later ask for information on this point. My own knowledge of the subject is far from satisfactory. I have therefore made an arrangement with an expert witness. If the court will adjourn for a meal, for instance, I am prepared to present this witness within an hour.

Colonel Orbal: Eat—God, that's the first sensible thing that's been said today. What are your cooks like, Pigafetta?

Colonel Pigafetta: Better than your plumbers, anyhow. And I've got female servants in the mess.

Colonel Orbal: The court is adjourned for two hours.

*   *   *

Lieutenant Brown: Is this extra-ordinary court martial prepared to continue the session?

Colonel Orbal: Of course.

Lieutenant Brown: The Prosecuting Officer requests to be allowed to call Max Gerthoffer, Laboratory Technologist, as witness.

Colonel Orbal: Let him in.

Lieutenant Brown: You are Max Gerthoffer, forty-two years old, employed in a civilian capacity at the Special Department of the Military Police. Do you swear by Almighty God to keep strictly to the truth?

Gerthoffer: I do.

Captain Schmidt: If I am correctly informed, you are connected with the Special Department of the Military Police in your capacity as an expert in interrogation.

Gerthoffer: That definition is not entirely correct.

Captain Schmidt: Anyhow, you have been in charge of the Velder case for a long time?

Gerthoffer: Yes. Erwin Velder and I met every day over a period of fourteen months.

Commander Kampenmann: What we wish to know is which interrogation techniques were used and to what degree torture was used to extract confessions from the accused.

Gerthoffer: I am convinced that on no occasion was Velder tortured in connection with the interviews.

Commander Kampenmann: In other words, you maintain that the accused quite voluntarily made these remarkably detailed and apparently exact confessions?

35

Gerthoffer: Yes and no.

Commander Kampenmann: Would you mind expressing yourself a little less cryptically?

Major von Peters: Here, here. Who the hell could understand that?

Gerthoffer: I do not like all these questions. In fact they irritate me intensely. If you gentlemen would stop interrupting me, I will, however, try to give you an exhaustive explanation. First of all, the definition of my assignment given by the Prosecuting Officer was incorrect. I am not an interrogation technician, at least not first and foremost. I have not, for instance, carried out a single interrogation of Velder. On the other hand, I have helped to prepare him spiritually and physically for the series of interviews which have been carried out during the last two years. This is the first time I've seen Velder since we parted in my office two years ago. Despite this, with almost a hundred per cent certainty, I can guarantee that Velder, in each and every one of the innumerable interviews he has undergone since then, has given truthful information. In all circumstances, he has himself been convinced that his statements have been exact and he has taken great trouble not to exclude anything of interest. The reservation I made with that 'almost a hundred per cent certainty' concerns a small but mostly unavoidable fault-percentage, which is due to defective memory-pictures. Not so that the memory-picture is disturbed or dimmed by later stratification in his consciousness; that type of complication we have long since overcome. No, if Velder today produces a faulty statement, or as it is popularly called, if he lies, that is only due to the fact that his own brain at the moment of occurrence made a defective registration. To correct this is not impossible in itself, as the registration of impressions occurs both in a conscious and an unconscious dimension. These can in themselves be different—but must they be or even are they that? No, by no means. Corrections can, then, be carried out in this field too, but they demand so much work and such complicated analyses, that they can still be recommended only in exceptional cases. In my view, Velder did not fall into that category.

I will now proceed to answer your question about the use of what you call torture; the inexact terminology you used in itself, 'to extract confessions' for instance, shows to what extent old-fashioned representations of a subject remain in circles that are occupied with war and other forms of professional extermination. Even empirical research ...

Colonel Orbal: Excuse me, but could you put things a little more simply?

Gerthoffer: Even empirical research, as I was saying, has long ago confirmed that the method of using different forms of torture to extract information and statements is both primitive and archaic. Nowadays, such methods might possibly—please observe that I say possibly—be motivated, against prisoners of war on the battlefield, for instance, or if the person being interviewed is dying. Even in such special and urgent situations, however, the method must be regarded as unreliable. On the other hand it can of course still be used to advantage by anyone who wishes to extract a confession at any price, and, *nota bene*, if that person is indifferent to whether the confession is true or false. But that has however nothing to do with modern interrogation techniques; perhaps it appertains only to politics. In addition, the process is so simple that anyone can achieve the result intended with practically any means of assistance whatsoever. As a means of persuasion in connection with interrogation, torture has no longer any practical significance. And in my view, conventional torture, by which I mean the kind that aims to torment the victim, that is, cause the object in question unendurable physical pain, has on the whole outlived its usefulness. Naturally, this is partly due to the fact that the individual's capacity to become inured to a sense of pain shows faster acceleration than the inventiveness of science when it comes to creating new physical sensations. So today's interrogators do not use torture, just as little as doctrinaire torture methods are brought into use during preparations; *nota bene*, if these are carried out by skilled men. Is that quite clear?

Colonel Pigafetta: Yes.

Gerthoffer: Excellent. I will now proceed to answer the first part of the question, which deals with Velder in particular. Incidentally, this is one of the most instructive and thoroughly prepared cases I have hitherto had the benefit of dealing with. Velder was handed over to our department three years and two months ago. He then came from a military hospital where he had been treated for a bullet wound in his neck. By the time of his convalescence, he had already

37

been interrogated by personnel from some office within the security services, and in connection with that also subjected to primitive forms of conventional torture. Amongst other things, they had smashed his right knee with a sledgehammer. The treatment had not, of course, had the slightest effect on Velder, anyhow not in the direction intended. He was in every way obstinate and unreliable, both deliberately and unconsciously. His experience during recent years had simplified his thinking and after the events that took place in the military hospital, he was adjusted to becoming the object of more complicated forms of primitive physical maltreatment. This way of thinking caused him no great worry. He was well equipped to face varying kinds of physical unpleasantness. The only anxiety he showed took the form of stubbornly asking now and again during the first weeks for the date of his execution.

Our assignment with Velder at first seemed to be fairly uncomplicated. The Minister of the Interior requested that we should prepare him for a series of interviews concerning his connections with a certain Janos Edner. The aim was clearly to ascertain whether Velder had certain information on this Edner's plans and whereabouts, information which the government at that time still had not been able to produce by any other means. Ironically enough, it turned out that on that particular point Velder was completely ignorant. However, shortly after that we received a new directive, because, I am told, the Chief of State himself was personally interested in the case. We were requested to prepare Velder for a much more comprehensive series of interviews, which aimed to account for his activities during the previous eight years of his life, from the day he joined the liberation movement. The assignment was given highest priority, which meant that I found myself called upon to deal with the matter personally.

Commander Kampenmann: Could it not possibly be that you were given orders to deal with the case personally?

Gerthoffer: One can, of course, express it that way, if necessary. It's a matter of interpretation. Thus the assignment before me was first and foremost to make Velder willing to co-operate, and then to persuade him to remember practically everything he had done, seen or heard during eight years of his life and finally to convince him that one or another way of thinking or acting was wrong and should result in legitimate punishment. Finally, he himself would have sufficient confidence to sieve out the episodes in which he himself considered he had acted criminally. The case was from the very first moment handled with the greatest possible care. The first five months were devoted to conversation. Velder was well looked after and we were soon able to break down the wall of rigidity which is common to all service personnel, and which in fact seems to be a pre-requisite for success within the profession. After that it was not long before I definitely won him over on to lines of co-operation. From that moment, we worked with a common aim in mind: to equip Velder mentally for the coming years' interviews. We succeeded beyond all our expectations in this and when Velder was handed over to the General Staff interrogation experts, we parted the best of friends.

Commander Kampenmann: But the torture?

Gerthoffer: The physical features in Velder which you wrongly interpreted as signs of his having endured torture are in fact the consequences of a series of operations, all carried out under anaesthetics and perfectly adequate forms of surgical expertise at the military hospital in Oswaldsburg.

Major von Peters: I don't really understand this.

Gerthoffer: To remember, gentlemen, is not quite so simple as it may seem. It was demanded of Velder that he should recall events, utterances and situations in detail, often matters lying so far back in time and which he himself, at the moment his brain registered them, judged as bagatelles and therefore unimportant. To peel away all intervening layers of memory demands a strength of will-power; surgical intervention in combination with periods of mental weakness has a certain capacity to stimulate the effort of will.

Commander Kampenmann: How many operations of that kind did Velder undergo?

Gerthoffer: Five amputations, one eye operation and partial castration. I personally checked that on each occasion he received the best possible attention. I was the last person Velder spoke to before the anaesthetic was administered and the first person he saw when he came round.

Commander Kampenmann: And you parted friends?

Gerthoffer: Of course. We had a stimulating time together and the results were excellent. The experts who led the interviews had a very easy job.

Commander Kampenmann: But Velder still pleads not guilty?

Gerthoffer: Only on one point, on which he finds himself in a kind of state of conscience. He considers he had been given permission to act as he did, but realises all the same that it was wrong. Unfortunately it is indeed a very important point.

Major von Peters: I've been sitting here thinking about a certain matter. Weren't we neighbours in Marbella two summers ago?

Gerthoffer: Yes, that's correct.

Major von Peters: Then it was your kids who kept hitting shuttlecocks over into my garden all day?

Gerthoffer: That's possible. They were only five and seven years old at the time, and hadn't yet really learnt the game. I hope that they didn't cause you any trouble.

Major von Peters: Not at all. Damned fine kids, anyhow.

Lieutenant Brown: Has the Prosecuting Officer anything to add?

Captain Schmidt: No questions.

Lieutenant Brown: And the Defending Officer?

Captain Endicott: No questions.

Gerthoffer: Goodbye.

Colonel Orbal: Odd profession.

Major von Peters: Seemed to be a good chap. But he wasn't easy to understand until the end, when he eventually came to the point.

Colonel Orbal: Odd witnesses you keep bringing in, Schmidt.

Major von Peters: I still haven't got over that dunderhead of this morning. What a picture of the national liberation.

Colonel Orbal: You look pale. And I've got a sore throat. Did you poison the beef, Pigafetta?

Major von Peters: The television broadcast of the final of the football cup is in fifteen minutes.

Colonel Orbal: Hell, yes, so it is. The Army versus the Air Force. The parties may leave. Session adjourned until eleven o'clock tomorrow.

Fourth Day

Lieutenant Brown: Present Colonel Orbal, Major von Peters, Colonel Pigafetta, Commander Kampenmann. Officer presenting the case, Lieutenant Brown.

Major von Peters: Isn't Haller here today either?

Lieutenant Brown: No, sir. Justice Haller is prevented from appearing.

Major von Peters: And who is Prosecuting Officer.

Lieutenant Brown: Captain Schmidt, sir.

Major von Peters: This really is damned bad. What's the general thinking about.

Colonel Orbal: Well, Pigafetta, how's the Air Force today? Ha, ha, after yesterday, I mean. You won't forget such a clobbering in a hurry, will you?

Colonel Pigafetta: As serving Chief of the Air Force, I've really got other things to think about besides football.

Major von Peters: What for instance?

Colonel Orbal: Did you hear that, Carl? He's a bad loser, too.

Colonel Pigafetta: How dare you sit there and discuss me with one of your subordinates? In the presence of one my own subalterns?

Commander Kampenmann: Calm down, now. Don't get excited.

Colonel Pigafetta: I'm tired of insults. There must be some limit even to boorishness.

Major von Peters: What the hell do you mean? Just say that again!

Colonel Pigafetta: The word was boorishness. An art developed by boors. And army officers.

Colonel Orbal: No, now that's bloody well enough, Pigafetta. If

41

you can't face being clobbered at football, then you'll have to get your men taught the harp instead. The men, incidentally ... what are they doing now? Standing around on jankers in some hangar or other?

Major von Peters: They haven't got the discipline for that.

Commander Kampenmann: Shut up.

Major von Peters: What the hell did you say? By God, what's this all about, for that matter? Are you sitting there trying to give me orders, Kampenmann? Anyway, you've been sitting there making yourself important for several days now. You shouldn't interfere with this, anyhow.

Commander Kampenmann: As an officer in the Navy, I refuse to ...

Major von Peters: Oh, you and your shitty Navy.

Colonel Pigafetta: Spare me your vulgarity, please. Ever since this session was opened, I've had to put up with far too much to make the odds even. As if it weren't enough with your platitudes and Kampenmann's officiousness, I also have to find myself daily being by-passed by a person of subordinate rank.

Coloner Orbal: When, for God's sake?

Colonel Pigafetta: At the daily enumeration of those present, for instance. Every time, I repeat—every time, von Peters' name is read out before mine.

Colonel Orbal: Listen to the man.

Colonel Pigafetta: The worst thing is that you've induced one of my own officers into this astonishing offence against decency and good tone.

Major von Peters: It would be the absolute limit if representatives of the Army, rank apart, were to be read out after those of the Air Force, wouldn't it?

Commander Kampenmann: I demand an apology from you, von Peters.

Major von Peters: What for? Because I said shitty Navy? Not on your life.

Colonel Orbal: Don't shout so damned loudly, Carl. They'll hear you all over the bloody Air Force Headquarters.

Commander Kampenmann: And from you, too, Colonel Pigafetta. I haven't come here to be insulted ...

Colonel Pigafetta: I refuse to stay a minute longer in this company. I'm leaving before I'm tempted to degrade myself with the type of argument which is evidently considered to part of good tone at Army Headquarters.

Commander Kampenmann: I demand an apology.

Major von Peters: Shut up.

Colonel Orbal: Demand and demand.

Colonel Pigafetta: Good-morning, gentlemen.

Commander Kampenmann: I still demand redress and I wish to have it here and now.

Colonel Orbal: Calm down, Kampenmann. Just because that lunatic from the Air Force is suffering from megalomania, there's no need for you to act like a bloody prima donna.

Commander Kampenmann: I really must request respect for my service. My honour as an officer ...

Major von Peters: Shut up, I said.

Colonel Orbal: This I'll have to stop. You'll have to settle this dispute between the two of you.

Major von Peters: It'll be a pleasure.

Colonel Orbal: Let's get to hell out of this today. Best to continue tomorrow.

Lieutenant Brown: What shall I tell the people waiting outside.

Colonel Orbal: Tell them what the hell you like.

Major von Peters: And Brown, not a word about this little dispute to anyone.

Lieutenant Brown: Sir, may I point out with incisiveness that as a Lieutenant in the Air Force I am on oath and like yourself have sworn that not a word shall be uttered outside these walls ...

Colonel Orbal: Oh, my God, don't you start, too. The session is adjourned until eleven o'clock tomorrow.

Fifth Day

Lieutenant Brown: Present Colonel Orbal, Colonel Pigafetta, Major von Peters, Commander Kampenmann. Officer presenting the case, Lieutenant Brown.

Colonel Orbal: I asked you all to come a quarter of an hour earlier.

Colonel Pigafetta: And we have, as you see, come.

Colonel Orbal: I've been thinking about this. Von Peters and I have had a discussion.

Major von Peters: We came to the conclusion that this assignment is far too important and ... well ...

Commander Kampenmann: Delicate?

Major von Peters: Exactly, much too delicate to be jeopardised by personal antagonisms.

Colonel Pigafetta: That should be fairly obvious.

Major von Peters: Yes, it should. Therefore, Colonel Orbal requests, not as President of the Court ...

Colonel Orbal: Exactly. Therefore I, as the senior officer present, would like to suggest that we draw a line through any discord that has occurred.

Major von Peters: And accept each other's apologies.

Colonel Orbal: Is that all right?

Commander Kampenmann: As far as I'm concerned, yes.

Colonel Orbal: And you, Pigafetta?

Colonel Pigafetta: All right. Though ...

Major von Peters: Though what?

Colonel Pigafetta: Oh, nothing. I'm prepared to accept your solution.

Colonel Orbal: Then the matter can now be considered closed.

44

Colonel Pigafetta: At least for the moment.

Major von Peters: Exactly.

Colonel Orbal: Good.

Major von Peters: I heard at Headquarters by the way, that the General is said to have given Schmidt a fearful dressing down for his way of presenting the prosecution. It probably won't be long now before he's forced to bring in Bratianu. In which case, Schmidt will just have to be more incisive.

Tadeusz Haller: Oh, you're already here, gentlemen?

Colonel Pigafetta: Yes, an internal military matter brought us together.

Tadeusz Haller: I see. I understand yesterday's session was rather short.

Colonel Orbal: Is the General ... I mean, has the Chief of State been ...

Tadeusz Haller: Irritated? Not at all. As I said on the first day, the Chief of State has from the start indicated that time is not that important. The main aim of this session is that the court informs itself so thoroughly on the background of the Velder case that the verdict on the various sections will be absolutely unassailable, even for scrutiny in the legislature.

Major von Peters: I still don't really see the point.

Tadeusz Haller: Between ourselves, I think the Chief of State intends to use the verdicts against Velder, and this whole investigation, as a club with which to beat the civil lawyers who are at present in the Ministry and the legislature.

Commander Kampenmann: You yourself are one of them.

Tadeusz Haller: My position is, as you will realise, somewhat different. I am the Chief of State's personal adviser. The Chief of State, however, is a soldier. He relies more on military than on civil justice.

Major von Peters: Thank God for that. Who is presenting the case today?

Tadeusz Haller: Schmidt. I was speaking to him just now in the hall.

Major von Peters: He probably won't be coming tomorrow. Get going, now, Mateo.

Colonel Orbal: Of course. Let the others in, Brown.

Captain Schmidt: We have now penetrated somewhat more deeply into our mission. The first thirty-two charges in the case against Velder, together with completely conclusive evidence have been submitted to the court. Before I proceed to the detailed submission concerning the continued criminal activities of the accused, I would like once again to take up the matter concerning which social and ethical factors impelled Velder along his course of crime and more and more deeply into moral decay. I request in this case to be allowed to refer to the registered documentation of the preliminary investigation.

Colonel Orbal: What? What did you say?

Major von Peters: More reading aloud?

Captain Schmidt: I intend to show, point by point, that it was the slackness and lack of moral responsibility in the existing form of society, its contempt for the fear of God and its indifference to the evident respect for firm leadership, which brought about Velder's —and that of many others—final ruin.

Colonel Pigafetta: Please keep your orations for the final summing up.

Captain Schmidt: To illustrate how the society that turned Velder into a criminal really functioned, I would like to refer to V II/13 of the preliminary investigation. This consists of a letter, written about two years after the liberation, by the then Councillor Aranca Peterson, later sentenced to death *in contumacia*.

Colonel Orbal: In what? What on earth did you say, man?

Captain Schmidt: Four years ago, she was sentenced to death for treason, in her absence.

Colonel Orbal: Well, we all know that.

Captain Schmidt: Aranca Peterson seems to have written this letter quite privately. You will find tendencies in it which indicate that even a fallen woman such as she was, suffered from subconscious pangs of conscience and felt a need, at least to herself, to show shame and regret over the conditions of chaos and criminal immorality which she and her fellow-conspirators had brought to the country. The letter is franked Zürich and addressed to another member of the Council, Janos Edner, with whom the aforementioned Aranca Peterson lived in unseemly circumstances.

Lieutenant Brown: Appendix V II/13. Marked secret according

46

to paragraph twenty-three. The text is as follows ...

Colonel Orbal: Twenty-three, is that the obscenity paragraph?

Captain Schmidt: Yes, that's correct.

Colonel Orbal: Loud and clear, now, Brown.

Lieutenant Brown: The text is as follows: My darling, this is a dismal windy town and I can't imagine why it is known for its beauty. And also I'm not sure I'm the right person for these international conferences. They talk and talk and I concentrate as best I can, but after a while I find myself sitting there longing for home, thinking about something quite different, mostly you, of course. The only consolation is that if you look round, you notice that all the others are also sitting day-dreaming and that the only person who is remotely paying attention is the one who is standing at the lectern, trying not to make mistakes as he reads from his manuscript, which usually someone else has written.

Anyhow, I have managed to find time to do quite a lot of useful things here these last two days. Met W yesterday and again today at lunch and late in the afternoon. He was very positive and optimistic and said that his government would ratify the agreement this week and that deliveries will get started at the end of next month. He thinks a lot about his percentage, avarice glistens in his eyes, and I'm sure he finds it hard to sleep at night, thinking about all that money he can make on the side. To judge from actual appearances—he dribbled at the mouth and at first I thought he was going to rape me—well, to judge from appearances, then we can probably be certain that the shipments will come as they should. 'With utmost punctuality' he said. We can also probably reckon that he himself 'with utmost punctuality' will be standing in front of his bank-deposit here in Zürich, waiting for the deposits to fall in.

I met him at his hotel, but then we went in separate cars to the congress hall. He was the first speaker of the afternoon, and he condemned us roundly in tremendous terms. He said, for instance; this (ours, that is) is a country which through its activities and spineless politics has lost all sympathy and placed itself outside every form of international co-operation. We demand immediate international sanctions against this impertinent little dictatorship and until our views gain general approval, we are thinking of continuing in our

47

rôle of the conscience of the world and of imposing a total and uncompromising blockade. Neither a pin nor a sewing-needle shall we export, for to trade with a country like this (he shouted) is as unthinkable to us (and here he achieved a really handsome metaphor) as for the famous camel to get through the needle's eye. A nation (he puffed, when he'd got his breath back) which gains its prosperity, its free life and its sovereignty with the aid of loans and generous investments from understanding, unsuspecting democracies such as our country, and which then rewards this gratitude (here he lost the thread completely) by a completely, ... I wanted to say unprecedented (he stopped and finally saved the situation by saying ...) well, I'm at a loss for words.

He stood there struggling for air, and naturally I did my duty without getting up, by taking the words from his mouth and saying: Well, it is quite true that we nationalised the foreign concessions which were making in-roads into our people's rights. We have never made a secret of that. We are not afraid to put our cards on the table and stand by our decisions (one in the eye for him, the bastard). In that way we have repulsed attempts by the capitalist and imperialist countries to get a foothold into what is for them virgin ground, in the same way as we have rejected every sign of international communism and other mass ideologies trying to sabotage our independence and make us into a pawn in the game between the power blocks.

A few people even applauded, although it was just after lunch and everyone was just sitting aching for some bicarbonate of soda. W didn't say anything else about us, but stood muttering for a while that they couldn't fulfil their deliveries and obligations before the agreement with the international steel union. When he went back to his place, he was stupid enough to wink at me, the idiot. It's a pity we need their damned steel, not to mention the other stuff.

Later on in the afternoon, when we met W again and settled the details in a meeting room at my hotel, the door was suddenly flung open and BM swept in with a whole lot of guys who he'd presumably been talking to about agricultural products. He stared at W and me as if he'd seen an apparition. They had made a muddle at the hotel and booked the same rooms for two different conferences at the same time. It didn't matter, of course, except that BM suspected something nasty in the woodshed, but I felt so incredibly silly and ashamed, rather like that time five years ago when we were sleeping together in your room and didn't know the lock was broken and that so-called head of the company came in with two English guests in black jackets and striped trousers, whom he was showing round his marvellous place. I can never laugh when such things happen—just feel foolish. At this moment I feel foolish and lonely.

The whole affair with BM is settled, anyhow. We'll get stocks that'll last for ten years.

Tomorrow I've promised to make a statement with an interview attached to some international women's organisation. It's being broadcast on several television networks, radio, of course, and all that. I know exactly what it'll be like. They'll ask about all the same old things and I know all the answers. It'll end by some of them getting annoyed and most of them pretending to be fearfully impressed.

Darling, will we really manage this? Did we know what we were letting ourselves in for four years ago, when this conspiracy began? Are you really so certain as you maintain when you say that it can't fail? Couldn't it get out of hand.

'Get out of hand' is exactly what I said to myself as I left home. The plane rose from the airport and—the airport building is really formidable now it's finished; Dr Stoloff and his guys have done a good job there—well, then it flew in a wide sweep in over Oswalds-burg. I was sitting on the inner curve, so to speak, and I saw all the houses, the finished ones and the unfinished ones, from straight above. All that upward-straining, astonishing building. I ask myself again: Will it get out of hand? *I* have a feeling, anyhow, of having neither it nor the island under control any longer. Nor Ludolfsport either, which we flew over twenty minutes later. Possibly Marbella, and although it's naturally the most complicated part of the country, I still feel most at home there. Sometimes I don't even like those ostentatious names—Oswaldsburg and Ludolfsport, for instance—although I myself was in on choosing them. It really is a bit of luck we didn't fall for the temptation (?) to call Marbella Ednaranca as Oswald and Ludolf wanted to at the time.

Don't know if I could've borne it today.

You must forgive me. I don't know why I'm thinking like this, when I'm alone and haven't got anything to do. Especially when everything has gone so well and has been such fun.

When I get home I must have all the people and all the materials for the new airport hotels in Marbella. And the other casino must be ready by March, even if it kills me. It can't be helped if our other projects have to remain at a standstill for a few weeks.

Apropos what I wrote ten minutes ago, I happened to think about one of our night talks long ago. I said: And what do we want it for? You said: We'll re-create it into a place where people like us and other people feel well. I said: What do you mean by feel well? You said: Simply thinking that it's fun to work, to feel yourself surrounded by people who understand and like you, naturally to have food, houseroom, what you think you need, all that, to have some point to your existence and a goal, and see others round about you who also have one. I said: And what shall we do with it when we've got it? You said: Live in it. I said: Is that the whole point of us and this island, which we presumably will never get? You said: That island, which we'll certainly get, you know just as well as I do, is a natural self-sufficient unit: it should and must be free and independent. I said: Of course, that's the point.

But we made those remarks as if they were tag-ends in some way, as if we'd said them out of shame. We both felt this, so after a while we went on with the argument and agreed on the following: today the island is the haunt of a small number of people who live a joyless and stupidly enough even an economically rather meagre life there. Lots of people who really belong there and who would like to be there are forced to move because of unemployment, lack of development, all that sort of thing. Fifty times that number of individuals could live really happily on that island, fifty times as many as those who live there now and are unhappy.

Do you remember that conversation? Yes, of course you remember everything of importance we've done and said together, just as well as I do. I've forgotten almost everything else. But as far as that argument is concerned, it seems to me now infinitely more important than what I thought then. I think that in that conversation lie the keys to both the past and the future, that on that occasion, we'd once and for all formulated both what is right and what is wrong in our thinking and our ideas. Or, anyhow, seen the truth without understanding it.

It's an unpleasant thought.

Anyhow, what will Oswald use three hundred jeeps for? It sounds crazy. But I suppose he can be crazy in his way if he wants to be. All that business about immigration he arranged perfectly. I've had compliments from international quarters about it as recently as today.

I love you so. Thanks for the fine pen you gave me on the airport. I'm writing this letter with it.

Please forgive this long and childish and disjointed letter, but I'm sitting here in the middle of the night in my hotel room. I'm feeling very randy, which respectable ladies shouldn't, I suppose, and so I'm homesick. I long for you. I don't want to go to bed alone among all those bolsters in that large elegant bed, but now I'm going to all the same. I love you, your Aranca.

Colonel Orbal: How old was this woman?

Captain Schmidt: Thirty-two. She had at the time an eight-month-old child by Janos Edner, but funnily enough, she does not mention it.

Colonel Orbal: What's funny about that?

Captain Schmidt: I didn't mean that literally.

Colonel Orbal: Seems to have been ardent sort of woman. What did she look like?

Captain Schmidt: Small, fair, lively. Blue eyes. Well developed, they say. There's a description here, four foot seven, eight stone three ...

Major von Peters: You know perfectly well what Aranca Peterson looked like, Mateo. You've seen thousands of pictures of her.

Captain Schmidt: Aranca Peterson did not send that letter off the next day. She obviously left it and then added something the next evening. That too, is of a certain interest. Continue, Lieutenant Brown.

Lieutenant Brown: My appearance this evening, as usual, was an extraordinary business. They asked questions until I nearly died. Unfortunately, I probably looked rather dreadful on television because the heat from the lights was terrible and my face was sweating as usual. I'll give you the main points; in comparison with all that rubbish I wrote yesterday, perhaps they'll be of some interest.

51

I warmed them up with the usual statement. Then the great bombardment began:

If your country considers that it follows a pacifist line, why do you refuse to ally yourselves to the block of states which has been formed along peaceful lines?

Because all power blocks at all times have believed or maintained that they were working for peace. The results speak for themselves.

So you dissociate yourself from the third world as an idea?

Yes. From the four and the fifth, too. For us, pacifism is a type of politics without any personal conception of life.

Do you consider it compatible with the idea of pacifism that your own party as long as two years ago started an armed revolution and took power by force?

The force that was used was extremely limited. The whole of the revolution cost fewer than ten lives. However, even that was deplorable, and I would be the first to admit it.

But if the attempts to suppress the liberation movement had been more forceful, the number of victims would naturally have been much greater?

Hardly. If anyone had attacked us with arms, we wouldn't have been so foolish as to have tried to use the same primitive means.

Do you mean that you wouldn't have wanted to defend yourselves, or that you wouldn't have been able to?

We neither wanted to nor were able to. In our case, the latter is dependent on the former and vice versa.

If you were attacked from outside today, would you also refuse to defend yourselves?

Who would want to attack us?

(After that there was a brief silence. Finally someone said):

That's no answer to the question. Would you offer military resistance?

Naturally not.

I think I know that your army today has put in discreet but relatively large orders for arms and other equipment?

What you think you know does not interest me very much, apart from the fact that it absolutely incorrect. First of all, we have no army. Secondly, we have neither bought nor ordered any military equipment.

Do you deny that less than a month ago your gendarmerie, or militia as you call it, ordered a very large number of military vehicles from a certain place abroad?

(Those damned jeeps!)

There's no reason to deny that. We have no car-factories and consequently have to import transport vehicles. Naturally we choose the type of vehicle that suits our terrain.

(End of the pacifist section. A madwoman from Ireland began to talk about God.)

I have, thank the Lord, never visited your country and neither shall I ever do so, but I have read and heard that you have no official religion.

Yes, that is correct.

They say that on the whole island there is not a single church. Why?

Presumably because there is no need for churches.

Then your people are completely secularised?

I don't know. I can't answer personally for every single individual.

Can you truly demand that the poor souls you've forced to live in spiritual darkness can exist under your anti-religious tyranny?

The question appears to me academic. If there are people who need a church, they will certainly build one themselves.

Would you then maintain that there is freedom of religious belief in your country?

Naturally.

I have brought with me a novel written by one of your authors and printed in Oswaldsburg. A dreadful book, but nevertheless I wish to quote a piece from it. This is word for word:

They find a guy called God, then, and in his honour they build a special building, which they go into at definite times and kneel and mumble incantations. This may seem somewhat strange at a time when we've learnt to control and make use of all known forces of nature, when vehicles made by human hands land on the moon and when ... I need read no further, I hope. Now I'm asking you: Does this author represent your country's official standpoint?

Our country has no official standpoints, either in matters of belief or any other matters.

(End of discussion, thank goodness.)

It seems to me that there are more interesting points in your speech than those concerning religion. Your country is, as far as I know, the only one in the world that lacks a constitution?

Yes. Neither are there any other laws or regulations.

So you make no claim to being regarded as a judicial state?

Yes, but not in that expression's conventional sense.

And despite this, you have a gendarmerie. Why?

The militia has two tasks. One is to see to passport and visa control, the other to function as a rescue service for accidents or in cases or illness or in other emergencies which lie outside the control of the individual. It's task vis-à-vis the ordinary citizen is to help, not to guard.

All this sounds very good, of course, but how does it function in practice? Is it not so that despite the absence of laws and regulations you have jurisdiction, a penal code, and some kind of courts.

It is incorrect to talk about a penal code. There is only one punishment for us—deportation. If you are deported, you may never return.

On what principle is this highly remarkable jurisdiction based?

The principle of good sense. It lies in the individual's own hands to determine what he or she can allow him or herself to do in relation to his or her fellow-human beings.

How often has this punishment had to be resorted to?

Hitherto, in ten or so cases.

And who decides when it shall be enforced?

We do. The people who live in the country.

Is it not so that an authority called the Council—of which you yourself are a member—decides such matters and other essential ones?

In principle, every citizen is a member of that Council.

I have heard that. But I've also heard that in practice the Council consists of a junta of five people and that only in exceptional cases has it happened that outsiders, so to speak, may take part in decisions. Is that so?

Of course.

Isn't that Fascism?

(I've heard that question several times before and I like it less each time.)

No, not in any respect whatsoever.

54

Anyhow, it's not democracy, is it?

Not if by democracy you mean a system committed to parties and politicians, which suffocates the individual's sense of responsibility, and thus also his initiative, with a flood of laws and hardened doctrines, with regulations which are meaningless from the beginning because they are not really self-evident, and the effect of which is that they make the individual feel incapacitated and gradually make him doubt his own mind. Democracy in the form you mean breeds nothing but a boundless, constantly-growing bureaucracy and a mind-paralysing bickering about trifles, so-called problems, which any normal ten-year-old could solve at the flick of a hand. Nor if you mean guidance of the people, the tea-party game for the chosen, in which outworn and old-fashioned concepts such as liberalism, reaction, social-democracy and radicalism are bounced back and forth as in a ping-pong match with neither a beginning nor an end.

This philosophy, so remarkably alien to reality, is, as you know, not new, but it would be highly interesting to see it working in practice.

(Sufficient sacrifices laid at the altar of demagogy. Then there was a short cross-examination.)

Official information on your country's financial status and the people's standard of living is indeed diffuse, but despite the artificial population explosion you have achieved through immigration, it seems as if you have succeeded in creating a certain economic balance. This appears remarkable, as the country in which you and your compeers caused a revolution was still a fairly backward agricultural province. On what factors is this relative well-being based?

On the fact that we created circumstances in which work was no longer regarded as a necessary evil but as a meaningful occupation.

Do you mean by that that you have no leisure-time problems?

Yes, amongst other things.

What is your largest source of income?

The tourist industry. To put it succinctly, you might say we undertake to solve other people's leisure-time problems. Thanks to good geographical and climatic conditions, in combination with the factors I named earlier, we seem to have succeeded in this to everyone's satisfaction.

55

(I'd taken the words out of her mouth there, and she didn't say anything else.)

You said just now that there are no churches or religious communities in your country. Nor any authorities. Have you also got rid of other cornerstones of society, marriage, for instance?

No, people who live together can naturally get married if they want to.

So they can enter into wedlock? In what way?

In any way they like. That's up to each person.

What proportion of those people who live together and create a family get married?

I don't think anyone has taken the trouble to compile such extremely pointless statistics. But among people who live together or move in together in order to create a family, I think I have noticed a general tendency to manifest their cohabitation in various ways.

How can they do that?

Through private agreement, for instance, verbal or written. They can also add their names to a list which is available to all.

Is it true that you do not tax individual citizens?

Yes, by the end of our second year, communally owned sources of income paid such good dividends that it was considered possible to make a distribution, instead of collecting taxes.

What are these communally owned sources of income?

The tourist trade and overseas communications. As I said in my preliminary statement, the aim is that only the south-western area round the town of Marbella is to be exploited for tourism. Otherwise all new building, as I mentioned, has been concentrated in the two other larger towns. The aim is partly to avoid unnecessary interference with the countryside, and partly to protect our agricultural areas. Thanks to intensified exploitation and specialisation, we have in fact, in spite of the increase in population, managed to maintain overproduction of foodstuffs. Quality products from agriculture are at present our main exports. In addition, we have had to—in consideration of the huge demand—limit the touristified area. Otherwise the whole country would gradually be flooded with foreigners, to no one's advantage.

When I visited your country. I had the impression that most things were very expensive, at least in Marbella.

Presumably you also had the opportunity to observe that our service is first-class.

Is it true that your immigration conditions nowadays are extremely severe?

To apply for citizenship you must have a recommendation from at least four people who are already living in the country. Despite this, the population is still increasing.

Your visa regulations are not particularly liberal either. As a foreigner, it is impossible to get permission to live in the country for any length of time. Why is that?

It's an economic matter. We issue visas in three categories, for fourteen days, a week and forty-eight hours. The latter service is intended for guests who use speedy communications, i.e. air travel and hovercraft, to enjoy our attractions for a shorter period.

You mean the gambling dens and brothels?

Yes, to some extent.

(The Irishwoman got her chance then.)

It appears that your country lives on the exploitation of sins and depravity.

I would not presume to judge what are sins or depravity, except on my own account.

You cannot deny you have what someone called a comprehensive brothel system, which is considered to be the bes ... I mean, the most extensive in the civilised world?

No, why should I do that? I myself organised it. What do you mean, by the way, by the civilised world?

(Then, thank heavens, time ran out. I was given thirty seconds to wind things up. The usual stuff.)

Now I'm off to bed at last. I don't see how I can stand it here for another week. I'll probably come home before it ends. Goodnight, your Aranca.

Major von Peters: Is that the end at last?

Captain Schmidt: No, not quite. The letter contains one more addition, a post-script.

Lieutenant Brown: P.S. It didn't work. When I tried to go to sleep, I had the most ghastly jealous vision ...

Major von Peters: Brown, for God's sake let's have a moment's peace. Is it really necessary to read that out as well?

Captain Schmidt: I consider that it is. The P.S. is quite short, but it presents a horrifying picture of the kind of exaggerated free speech and the wholly disintegrated morality which flourished under the régime, even among the women, and within the leadership.

Colonel Orbal: This sounds interesting.

Captain Schmidt: It is frightening rather than interesting. I am warning the court that this bit of the appendix is extremely distasteful. But it illuminates, as I said, the total lack of ordinary decency at the time and at the same time it portrays the environment in which the accused was to live in the future.

Colonel Orbal: Yes, yes. Get going now, Brown.

Lieutenant Brown: P.S. It didn't work. When I tried to go to sleep, I had the most ghastly jealous vision. Darling, it's horrible, but I must try to tell you everything. I must ask you one thing. That you try to avoid sleeping with Dana. And *if* you do (but try not to!) then tell me at once, because I'll notice at once anyhow, I'm certain of that. I wouldn't ask you if I didn't know, really know that it could happen so easily, some time when I was away like this, or not around.

The vision I had was just that you suddenly went over to her and stood behind her and then you suddenly undid the belt of her white overall and she stood quite still while you did it, her arms hanging down her sides. She had nothing on underneath and when you let the overall fall to the floor, she was naked and then she stepped out of her white clogs and turned round. I was afraid because now I knew you couldn't stop. You've never seen her naked, but I have, several times in the sauna, when we've been bathing together.

I know a little about her which I don't think you know. And I also know exactly what she looks like. She's narrower across the shoulders and hips than I am, and slightly taller. Her breasts are much smaller, but her nipples at least three times as large as mine and dark brown. Every time I've seen her without clothes, they've stood straight up from her breasts, or straight out if you like, at least half an inch. Her skin is quite brown and from her navel downwards she's got a string of short black hairs. You say my cunt is large, but hers is larger, at least it looks it. The hair is quite black and thick and in round tight curls. It goes further up on her stomach than on any other person I've ever seen. Once, about six months ago.

she fell asleep in the sauna and I sat looking at her. She was lying on her back, sleeping very uneasily, moving her thighs all the time and fumbling with her hands all over her hips and breasts. I saw exactly how she felt and why, and when she woke I asked her straight out. She said at once that she hadn't had a man for seven months and then it was someone she didn't even know what he looked like, someone she'd met on the beach in the middle of the night when she was out walking, because she couldn't bear being indoors lying in bed. She said that she'd just felt dispirited afterwards and that she didn't want to do that again. She also told me she'd been married once and had lots of affairs before she came here, but that everything had gone wrong and ended badly in some way. People had died and been destroyed all round her, and the ones she'd really wanted to be with, she'd just done harm to, and she herself had always been unhappy. When she came here she had decided to try to live without sex, and she had done so too, almost completely. What had happened on the shore wasn't that. But it wasn't easy, she said, and I know that only too well.

Now I'll tell you why I had that vision, too. It seemed a bit shabby towards her, which is why I didn't tell you before. It was last summer, when it was so terribly hot and we were in the little house down by the shore. I was busy with something in the inner room and out there you were walking to and fro in your shirt and bathing trunks, dictating something. She was sitting at the table writing and she was wearing those white clogs and that white overall. I came out to fetch something and happened to look at her. She seemed strange in some way and when she looked at me her eyes were quite cloudy. Suddenly she let everything fall from her hands and said to me: I must talk to you for a moment. She sounded hoarse and peculiar, but you didn't notice anything, but just shrugged your shoulders and went out. She came in with me and locked the door behind her and I hadn't a clue what was going on. She kicked off her clogs and tore off her overall. She was wearing nothing underneath. Without saying a word, she threw herself down on her back on the bed and began to masturbate. I was absolutely nonplussed (for once) and didn't know what to do, so I went over to the window and stood there looking out. It took about ten minutes before she got an orgasm and then it went on for quite a time. Then she lay quite still for a while and neither of us said anything until she got up and dressed. Then she looked at me and said: Sorry. I just couldn't bear it. And I said: I understand.

I just felt bloody sorry for her and also a little ashamed too, because you and I had been together only a few hours earlier.

For many people it might well seem unusually stupid of me to write like this to you, but I don't think so. I just want to tell you that it's slightly dangerous. Now I really will go to bed. 'Bye darling. A.

Colonel Orbal: What page is that on?

Captain Schmidt: Page nine hundred and twenty-two.

Colonel Orbal: Give me that book, Carl.

Major von Peters: Is it possible that we've now come to an end of all these perversions, smut and filth?

Captain Schmidt: The appendix ends there.

Colonel Orbal: Who was this woman?

Captain Schmidt: Danica Rodriguez. Secretary to Janos Edner.

Colonel Orbal: Was that the one with the moustache?

Captain Schmidt: Exactly.

Colonel Orbal: Oh, hell.

Major von Peters: I must say, Schmidt, that you're well on the way to transforming this court martial into ... well, I don't know what. I'm at a loss for words.

Colonel Pigafetta: In that case that's the most remarkable and fortunate thing that's happened in this room for a long time.

Major von Peters: What do you mean?

Colonel Pigafetta: Nothing, of course.

Major von Peters: I've noticed one very strange thing, Schmidt. During the whole of all that reading, I never heard Velder's name mentioned once. Why is the accused sitting here at all? Because it amuses him? It doesn't amuse me in the slightest.

Colonel Pigafetta: The trial is in fact advancing somewhat slowly.

Colonel Orbal: Peculiar person.

Colonel Pigafetta: Who?

Colonel Orbal: That Edner. That he didn't notice anything, I mean. The woman was almost naked and just about dying of ... oh, well, continue.

Major von Peters: What with? Reading aloud?

Commander Kampenmann: I was just thinking about something.

60

How did the brothels function in fact?

Colonel Orbal: Excellently. They were still here when I came here.

Commander Kampenmann: I meant organisationally.

Colonel Orbal: I really have no idea about that.

Tadeusz Haller: I can inform you on that matter. Briefly, women from abroad were found, chosen very carefully and given work-permits here for periods of three months. If they behaved well, the permit was renewed. They had a fairly good monthly salary, but a lot was demanded of them and medical control was very thorough.

Commander Kampenmann: In other words, the State acted as procurers?

Tadeusz Haller: That is a matter of judgement. Their salaries were tax-free.

Commander Kampenmann: Where did the profit come in?

Tadeusz Haller: Oh, their salaries made up only about two or three per cent of the customers' expenses. The establishments were exclusive and the service quite advanced. If there had been a register of customers, it would certainly have astounded you.

Commander Kampenmann: Did the country's own inhabitants use this—er—service?

Tadeusz Haller: It wasn't forbidden, but presumably very seldom.

Commander Kampenmann: Where did the women go then?

Tadeusz Haller: The overwhelming majority were dispatched out of the country when their contracts ran out. But there were some who applied for citizenship and stayed here. Some are still here, as married women.

Major von Peters: I request that we drop this subject immediately. It has nothing to do with Velder. Go on, Schmidt.

Captain Schmidt: After his first thirteen months' service, Velder was transferred to what was called the militia's emergency corps, in which he remained for a year. During this time, he committed twelve offences, which in the detailed charge sheet are taken up under points thirty-three to and including forty-four. The charges in five cases are dereliction of duty, in three theft from military stores, and in three cases drunkenness on duty and finally in one case abuse of rank. I request that as in the earlier consideration of the first complex of offences, to be allowed to lay these before you without further evidence. The accused's signed confessions, witnessed on oath, are submitted.

Major von Peters: Uhuh. Endicott, does the accused adhere to his confessions?

Captain Endicott: He does.

Major von Peters: Then we'll add these to the proceedings. That's it. That's something, anyhow.

Commander Kampenmann: Shouldn't the kind of offence be described more extensively, at least briefly?

Major von Peters: Christ, you are awkward. Theft of twenty-six packets of biscuits on sixteen different occasions, theft of a first-aid box, theft of sixteen tins of food, he's got a good memory, I must say, drunk in action, what action for Christ's sake?

Captain Schmidt: The militia's emergency corps also acted in the capacity of fire brigade.

Major von Peters: Oh, yes. And drunkenness while on duty as a driving-instructor. Oh, hell, take this rubbish away and read it for yourself.

Commander Kampenmann: Thank you.

Captain Endicott: As far as the charges of theft are concerned, I should like to point out one detail, despite Velder's confession. There were no military stores in existence as such. On special assignments, however, provisions and other consumer material were issued and it was customary that the men shared out between them what was left over.

Major von Peters: Uhuh. Now you've pointed that out, haven't you?

Captain Schmidt: Velder, do you admit gross theft on these three occasions?

Velder: Yes, sir.

Major von Peters: Stand to attention.

Velder: I'm doing my best to, sir.

Captain Schmidt: After his service in the emergency corps, Velder was transferred to General Oswald's bodyguard. With that, his criminal activities took on a character which was more serious and damaging to society.

Major von Peters: We can't cope with any more today. Mateo, let the parties right left turn forward march.

Colonel Orbal: What? What did you say?

Colonel Pigafetta: The parties may leave.

Major von Peters: It's tough on Endicott, I must say. What a bloody awful posting. And I consider we must get rid of Schmidt. I can't stand him another day.

Colonel Orbal: Have we finished now?

Major von Peters: Do stop reading that book now, Mateo. Adjourn the session.

Colonel Orbal: The session is adjourned.

Sixth Day

Lieutenant Brown: Those present: Colonel Orbal, Colonel Pigafetta, Major von Peters, Commander Kampenmann and Justice Tadeusz Haller. Officer presenting the case, Lieutenant Brown.

Colonel Orbal: Hellish cold in here.

Colonel Pigafetta: The heating isn't working.

Colonel Orbal: Why don't you try getting it repaired?

Colonel Pigafetta: We are. Please note, I said *we*. I've got our own technicians on to it this time. As long as the whole system isn't wholly useless or too hopelessly installed, we should have it functioning within an hour. My men know their job.

Major von Peters: That remains to be seen.

Colonel Pigafetta: What do you mean by that?

Major von Peters: I was just sitting here thinking about the accident statistics in the Air Force.

Colonel Pigafetta: In relation to the size of the country, our Air Force is one of the strongest in the world. If you compare the accident rates in the best equipped of the great powers, then our figures are in no way remarkable. You know that perfectly well, Major von Peters. I take your remarks as malicious and insulting.

Tadeusz Haller: Gentlemen, gentlemen ...

Colonel Orbal: Yes, calm down now, Pigafetta. You too, Carl. Return to order.

Lieutenant Brown: Captain Schmidt is unable to be present. He has had an urgent and important posting. The prosecution will be presented by Prosecuting Officer, Lieutenant Mihail Bratianu.

Major von Peters: Good.

Commander Kampenmann: You don't sound very surprised, Major von Peters. Is this a manoeuvre to enrich the court martial with yet another representative of the Army?

Colonel Orbal: You're all hellish bad-tempered today. And it's as cold as an Eskimo cunt in here, as General Winckelman used to say when we opened the mess windows. Now we must get going. Call in the parties, Brown.

Lieutenant Bratianu: Colonel Orbal, Major von Peters, Colonel Pigafetta, Commander Kampenmann, Justice Haller, I request to be allowed to continue the case from the point where Captain Schmidt found it necessary to interrupt it.

Major von Peters: Excellent demeanour.

Colonel Orbal: What are you whispering about, Carl?

Major von Peters: I said: Damned fine demeanour. Bratianu's, I mean.

Colonel Orbal: Good bearing, that lad, what?

Colonel Pigafetta: What are you gentlemen mumbling about? Granted, Bratianu.

Colonel Orbal: Of course. Granted.

Lieutenant Bratianu: Charge forty-five. Insubordination and dereliction of duty combined with want of common sense and carelessness on duty. Corporal Velder.

Velder: Yes, sir.

Lieutenant Bratianu: Stand to attention, Velder. I'm sure you can do better than that. That's right. On the third of May seven years ago, Corporal Velder, in his capacity of chauffeur and bodyguard, accompanied General Oswald on an official journey to what was then Ludolfsport. The General visited a building in the old part of the town. This occurred at fifteen thirty hours. Corporal Velder was posted as guard by the jeep. Forty-five minutes later the General returned and found that Corporal Velder had left his post. The General had to search for over ten minutes before he found Corporal Velder three blocks away. On their return to militia headquarters, it appeared that Corporal Velder's map-holder was missing. The accused's own motivation for his action is so astonishing that the honoured presidium should hear it with their own ears. I request that Corporal Erwin Velder be called as witness.

Major von Peters: Granted.

Lieutenant Brown: Erwin Velder, do you swear by Almighty God to keep strictly to the truth?

Velder: I do, sir.

Lieutenant Bratianu: Why did you leave your post?

Velder: I knew that Oswal ...

Lieutenant Bratianu: *General* Oswald.

Velder: Sorry, sir. He didn't call himself General then.

Lieutenant Bratianu: No comments. Answer clearly and concisely.

Velder: I knew from experience that General Oswald would be away for about an hour. Four boys of about ten years of age were playing ball in the street and after about ten minutes one of them came up to me and asked if I would be goalie. They were playing one-ended goal, as they called it those days.

Lieutenant Bratianu: Skip the linguistics.

Velder: Yes, sir. I did as I was asked.

Lieutenant Bratianu: How far did you go away from your post?

Velder: About seventy yards.

Lieutenant Bratianu: And what happened then?

Velder: It was a warm day and although I left my tunic in the vehicle, I got very sweaty.

Lieutenant Bratianu: Do you consider yourself to have broken military regulations by beginning to undress in the street?

Velder: Yes, sir.

Lieutenant Bratianu: I request to extend the charge with one more point concerning the transgression of paragraph two in military regulations. I further request that the charge of want of common sense and carelessness on duty be changed to gross want of sense respectively gross carelessness.

Major von Peters: Granted. Continue, Velder.

Velder: The ball game ended at about twenty past four. The boys went on playing something else and one of them asked if he could borrow my map-holder, which was lying on the front seat of the the jeep. I gave it to him and went to the nearest bar to have a cold beer. When I'd been sitting there for ten minutes, the General came and fetched me. When he left, I forgot I'd lent the map-holder.

Lieutenant Bratianu: What did the map-holder contain?

Velder: A map of the area east of Oswaldsburg.

Lieutenant Bratianu: On which the headquarters of the militia and surrounding posts were carefully marked?

Velder: Yes, sir. And a list on which Osw ... on which General

66

Oswald had written down what we were to do during the coming week, a bar of chocolate and a letter I was going to post.

Lieutenant Bratianu: A letter which the General had written by hand and entrusted to you?

Velder: Yes, sir.

Lieutenant Bratianu: Did you manage to retrieve the map-holder?

Velder: No, sir.

Lieutenant Bratianu: Did you try?

Velder: No, sir. But the letter got there all the same. The boy himself or his father must have posted it.

Lieutenant Bratianu: Do you presume to stand there making excuses in front of two colonels, one major and a commander in the Navy? Look me in the eyes, Corporal Velder. You have already confessed, but do you realise what risks your criminal activities in another situation might have signified for the security of the State and the General personally?

Velder: Yes, sir.

Lieutenant Bratianu: Your witness, Captain Endicott.

Captain Endicott: What were relations like between you and the General?

Velder: Very good.

Captain Endicott: What did the General do when he found you in the bar?

Velder: He sat down and had a beer.

Captain Endicott: Did he criticise or punish you?

Velder: No, not then. That evening he was a bit cross about the letter.

Captain Endicott: Do you know whether the General's visit to that building was in the line of duty?

Velder: No, it was quite priv ...

Lieutenant Bratianu: I protest. The question has nothing to do with the case.

Colonel Pigafetta: Yes, that's enough now, Endicott.

Captain Endicott: No more questions.

Lieutenant Bratianu: Although there is no doubt justification at this point for extending the charge to threat to the security of the State, from a time point of view I request to be allowed to place this section of the case before the court.

Colonel Orbal: Excellent, Bratianu. Granted.

Lieutenant Bratianu: Stay standing to attention, Corporal Velder. Charges numbers forty-six to sixty-four. Nineteen cases of insubordination, drunkenness on duty, gross dereliction of duty, gross want of sense on duty, gross carelessness on duty, carelessness with military equipment, fornication and theft from military stores. In some cases, the charge is concerned with two or more of these offences in combination and committed at the same time. Most of the charges refer to events of the same or of a similar nature as charge number forty-five, which has just been thoroughly dealt with. Corporal Velder pleads guilty to all charges. To avoid unnecessary waste of time, I request that the procedure be simplified in the same way as before. I request that I be allowed to lay this section of the case before the court immediately.

Colonel Orbal: Fornication?

Lieutenant Bratianu: That point will be taken up as evidence in charge number seventy-seven of the case, that is, the section of the case in which Corporal Velder still contests his guilt. I request to be allowed to place before you section forty-six to sixty-four.

Major von Peters: Excellent. Now things are shaping up.

Lieutenant Bratianu: Keep your head still, there, Corporal Velder. Pull in your chin. Remember that you're still a soldier and stand to attention. Corporal Velder, do you agree to your confession to the nineteen charges which will now be laid before this court martial.

Velder: Yes, sir.

Lieutenant Bratianu: Do you feel any regret or shame for the way in which you betrayed the General's trust and your duty as a soldier?

Velder: Yes, sir.

Lieutenant Bratianu: Then turn to the presidium of this court martial and explain what you feel!

Velder: I regret the way in which I betrayed the General's trust and my duty as a soldier. I feel deeply ashamed.

Commander Kampenmann: Not frightfully good phraseology, but it was your own, wasn't it, Lieutenant Bratianu?

Colonel Orbal: What? I don't understand a thing.

Lieutenant Bratianu: This section of the case is now concluded. Charge number sixty-five. Offences against the secrets act, and illicit intelligence activity. At the time of the offence, Corporal Velder had belonged to General Oswald's personal bodyguard for more than two years.

Commander Kampenmann: Permit me to intervene with one question. Why and by whom was Velder chosen as the General's bodyguard?

Lieutenant Bratianu: Corporal Velder was a relatively skilled shot and his physique was good. People around the General had recommended Velder and had also said that he was trustworthy and intelligent. General Oswald relied on these people. To the utmost. He also relied on Corporal Velder.

Colonel Pigafetta: I would be grateful if you would not repeat that word corporal ten times a minute. It's extremely irritating. If you don't mind.

Lieutenant Bratianu: Naturally, sir.

Commander Kampenmann: Just one more thing. In charge after charge, it has been maintained that through his in itself unprecedented and inexcusably undisciplined behaviour, Velder offended against militia regulations. Earlier in the session, however, one of the Prosecuting Officer's own witnesses maintained unchallenged that no such regulations existed.

Major von Peters: You're being hellish awkward again, Kampenmann. And just now, too, when we're at last getting going.

Lieutenant Bratianu: The witness was lying or mistaken. In a general order, signed four years ago, General Oswald laid down for everyone that military instructions and service regulations which were put into practice when he himself had received his basic military training, were applicable to the militia from half-past five on the morning of the liberation. In that general order, it was also stated that the militia was a military organisation from that time on, equivalent of regular troops. I hold the evidence in my hand. Here you are, sir.

Commander Kampenmann: Strange that this important confirmation wasn't signed until five years after the liberation.

Colonel Orbal: Not at all. I remember that order. I was here then. It came at the beginning of the disturbances, to enable us to clear the place of deserters. It came as a relief.

Commander Kampenmann: I see. Incidentally, what basic training did the General have before the national liberation?

Tadeusz Haller: He'd been a national service lance-corporal in a service regiment.

Colonel Orbal: What?

Major von Peters: Think about what you're saying, Mr Haller.

Tadeusz Haller: It was a joke, of course.

Colonel Orbal: Singularly out of place.

Major von Peters: May I remind you, Mr Haller, that this is a military court and not a music-hall act. You may continue now, Bratianu.

Lieutenant Bratianu: Think about your bearing, Velder. I repeat: Charge number sixty-five. Offences against the secrets act and illicit intelligence activity. I request to be allowed to extend the charge to preparation for high treason.

Major von Peters: Granted.

Lieutenant Bratianu: Velder had, as I said, for more than two years belonged to the General's bodyguard at the time of the offence. In this capacity, he had automatic access to secret material and was often in a position to listen to conversations and conferences dealing with matters of weight to the security of the armed forces and thus also to the State. The case I am now to lay before you is far more serious than the original charge implies. It is also hitherto the grossest of all the offences. I request to be allowed to call and interrogate two witnesses, Corporal Velder and Justice Tadeusz Haller.

Colonel Orbal: Are you appearing this time, Haller?

Tadeusz Haller: Yes. In this case, I can see no objections.

Colonel Orbal: Then that's all right. Granted.

Lieutenant Bratianu: The background to the case is as follows. The militia, shortly before this actual moment in time, had been equipped with a number of helicopters. They were of foreign manufacture and were intended first and foremost for guarding the borders. On the twelfth of July in the afternoon, one of these machines crashed. Velder, remember that you're on oath. I want clear but exhaustive answers. Were you a witness to this event?

Velder: Yes, sir.

Lieutenant Bratianu: Where were you?

Velder: I was standing on the edge of the shore plateau, above the high grass slopes about three quarters of a mile west of Marbella harbour. As you know the land on this stretch of the island rises steeply out of the sea.

Lieutenant Bratianu: Why were you standing on this veritable look-out place?

Velder: I was on my way to the lighthouse.

Lieutenant Bratianu: In the course of duty?

Velder: Yes, sir.

Lieutenant Bratianu: Remember that you're on oath. Are you telling the truth?

Velder: Yes, sir.

Lieutenant Bratianu: Stand to attention. How many times do I have to tell you? What kind of duty?

Velder: I was to leave a message with the lighthouse staff, about a boat that was to board a passing ship.

Lieutenant Bratianu: Is that the truth?

Velder: Yes, sir.

Lieutenant Bratianu: Remember your oath! Are you speaking the truth?

Colonel Orbal: What's going on? Why is he shouting like that?

Major von Peters: Ssh, Mateo, wait a moment.

Velder: Yes, sir.

Lieutenant Bratianu: What would you say if I maintain that I don't believe you?

Velder: That you're wrong, sir.

Lieutenant Bratianu: Don't be insolent. Keep your head still. So you still maintain that you were going there on an official errand?

Velder: Yes, sir.

Commander Kampenmann: May I ask why the Prosecuting Officer is pressing this point so hard?

Lieutenant Bratianu: Because I doubt the accused's word.

Colonel Orbal: Yes, for Christ's sake, what are you waving that about for, Endicott?

Captain Endicott: I would like to point out that this point is thoroughly accounted for in the preliminary investigation. There is no material evidence to show that Velder is telling the truth, as the errand referred to is not recorded, but the interrogation-psychologists can find no reason to question the truth of his story.

Lieutenant Bratianu: Interrogation-psychologists are not infallible.

Velder, I'll ask you once more only. Are you speaking the truth?

Velder: Yes, sir.

Commander Kampenmann: I can't imagine that we'll get much further along these lines.

Lieutenant Bratianu: I will leave the matter for the moment. So, what did you see from up there?

Velder: I saw the helicopter flying along the shore from west to east. In the middle of the harbour in Marbella, it turned out to sea. When it got about a thousand yards from the outer break-water, it sort of heeled over and crashed into the sea. The engines seemed to be still running. Everything happened very quickly. It was three or four minutes past two in the afternoon.

Lieutenant Bratianu: How was it that you were standing watching so carefully that even now, so long afterwards, you can give such a detailed account of it?

Velder: We hadn't had the helicopters all that long. I was curious, sir. And my memory has been well exercised too.

Lieutenant Bratianu: I think it seems extremely unlikely that you were standing there in order to stare at an aeroplane, when according to your own evidence—do you hear, your own evidence—you were on your way to carry out an important official duty.

Colonel Pigafetta: It seems to be quite analogous with Velder's way of carrying out his duties in general, I think. Anyhow, a helicopter isn't an aeroplane, Lieutenant Bratianu.

Lieutenant Bratianu: I beg your pardon, sir. Well, Velder, let us continue, even if I'm not satisfied with your answers. On the following evening, the so-called Council met. Were you present?

Velder: Yes, sir. For some time Osw ... the General had got into the habit of asking me to come with him as a personal bodyguard to Council meetings, too.

Lieutenant Bratianu: Asking you? What sort of expression is that? Have you no manners or respect? What had the General done? He had got into the habit of what?

Velder: Allowing me to go with him to Council meetings as bodyguard.

Lieutenant Bratianu: Who was present at the meeting, apart from the General and yourself? Don't stand there sleeping, Velder. Answer. I want speedy replies.

Colonel Orbal: What frightful shouting.

Velder: The usual, sir. Aranca Peterson, Joakim Ludolf, Janos Edner and Tadeusz Haller.

Lieutenant Bratianu: I request to be allowed to call Justice Haller as witness.

Major von Peters: Granted.

Lieutenant Brown: Justice Haller, do you swear by Almighty God to keep strictly to the truth?

Tadeusz Haller: I do.

Lieutenant Bratianu: So you were present at this actual meeting, Mr Haller. Would you be kind enough to tell us what happened there?

Tadeusz Haller: Well, with some reservations as to failure of memory. This happened almost six years ago, after all.

Lieutenant Bratianu: Naturally.

Tadeusz Haller: The Council was meeting as usual in the building in Oswaldsburg which was then used as a kind of government office. Today the National Christian Youth Guard's offices are in the same building. No special agenda was followed at these meetings, and affairs and matters sent in by individual citizens used to be dealt with and discussed, after which decisions were made in one direction or another. Usually the matter was referred back to the person who had sent it in to settle himself.

Lieutenant Bratianu: And decisions were made by voting?

Tadeusz Haller: No, that hardly ever happened. Voting is democratic and according to the ideas of the régime of the time, was to be avoided. According to the philosophy developed largely by Janos Edner and Aranca Peterson, unnecessary voting led to situations in which more or less against their own will, people were driven into traps and divided into groups and parties, which came about from an artificial drawing of boundaries and therefore constituted obstacles for personal thinking and a threat to freedom. In actual fact, voting was only brought up once, as far as I remember. That was far earlier and then it was over a suggestion made by General Oswald to purchase motor-vehicles suited to our terrain, jeeps for the militia, seven hundred of them, I think. The members of the Council who later became traitors were opposed to the suggestion and the General himself requested a vote. But it was never

73

carried out. The decision to buy was taken all the same.

Lieutenant Bratianu: This is of little importance. I apologise for my ill-thought-out question which led to this digression.

Major von Peters: The Prosecuting Officer's apology is accepted.

Tadeusz Haller: At the meeting, the matter of the crashed helicopter was taken up. The atmosphere grew very irritable, which was unusual. The immediate cause of this was that the newspapers had that same day contained a communiqué on the accident from militia headquarters. I don't remember the exact words, but ...

Lieutenant Bratianu: I have the communiqué here. I request the officer presenting the case to read it.

Lieutenant Brown: Appendix V III/12xxx. Communiqué from General Oswald. Oswaldsburg, Militia Headquarters, Wednesday. On account of persistent rumours that an accident has occurred to one of the helicopters belonging to the Militia, it is announced that no unit of our Air Detachment is missing or reported crashed. On the other hand, information has been received from the Coastguard Force that a plane of unknown origin had been seen to crash into the sea. Whether this occurred in international waters or within the country's territorial waters cannot be ascertained.

Tadeusz Haller: Yes, that's much as I remember the text. Janos Edner and Aranca were the ones who criticised the communiqué most. Their motivation was that between fifty and a hundred thousand people, most of whom were foreigners, had seen the helicopter flying low along the shore and had still had it within view when the accident happened. It had happened in the middle of the high season and after midday, when the beaches were packed with people. In addition to that, they added what they called the moral aspect. I remember Aranca Peterson said that lies were an aid which we could use against foreigners and foreign powers, but which should not be used between citizens.

Lieutenant Bratianu: And what did the General reply?

Tadeusz Haller: That the event must be kept secret as it would damage our international reputation. It could make the militia look foolish—as it had only three or four helicopters at the time—and involved a loss of prestige which would be difficult to recover. Janos Edner repeated that it was meaningless to try to keep secret an event that about a hundred thousand people had witnessed. The General replied that experience had shown him that that didn't make the slightest difference.

Commander Kampenmann: On that point, the General was undoubtedly right. During the Russo-Japanese war in 1904, by a cunning and skilfully carried out manoeuvre, the Russians sank two of the best warships the Japanese had, the *Hatsuse* and the *Yashima*, outside Port Arthur. Despite this, by obstinately keeping their losses secret and denying facts, the Japs managed to get the Russians to doubt what they'd seen with their own eyes. So the Russian success could never be followed up.

Tadeusz Haller: Thanks for the lecture. It says a great deal about military thinking. Edner and Aranca Peterson, however, stuck to their opinion and amongst other things had the audacity to imply that the General was behaving as he did because he feared for his own personal prestige. They also tried to pass the whole matter off as a joke and called the General alternatively childish or senile.

Colonel Orbal: Peculiar joke.

Major von Peters: Yes, indeed. That the General didn't at once arrest the rogues, what!

Tadeusz Haller: The tone of the Council was very special. In the light of today, it's rather difficult to understand how this could be so and how a country could be governed in this way.

Commander Kampenmann: What attitude did the other members of the Council take?

Tadeusz Haller: Joakim Ludolf was much too drunk to say anything, on the whole. That in itself wasn't all that unusual. He had a bottle of spirits with him, which he took continuous toll of. Now and again he tried to interrupt or interject something but the only thing he managed to say was phrases like 'No, stop there' or 'Listen a moment'.

Colonel Pigafetta: What functions did this extraordinary example of the human race fulfil?

Tadeusz Haller: Ludolf was in charge of several of our overseas connections, absurdly enough.

Commander Kampenmann: And you yourself, Mr Haller? What did you say?

Tadeusz Haller: Practically nothing. General Oswald had not yet

75

initiated me into his plans for reform. We were working separately, so to speak.

Lieutenant Bratianu: How did the meeting end?

Tadeusz Haller: Edner and Aranca Peterson wanted to send out a message that contradicted the communiqué, but the General maintained sharply that for reasons of secrecy, this should on no account happen, and that the matter mustn't become known. Finally the others agreed with this, only so as not to cause open disunity, as they put it, but the members parted in obvious discord, which had not happened before. The discussion had then gone on for many hours.

Lieutenant Bratianu: Was Velder present all the time?

Tadeusz Haller: Yes.

Lieutenant Bratianu: The defence's witness.

Captain Endicott: No questions.

Lieutenant Bratianu: I would like to bring to the presidium's notice the General's words 'that for reasons of secrecy the matter should not be made known.' Velder!

Velder: Yes, sir.

Lieutenant Bratianu: What did the General say, then?

Velder: The General said, word for word: 'Are you so bloody naïve that you don't understand that I'm right? This must be kept secret, especially now that that communiqué's already got into the papers. I won't agree with anything else, do you hear?'

Lieutenant Bratianu: Velder, I won't tolerate insolence. You've just heard what the General said, according to Justice Haller. What exactly did the General say?

Velder: That a contradiction mustn't be sent out for reasons of secrecy and that the matter mustn't be made known.

Major von Peters: That's right, Bratianu. Exactness before everything else.

Lieutenant Bratianu: So you heard your most senior officer express an opinion which to you as a soldier constituted a direct order.

Colonel Orbal: Oh, God, now he's started shouting again.

Lieutenant Bratianu: And how did you carry out this order? *How*, I'm asking you. Stand up straight, man!

Velder: Yes, sir.

Lieutenant Bratianu: What do you mean by 'yes, sir'? Do you

76

mean the fact that you not only passed on a state secret to what you called your family and several other people, but you also reported the matter to a foreign journalist whom you visited?

Velder: Yes ...

Lieutenant Bratianu: Shut up, you swine. Don't take liberties. You offended against the secrets act and were guilty of illicit intelligence activity. You gave information on the armed forces to a person who was probably an agent for a foreign power. This you have admitted.

Velder: Yes, s ...

Lieutenant Bratianu: Shut up, I said. I appeal to the presidium to exhort the Defending Officer to discipline his ... client.

Major von Peters: Endicott, I've already pointed out that you are responsible for the accused's behaviour and discipline before his superiors.

Lieutenant Bratianu: You realised, Velder, that the General already suspected that the helicopter had been sabotaged and that it was vital to the security of the nation that the espionage that lay behind this deed should be put an end to. It is tempting to go once again into the question of why you were standing on the highest point between Marbella and the lighthouse, with the lighthouse within view. Thus it is also tempting to go into the question of who it was who committed sabotage. But I'll desist.

Colonel Pigafetta: Yes, Endicott. What do you want to say?

Captain Endicott: I would like to say that the wreck was raised and that the notes from the technical investigation by the Wrecks Commission have been kept. These point to the helicopter having crashed because of a faulty manoeuvre.

Lieutenant Bratianu: With all due respect to the presidium, I must say you surprise me, Captain Endicott? The Wrecks Commission? Appointed by whom? Technical investigation? Carried out by whom and under whose direction? By the nation's most dangerous enemies, Captain Endicott. By the traitors.

Captain Endicott: And it wasn't Velder who visited the foreign newspaperman, but the other way round.

Lieutenant Bratianu: You're probably wrong, but that detail is of no importance. Velder? So you confess to offending against the secrets act and carrying out illicit intelligence activities?

Velder: Yes, sir. I confess.

Lieutenant Bratianu: And with that you consider that you've come off lightly, I suppose. But you're deceiving yourself. Honoured members of the presidium, I will now proceed to the amplification of the charge, a point which in my opinion has been unsatisfactorily accounted for in the preliminary investigations. I maintain that even at this time Erwin Velder was conspiring against General Oswald and thus also against the security of the State; that his offence against the secrets act and his illicit intelligence activities in actual fact were only a small part of a far more serious crime: preparation for high treason. I am sure that the accused will deny this, but I do not accept that.

Major von Peters: This looks like coming to something. Go on.

Lieutenant Bratianu: Velder, do you admit that even at this time you had already decided in your own mind to deceive General Oswald in every way and that you were seeking to take his life?

Colonel Orbal: At first he was shouting, and now he's whispering. What did you say, Bratianu?

Lieutenant Bratianu: That Velder was planning high treason and wished the General's death. I asked the accused if he admitted it. Well, Velder, do you admit it?

Velder: Yes, sir.

Lieutenant Bratianu: What? What? It's not that simple, Velder. Expound on your confession.

Velder: Perhaps I hadn't realised it before, mostly because the matter wasn't taken up during the interrogations. But you must be right, sir. I'm convinced that already then I had lost confidence in Oswald and his ideas, which grew more and more clear to me and seemed more and more frightening.

Lieutenant Bratianu: What ... what do you mean by the expression 'I'm convinced that', and what do you mean by not saying General Oswald, anyhow?

Velder: I beg your pardon, sir. I confess without reservations. I knew already then that I was going to turn against General Oswald.

Colonel Pigafetta: What's the matter with you, Bratianu? Don't you feel well? The charge can be laid before the court now, can't it?

Lieutenant Bratianu: Pray forgive me, sir. A temporary giddiness.

Probably from an old wound. It is over now.

Commander Kampenmann: The accused has confessed. Are you laying the charge before the court?

Colonel Orbal: It can't ever be a good thing to shout like that.

Lieutenant Bratianu: There is just one more detail. Velder, do you regret anything? Do you realise how appalling your actions were? How base and treacherous? How vile you were?

Velder: Yes, sir.

Lieutenant Bratianu: Turn towards the President of the Court and explain what you feel.

Velder: I regret my crimes and realise how appalling, base and treacherous my actions were. I also realise my vileness.

Major von Peters: Fine. Lay the charge before the court now, Bratianu.

Colonel Orbal: Yes, do that.

Lieutenant Bratianu: I request to be allowed to lay the charge before this special court martial.

Major von Peters: Granted. This is going along fine. We can more or less finish for today, Mateo.

Lieutenant Bratianu: Already?

Colonel Orbal: What? Yes, of course.

Major von Peters: Short working day, Bratianu. The fruits of a good job done.

Colonel Orbal: The parties may leave.

*   *   *

Lieutenant Brown: The parties have left the hall. Does the court now wish to go over to internal deliberations?

Colonel Orbal: On what?

Major von Peters: Didn't I tell you that things would be quite different when Bratianu took over? Excellent Prosecuting Officer. He's taken things as far in one day as Schmidt did in five.

Colonel Orbal: Good lad, but he shouts too much.

Major von Peters: Nonsense, Mateo. He's giving Velder the gruelling he thoroughly deserves.

Commander Kampenmann: He surprised me a bit. I wonder what he's after?

Colonel Pigafetta: Funny that you should say that. I also got the impression that he was trying to press the session to a certain point.

Commander Kampenmann: In that case, he hasn't much time. Captain Schmidt will be back the day after tomorrow.

Major von Peters: Do you know that for certain?

Commander Kampenmann: Yes, with absolute certainty.

Tadeusz Haller: I think I know.

Colonel Orbal: Know what?

Tadeusz Haller: What Lieutenant Bratianu is after.

Major von Peters: It's all the same to me, really. The main thing is that we've got a move on. Is there anything left in the mess, Mateo?

Colonel Orbal: Think so. Though no females as Pigafetta has. We should introduce that. Something to feast the eyes on is necessary for a man, as General Winckelman used to say. He never went into action without his books.

Major von Peters: Anyhow, it would be a good thing if the ban were lifted. Finish this off now, Mateo.

Colonel Orbal: Thank you, gentlemen. This session of the extraordinary court martial is adjourned until eleven o'clock tomorrow.

Seventh Day

Lieutenant Brown: Those present: Colonel Orbal, Colonel Pigafetta, Major von Peters, Commander Kampenmann and Justice Tadeusz Haller. Officer presenting the case, Lieutenant Brown. Captain Schmidt has reported his absence, but has telegraphed a message to say he will be presenting the case for the prosecution tomorrow. Prosecuting Officer at today's session will be Lieutenant Bratianu.

Major von Peters: Excellent. Call in the parties.

Lieutenant Bratianu: Sir, honoured members of the presidium, I request to be allowed to continue the case of the Armed Forces versus Corporal Erwin Velder from the point at which yesterday's session was adjourned.

Colonel Orbal: Of course. Granted.

Lieutenant Bratianu: I exhort the accused to stand to attention and remain thus until the adjournment of this session. I request that the presidium points out to the accused that he is still bound by his oath when called as a witness.

Colonel Orbal: Granted. Now those instructions are lost again. Oh, there they are, thank you. You are testifying under oath to tell the truth and I hereby remind you of the significance of the oath. I said all that to you, Velder. Yes, Bratianu, go on.

Lieutenant Bratianu: Charge numbers sixty-six to and including seventy-six. Eleven charges of repudiation of God, atheism, blasphemy and the spreading of heresy. The offences did not occur in wholly chronological order if one places them in relation to the group of charges which have been gathered together in the last complex. This is for purely practical reasons. To avoid unnecessary waste of time and to facilitate a summary of jurisdiction, offences of a similar nature have been brought together in separate complexes.

Colonel Orbal: That sounds all right, what?

Lieutenant Bratianu: Briefly, I shall now express more precisely the different charges. Velder's behaviour and attitudes towards spiritual and religious matters have been closely analysed in relation to a period of two years, to be more exact, the twenty-four months prior to his desertion from the Army. During all that time he was a member of General Oswald's bodyguard and also held a position of special responsibility, which should have induced him to behave as an example to others. During that time, he committed innumerable indiscretions against Christian morality, he blasphemed, he profaned, and he spread infamous heresy. The general spirit of secularisation and irreligion created by the traitors Edner, Ludolf and Aranca Peterson are thoroughly described and documented in the preliminary investigation's various appendices, but I shall not weary the presidium by taking these matters up at this particular moment.

Major von Peters: Thank God for that.

Lieutenant Bratianu: I request that this side of the case is left at that.

Major von Peters: For Christ's sake, yes. Granted.

Lieutenant Bratianu: Of greater interest, of course, are the offences to which the accused has confessed. Complete statements and confessions in each separate case lie here before me. What we have now to establish is the accused's attitude today, and to what extent he has acquired correction and wisdom. And also whether he feels due shame and regret.

Colonel Orbal: This is all deadly dull.

Lieutenant Bratianu: Velder, I will take a few samples from your register of sins. Stand to attention and listen carefully. You have on several occasions abused the name of God, the Holy Virgin and the Saviour. You have used expressions which an honest and righteous man is scarcely capable of uttering. It is with considerable reluctance and genuine anxiety that I now force myself to do so. The expressions 'Jesus Christ and all the Demons in Hell', 'God's Curses', 'Bloody Plastic Jesus', 'Christ in Heaven', just to mention a few. Is that right?

Velder: Yes, sir.

Lieutenant Bratianu: You have also—according to your own

82

sworn statement—said to a certain named person: 'I don't care if there's only one or there are a thousand gods. The question doesn't interest me and it doesn't interest anyone else either.' This is an example of your criminal atheism and spreading of heresy. Do you admit to that too?

Velder: Yes, sir. I admit that.

Lieutenant Bratianu: You have also violated and grossly desecrated one of the two remaining churches which at the time existed in the country, you played cards on the altar, spat on the floor, washed yourself in the font, killed animals in the choirstalls, committed the most gross obscenity by fornicating in the sacristy and urinating on the church wall. Do you admit to this?

Captain Endicott: In the name of exactitude, I must point out just one thing. The building to which the Prosecuting Officer is referring had not been used as a church for many years. It was derelict and functioned at first as a temporary school, then as a guard-post for the militia, and finally as a pig-sty and hen-house for the militia. It was during the latter time that Velder occasionally supervised the building.

Colonel Orbal: Did he say on the floor of the sacristy?

Major von Peters: Yes, Mateo.

Colonel Orbal: Good God ...

Lieutenant Bratianu: I will not tolerate these quite unwarranted interruptions from the defence! Captain Endicott, think of whom you are ordered to defend. A monster of degeneration, debauchery and ...

Colonel Orbal: Oh, now he's beginning to shout again.

Lieutenant Bratianu: Should the anti-religiousness and infamous actions of a perverted régime rob a sacred place of its sacredness? Can human evil change the character of an institution ordained by God? You surprise, me, Captain Endicott. You should apologise to the presidium.

Captain Endicott: Colonel Pigafetta?

Colonel Pigafetta: Yes, do that, Endicott.

Captain Endicott: I apologise.

Colonel Pigafetta: Accepted.

Lieutenant Bratianu: Velder! Look me in the eye! Stand up straight! Do you regret what you have done?

83

Velder: Yes, sir. I regret what I have done.

Lieutenant Bratianu: I don't believe you.

Velder: What, sir?

Lieutenant Bratianu: Don't speak until you're spoken to. I don't believe you, Velder. You're lying and trying to get out of it. Admit that you're lying.

Velder: I'm telling the truth. I am prepared to reply truthfully to all questions.

Lieutenant Bratianu: You're lying straight in the face of both myself and the presidium.

Velder: Sir, I assure ...

Lieutenant Bratianu: Are you out of your mind? You break in on me, you almost interrupt me. When are you to speak? Answer me!

Colonel Orbal: Why does he keep shouting like that, Carl?

Major von Peters: Don't keep fretting, Mateo. This is just what Velder needs.

Lieutenant Bratianu: Answer me, man! When are you to speak?

Velder: When I'm spoken to, sir.

Lieutenant Bratianu: Admit now that you're lying. For your own sake. Turn to face the presidium.

Velder: I assure you that I'm not lying. I have during recent years, thanks to a man called Gerthoffer, learnt to be aware of the faults I have been guilty of. I regret them truly. I also feel ashamed.

Lieutenant Bratianu: Faults? You have the face to call these monstrous offences faults? It's unheard of. Stand to attention, Velder. You're not even capable of accepting the simplest disciplinary axiom. You're hardly worthy of the word human!

Velder: No, sir.

Major von Peters: Why don't you say anything, Bratianu?

Lieutenant Bratianu: I leave the case with the court.

Major von Peters: Granted.

Lieutenant Bratianu: I request thirty minutes' adjournment of the session in order to give the accused the opportunity to collect himself before the presentation of the next charge. This concerns section seventy-seven, the charge to which Velder still pleads not guilty.

Colonel Orbal: Must you shout so loudly, Bratianu?

84

Lieutenant Bratianu: I assure you that there will be no reason to raise my voice during the rest of today's proceedings, sir.

Colonel Orbal: That's good.

Lieutenant Bratianu: I requested a pause in the proceedings.

Colonel Orbal: Oh, of course. Granted. The parties may leave.

Major von Peters: Brilliant prosecutor. He's achieved five times as much as Schmidt in a fifth of the time.

Colonel Orbal: Have you got any beer in the mess, Pigafetta?

Colonel Pigafetta: Yes, there's beer in the mess.

Colonel Orbal: Then let's go there. The session is adjourned for thirty minutes.

*   *   *

Major von Peters: He makes a really good prosecutor, Bratianu does. He's ...

Colonel Pigafetta: I hope you're not going to say yet again that he's achieved five times as much work as Captain Schmidt has, and in addition in a fifth of the time ...

Major von Peters: Pity we didn't have him from the start. It would all be over by now, presumably. It's extremely annoying, not least because I'll miss a good official trip. It would have started the day after tomorrow.

Lieutenant Brown: Is this extra-ordinary court martial prepared to continue the proceedings?

Colonel Orbal: Now all that gassing starts again.

Tadeusz Haller: I don't think it'll be too bad.

Colonel Orbal: What? What d'you mean?

Tadeusz Haller: Anyhow, not if my interpretation of Bratianu's intentions is correct.

Colonel Orbal: I don't know what you mean by that. Let the parties in, Brown.

Lieutenant Brown: Sir, honoured members of the presidium. Charge number seventy-seven. Fornication, obscene behaviour and bigamy. Does the accused plead guilty? No, you may remain seated, Velder. Let the Defending Officer bring your case.

Captain Endicott: Velder owns to the behaviour as fact but does not admit to the criminality of it.

Colonel Orbal: Did you say bigamy? Then he married two people?

Lieutenant Bratianu: Yes, sir. It is a matter of bigamy. In addition to that, of an extraordinarily unpleasant and detestable kind. This is the main point of the charge. If I understand you correctly, Captain Endicott, the accused does not admit to the criminality of the charge.

Captain Endicott: The accused pleads not guilty.

Lieutenant Bratianu: He does not consider himself liable to lawful punishment.

Captain Endicott: No.

Lieutenant Bratianu: The accused's attitude forces me to go to the root of the case. I request to be allowed to call Justice Tadeusz Haller once again as witness.

Colonel Orbal: What about it, Haller?

Tadeusz Haller: The situation gives me no choice.

Colonel Orbal: Granted.

Lieutenant Brown: You have already taken the oath, Mr Haller. As a formality, I must remind you of the significance of the oath.

Tadeusz Haller: Naturally.

Lieutenant Bratianu: To bring some order into the complex of offences which are included in charge seventy-seven of the case, I consider it appropriate to assail the task with a starting point from the moment when the circumstances were first discovered. About a month after the event with the helicopter, Velder came in to the Council with a letter, didn't he?

Tadeusz Haller: That's correct. His letter was one of many which people sent in to the Council. They were collected in a heap, so to speak, in the office and then read by one of the Council members. In most cases, it was considered that the person who happened to receive a letter was also capable of dealing with it. It may seem unlikely, but this system functioned for more than five years.

Lieutenant Bratianu: Which of the members dealt with Velder's letter?

Tadeusz Haller: The letter happened to come into Janos Edner's hands. He read it and clearly found the contents so remarkable that a few days later he took the matter up at a meeting, at which apart from himself, both Aranca Peterson and myself were present.

86

Lieutenant Bratianu: The letter has not been kept. Do you remember how it ran?

Tadeusz Haller: I don't remember it word for word, but I do remember the contents. To avoid obscurity, I should first like to point out—as in previous circumstances—that there existed means of proclaiming a marriage, or as it was called, manifesting mutual affinity between two people. In time the most usual way became to send a letter to the Council, who then placed the names on a public register. People who wished to separate often did the same thing and their names were struck off. The number of separations, however, was astonishingly low.

Lieutenant Bratianu: And now to the contents of the letter, Mr Haller.

Tadeusz Haller: Velder asked, quite politely actually, that the Council should register his marriage and family. Up to that point, everything was part of the routine of the times. The remarkable thing was that he asked if it was all right if he registered a marriage *à troise*, consisting of himself and two women. The two women were sisters, he wrote, and all three of them had lived together for some time, how long for I do not know. He had children by both of them, how many I do not remember.

Lieutenant Bratianu: What reaction did the letter bring about?

Tadeusz Haller: Well, I seem to remember that I made the remark that the man must be insane. Janos Edner seemed slightly thoughtful. Even Aranca Peterson, to whom it always seemed to be a point of honour to beat all records in so-called freedom of prejudice, was hesitant. After a while, she shrugged her shoulders and said: 'Why not? Register them.' I remember that despite everything, she didn't sound all that wholehearted. Naturally I was strongly opposed to it. We didn't discuss the matter either thoroughly or for any length of time. The whole thing ended by Janos Edner saying: 'As soon as I get the time, I'll go there and see how things are with them.'

Lieutenant Bratianu: Did all the members of the Council know Velder at the time?

Tadeusz Haller: Yes and no. He had been in on everything from the beginning and naturally we knew him in so far as we had spoken to him many times and knew who he was. The person who

87

saw most of him was naturally General Oswald. But none of us knew anything about his private life. In those days, anyhow, very few people had the opportunity to observe other people's home circumstances. That was one of the many unspoken principles.

Lieutenant Bratianu: Did Janos Edner ever visit Velder and what he called his family?

Tadeusz Haller: It appears so. I know for certain that he did, actually, because about a week later he wrote a letter to me on the matter. He and Aranca Peterson were to go abroad and the point of the letter was to inform me and the others, in case the matter had to be dealt with during their absence. That didn't happen then, of course.

Lieutenant Bratianu: This letter is news to me. It is no longer in existence, I presume.

Tadeusz Haller: I have in fact got it in my pocket. It was kept among my papers and yesterday I suddenly remembered it and hunted it out. It is well worth reading out, in contrast to many other documents, because it gives a summary which would otherwise be difficult to achieve. Lieutenant Brown, you are the authorised reader, please would you ...

Lieutenant Brown: If the presidium will permit ...

Colonel Orbal: Yes, I want to hear it.

Tadeusz Haller: The beginning isn't especially interesting.

Colonel Orbal: I want to hear it all.

Lieutenant Brown: Old friend, herewith some information on the little I know about Velder, the man with the two sisters. I went there yesterday evening. They live in the northern section of the town, so I had to walk right through it. It was unusually warm last night, that kind of soft dry heat which is pleasant because you don't sweat. You probably don't see much of that sort of climate down in Marbella. As I walked through the streets in this silent upside-down science-fiction town which we've achieved, it struck me for the umpteenth time that Oswaldsburg really is a success. Stoloff is a genius. Just think of the way he shortens all distances with his mysterious apartment system. But back to Erwin Velder. I had carefully made my intended arrival known two days before-hand, and you could see at once they'd made some preparations. They live in a pleasant and spacious dwelling, and of course in a

88

good position, like everyone else here.

All of them were at home. Velder was clearly off duty from his job as daddy to Oswald and was trotting around in his stockinged feet and smoking a pipe. He seemed perfectly relaxed and thank God wasn't taking it all that seriously. The women seemed rather more cautious. The children, three of them, all looked about the same age, two or three, or thereabouts. They came in in their nightshirts to say hullo and then went off to bed. As he has children by both these women, two of them must belong to one, but I couldn't bring myself to ask which. The women are sisters, twenty-seven and twenty-nine, eighteen months difference between them in age. They were in some way a fascinating sight, dark, well-built women, mature, almost beautiful. Both of them seemed intelligent, even by our standards. They are astonishingly alike in appearance and build, but after a very short while with them, you could see their characters were different in essential points. The elder is more joyful, livelier, much more spontaneous and optimistic than the younger one, who often frowns and thinks, and who also occasionally had a glint of doubt in her eyes. Both of them have brown eyes, by the way. Both seemed to have a sense of humour and are quick-thinking to an equal extent. All of them seemed almost foolishly harmonious. They seem to get up to all sorts of things, different hobbies; they like working with their hands and they've a big workshop in the basement which is full of model boats and model planes and batik dresses. It turned out to be impossible to find out who did what, though strangely enough, it seemed to be Velder who mostly made the dresses. What's so strange about that, anyhow? Tade, we must constantly be on our guard against thinking in clichés. When I'd got over my initial feeling of distaste—this business of inspecting another person's home—reason soon prevailed. They assured me, almost in chorus, how happy they were. I gradually realised that this registering business meant a great deal to them. In parenthesis, this seems to be a deeply rooted instinct which we hadn't reckoned with at first. Velder gradually became very unreserved. He told me he'd first been with the elder one, then with the younger one, and then with the elder again. He said that they were so alike that he was constantly muddling them up, but that they both had small traits, not least physical, which he always missed, whichever one he tried to live with. Neither of the women had been able to adapt herself to living without him, and after a colossal amount of toing and froing, dotted with unspoken tragedies, all three of them had moved in together. This had solved the problem like a magic wand, they said. Since then they hadn't even quarrelled. I think they were telling the truth. Why *shouldn't* they be? I was there for about two hours, had some tea and something to eat—one of them seems to be more domestic than the other, by the way. And had some whisky. When I left and saw Velder standing there with his two (almost) identical wives, it was on the tip of my tongue to ask if they had a communal bedroom. I didn't, of course, but just said goodnight. On the way home I noticed how the thought of these two (almost) identical women set my imagination whirling. Enough of that. My attitude should be clear. See you next Monday. Hi, Janos.

Lieutenant Bratianu: May I borrow that letter?

Tadeusz Haller: Certainly.

Lieutenant Bratianu: What happened then?

Tadeusz Haller: A few weeks later, Aranca Peterson brought the matter up at a Council meeting. General Oswald, myself, Janos Edner and Joakim Ludolf were present. Velder was there too, at first, but he left when he saw that his own case was to be discussed. Aranca Peterson wanted to register this extremely bigamous marriage at once and Janos Edner agreed with her, though not quite so enthusiastically. Joakim Ludolf seemed cautious—the General was categorically opposed. I myself pointed out where this precedent could lead. Aranca Peterson said that people in our country were such that even if there did happen to be men who wanted a harem, there were certainly no women who wanted to inhabit it. The most apocryphal remark was made by Joakim Ludolf, who said that in his view Velder wasn't living with two women, but with one who was divided into two guises. The General clarified the moral aspects and refused to be drawn into this mindless discussion, as he expressed it.

Commander Kampenmann: What did you say yourself, Mr Haller?

Tadeusz Haller: Very little. The General's attitude was just as clear as my own and we both trusted Joakim Ludolf's good sense. At the time, we did not realise the extent of the conspiracy.

Lieutenant Bratianu: How did the meeting end?

Tadeusz Haller: A vote was taken for the very first time, requested by me, by the way. General Oswald and I voted against, of course, but Edner, Aranca Peterson and Ludolf voted for. In this way, the traitor element pushed through a decision which I personally, despite what had happened before and what happened later, consider was the most degrading in the history of the nation. Velder's bigamous marriage was registered. From that moment on, however, both General Oswald and myself were aware of the traitors' intrigues and of the abyss into which they were thinking of casting the nation.

Lieutenant Bratianu: Thank you. The defence's witness.

Captain Endicott: Do you consider that this decision can be regarded as judicially valid?

Tadeusz Haller: Of course not. To avoid retroactive legislation, the case would have to be placed before a military court. Velder was a soldier.

Captain Endicott: No more questions.

Colonel Orbal: Is all that in the book?

Lieutenant Bratianu: Yes, sir. Volume Three of the preliminary investigation, page five hundred and twenty-three.

Colonel Orbal: Give me that part, Carl. This must be looked into.

Lieutenant Bratianu: I request to call Corporal Erwin Velder as witness.

Major von Peters: Granted.

Lieutenant Bratianu: Yes, you can get up, Velder. Naturally, you're still on oath. I have some questions for you. Are you prepared to answer them?

Velder: I don't know, sir.

Lieutenant Bratianu: Well, we'll just have to try, won't we? How long had this obscenity been going on when the traitor Janos Edner visited you?

Velder: I'd lived with my wives for four years, sir.

Lieutenant Bratianu: You call these women your wives and yet you won't admit that you have committed criminal bigamy.

Velder: No, sir.

Lieutenant Bratianu: So you deny it?

Velder: Yes, sir.

Lieutenant Bratianu: Has the Defending Officer any comments on the attitude of the accused?

Captain Endicott: Velder denies that his bigamy was criminal. He asserts even in the preliminary investigation that he contracted a marriage with these two women that was authorised by the authorities of the day.

Lieutenant Bratianu: Well, Velder, wasn't it with one of these two women that you committed the innumerable sexual offences which earlier in the session you admitted.

Velder: Yes, sir.

Lieutenant Bratianu: Or perhaps with yet another?

Velder: I never deceived them, sir.

Lieutenant Bratianu: Who was it, for instance, you fornicated with on the beach, when you should have been on guard?

Velder: Doris, sir.

Lieutenant Bratianu: So it was the elder of the sisters, then? Who were you with when you desecrated the church?

Velder: That was Doris, too, sir.

Lieutenant Bratianu: Was this Doris always the one who made herself available in the church. It seems to have happened several times.

Velder: Yes, sir.

Lieutenant Bratianu: And in the guard-post and the ammunition depôt, was that also Doris?

Velder: Yes, sir.

Lieutenant Bratianu: But the other one, then, whatever her name is, let's see, Carla. Weren't you having intimate relations with her during the same period?

Velder: Yes, sir.

Lieutenant Bratianu: Where? And when?

Lieutenant Bratianu: Why don't you answer?

Velder: This has nothing to do with my criminal activities.

Lieutenant Bratianu: So you refuse to answer?

Velder: Yes, sir.

Lieutenant Bratianu: So ... that's how things are, then. The preliminary investigation does not offer any information on this point either. I will leave the matter now and go over to a later point in time. Will you as thoroughly as possible account for the criminal circumstances in your house while you were living with these two tarts.

Velder: No, sir. Anyhow, I must protest at your choice of words.

Lieutenant Bratianu: So you refuse to answer again?

Velder: Yes, sir.

Lieutenant Bratianu: And you deny that you are guilty of criminal bigamy and an endless series of obscene activities in what you call your home?

Velder: Yes, sir.

Colonel Orbal: I must say Bratianu, this interrogation is going off the rails a bit. Velder, now I'm going to ask you a few things. For instance, that question the Edner fellow was too cowardly to ask. Did you have a communal bedroom with those women?

Velder: I cannot answer that question, sir.

Colonel Orbal: What? What's this nonsense? Did you have a communal bedroom or didn't you?

Velder: With all due respect to this court martial ...

Major von Peters: Endicott, what's the matter with the man? Has he gone crazy?

Colonel Orbal: In that letter it said that you babbled something about small physical traits which you couldn't bear to live without. What were they?

Lieutenant Bratianu: Aren't you going to answer, Velder?

Captain Endicott: The accused considers that he is not bound to answer questions which in his view have no connection with his criminal activities.

Lieutenant Bratianu: Is that correct, Velder?

Velder: Yes, sir. And the respect I felt and still do feel for my wives makes ...

Colonel Orbal: What's all this crap? Respect for a couple of tarts, which you clearly simultaneously fucked for several years!

Major von Peters: Mateo, do cool off a bit.

Colonel Orbal: This circus must be brought to an end. Velder, account for everything on this point. Immediately and in a loud and clear voice.

Lieutenant Bratianu: Velder! The President of the court martial has asked you a question! I order you to answer!

Velder: I'm sorry, sir, but I've nothing to say. If I'm to be sentenced on this charge, then it will be against my own denial.

Lieutenant Bratianu: So that's it. The defence's witness.

Captain Endicott: No questions.

Colonel Orbal: Are we really supposed to rest content with that?

Lieutenant Bratianu: The preliminary investigation does not say much on this charge. Nonetheless, I consider this section of the case important. Does the presidium agree with me?

Major von Peters: Naturally. What's the matter, Bratianu? Have you lost heart?

Lieutenant Bratianu: I request five minutes' adjournment, while the prosecution gathers more complete evidence.

Major von Peters: We needn't adjourn just for that. The parties can leave the room. Five minutes break.

Colonel Orbal: I don't understand a thing. In the middle of this extremely interesting bit, Bratianu is suddenly as if transformed. He didn't even raise his voice more than once at the end.

Major von Peters: He's probably got something up his sleeve.

Tadeusz Haller: Certainly.

Colonel Orbal: What happened to the sisters?

Tadeusz Haller: One of them is dead, they know that. The other one probably fled the country.

Lieutenant Brown: The Prosecuting Officer has returned now.

Major von Peters: Call in the parties.

Commander Kampenmann: Velder, just one question. What happened to your children?

Velder: I don't know, sir.

Captain Endicott: I can partially answer that question. One is dead and one is still here in the protective care of the authorities. The third disappeared, presumably with Janos Edner and his people.

Major von Peters: Pack would be a better word, Endicott.

Lieutenant Bratianu: May I have the presidium's attention. Sir, honoured members of the presidium. The extremely important part of this case we are now dealing with has unavoidably landed in a cul-de-sac. The accused evades all questioning with a series of denials and lies which make the matter impossible to survey. The reason for this is obvious. The preliminary investigation in this section, that is, charge seventy-seven, is incomplete, in fact positively inadequate. To enable me to complete the case in a satisfactory

94

manner, it is necessary that the prosecution be granted a certain time to gather up more complete evidence.

Colonel Pigafetta: How long?

Lieutenant Bratianu: With reference to court martial regulations, paragraph eleven, part two, I request a month's postponement to carry out further preliminary investigations.

Major von Peters: Damn it, that'd be first rate.

Colonel Pigafetta: Would it?

Colonel Orbal: A month, what can one say about that?

Lieutenant Bratianu: Allow me to point out that the regulation is unmistakable and absolutely definite on this point.

Commander Kampenmann: You're a lawyer, Mr Haller. What do you think?

Tadeusz Haller: Lieutenant Bratianu is no doubt right.

Major von Peters: So there's nothing we can do except grant a postponement?

Tadeusz Haller: Not as far as I can see.

Major von Peters: Mateo, grant a postponement.

Colonel Orbal: Granted.

Lieutenant Bratianu: I request further, with reference to paragraph fourteen in the regulations, that the accused is ordered to be at the disposal of the prosecution during renewed preliminary investigations. Also that the accused is transferred to the Investigation Bureau of the Security Service for further interrogations.

Colonel Orbal: Yes, yes. Granted.

Lieutenant Bratianu: My plea then is concluded. The prosecution anticipates a return to normal order when the session is resumed. Colonel Orbal! Major von Peters! Colonel Pigafetta! Commander Kampenmann!

Major von Peters: Damned fine conduct. Let the parties go now, Mateo.

Colonel Orbal: The parties may leave

Major von Peters: Well, I didn't think that'd happen. But I've nothing against it. I'll get my trip now.

Colonel Orbal: Yes, indeed. An unexpected turn of events.

Tadeusz Haller: Not really.

Commander Kampenmann: Was this what you thought might happen, Mr Haller?

Tadeusz Haller: Exactly. Lieutenant Bratianu wished to force a postponement and a new investigation at any price. So he chose several sections which he tried with every means to get Velder to deny. As soon as he saw that he wasn't going to succeed, he rushed through the charges to get through to charge number seventy-seven before Captain Schmidt returned.

Commander Kampenmann: Because he knew that that was the only one Velder would be certain to deny?

Tadeusz Haller: Naturally. He also pressed the accused very mildly during the later questioning. Tactically and judicially, it was very skilfully done.

Commander Kampenmann: But why?

Tadeusz Haller: Unfortunately, it was probably for purely personal reasons.

Major von Peters: Personal reasons? What do you mean?

Tadeusz Haller: It seems as if I know more about your officers than you do yourself, Major von Peters. Perhaps that's not all that peculiar. I have in fact taken the trouble to study Lieutenant Bratianu's dossier.

Major von Peters: And so?

Tadeusz Haller: Before Lieutenant Bratianu became an army officer on the active list, he served in the Investigation Bureau of the Security Service. He handled the Velder case over three years ago, while Velder was still in military hospital. Lieutenant Bratianu clearly failed almost completely at the time, despite the fact that he used various forms of force. Velder was handed over to the Special Department of the Military Police and that meant, in fact, the end of Bratianu's career within the Security Service.

Commander Kampenmann: Do you mean his motive was quite simply a desire for revenge?

Tadeusz Haller: Well, perhaps more of a wish to get his own back ... on the Security Service, too, for that matter. The Special Department of the Military Police and the Investigation Bureau of the Security Service have different views on various matters.

Colonel Orbal: I've been listening, in fact. And so he saw to it that he got the prisoner to himself again. He's a smart boy, I must say. He'll make a good officer. What are you dreaming about, Pigafetta?

96

Colonel Pigafetta: Whatever I may do, it certainly isn't dreaming.

Lieutenant Brown: Allow me to point out that the session has still not yet been officially adjourned.

Colonel Orbal: No, nor it has. This extra-ordinary court martial is hereby adjourned until Monday the fifth of April at eleven o'clock.

Eighth Day

Lieutenant Brown: Those present: Colonel Orbal, Colonel Pigafetta, Major von Peters, Commander Kampenmann and Justice Tadeusz Haller. Officer presenting the case, Lieutenant Brown.

Colonel Orbal: Welcome, gentlemen. Ghastly hot in here, Pigafetta.

Colonel Pigafetta: In that case, I must blame the fine weather. And Army engineers presumably played no part?

Colonel Orbal: Isn't there any ventilation?

Colonel Pigafetta: Naturally. Switch on the fans, Brown.

Tadeusz Haller: Well, Major von Peters, was your trip to your satisfaction?

Major von Peters: Yes, in every respect. Excellent, quite simply. A lot of news over there. Good to be away from home, actually. All those strikes and miseries.

Tadeusz Haller: They're all over now.

Colonel Orbal: The Army cleared the whole business up in twenty-four hours.

Major von Peters: It's an old truth. A régime which has the support of the Army has nothing to worry about.

Colonel Orbal: Those fans are powerful. Hellish draughty.

Colonel Pigafetta: Shall I get Brown to switch them off again?

Colonel Orbal: So we've either got to suffocate or be blown out of our seats, have we? Aren't there any half-measures?

Lieutenant Brown: Unfortunately not.

Colonel Orbal: This fan business and Carl here, who's been away from his old woman for more than three weeks, made me think of Swift Slim and Speedy Gonzales. Swift Slim was a tremendously fast worker, both on horseback and at laying other men's wives. Speedy

98

Gonzales was also tremendously fast. When Speedy Gonzales heard that Swift Slim was in the neighbourhood, he took safety precautions and got into firing position on his verandah with his '45 in his right hand and his left thumb in his old woman. He just sat there. Suddenly he saw a cloud of dust on the horizon and at that moment a fly came and settled on his nose. It was, as General Winckelman used to say, a difficult and very technical decision. Speedy Gonzales didn't want to let the '45 go, so swatted, yes, just swatted away the mosquito with his left hand. A tenth of a second later, he was sticking his thumb into Swift Slim's arse.

Colonel Pigafetta: It pains me to have to admit that that story was among the very first I heard when as a young subaltern I went into the mess for the very first time.

Colonel Orbal: It's a bloody good story, anyhow.

Commander Kampenmann: For me, it is fortunately quite new.

Major von Peters: I've always said that about the Navy. It's not great but it's bloody refined.

Colonel Orbal: Well, we'd better get going then, hadn't we?

Major von Peters: Is Bratianu still Prosecuting Officer?

Lieutenant Brown: No. Captain Schmidt is presenting the case for the armed forces.

Colonel Orbal: Call in the parties.

Commander Kampenmann: Is this really absolutely necessary?

Colonel Orbal: What's this now? What the hell's going on? Why is he sitting in that apparatus, Endicott? Can't he walk by himself?

Captain Endicott: No, sir, the accused cannot walk.

Captain Schmidt: My replacement requested a postponement a month ago to complete the evidence for charge seventy-seven. Despite intensive interrogation, partly under the personal supervision of Lieutenant Bratianu himself, Velder has, however, not made any admission which to any great extent makes the judgement of the case any easier.

Major von Peters: Oh, yes, not even Bratianu could get it out of him, then? Does the swine still deny it?

Captain Endicott: Yes, the accused pleads not guilty.

Captain Schmidt: As charge number seventy-seven, concerning fornication, obscenity and bigamy has already been dealt with thoroughly and also is hardly of such significance as my replacement seems to have considered, I request to be allowed to lay this section of the case before the court. All the facts of the matter are clear and Velder's plea of not guilty is unimportant. I demand a conviction.

Major von Peters: Yes, that'll probably be all right. Go on.

Captain Schmidt: Considerably more than half the charges against Erwin Velder have now been considered. The sections that remain include, however, far more serious offences. The next group of charges, numbers seventy-eight to and including eighty-two, concerns Velder's high treason and desertion from the Army. The accused admits these offences, just as he admits to all the other remaining charges in the case. The essential point, however, is not these confessions in themselves. What must be set out as the basis for judicial argument and the prejudicial judgements are Velder's intentions and motives. These can hardly be made clear unless we try to reconstruct the atmosphere within what was called the Council and the situation in the country as a whole at the actual time.

Colonel Orbal: Damned long-winded, he is, what?

Major von Peters: Yes, thank the Lord for Bratianu.

Captain Schmidt: To make the country's situation clear, I refer to Appendix V IV/14, which consists of a summary of a descriptive outline drawn up by the National Historical Department of the General Staff. Marked Top Secret. I request the officer presenting the case to read the actual appendix.

Major von Peters: Here we go again.

Lieutenant Brown: Appendix V IV/14, concerning the social and economic development of the country during the period of domination by the traitors. Compiled from Volume Eleven, drawn up by the National Historical Department of the General Staff. Marked Secret according to paragraphs eight and eleven. The text is as follows:

Major von Peters: You might at least spare us the preliminaries?

Lieutenant Brown: The five years of misgovernment which had been maintained because the traitors Janos Edner, Joakim Ludolf and Aranca Peterson were in a majority on the Council, had left the country in a state of moral chaos and total defencelessness. General Oswald's efforts to put the defence of the nation on its feet had been systematically sabotaged. In the whole country, there were only a few thousand militiamen, whose training and equipment scarcely made them suitable as the core of a modern army. The militia had about thirty helicopters and slow reconnaissance planes at their disposal. On the other hand, they completely lacked assault planes and fighters. For defensive weapons, they had about ten old-fashioned artillery pieces, though supplies of mines were relatively large and the already mined barriers, intended for electrical release, were fairly well maintained. There was, however, not a single anti-aircraft battery on the whole island, nor any tanks, and the old permanent coastal defences had been either blown up or allowed to decay. The Navy, which was also administered by the militia, consisted of about twenty patrol boats. These were small but fast and comparable to Customs boats. The militia, apart from considerable stores of hand firearms and ammunition, also had a number of machine-guns. There were no infantry guns or anti-tank weapons, nor any other modern weapons of war, i.e. atomic weapons, robots, nerve-gas and napalm. There were not even any mortars or flame-throwers. On the other hand, thanks to the General's far-sighted planning, they were well supplied with transport vehicles in the form of a large number of armoured cars with tracks for use in the terrain and suitable for moving troops. Access to motor-cycles and cars was also quite good. These rudimentary defences, however, left the country wholly exposed to attack, especially from the air, and if a presumptive attacker had established a bridgehead, for instance by parachute landings, the small and scattered militia forces lacked any means of launching a counter-attack. Even more precarious than the military situation—catastrophic in itself—was the moral situation. In treasonable circles in the Council, a spirit of defeat and pacifism, irreligiousness and anarchy had spread. Sexual aberrations were as apparent as religious ones. The free Health Service, for instance, included free abortions, and various forms of criminal perversions occurred freely and openly. Finally, these treasonable circles went so far in their laxity that even bigamy was accepted. On the other hand, deportation, the only kind of jurisdiction exercised, was extended to people who had done nothing more serious than to have been guilty of breaking a simple promise or business transaction, which in any other country would be regarded as common practice. Industrial development was neglected completely; not a single armament factory existed in the whole country. On the other hand, what was called cultural production flourished enormously. The number of books printed increased five-fold from year to year, as did the number of films produced in the country. By totally neglecting defence and administration—apart from the few militiamen, there was hardly a single government servant in the country—they managed to create an apparently high economic standard of living. The main part of the national income came from the constantly expanding tourist trade; through luxury hotels, gambling dens and brothels, foreign currencies were poured into the country and the food industry included a considerable export of luxury articles. This commercialised depravity, however, had transformed the Marbella district—which at the time had more than a hundred daily air and hovercraft links with larger centres in the neighbouring countries and with most of the cities in the rest of the world—into a nest of vice which a foreign commentator described as 'without precedent in the history of the world'. The nation's international reputation sank very rapidly. It was possible, nevertheless, to keep official relations with foreign powers relatively intact through a well-developed system of bribery.

Colonel Pigafetta: What does that last sentence mean?

Tadeusz Haller: Entertainment opportunities exercised a remark-able enticement to many famous people, not least statesmen. Marbella was in certain respects similar to one of the free cities in the Middle Ages. Everything and anything could be done there and discretion was absolute.

Colonel Orbal: It certainly was.

Lieutenant Brown: I have only a few lines left. Such was the situation then in the country five years after the liberation; drink in plenty, all kinds of drugs were sold freely and openly, sexual orgies succeeded each other and everything saleable was there to buy. The reputation of the country grew worse and worse and moral dissolution more and more obvious, while at the same time by their mole-like activities, the traitors made the country militarily power-less and undermined the individual's will to defend it.

Captain Schmidt: The document marked V IV/23x of the pre-liminary investigation also illuminates the developments and chain of events which led to Velder's desertion and high treason. It concerns a letter from Joakim Ludolf to Janos Edner, sent from a place abroad three months before the outbreak of the disturbances. There are also three comments on the letter, which were undoubtedly written by Janos Edner and Aranca Peterson. Joakim Ludolf was not a writing man and this is one of the extremely few surviving documents in his hand.

Colonel Orbal: There's almost a hurricane blowing in here. For God's sake, switch that fan off, Brown.

Lieutenant Brown: Done, sir. Appendix V IV/23x, concerning ...

Major von Peters: Cut the preliminaries.

Lieutenant Brown: The letter runs as follows: Hi. Watch out for Oswald. I think he's cooking something up. Don't like his behaviour. Have observed him all this last year. Think this business with the militia has gone to his head. It began as a necessity. Went on as a joke. It was a joke when he got himself a uniform and stainless steel teeth. But now? If he wants to play at generals and have the militia as his private army, then we can let him do it. He can even call himself General or Field-Marshal. But it could get more dangerous than that. Think about it. Talk to Velder. He's shrewd and knows more about Oswald than we do. This has not come to me suddenly. I've been thinking about it for a long time. Have known Oswald for twenty years. Know there's always been something deep down inside him. Bigotry? Megalomania? Arrogance? Don't know. But something. Send Stoloff back home for safety's sake and let him take this letter with him. Everything's going well here otherwise. Have been stone cold sober for three days. Hi. J.L.

Below this, in handwriting which has been identified as Janos Edner's, is the following:

Paul has been a bit strange, it's true, but I refuse to believe that it's anything serious. We'll talk to him.

Another person, identified as Aranca Peterson, has added:

Ludolf is fairly strange himself, may I say, and it's not just drink.

Colonel Pigafetta: In the light of what happened later, this Joakim

Ludolf seems to be a highly astonishing personality. What did he look like, really?

Captain Schmidt: There's a contemporary description of him among the appendices, written by a foreign journalist. A small man whose hands tremble. He has a brown beard and protruding eyes which are restless. He is not especially clean and tidy, nor at all impressive, but he seems stubborn and was given an impression of steadfastness.

Commander Kampenmann: Who was this Stoloff?

Major von Peters: A demon in human form.

Tadeusz Haller: That's true. And he was Joakim Ludolf's closest friend and confidant. He was in on it all from the beginning and functioned as a construction and planning technologist. In his particular field, he was a genius. He organised all supplies and building in the country. He was also a fortifications expert.

Major von Peters: We know that, thank you.

Colonel Orbal: Yes, by God, we do.

Captain Schmidt: I call Corporal Erwin Velder as witness.

Colonel Orbal: Yes, what? What is it, Endicott? Can't you speak so that we can hear? Yes, of course he can remain seated if he can't stand up. Push him forward into the middle of the floor. That's right.

Lieutenant Brown: May I remind you of the significance of the oath, Velder.

Velder: Yes, I know.

Captain Schmidt: After the bizarre events which were dealt with in the seventy-seventh charge, you continued to serve as the General's bodyguard and you were also present at Council meetings.

Velder: Yes, that is true.

Colonel Orbal: For Christ's sake, Velder, you sound like an old steam engine. Speak like a soldier, man.

Captain Endicott: The accused has an injury to his larynx, sir, which prevents him from speaking normally. A week ago, he could not speak at all.

Colonel Orbal: Oh, hell.

Captain Schmidt: Describe briefly the events which led to your desertion from the Army.

Velder: As the General's bodyguard ...

Colonel Pigafetta: Why did General Oswald keep you near to him?

Velder: We always got on well together. I imagine that the General trusted me.

Colonel Pigafetta: Highly remarkable.

Captain Schmidt: Well, Velder. Go on.

Velder: As the General's bodyguard, I noticed a number of things. After the Council meeting concerned with my circumstances, the General didn't actually show aversion to me, but the tone of the meetings grew more tense. There weren't any votes taken, of course.

Captain Schmidt: We are primarily interested in what happened to you personally.

Velder: The General began to take certain measures which he didn't bother to tell the others about. In two months, the strength of the militia was doubled and stores replenished. They were placed at three new depôts too, near Oswaldsburg, Marbella and Ludolfsport. Otherwise everything was as usual. The General often used to talk to me, of course, and he said he was worried about our vulnerability and our poor defences. Discipline within the militia was improved and training became more systematic. A lot of new officers were found; I remember that both Colonel Orbal and Major von Peters came with the first contingent. At the same juncture, the militia was reorganised into a regular army. That was when I became a corporal.

Captain Schmidt: Were you already planning high treason then?

Velder: Yes, but not consciously. I didn't realise what was happening. I didn't really begin to think seriously about it until after the Council meeting on the thirteenth of November.

Captain Schmidt: Describe in your own words what happened there.

Velder: It was very rowdy—the rowdiest I've been present at at any time.

Captain Schmidt: Who was rowdy?

Velder: Janos Edner mostly. He had discovered that there were several religious sects in the country, both in Oswaldsburg and Ludolfsport. They had already been in existence for a long time and were holding regular services in private houses. Janos Edner was furious. He behaved in a very unbalanced manner, swearing and cursing.

Captain Schmidt: What was he so agitated about? That there were people who believed in God?

Velder: He said he didn't care a bloody fig about that. But he was livid over the secrecy, he said. He seemed fearfully disappointed. Aranca Peterson agreed with him, as usual. The others didn't say anything. He also quarrelled with the General, who he considered must have known about the matter. Especially as so many of the members were from the militia. The General was very calm. When Edner had come to an end, the General brought up his suggestion.

Major von Peters: Can't you speak up a bit, man?

Captain Schmidt: One moment. I will interrupt Velder's testimony here and call Justice Tadeusz Haller instead.

Lieutenant Brown: Mr Haller, may I remind you of the significance of the oath.

Tadeusz Haller: I realise the significance of the oath.

Captain Schmidt: You were present at this meeting. What happened then?

Tadeusz Haller: The General was—just as Velder said—very calm. He didn't reply to the accusation at all. But when Janos Edner had finished, he got up and said: 'Isn't this evidence of something I've long suspected? That we've got to review the question of the country's method of government and administration.' Aranca Peterson at once asked how this reviewing was to be done and the General replied that it should happen by public vote. The others stared at him as if they'd seen a ghost. Naturally, I supported the General and pointed out that it was possible that the country had got to the point when its leadership should be entrusted to a president and a democratically chosen government. Aranca Peterson and Janos Edner laughed at me and asked who was going to be the president. Naturally, I answered that the president should be whoever the people chose. The whole thing culminated in a discussion which went on all night and a good way into the next morning. The General's decisive behaviour, perhaps to some extent my own too, made a certain impression on the others. They felt that the very foundations of their ridiculous doctrines were collapsing.

Commander Kampenmann: Weren't you yourself from the start

one of the supporters of these doctrines?

Tadeusz Haller: Never seriously. I saw them only as a means of swiftly carrying out national liberation.

Captain Schmidt: Was Velder present all through that meeting?

Tadeusz Haller: I think so. In the end, when it was almost lunch time, we arrived at a compromise. This was that the matter should be settled by a referendum. The people should be allowed to choose between two alternatives; the first to keep the old form of government, the second to choose a president at a later election and form a conventional government. The voting was to be carried out four weeks later. The timing was especially suitable, as winter had just begun and the number of foreign tourists wasn't so great.

Captain Schmidt: Did everyone agree to this?

Tadeusz Haller: Everyone except Joakim Ludolf. He was quite adamant and on this occasion showed his true nature for the first time.

Captain Schmidt: Thank you, Mr Haller. I will now return to questioning Erwin Velder. Was it at this moment in time that you definitely decided to turn against the General?

Velder: I wasn't really certain until I'd heard his big speech two weeks later, on the twenty-seventh of November.

Captain Schmidt: The speech Velder refers to was the first of a series by General Oswald which went out to the whole country on radio and television. The text of the speech is contained in Appendix V IV/50. If you don't mind, Lieutenant Brown.

Lieutenant Brown: Appendix V IV/50. Speech by General Oswald, held at Radio Headquarters, Oswaldsburg, twenty-seventh of November at seven o'clock in the evening. The text is as follows:

Citizens! As I turn directly to you for the first time, it is after lengthy hesitation and consideration. As you all know, I personally was in the vanguard of the action which liberated this country from the tyranny and oppression of colonialism.

Since then, not a single general election or referendum has been held in the country. Despite this, the nation is faced every day with questions of critical importance, questions which concern the lives and welfare of all of us. Now, for the first time, we have an election ahead of us, or a referendum, if you so wish. Two alternatives are before us—but the most important thing is not the choosing of one form of government or the other. Fundamentally, the election is between keeping watch over our freedom and dignity on the one hand, and on the other hand continuing on the route already embarked on towards chaos and self-degradation.

With increasing anxiety, I have watched recent developments. Our international reputation has fallen a long way below par. Hundreds of millions of people now already regard our island as a spot of shame upon the map of the world. Worst is that none of us can hold our heads up and maintain that our accusers are wrong. We are developing into a chaotic and spineless nation, we have deliberately torn down what would have held us up, the three cornerstones of human existence, contained in the concepts of Religion, Morality and Dignity.

Our way of life has also created external enemies, far too many of them and far too strong to enable any of us to sleep soundly at night. I know that many of you do so—but that is due to ignorance and laxity.

Are you secure in your own homes? Can we even guarantee the lives of our children and our loved ones? The answer is no. As the person ultimately responsible for the internal and external security of the nation, I am forced to say that we lack the means to repel the annihilating attack from outside which any day, indeed any minute, could become a nightmare reality. In our blind faith in naïve doctrines, we have neglected to take the most elementary safety precautions. Many people covet our land and our lives, and we have robbed ourselves of the means of defending ourselves.

At root, all this is the result of our laxity and moral decay, of our retreat from the only true God, and our contempt for the rules of personal human behaviour. Yet these rules have been formed over the centuries and it is impossible to live without them. The developments here are definite and conclusive evidence of this. We gained our independence and founded this state in order to live in freedom. But what does that freedom look like today? Is it possible to speak of freedom in a country in which people to whom religion is a vital condition of life are forced to meet in secret places, like thieves in the night, to pray to their Creator? A country led by irresponsible people whose idea of freedom is chaos?

What is freedom worth in a state during whose whole existence its citizens have had no opportunity to have their say in free elections? Not until now, as our beautiful and flourishing island is on the way to being transformed into an Augean stables, stinking of excrement and immorality, as we lie defenceless, helplessly exposed to the first attacker—not until this moment of remorse and anxiety in face of the future, have I succeeded in convincing my opponents that a referendum is necessary.

Citizens, our old form of government has always been dubious, and now it has finally outlived itself. Its rôle is for ever and irretrievably played out. What we need today is a firm republican organisation, a president and a government which has the courage and strength to return the country to a tolerable and acceptable existence. A system in which freedom isn't just a meaningless phrase. We need an army, a force that can defend us against external aggressors. We must recover all the spiritual values that have already been dragged through the mud and which will soon be irretrievably lost.

Perhaps you are asking: who today has sufficient courage and sufficient spirit of sacrifice to lead the way? My answer is: if you, citizens, offer me this onerous task, I am prepared to accept it.

In the referendum in two weeks' time you will be given two alternatives—to vote yes or no, that is, for or against the subversive system which has brought us to the piteous state of vegetation we are now forced to endure. But it is not yet too late to stem the avalanche. You must vote no. Every no-vote is also, if you so wish it, a vote for me personally. Listen to me! Listen to me! Listen to God's truth! He who votes no is helping to sweep away immorality and corrupt administration. He who votes no is choosing freedom and security for himself and his kin. He who votes no professes himself an adherent to the triumvirate Religion—Morality—Dignity. That is all, citizens. The decision is yours.

Colonel Orbal: Extremely good speech.

Major von Peters: Magnificent. What's wrong with Velder? Has he fallen asleep?

Captain Endicott: Exhaustion, sir.

Colonel Orbal: Take the wretch out and shake some life into him. Try cold water if nothing else helps. Anyhow, I must have a cold beer before I get heat-stroke. The session is adjourned for one hour.

* * *

Colonel Orbal: Get the parties called in now, Brown.

Lieutenant Brown: There's only Captain Endicott out there now, sir.

Colonel Orbal: What? Why's that?

Major von Peters: Call him in then, Brown. And don't stand there staring. This is a court martial, not an agricultural show.

Colonel Orbal: Well, Endicott, what's the matter?

Captain Endicott: The guards did not succeed in rousing the accused from unconsciousness. Perhaps their methods were ... somewhat primitive, if I may use that expression.

Major von Peters: Are you standing there insinuating that Bratianu's men don't know their job?

Colonel Orbal: Bratianu is first class.

Commander Kampenmann: What happened?

Captain Endicott: Velder collapsed and had to be taken to the military hospital. I've just spoken to the doctor and he couldn't guarantee to have Velder on his feet by tomorrow.

Major von Peters: What sort of doctor?

Captain Endicott: Surgeon-Lieutenant Mogensen of the Naval General Staff.

Major von Peters: Take a note of his name. You'll have to see to this, Kampenmann.

Colonel Orbal: This really is the limit.

Major von Peters: You can go, Endicott. We must have an internal discussion on this matter.

Colonel Orbal: Exactly.

Commander Kampenmann: What are we going to talk about now, then?

Major von Peters: I don't like this business. Not a bit. It's almost as if someone were having us on. Colonel Pigafetta, is this Endicott absolutely reliable?

Colonel Pigafetta: Are you sitting there saying straight to my face that you're questioning the loyalty of my officers?

Colonel Orbal: Now, now, keep calm, you two.

Major von Peters: I just wondered how the hell we can try and sentence a murderer, deserter and traitor who, without punishment, uses every opportunity to malinger and give himself breathing space to find new lies. If he isn't falling over on to the floor, he's sitting sleeping in a wheelchair. And both Schmidt and Endicott treat him as if he were a new laid egg.

Commander Kampenmann: A lightly boiled egg, people usually say.

Major von Peters: To hell with what people usually say. What's actually wrong with the swine?

Tadeusz Haller: I think I can dispel your uncertainty on this matter. Velder has in fact spent the last three weeks in the military hospital. After five days' interrogation by the Security Service, he was practically dying. Fortunately, Lieutenant Bratianu realised at the last moment that he was adding yet one more blunder to his previous ones, and he had Velder taken to hospital. The doctors had an extremely difficult job, and it was only by the skin of their teeth and great efforts that they finally managed to keep him alive.

Major von Peters: Pretty meaningless occupation, I should've thought.

Tadeusz Haller: I don't think the General shares your opinion on that point.

Major von Peters: You seem to be suspiciously well-informed, Haller.

Colonel Orbal: Yes, you seem to know everything. But I bet you've never heard this one before. Once when Speedy Gonzales ...

Major von Peters: For Christ's sake, Mateo, at least wait till we've switched the tape-recorder off.

Colonel Pigafetta: Before I forget, Mr Haller. It would be a good thing if we could meet an hour earlier than we agreed to this evening.

Tadeusz Haller: That's fine by me.

Major von Peters: Oh, so there's to be high jinks at the Air Force again, is there?

Colonel Pigafetta: Not at all. Just a little bridge evening with the family.

Colonel Orbal: Bridge evening. Doesn't sound much fun.

Commander Kampenmann: Shouldn't we adjourn the session.

Colonel Orbal: Yes. Yes, of course. This extra-ordinary court martial is hereby adjourned until ... what's the date the day after tomorrow, Carl?

Major von Peters: The seventh.

Colonel Orbal: Until Wednesday the seventh of April at eleven o'clock. Then the wretch gets an extra day to pull round.

Ninth Day

Lieutenant Brown: Those present, Colonel Orbal, Colonel Pigafetta Major von Peters, Commander Kampenmann and Justice Haller. Officer presenting the case, Lieutenant Brown.

Commander Kampenmann: I hear that disturbances in the Eastern Province have broken out again.

Major von Peters: The plastics factories, as usual. Nothing serious.

Colonel Pigafetta: I haven't had any reports on that.

Colonel Orbal: There's no need to be so sour about it. We don't need the Air Force. The emergency regiment in the second military area has already cleared things up. The whole mob were back at their machines within an hour.

Commander Kampenmann: It seems that these things have begun to happen somewhat frequently of late.

Tadeusz Haller: Remains of the bad old days, gentlemen. Exactly what this trial can eradicate at root. Or rather, the legislation the verdicts on Velder will lead to.

Colonel Orbal: Oh, yes. Call in the parties, Brown.

Major von Peters: Velder, for God's sake pull yourself together now.

Velder: I'll do my best, sir.

Major von Peters: For Christ's sake, man, stand to atten ... to think that I've lived to see this, too. A corporal sitting like a sack of potatoes when you speak to him.

Colonel Orbal: Get going, now, Schmidt.

Captain Schmidt: I request to be allowed to continue the questioning of the accused from the point where it was interrupted on Monday.

Major von Peters: Granted. Push him forward, Endicott.

Captain Schmidt: Corporal Velder. You say that General Oswald's speech of the twenty-seventh of November—i.e. the speech which we heard read out word for word in this room—was decisive to your actions. Why?

Velder: I realised that the General's attitude had changed and that he was preparing to smash something which not just he himself, but I and many others had created together.

Captain Schmidt: Why do you use the expression 'changed his attitude'? Don't you understand that the General has always had the same attitude, but for the public good and in consideration of the perpetuation and security of the nation, he had been forced to keep a good countenance in the face of evil?

Velder: I didn't realise that at the time, anyhow.

Captain Schmidt: You just thought that the General was wrong then, when he attacked immorality, irreligiousness and slack administration?

Velder: Yes, sir.

Captain Schmidt: That should be sufficient to demonstrate the accused's receptivity to spiritual and moral rearmament.

Colonel Orbal: What do you keep mumbling about, Schmidt? I can't hear a word you're saying.

Captain Schmidt: I beg your pardon, sir. I was pointing out the state of moral dissolution which Velder—like so many others—found himself in at the actual time.

Colonel Orbal: Oh.

Captain Schmidt: So as early as the twenty-seventh of November, then, you decided more or less unconsciously to desert and to commit high treason. And yet you remained in the service for some time onwards. Why?

Velder: I didn't know what was going to happen. And although I didn't like the General's ideas, I didn't see through his plans.

Captain Schmidt: What were conditions within the militia like at the time?

Velder: The new officers tightened up discipline. Both original militiamen and new recruits were driven very hard. The training was intensive.

Major von Peters: A true word at last. Never have bunches of blackguardly civilians been transformed into active troops so quickly. It ...

Velder: But both officers and men were kept in their garrison areas. No leave was granted.

Major von Peters: Velder, if you interrupt me once more before I've had a chance to finish was I was saying, I'll draw my pistol and shoot you through the head.

Colonel Orbal: What's going on now? Why are you shouting like that, Carl?

Velder: I beg your pardon, sir. I don't understand ...

Captain Endicott: May I interject here that the doctor has said that since his last interrogation, Velder has been affected by aphasic disturbances. Contacts fail to function between his hearing on the one side and his speech organs and certain centra on the other.

Major von Peters: To hell with that. If he interrupts me again I'll shoot him.

Colonel Pigafetta: Show at least a grain of sense, von Peters.

Major von Peters: What the hell did you say?

Tadeusz Haller: Gentlemen, gentlemen ...

Colonel Orbal: Quiet, Carl. Velder, show respect to your superiors, whatever you're suffering from. Go on, Schmidt.

Captain Schmidt: Were you present on any occasion when the General spoke to the nation.

Velder: Yes, on every occasion. The referendum was held on the twelfth of December. During the two weeks before it, the General made six speeches; three broadcasts on radio and television and three in public, in Oswaldsburg, Marbella and Ludolfsport. I was with him all the time, as I'd been posted as his personal bodyguard. Yes, indeed I was there and it was then I realised that it was exactly that, seeing him as he spoke, close to as well, which influenced my actions.

Colonel Orbal: Some people shout and others mumble like old women. What a performance.

Colonel Pigafetta: It is, in fact, very difficult to hear what the accused is saying.

Captain Endicott: We're working on acquiring a strengthener, sir. Some kind of throat-microphone.

Captain Schmidt: How could the General's appearance influence you?

Velder: It was something to do with his bearing. And his look. When you saw him close to, you realised that he really meant every word. Believed it all. He seemed taller, broader. His eyes shone. His teeth flashed.

Major von Peters: Of course the General meant what he was saying. Why should he say it otherwise? I've never heard such bloody nonsense in my life.

Captain Schmidt: And this influenced you in a negative direction? Made you betray the General?

Velder: Yes, I'm convinced of that. He made an impression that was almost overwhelming. All the speeches ended with the same phrase: 'Listen to me, listen to God's truth.' In some way, that frightened me.

Captain Schmidt: I would like to draw the court's attention to this in particular. Velder's mind as well as the minds of many others were so twisted by heresy and inverted moral values that the truth frightened them and offers of help bred hatred and aversion instead of gratitude.

Colonel Orbal: What?

Velder: Strangely enough.

Captain Schmidt: Why do you say that?

Velder: Strange that he frightened me, I mean. I'd known him for many years. I'd always seen him as someone quite different. Friendly and quiet. Not at all impressive. Least of all vain. Almost careless in his dress. Never one for giving orders and blustering. I suddenly realised ... I mean that then I thought I understood that the desire for power had always been in him and it'd kept in step with his progress. I mean that now the country really was something to rule over. To reform and change.

Captain Schmidt: So that was the way you took the General's efforts to save the nation?

Major von Peters: It's repulsive listening to all this.

Captain Schmidt: Nonetheless, it is valuable for the future. Well, Velder, did the General talk to you at all during those weeks?

Velder: Yes, of course. Every day. We knew each other well. He was always talking to me.

Captain Schmidt: During the preliminary investigation, you made special mention of a conversation that occurred a week before the referendum.

Velder: Yes, on the fifth of December. He asked me if I wanted to be an officer.

Colonel Pigafetta: Just one moment. You maintain that the General offered you a commission?

Major von Peters: This is too much, even regarded as a lie. I refuse to concern myself with this.

Velder: Yes, he asked me if I wanted to.

Captain Schmidt: And what did you reply?

Velder: That I would prefer not to. He looked at me with a sort of smile then. Ambiguous, they used to say, I think. Then he mumbled: 'Well, perhaps you're not suitable.' Soon after that he gave me a sealed envelope and said that I wasn't to open it until I received a certain order in code. A code-signal, really.

Major von Peters: That may well be true. That secret Army order was distributed just about then. I didn't think, of course, that it was for corporals.

Velder: Then the General said: 'It's ninety-nine per cent certain that you won't need to open that envelope. A week tonight, you can burn it.' He meant the day after the referendum.

Major von Peters: Have you by any chance observed, Captain Schmidt, that the accused's behaviour is beneath all comment. He hasn't given a formal reply to a single one of your questions. He keeps saying 'he' about the General, and maintains the General used his first name. Are you going to tolerate such things?

Captain Schmidt: In consideration of Velder's general condition and how easy it is for him to lose the thread, I prefer that his replies are factually correct. This is hardly the right occasion to start insisting on military regulations.

Major von Peters: What do you mean? Kindly spare me your sarcasms. An apology would be in order, I must say.

Commander Kampenmann: Schmidt, apologise to the major.

Captain Schmidt: I apologise for my thoughtless choice of words.

Major von Peters: Good. Continue.

Captain Schmidt: I will now interrupt the interrogation of the accused and ask to be allowed to put a few questions to Justice Haller.

Tadeusz Haller: Certainly.

Captain Schmidt: We have now heard the accused's version of events of the crisis weeks before the referendum. As you, Mr Haller, were close to the centre of events all the time, you should be able to give us a more general account of the situation which ended in Velder first deserting the armed forces and then committing high treason.

Tadeusz Haller: Several of the facts the accused has given appear to me to be correct. During the fortnight prior to the referendum, General Oswald made six big speeches to the nation. Personally, I supported the General's campaign with a series of articles and public appearances, how many I no longer remember. Both the General and I myself were at this point convinced that the majority of citizens would come to their senses and with their votes give the no-side a firm and comfortable majority. We didn't know then to what extent defeatism and apathy had managed to spread throughout the treasonable element. The General appeared very calm and certain of victory all the time. Council meetings were still held, the last one, as far as I remember, three days before the referendum. Apart from the General and myself, Janos Edner and Aranca Peterson were there. Joakim Ludolf was abroad then. No questions of importance were ventilated and the atmosphere was noticeably tense. The General, however, was formal and balanced, but Janos Edner repeatedly showed evidence of ill-temper and made one outburst after another. Clearly his defeat in the vote in Council on the thirteenth of November had grieved him sorely. Aranca Peterson seemed more conciliatory and kept saying that we must patch up the differences that had appeared in the Council. To one question from the General, that whether by this she meant that everything should return to the old ways, she replied very characteristically: 'Naturally', as if that were absolutely obvious.

Captain Schmidt: Do you consider that the counter-propaganda by the enemies of the people before the coming referendum was of such a nature that it could have influenced Velder's attitude?

Tadeusz Haller: That's hard to say. The activities of the traitors were so devilishly well calculated and so insidious that even today they are difficult to analyse. Their plans were simply to ignore democratic elections completely. According to available information,

Janos Edner refused to carry out any kind of propaganda whatsoever. He is said to have stated that he found it absolutely out of the question that stupidity had spread to such an extent that more than at most ten or so people in the whole country would consider voting no. Aranca Peterson said on some public occasion that she hoped and believed that all citizens would simply not bother to vote. Joakim Ludolf demonstrated his utter indifference to the will of the people by going abroad to conclude some agreement. For these so-called theoreticians of the old system, this attitude was of course a necessity. They couldn't urge their eventual supporters to deprive themselves of all democratic rights through a majority in a democratic election.

Commander Kampenmann: I remember a similar dilemma in my early youth, in a political student society in which we were discussing the question of the mass's ability to dominate elections. The result was that with an overwhelming majority the meeting decided that the majority is always wrong.

Major von Peters: That wasn't all that amusing, was it?

Tadeusz Haller: The insidiousness of these tactics naturally lay in that the traitors, relying on the remains of their prestige and authority, succeeded in giving the impression to some people that the referendum was nothing but a ridiculous whim, lacking any significance. Thanks to the General's foresight, however, in the end they fell into their own cunningly contrived trap.

Major von Peters: What's wrong with Velder now?

Captain Endicott: He seems to have fallen into some kind of coma. Exhaustion, I imagine.

Major von Peters: Exhaustion? From what, may I ask? God, what a sight! An extra-ordinary court martial in which the accused sits and sleeps. Or simulates sleep, more likely.

Captain Schmidt: Velder's condition is causing me some anxiety. These repeated faintings and mental blackouts upset both the timetable and procedure of the court martial. I request two hours' adjournment to allow an expert to examine the man.

Colonel Pigafetta: The accused is not alone in that state. The President of the Court has not been heard of much during the last hour. If you look at him more closely, you will find that this phenomenon has a highly natural explanation.

Major von Peters: Mateo! Yes, my God, he's fallen asleep ...

this won't be easy ... I know no one who sleeps as heavily as he does.

Colonel Pigafetta: I suggest that you use the gentleman in question's own methods. Take the bloody fool out and pour cold water over him, if nothing else helps.

Major von Peters: This really isn't very amusing, is it?

Colonel Pigafetta: Isn't it?

Major von Peters: Mateo, wake up, for God's sake!

Colonel Orbal: What ... what ... leave me alone ...

Major von Peters: Adjourn the session.

Colonel Orbal: Already? Yes, of course, the session is adjourned until tomorrow at eleven o'clock.

Major von Peters: No, for two hours.

Colonel Orbal: Oh?

Colonel Pigafetta: Now, that's enough. We meet again at three. Good-day, gentlemen.

*   *   *

Colonel Orbal: Damned embarrassing that business this morning. But it was Schmidt's fault. He stands there mumbling on like an old monk.

Major von Peters: To put it briefly, he's damnable. All right, I'm sorry, Kampenmann, perhaps he's better at sea.

Colonel Orbal: Brown, is there still no one out there in the hall?

Lieutenant Brown: No, sir.

Colonel Orbal: This is absolutely appalling, of course. It's already a quarter past three and not a sign of either Pigafetta or Haller or any of the parties.

Commander Kampenmann: There is one thing that surprises me and that's why Justice Haller isn't in the government.

Colonel Orbal: Oh, he's been both Minister of Foreign Affairs and Minister of War. Then the Chief of State took on Foreign Affairs himself and General Winckelman got the Ministry of War. Haller is very close to the Chief of State, all the same, as adviser.

Major von Peters: And then he's in charge of this business of legislation. It seems to be tremendously important.

Colonel Orbal: Ach, in any case it's the Army that decides.

Commander Kampenmann: Is the strike over?

Colonel Orbal: No idea. Here are Pigafetta and Haller, anyhow.

Colonel Pigafetta: I apologise for the delay, gentlemen. The troops in the strike area had asked for a division of assault planes and I was forced to deal with the matter personally.

Colonel Orbal: Oh, God.

Major von Peters: And your aeroplanes got there as they should?

Colonel Pigafetta: I'm prepared to overlook a lot, von Peters, but not the expression you've just chosen to use.

Major von Peters: Aeroplanes?

Colonel Orbal: Keep your hair on, now, Carl. How did it go?

Colonel Pigafetta: The strike? It's blown over.

Major von Peters: Blown away, I presume.

Colonel Pigafetta: Not at all. Colonel Orbal was absolutely right, this morning. There was no real need for air support, but the commander of the military area over there didn't want to waste people unnecessarily by storming one of Ludolf's old bunkers, where the worst element was entrenched.

Commander Kampenmann: Strange that we never get rid of these communist fanatics.

Colonel Pigafetta: We got rid of a number of them today.

Lieutenant Brown: The parties are here, now, sir.

Colonel Orbal: Call them in, then.

Captain Schmidt: I have now consulted an expert on Velder's condition. I request that he may render his statement to the court martial.

Colonel Orbal: Of course. As long as he's not too long-winded. Who is it, but the way?

Captain Schmidt: Max Gerthoffer, technologist from the Special Department of the Military Police. He has previously given evidence.

Lieutenant Brown: Would you step forward, please, Mr Gerthoffer. You are to make a statement only, so you need not take the oath.

Gerthoffer: I tell the truth on principle. Unfortunately my time is limited and I must be extremely brief. It surprises me that this court martial, despite my careful elucidation of these matters, has allowed Velder to undergo anything so utterly pointless as physical torture. Fortunately the object of examination in this case was so well prepared that the primitive treatment has not to any noticeable degree been able to disturb its mental balance. Its memory seems to be intact still. On the other hand two other matters give cause for anxiety. Firstly, these measures have to a considerable extent weakened Velder's physique, which seems particularly absurd when one thinks of the trouble to which we went earlier on to respond to and build up his central life function, naturally with exactly the thought in mind that he would be in the best possible condition for interrogation and court martial sessions. As things are now, the greatest care must be devoted to the task of keeping him physically alive, as in their stupidity—I cannot use a milder expression—they have also punctured his eardrums and exposed him to the most unsystematic maltreatment with batons and rubber clubs. These have caused aphasic disturbances. He finds it difficult to connect immediately what he hears with his own thoughts. It is particularly inappropriate to expose him to too intensive interrogation. So-called questioning, or even worse, cross-examination, has a very exhausting effect, as swift adjustments of thought cause such great strain that they quickly lead to a state of coma or complete unconsciousness. If on the other hand, Velder is given the opportunity to produce his memory-pictures in larger complexes and in correct order, you will notice that his ability to remember will remain unbroken, and at the same time the risk of mental exhaustion is more or less eliminated. For a while, I considered the possibility of allowing Velder to go through some kind of will-stimulating surgery, but I don't think there would be much to gain from that, and also the Special Department is at the moment overwhelmed with work. As recently as today we received several objects of investigation from the riot areas in the Eastern Province. That is largely all I have to say.

Major von Peters: How are your children?

Gerthoffer: They're very well, thank you, though the girl has had a cold nearly all winter. And unfortunately my work stops me from being with them as much as I should wish.

Major von Peters: Well, it'll be better when we've finally winkled out all those Reds. Thanks for taking the trouble to come here.

Colonel Orbal: Quite.

Captain Schmidt: I call Erwin Velder as witness. With regard to Mr Gerthoffer's indisputable professional knowledge I shall in so far as possible lead the questioning according to his recommendations.

Colonel Orbal: I didn't understand all that.

Commander Kampenmann: The idea is virtually to let Velder talk and interrupt him as little as possible.

Major von Peters: Fine, what? Now you can't even ask the ac-accused questions. Soon we'll have to begin feeding him and blowing his nose for him, I suppose.

Captain Schmidt: Brown, would you mind pushing the accused forward. Put him as close to the bar as possible. That's right. Now, Corporal Velder, can you in your own words describe the events and circumstances surrounding your desertion, beginning from the twelfth of December, the day before the referendum. Try to speak as clearly as possible.

Velder: Election day, yes. The twelfth of December. That's right. It was sunny and quite a warm day for winter time.

Major von Peters: What the hell's that to do with us?

Colonel Pigafetta: Can't you stop interrupting the witness? You've seen for yourself what the consequences are.

Major von Peters: Huh.

Captain Schmidt: Go on, Velder.

Velder: Excuse me?

Captain Schmidt: Election day, the twelfth of December, a sunny and warm day ...

Velder: Fifty-three degrees in the shade. The General cast his vote at the polling station in Oswaldsburg early in the morning. Then I drove him in a jeep to Ludolfsport and some smaller places. He travelled around to encourage the voters. It was important to give them a push at the last moment, he said. All citizens over fifteen had received printed ballot papers and a register of electors had been set up. There weren't very many people about round the polling stations. But at one place in Ludolfsport there was a group of supporters who cheered as we drove past. In the afternoon we took the coastal road to Marbella. Things looked about the same there. The General seemed exhilarated and optimistic. He said several times that whatever happened, Janos Edner and the others had made a mistake in ignoring the referendum. But he also said that he was certain that the no-alternative would get a majority. Absolutely certain. There were hardly any militiamen about. For some reason

123

which I don't understand, large numbers of militiamen had had orders not to take part in the referendum. Soon after five o'clock, we got back to Oswaldsburg, where the General had dinner with Tadeusz Haller. I wasn't present at the meal, but took the opportunity to go home for a while. I remember that I observed that militia signalmen had put loudspeakers up all over the town and that people were told over and over again to go and exercise their rights as citizens by voting no. After eating with my wives and children, I went back to fetch the General. It was about ten minutes to seven and already dark. Then I went with the General and Haller to the office. We got there just after seven.

In the office building, Janos Edner and Aranca Peterson, who lived in the flat above, by the way, were already there. Danica Rodriguez, who was Edner's secretary, was also there. The polling stations were closed at half-past seven and the count was to begin half an hour later. Eight o'clock, then. There was a teleprinter in the meeting room and as they were counted, the results from the different districts were to come in on that. Aranca Peterson went upstairs and made some coffee. Then we all sat round the big table in the room and drank it. Very little was said but the atmosphere was neither jarring nor hostile. Everything seemed much as usual. Janos Edner was the only one who looked sour and discontented, but he had already seemed sullen for quite a long time. Aranca Peterson was calm and untroubled. She had a fantastically calm disposition anyhow, almost always. All I know is that I saw her lose her temper only once in all the years I knew her. Only Tadeusz Haller seemed to be nervous, but I'd been used to that for quite a time, too. He got up several times and walked up and down the room. The General was very friendly towards the others and absolutely dead calm. I remember that in passing he asked when Ludolf was coming back. Aranca Peterson replied that he was expected in Oswaldsburg on an early morning flight the next day, due in at a quarter past eight. The General said he thought that was excellent. Then they all sat in silence for a while again, but when a little later Edner filled the General's cup, he said: 'I must ask you something, Paul. If this utterly idiotic referendum had given the absurd result that the people here had voted no, so that you had become president, what would you have done? Would you have let loose all the shit that we've moved here to avoid? Would you personally have smuggled in political and religious fanatics and thrust Christianity and Buddhism and Catholicism or whatever they're called on to the people? Would you have set up political parties and forced people into choosing between Fascism and social-democracy and liberalism and communism and all the other idiotic ideologies?' The General laughed and said: 'No, I don't intend to go that far.' Then soon after that Edner said: 'Why haven't you got your uniform on and your steel teeth in?' The General laughed again and at first said nothing. He was in civilian clothes—it was actually only during the last two weeks that he had been wearing his uniform and decorations—and I think he'd left his dentures at home because they irritated him. He'd told me they rubbed.

Major von Peters: No, now look here, I can't stand this a moment longer.

Colonel Orbal: Let him talk, Carl.

Velder: I'm sorry but ...

Captain Schmidt: Go on, Velder. General Oswald didn't reply, you said.

Velder: Yes. Yes, of course. Well, after a while he said that they were equipment he didn't usually use amongst friends. Then Janos Edner actually laughed too, but Aranca grew thoughtful and said that she thought that last remark had been a strange thing to say. I presumed she was referring to the fact that the General never went abroad, that he doesn't like flying, and that because of this he always ought to be among friends. After yet another while, when it was quite quiet, Edner suddenly burst out with: 'Why the hell have you done all this?' The General and Tadeusz Haller looked at each other and finally the General said: 'You can rest assured that there is no evil intent.' Then Danica Rodriguez said: 'While you're here you don't have to stand on ceremony. Save that for the next time you need to make a speech. I happened to hear one of them, by mistake.' The General looked at her with distaste. I had a feeling that he'd never liked Dana very much.

Colonel Orbal: Was that the woman with a moustache? The sexy one?

Major von Peters: Did a tart like that dare to be so familiar with the General? No, now that's enough. Am I the only one here

125

who sees that we must put an end to this deluge of lies?

Commander Kampenmann: Can't we agree once and for all to let the accused tell his story without interrupting him all the time?

Colonel Orbal: You're being damned officious, Kampenmann. Oh, well, go on talking now, Velder.

Major von Peters: God, that one should have to endure this, sitting here hour after hour, listening to this swine.

Colonel Pigafetta: What's wrong now, Captain Endicott.

Colonel Orbal: What? What's the matter with the man?

Captain Endicott: He seems to have lost the thread, sir.

Major von Peters: Thank God for that.

Captain Endicott: One moment. I have some injection ampules here which Doctor Mogensen gave me for just this kind of situation. Give me a hand, will you, Brown. In the thigh, he said. That's it.

Colonel Orbal: Do we have to sit here staring at all this? Damned unpleasant. Disgusting.

Colonel Pigafetta: Not very aesthetic, I must say.

Colonel Orbal: They've stuck it in the wrong place, of course.

Colonel Pigafetta: My officers are usually capable of carrying out their tasks.

Major von Peters: They're experts at opening their parachutes, anyhow.

Lieutenant Brown: He's coming round now, I think.

Velder: On the thirty-fifth day, the communication system between the different defence units began to collapse. We couldn't reach the bunker system in the west and south-west any longer. The whole of the surface of the ground was burning.

Captain Endicott: One moment, Velder. You must go back in time. See if you can.

Major von Peters: He talks like a children's nurse. Is he supposed to be an officer?

Colonel Pigafetta: Yes.

Captain Schmidt: You said you had a feeling that the General had never liked Danica Rodriguez very much.

Velder: He said nothing to Dana, didn't reply, but just glared at her. At seven minutes past eight, the first result came in on the teleprinter. It came from one of the smallest districts, near Marbella. Three people there had voted yes and eleven no. At thirteen minutes past eight, the next one came, from the same area. Three had voted yes and six no. Dana and I—that's Danica Rodriguez, Edner's secretary—did the counting. We took it in turns to pull the telex strips off the machine and write the figures up on a large blackboard, where we totted them up. Twenty minutes later, another small district result came in. There the figures were seven-seven. Janos Edner had sat around yawning for a while and at half-past eight he said he was ready to go up to bed. He said to Aranca that she could wake him up if anything interesting happened, or when the count was complete. I remember that Tadeusz Haller stared at him as if he didn't believe his ears. Shortly before nine, the first Oswaldsburg town district result came in, and there the figures were ninety-six yes and four no. A few minutes later, another one came and the figures were eighty-two yes and seventeen no. That was the fifth district in Ludolfsport, and I remember it especially because it turned out to be an almost exact average figure. Haller was noticeably nervous now, but Oswald took it all quite calmly. Then the figures began to pour in at great speed and all of them showed roughly the same tendency. At about ten, Aranca said she'd go and get some beer and sandwiches, and the General—I remember this especially—went with her to help. When they came down, the figures were seventy-three thousand four hundred and two yes against fifteen thousand six hundred and sixty-three no. Everyone had some beer and sandwiches then and we let the teleprinter look after itself, collecting up paper in a heap below. The General and Aranca Peterson and Danica Rodriguez were just as usual, but Tadeusz Haller was very nervous. He didn't want anything to eat and spilt his beer. Soon after eleven ...

Major von Peters: Are you going to tolerate this, Mr Haller?

Tadeusz Haller: I suppose so.

Captain Schmidt: Soon after eleven ...

Velder: Soon after eleven, the count was complete, percentages and all. One hundred and forty-two thousand one hundred and twenty-two had voted yes, and thirty-one thousand seven hundred and six no. That meant, Dana and I calculated, that only seventeen per cent of all the people who could vote had done so. And of those who had, eighty per cent had voted yes and eighteen per cent no.

Colonel Orbal: Damned difficult to hear what the man's saying.

Captain Endicott: With permission from the court, I should like to request a pause in the interrogation to allow the accused to rest his vocal chords.

Major von Peters: Interrogation—huh.

Colonel Pigafetta: Yes, Endicott. Granted.

Colonel Orbal: What's going on? I ought to have said that, Pigafetta.

Colonel Pigafetta: Yes, you ought.

Commander Kampenmann: Are those figures correct?

Tadeusz Haller: Yes, as far as I remember. With cunning propaganda, they'd managed to persuade over eighty per cent of the population to abstain from exercising their rights as citizens. And the others ... well, you've got the exact figures in your papers, haven't you, Captain Schmidt?

Captain Schmidt: One moment. Yes, here they are. Of all those entitled to vote, eighty-two point four per cent abstained. Fourteen point one voted yes and three per cent voted no.

Tadeusz Haller: So it wasn't a vote at all, quite simply. Apathy was so great that most people didn't even bother to vote in the referendum.

Commander Kampenmann: There is one point in the accused's statement that I didn't really understand. Why were large numbers of the militia not allowed to partake in this referendum?

Tadeusz Haller: That was a well-considered measure taken by General Oswald. The strength of the militia had been tripled in a very short time. Naturally I was informed on this point, but otherwise very few people knew about it. The General was the only person who had full control over the immigration frequency.

Major von Peters: You're talking about the Army, Mr Haller. By this time, the militia had ceased to exist. Otherwise, you're right, of course. The troops were ordered to stay in their barracks or training areas, and their numbers were held secret. It was a kind of precaution against a coup, should anything happen, a surprise attack, for instance, from outside or from within.

Tadeusz Haller: Exactly. And if the new troops had taken part in the referendum, they would have to have had ballot papers, to have been included on the electoral rolls, and also the soldiers would have had to leave their camps to go to the polling booths. So the whole arrangement would have been disclosed.

Major von Peters: Yes. Briefly, it was a military safety precaution.

Colonel Orbal: What in heaven's name is Endicott up to now?

Major von Peters: He's busy with his protégé, can't you see? He'll start singing him a lullaby soon.

Captain Endicott: I think we can go on now, sir.

Major von Peters: One doesn't think in the forces. Even your men ought to have learnt that, Pigafetta.

Captain Schmidt: I would like to take this opportunity to point out that Velder—according to a scientifically based opinion given to me by Gerthoffer—is now speaking more or less directly from memory, without being able to make any later thought-constructions or manipulated valuations.

Commander Kampenmann: How do you know that this opinion is scientifically based?

Major von Peters: For God's sake, Kampenmann.

Colonel Orbal: Yes, yes. Go on, now, so that we get somewhere sometime.

Captain Schmidt: Please go on, Velder.

Major von Peters: He's not that polite even to us. If only we had Bratianu here still, for God's sake.

Colonel Orbal: What are you whispering about, Carl?

Major von Peters: I said we ought to have Bratianu here.

Colonel Orbal: Yes, I'll say ...

Captain Schmidt: If the presidium permits ...

Colonel Orbal: Yes, what are you dithering on about, Schmidt? And Endicott, standing there fiddling about with that wretch as if he had a tart in bed with him. Get going, now.

Velder: Then Janos Edner came down. Aranca had been up to wake him, I suppose. He looked at the figures and then began to swear. His reaction was very surprising. When Aranca said that everything had gone much as they'd expected, he replied that he hadn't expected to find that there were over thirty thousand people on the island who were so crazy that they sympathized with Oswald and his twisted ideas. And—he said—the other figure was nothing to get excited about either. It just showed that on our island—he emphasised the *our*—there were a hundred and forty thousand individuals who let themselves be duped into partaking in a meaningless referendum. Aranca gradually calmed him down and then everyone talked for about quarter of an hour, except Haller, who had already gone. Danica Rodriguez asked the General what he considered he had demonstrated with all this nonsense. The General answered absently: 'Nothing, my dear, nothing ...' Then he yawned and said goodnight to the others. 'See you tomorrow,' he said, too. I went out with him and we went to a small apartment which he had a few blocks away. It was a lovely, warm evening and the whole town was calm and quiet. I think the results of the referendum were being broadcast over the radio and television, but no one seemed to bother about them. When we got up to the apartment, Oswald got two beers out of the refrigerator. Then he got out his portable typewriter and typed out something from a handwritten note he'd had in his pocket. I'd seen him making notes on that piece of paper earlier in the evening. He drank his beer as he worked. Then he rang headquarters and sent for a jeep to come and fetch him. He folded up the paper he'd written on, put it in an envelope together with another piece of paper and stuck it up. Then he wrote on the front that it should only be opened on an order which had a code-signal ...

Major von Peters: Night exercise.

Velder: A code-signal that was the same as for the other sealed order I'd been given. We stood there drinking our beer and Oswald was absolutely dead calm. He said he didn't need me any more for the moment, as he was thinking of going to headquarters and staying there overnight, but that I should take the new instruction, with the old one, and go to a place called Checkpoint C—that was a military post east of the town, usually unmanned—and take command over the men there and stay until I was given further orders. As he said that, he began to take off his suit and change into uniform, a brand new one, by the way, which I'd never seen before. When he'd put on the cap, he clamped his dentures in and stood for a moment—probably only a few seconds—looking straight ahead. As if to himself, he said—he'd often done that together with me during the past year, talked to himself, I mean. 'I've waited for this moment for years,' he said. Then he seemed to wake up and said to me: 'See you tomorrow. I rely on you to follow these instructions if anything happens. And you should think again about that business of becoming an officer. The offer is still open.' We shook hands and parted outside the building. I went to the place where we'd parked the jeep, down in one of the car tunnels, and it was still warm and a little damp in the air. The town was quite empty and silent now and there was hardly a light to be seen in any of the windows. When I got to that post, Checkpoint C as it was called, there were thirty men there all ready for action. They had two large trucks full of materials, troop transports, automatic weapons and two walkie-talkies. I didn't know a single one of them. They belonged to some recently set up force. I got there at five minutes past one and at exactly half-past one, the 'phone rang in the office. It was headquarters and I gave the code-word 'Night exercise', which the major here said quite correctly. I took out the two envelopes and opened them. One was an action-order, which was to be carried out immediately, and the other was a message I was to pass on as soon as the measures in the action-order had been taken.

Captain Schmidt: You can stop there, Velder.

Colonel Orbal: Good. He sounds like a gramophone record from the turn of the century.

Captain Schmidt: The contents and wording of both documents named by the accused are extremely important. A copy of the action-order has been kept in the Army archives and the message written personally by the General has also been retrieved. Both are included in the Appendices of the preliminary investigation marked V V/17xx and V V/17xxx. I request that the officer presenting the case should read them both.

Major von Peters: Without all those formalities, may I suggest.

Lieutenant Brown: Appendix V V/17xx. Secret action-order, reference Operation Night Exercise, sent 5th December. Concerning Corporal Velder and his subordinates. Marked Secret according ... sorry ... the text is as follows:

At Checkpoint C troops collected shall at 0200 hours on 13th December proceed to point on north road between Oswaldsburg and Ludolfsport three hundred yards east crossroads by inn in square forty-seven. Two road barriers to be constructed fifty yards apart, the western facing Oswaldsburg, the eastern facing Ludolfsport. Apart from blockade materials already issued, it is appropriate that vehicles form part of the barriers, which must be a hundred per cent efficient. The barriers shall be of a depth of at least fifty yards north and south of the road. Only military personnel with passes of enclosed type may go through. Every effort to force or circumnavigate the barriers is to be met with decisive and effective action. The road barriers are to be held until further instructions are given. Radio silence until 0230 hours.

Colonel Orbal: Yes, we really were that short of men. Thirty men and a corporal, what?

Lieutenant Brown: Appendix V V/17xxx. Instruction and secret message from General Oswald, entrusted to Corporal Erwin Velder, 13th December, 0015 hours. The text is as follows:

... I should perhaps insert here that the first part is in the form of a letter from the General to Velder, the second part in the form of a proclamation. Velder—when you've carried out the measures in your action-order you must do the following. Put someone in command of the whole barricade area and a second-in-command for each separate barrier. The men you've got under your command are guaranteed trustworthy, so there's no risk. Then take the jeep and go to Radio Headquarters in Oswaldsburg, which should then be in the hands of loyal troops. See that the text of the enclosed manuscript is broadcast over the radio, television and the entire loudspeaker network every half hour from half-past eight in the morning today onwards. As soon as you're convinced that this will be done, return to the road barriers. I need hardly point out that I am relying on you. Signed. P.O.

Colonel Pigafetta: Highly informal, I must say.

Major von Peters: A forgery, of course.

Lieutenant Brown: General Oswald's message to the nation runs as follows:

Citizens. The attempt via democratic and rational means to make the government of the country understand and act according to the serious and exposed situation the nation is in, has failed. By infamous underground propaganda and systematic election frauds, yesterday's referendum became of such a character that it can be declared totally invalid. Supported by the Army and an overwhelming majority of right-thinking citizens, I have decided to accept the responsible task of Chief of State. Until a legal government can be

132

appointed through public elections and according to democratic principles, I shall also undertake the position of head of the interim government. I see my task as one of leading the nation out of its present depraved and dangerous state. The Army has taken over the responsibility for the personal safety of the individual in our new national democratic state. In return, it is up to every citizen to follow carefully the instructions issued by the military authorities. Complete calm reigns over the whole country. Every attempt from the side of the traitors or from foreign powers to rob the nation of its newly won freedom will however be dealt with with all strength. Long live our new fatherland, founded on the triumvirate Religion—Morality—Dignity. Paul Oswald. General. Chief of State.

Colonel Orbal: Very forceful.

Captain Schmidt: The contents of both these documents show to what extent the General and the new State relied on Erwin Velder. Naturally it did not occur to the General that a man who had for years served in his immediate proximity and who had him to thank for everything, would turn out to be a simple deserter and a cold, calculating traitor. We shall now hear Velder's own story of how he carried out his responsible task. Captain Endicott, has the accused grasped what has been said?

Captain Endicott: I think so.

Major von Peters: Think!

Captain Schmidt: Well, Velder, go on with your story. You've just opened your sealed orders and find yourself a responsible military officer at Checkpoint C.

Velder: Oh, yes. Of course I remember the text. I shut myself in the office at the guard-post and read through the different papers over and over again. In spite of everything that had happened, I hadn't really believed that this could ever happen. I couldn't believe, either, that people like Aranca Peterson or Janos Edner—despite their pacifist attitude—would just give in to this sort of change of régime. Not even Tadeusz Haller, although he'd taken the General's side during the preparation for the referendum. I saw at once that I wouldn't obey the instructions I'd received. What forbade me to do so, I don't know, perhaps something which at that time I thought was my conscience, but which in fact was probably my general attitude.

133

Colonel Orbal: I don't understand that.

Velder: My first thought was to go to headquarters at once and try to convince General Oswald of the absurdity of his actions. But on second thoughts, however, I saw that this wasn't possible, mostly because of what I knew about the General and his gradual change of attitude. I also considered the possibility of large numbers of the militia, like myself, refusing to obey orders. After a few minutes, I realised that this, too, was unlikely. The new Army could in no way be compared with or considered equal to the militia such as it had been only six months earlier. And also by that time, I was one of the few remaining militiamen and had been in it since it first started. Through new recruiting, which I knew quite a lot about, at least two thirds of the men were now what could be more or less regarded as professional soldiers. I had no illusions about them. As far as the others were concerned, presumably the last six months' strict discipline and hard training had been enough to change their attitude. I remember how time and time again I read through those papers lying in front of me in that bare office. The window had an ordinary fine mosquito net of steel wire. Outside it was as black as ink and quiet, but I heard the men moving about and rattling their arms in the guard-room. I should perhaps also say that I understood very well that although the task I'd been given was important, it was not the most important of all. There were two roads between Oswaldsburg and Ludolfsport, and of these two, the northern one was the oldest and least used. It must have been much more important to barricade the southern road, which was a large motorway with double four-lane roads, and also to advance directly into the towns to take over points like telecommunications centres and depôts. And naturally to stop armed counter-action and neutralise untrustworthy groups of people. And yet the barrier on the northern road was naturally a key position. It did not surprise me that the General had given me this task, though most people would have found it more natural if it had been entrusted to an officer. And yet I was a little surprised ...

Major von Peters: Oh, yes. That's nothing to what I and the others here have be ...

Velder: Of course, I thought about my wives and children in town and about how things would go for them if I ... well, I was thinking about their safety.

Major von Peters: Now the man is interrupting me again. I really can't be responsible for the consequences. Isn't it soon time to stop, anyhow?

Velder: As late as five to two, I still didn't know what to do ...

Captain Schmidt: I suggest that we leave Velder and his thoughts for a moment and ...

Major von Peters: ... and end for today. This has all been a bit much for an honest man all in one day. Adjourn the session now, Mateo.

Colonel Orbal: Of course. This extra-ordinary court martial is adjourned until tomorrow at eleven o'clock.

Tenth Day

Lieutenant Brown: Members of the presidium present: Colonel Mateo Orbal, Army, Colonel Nicola Pigafetta, Air Force, Major Carl von Peters, Army, and Commander Arnold Kampenmann, Navy. As adviser, Justice Tadeusz Haller, Ministry of Justice. Officer presenting the case, Lieutenant Arie Brown, Air Force. Prosecuting Officer, Captain Wilfred Schmidt, Navy, Defending Officer, Captain Roger Endicott, Air Force. At today's session, Assistant Prosecuting Officer, Lieutenant Mihail Bratianu, Army, will also be present.

Major von Peters: What about listing our ages, weights and years of service while you're at it, Brown? Just to extend the pleasure, I mean.

Lieutenant Brown: To tell you the truth, sir, I have received a reprimand for irregular presentation of the case.

Major von Peters: To tell the truth? What sort of expression is that?

Colonel Pigafetta: Who issued this reprimand, Brown?

Tadeusz Haller: Perhaps I'm best qualified to answer that question. The comment probably emanated from the Joint Commission from the Ministry of Justice and the General Staff Judicial Department which is at present occupied with formulating the verdicts which will form the basis of the sentences of the court martial in the case against Velder.

Commander Kampenmann: Are the sentences already being worked out?

Tadeusz Haller: Verdicts. Yes, naturally. Otherwise it would take months, perhaps years after the session is over before they could be laid before the presidium for consideration.

136

Colonel Pigafetta: Shouldn't any complaint against one of my officers be put through the usual channels?

Commander Kampenmann: Isn't Lieutenant Brown attached to the Operational Department of the General Staff?

Colonel Pigafetta: Nonetheless, he's an Air Force officer. The matter should have gone through service channels.

Tadeusz Haller: I'll look into the matter.

Colonel Orbal: This is going to be an extraordinary day. The heat! Like cutting through cheese.

Major von Peters: Good to see Bratianu again, anyhow.

Colonel Orbal: I say, Pigafetta, I was lying awake last night thinking about something. The air in here is absolutely bloody awful and if you switch on the fans, you're almost blown away. For several days, I've had a draught down my neck. Well, I was lying there thinking and finally something came to me.

Colonel Pigafetta: Yes?

Colonel Orbal: Well, it came to me suddenly. As there's no middle way with the fans, they're absolutely useless. I've asked the Commander of the Engineer Corps and he says the only thing you can do is change the whole fan system and that would take at least two weeks, perhaps longer, because the most suitable type of fan isn't in stock and has to be ordered from elsewhere.

Colonel Pigafetta: What was it that came to you?

Colonel Orbal: Well, that there is in fact a middle way. You could open the windows. I've checked that they open inwards, so we could leave the shutters closed in any case. If, for instance, you open one half of the windows over there in the corner and then the other window to the right, the one diagonally behind Kampenmann, then you'd get an even and satisfactory movement of air. Don't you think so, Carl? Of course, if the wind ...

Major von Peters: Call in the parties now, Mateo.

Colonel Pigafetta: Brown, open the windows.

Major von Peters: Get going now, Mateo. Call in the parties.

Colonel Orbal: What's all the damned hurry? Yes, call in the parties now, Brown.

Captain Schmidt: At yesterday's session, the case against Velder was brought to the point just prior to the accused's desertion from the armed forces. We are still concerned with points seventy-eight to and including eighty-two in the case, reference to desertion and high treason. When Velder's story was interrupted yesterday he had just opened his sealed orders. He was still in the office at Checkpoint C, where, according to his own statement, he was what is called a prey to his own conflicting thoughts. The time was five minutes to two and by delaying carrying out the action-order he had already grossly failed in his duty. Velder's next actions to a certain extent influenced the future of the nation. So it is important that we create a clear picture of the situation in general. To enable me to do this, I will refer to some written documents, first and foremost a fragment from a diary written by Aranca Peterson and presumably intended as the basis for the aforementioned memoirs, which she and Janos Edner together planned to publish, but which they clearly never completed. If you please, Lieutenant Brown.

Lieutenant Brown: Appendix V V/33. Concerning the situation in Oswaldsburg on the night of December 13th. Confiscated documentation written by the traitor Aranca Peterson. Marked Secret according to paragraphs eight, eleven and fourteen to twenty-two.

Major von Peters: Is all that going to start again now?

Lieutenant Brown: Orders, sir. The text is as follows: I'll now try to remember what happened during that decisive night, the night of the thirteenth, how and in what order it happened and how we understood it. Tadeusz left the Council buildings at about half-past eleven, soon after the final count had been made. Oswald must have gone at about midnight, followed by his constant companion Velder, the man whose, as far as I can make out, quite worthy sex life had caused us so much trouble and discord. Thus Janos, Dana and I were left behind in the room. We sat there for a while drinking beer and not saying much. Janos had collected himself from his in itself understandable but unnecessarily violent reaction (perhaps I'll have to look after him better, I thought) and when we had looked at the figures for a while, a conversation developed of which, despite the short time which has elapsed since then, I can remember only the bare outlines.

Dana: Oswald seemed astonishingly satisfied.

Janos: He had good reason to. Thirty thousand sympathisers to build on. Not so dusty.

Me: Do you think he'll go on building on to them?

138

Janos: I'm sure he will. He certainly hasn't acquired those uniforms and general's teeth just for fun.

Me: But the referendum was an overwhelming manifestation in favour of us, after all. He got three per cent of the votes. A defeat in an election can hardly be greater than that.

Janos: And we got eighty per cent.

Me: What do you mean?

Janos: The fourteen per cent who voted for us we can't rely on at all. The fact that they voted at all shows that they haven't grasped the idea—or that they don't sympathise with it, possibly with us personally. Consequently they might just as well have voted for Oswald. In practice, then, seventeen per cent of the people are not to be trusted. That's not all that few. Just think, seventeen out of a hundred.

Dana: I'm scared of Oswald.

(She said this very suddenly.)

Janos: You mean that you don't trust him.

Dana: No, I mean just what I said. I'm scared of him. I'm not usually scared, as you know, but I've seen people like him before, in different circumstances and a long way away from here.

Me: But what is it he's after?

Dana: Power.

Janos: But he's got it. He's got everything he could possibly want, from uniforms and medals to aeroplanes and guns.

Dana: Perhaps that's not what he primarily wants—but simply power. In that case ...

Me: In that case what?

Dana: In that case it is a matter of indifference to him whether he takes power by force over a barren desert or over an ideal society. The main thing is power in itself, as a phenomenon.

Janos: Oswald has never been like that.

Dana: Perhaps he wasn't, but he may have become so. He lives alone, doesn't he? The seeds to this are in everyone, but I think they grow more easily in someone who is alone. I know that. I live alone too.

Me: No one can be very much alone here. They're not meant to.

(Naïve, I admit, but I said that.)

139

Dana: I've been damned alone here, many a time.

Janos: Perhaps Oswald is going mad. In that case we must help him. But I must say that Tadeusz annoys me more. His spinelessness has always irritated me and it's got worse over the years.

Dana: Tadeusz Haller is a second-tier person. He's always been so, and he'll always latch on to new opportunities in the vain hope that they will eventually carry him up to that top step which he'll never reach. I don't understand why you allied yourself with him in the first place.

Me: There's a lot you don't understand. We've known Tadeusz for a long time. He's intelligent and his fundamental attitude is right.

Dana: I'll agree that he's gifted, but what for? And fundamental attitudes can be changed.

(Where have I heard that before? Naturally, from myself, long ago.)

Dana: And also, it's not impossible that Oswald isn't right on a number of points. There is perhaps a fundamental moral sense of belonging which one can stand outside of for a while—but not in the long run.

Janos: What would that be?

Dana: I don't know. If I'd known that I wouldn't be sitting here.

We sat on for a while longer, chatting about this and that, the irritableness still there. Janos repeated several times that Oswald and Tade had had a set-back and that tomorrow they'd shrug their shoulders and then we'd soon all shrug our shoulders at this odd interlude and laugh at it. He also said that if Oswald wanted to be dictator then he only had to say so, then we could just fix it in some way. If he wanted to play Leader, why not? He ought to realise that himself, too, Janos said, still as if he wanted to convince himself at any price. 'Ought to and ought to,' said Dana. Suddenly she shuddered. (She has an unpleasant way of being over-sensitive, as if her nerve-ends were outside her skin.)

'I wish Ludolf were here,' she said.

I asked why, but she didn't answer. Janos sat thinking for a while. Outside, it was absolutely deathly quiet and I felt as if we three were alone in the whole universe. (What peculiar things I do think up.)

Then Janos said:

'Ludolf, yes. We could send him a telegram, couldn't we—if he's sober enough to be able to read it?'

We wrote it out together and Danica went over to the 'phone to ring it through. She clicked the cradle several times. Finally she said:

'It's dead.'

'Send it on the telex then,' said Janos, yawning. (He looked pointedly at me, as if I hadn't known a long time ago that he wanted us to go to bed.)

'That's dead, too,' said Dana, after a minute or two.

'The hell it is,' said Janos. 'Has the whole damned tele-system collapsed? Oh, well, I'll trot over to the tele-centre with it.'

'No,' said Dana. 'I'll go. I'm an old hand at night-wandering.'

She took the telegram form and left. It was then five to two. When Janos and I were alone, he looked at the referendum figures and smiled. That was the first time that evening. Then we went up and looked in on the kids, who were asleep, and went on into our bedroom.

We began to get undressed. I was standing naked in the middle of the floor and Janos was still in his shirt and trousers in the bathroom when the door was jerked open. Quite without any warning. It was Dana. She was panting and said:

'The tele-centre is occupied by police troops. Oswald's people. All external lines are closed. They've put an emplacement with sandbags and machine-guns outside the building. I only got away by the skin of my teeth, presumably only because none of the soldiers recognised me. An officer told me that I should go home and keep calm. Everything would be cleared up early tomorrow morning and then I could send my telegram. I ran back here.'

'Did you see anything else?'

'No, nothing. It was quiet and calm everywhere.'

'What the hell?' said Janos.

'Yes,' said Dana. 'Exactly. What the hell?'

I got my clothes on faster than Janos did, although he only had to pull on his socks, shoes and jacket. We went down to the ground

141

floor. Janos put on his cap and opened the outer door. There were three soldiers on the steps. They had firearms in their hands. I had never seen any of them before. One of them saluted and said very courteously:

'I must ask you not to leave the building. The whole block is surrounded. We have orders to shoot if you attempt to leave.'

'What's all this nonsense?' said Janos, and he began walking down the steps.

The soldier who had spoken raised his rifle and cocked it; the others did the same.

'You're putting me in an untenable position,' he said. 'You leave me no choice.'

Janos stopped. I saw then that the soldier who had spoken had stars on his collar.

'A state of emergency has been declared,' said the soldier. 'The Army has taken over responsibility for safety and that applies to everyone. As long as you stay indoors nothing will happen to you. If on the other hand ...'

Colonel Orbal: Who was that officer?

Major von Peters: Lieutenant de Wilde, you must remember. He was demoted the next day. Killed at Ludolfsport.

Colonel Orbal: Oh, was he? Good demeanour, nevertheless.

Major von Peters: Too good.

Lieutenant Brown: I shall continue ... with the permission of the presidium.

Finally we went back into the building and stood staring at each other. Janos mumbled over and over again: 'A military coup ... the most impossible of everything that's impossible ... the most distasteful ... a military coup.'

'Are there any weapons in this place?' said Dana.

'You know as well as I do that there aren't,' I said. 'There's nothing here except ourselves, the kids and their nurse.'

'We must get away,' said Janos.

'Yes,' said Dana. 'But how?'

Janos went over to the window and looked out. There were soldiers everywhere.

'Has that idiot really enough men to manage this?' he said.

'Obviously,' said Dana. 'I've seen about forty uniformed men now. Here and at the tele-centre. And I didn't recognise a single one of them. Something has just passed us by.'

'Yes, it certainly has,' said Janos. 'We're casualties of one of our basic principles, limited supervision. And Ludolf ...'

'Will they take over the airport early tomorrow morning?' I said.

We looked at each other, but none of us was adjusted to the situation being hopeless or definitely catastrophic. If it had all suddenly turned out to be a gigantic practical joke, we wouldn't have been especially surprised; anyhow, I wouldn't.

At exactly ten to three, someone in military boots came stumping up the stairs. There was a bang on the door and a voice shouted: 'Military! Open up!'

'It's not locked,' I called. (We didn't usually lock up. I don't even think there was a key.)

The door was opened and a soldier came in. He had a machine-gun on a strap across his chest and a steel helmet on his head. We recognised him at once. It was Erwin Velder, Oswald's private bloodhound.

Captain Schmidt: That's enough. You can stop there, Brown. The notes in the fragment do in fact cover several more pages, but it would be perhaps of greater interest to hear Velder's version of the course of events.

Major von Peters: Frightfully interesting. So now we've got to listen to the same thing, which we already know about anyhow, all over again, have we?

Colonel Pigafetta: That undeniably doesn't sound particularly cheering.

Captain Schmidt: Captain Endicott, have you prepared the accused and tried to persuade him to be brief?

Major von Peters: 'Tried to persuade him' is delightful.

Captain Endicott: Yes, as far as is possible.

Major von Peters: 'As far as is possible' is delightful too. What the hell is this? A court martial or a nursery school?

Captain Schmidt: And he knows where he's to begin?

Captain Endicott: I think so.

Major von Peters: This eternal thinking is getting on my nerves. Push the swine forward now, Brown, so something gets done.

Colonel Orbal: Exactly. Just get going.

Captain Schmidt: Velder, will you describe what happened from fifty-five minutes past one onwards on the thirteenth of December.

Colonel Orbal: That window idea was brilliant. Works excellently. Doesn't it?

Captain Schmidt: Yes, sir. Well, Velder. At five to two, you still didn't know what to do.

Velder: I was sitting at the little table in the office at the post and listening to the men moving about outside. At exactly two o'clock, when according to that order, we ought already to have been in place at the road barriers, I went out. I gave orders for embarkation, formation and departure. The convoy consisted of a jeep, the two large trucks and two light armoured cars for troop transport. We drove the only possible way, crossing the southern autostrad, as both sides of the crossroads were blocked with tank barriers and trucks placed across the traffic lanes. The barriers were well manned. An officer standing at the crossroads irritably indicated that we were nearly fifteen minutes late and that the northern road was thus still open. When he recognised me, he moderated his tone considerably. We touched on Oswaldsburg's eastern outskirts and swung in on to the old road to Ludolfsport. When we passed the inn in square forty-seven we were stopped by a signaller, who once again pointed out that we were a quarter of an hour late. He was the only soldier I saw all the way. I let the convoy continue for three kilometres past the barrier positions and swung into a side road to the south. It led to an ex-church which earlier had been used as a pig-shed, but had now been abandoned. The roof had fallen in and it was useless. After getting the vehicles parked in the terrain round about, I set up guard-posts and let the rest of the men bivouac in the ruined church. Then I went from vehicle to vehicle, removing the distributor-heads from the jeep and one of the armoured cars. I left the trucks as they were. They had to be unloaded anyhow, before they could be used as troop transports. I put one of the walkie-talkies out of action. The other I took with me. Then I appointed someone in command and a second-in-command, gave orders that the area round the church was at all costs to be held in case of attack, and drove back towards Oswaldsburg in the remaining armoured car. After I had passed the signaller by the inn, I stopped at a safe distance and began working on the radio-receiver. Radio silence was still being maintained and nothing could be heard when I plugged into several frequencies I knew within the first and third military areas, that is, the regions round Oswaldsburg and Marbella.

Major von Peters: Correct. Military divisions were the same as they are now.

Velder: Excuse me.

Major von Peters: Nothing, for Christ's sake. Can't one even say one word any longer.

Velder: Excuse me, but ...

Commander Kampenmann: Nothing was heard from the first and third military areas. Go on, Velder ...

Velder: But gradually I got radio signals from other military areas. As I sat there, I intercepted a message from some group that must have been about forty kilometres west of Ludolfsport on the road to Oswaldsburg. I just heard what they sent out, but from that it seemed that street fighting was raging in Ludolfsport and that the Army was not in control of the situation. I thought at first it was an Army transmitter I was listening to, but I soon realised that radio-communication was going on between several organised groups who were resisting the Army. I came to the conclusion that the Army was in control of Oswaldsburg and Marbella and the surrounding areas, but that the situation in Ludolfsport must be different. Then I went down into the traffic tunnel towards Oswaldsburg. There were only a few odd guard-posts there and my pass fastened on the windscreen got me through unchallenged. My first thought was to fetch my family, but as soon as I'd parked and come up into the town, I changed my mind and went to the government office. This was guarded by a force of about forty men, commanded by Lieutenant de Wilde, who at once recognised me. Despite my lower rank, I'd often had a kind of psychological advantage over officers, because of the position I held with the General and at headquarters after the reorganisation of the Army. I was allowed through without question and went into the meeting room. Janos Edner, Aranca Peterson and Danica Rodriquez were there, obviously under house-arrest. At first they were suspicious when I told them the little I knew. In the end, Janos Edner said: 'If thing's are as you say, then let's drive to Ludolfsport, for God's sake.' I agreed with this, after thinking for a moment. Aranca Peterson woke the children's nurse and the children were dressed and I took all of them through the chain of soldiers outside without anyone even questioning that I was doing anything else but taking the prisoners to headquarters. The officer in command, de Wilde, just asked me whether I needed extra escort and whether he should continue guarding the government office. I replied no to the first question and told him an escort was waiting at the car, and yes to the second. I said there were still people in the building. He seemed satisfied with that. Once again I considered fetching my family, but I decided not to. There seemed to be a lot of military patrols in the streets. Otherwise it seemed as if the whole of Oswaldsburg was asleep. It was dark and quiet. We went down into the traffic tunnel and stowed ourselves into the armoured car, Janos Edner, Aranca Peterson, Danica Rodriguez, Janos and Aranca's children, who were two and four years old, a children's nurse called Irene Miller, and myself. The northern road was still open and radio silence favoured us, of course. I wasn't clear about the situation and neither could Janos Edner make sense of the confused messages between weak transmitters in and around Ludolfsport. However, we proceeded from the fact that Oswaldsburg and Marbella, and thus also the first and third military areas, the two largest towns and more than half the island's total area in other words, were under the control of the Army.

Captain Schmidt: That's sufficient, Velder. Push him away, Brown.

Major von Peters: Now let's have lunch.

Captain Schmidt: It would be an advantage if we could complete this point before adjourning. It seems superfluous that Velder should sit and describe the military situation which is accounted for in an Appendix numbered V VI/1 from which I shall herewith quote. Lieutenant Brown ...

Major von Peters: That seems superfluous on the whole.

Captain Schmidt: With all due respect to the presidium, sir, I should like to point out that not everyone present is as well acquainted with these events as you yourself are. A number of us had not yet returned to the country at the time. Mr President, sir ...

146

Colonel Orbal: Yes, for God's sake. Granted. But lunch after that, whatever happens.

Lieutenant Brown: Appendix V VI/1, concerning the disturbances, compiled from the summary drawn up by the National Historical Department of the General Staff. Marked Secret according to paragraphs eight, eleven and twenty-two. The document is included in the twelfth volume of ...

Colonel Orbal: Get going, Brown, get going.

Lieutenant Brown: The traitor element, led by Janos Edner, Joakim Ludolf and Aranca Peterson, had placed the country in a state of defencelessness and moral decay. Their preparations to eject General Oswald and his supporters from what was called the Council by a coup and after that set up an anarchic or Bolshevik régime of terror had already been under way for a long time. Partly to meet the expected Red revolution, partly to stop the country from simply being colonised by some external enemy, during the summer and autumn, General Oswald had reorganised the militia under strict security measures into a regular Army and more than tripled its numbers. Relatively large supplies of arms and ammunition had been acquired from friendly nations, which, like General Oswald, wished to stop the island falling into the hands of the Red hordes. A number of secret emergency depôts were set up and the reorganised ex-militia was put through an intensive training programme during the autumn. The Air Force and the Navy were still so ill-provided for that they could scarcely be relied on as efficient instruments, even in an internal conflict situation.

The country was divided into three military areas, with headquarters in Oswaldsburg, the capital and centre for the western and north-western part of the island, Ludolfsport on the east coast and Marbella in the south-west. Each military area covered about a third of the country's total area.

In command of the three military areas were the following:

First military area (Oswaldsburg and Central Province): Colonel, later Major-General Henry Winckelman.

Second military area (Ludolfsport and Eastern Province and the archipelago off the east coast): Colonel Milton Fox.

Third military area (Marbella and South-Western Province): Lieutenant-Colonel, later Colonel Mateo Orbal.

Material and manpower resources of the armed forces were more or less equally divided between the three military areas. On the fourth of December, after a series of provocations from groups hostile to the people, General Oswald increased his preparations against a coup.

These provocations, which had continued virtually throughout the whole year, culminated in the sabotaging of the democratic elections on the twelfth of December, when over eighty per cent of the country's inhabitants abstained from exercising their rights as citizens out of apathy, ignorance and fear of reprisals. This was the situation, with the future of the whole nation at stake, when General Oswald decided to allow the Army to intervene, despite the fact that the small numbers of regular troops and still inadequate equipment made the operation a risky undertaking. The detailed plans for taking over power had been worked out under the General's supervision separately from the three military area commands. As a general principle, it was a matter of control over the state machinery being taken over with the minimum possible bloodshed.

With consideration of the small numbers of troops, the element of surprise was of great importance. It was a matter of striking swiftly and taking vital positions before opponents had time to organise the mob into armed resistance. A state of emergency was proclaimed at 0130 hours on the night of the thirteenth of December. Half an hour later, 'Operation Night-Exercise' began. The crusade against the enemies of the people had begun.

Within the first military area, everything went according to plan. When the roads into Oswaldsburg were blocked, Colonel Winckelman's troops advanced into the capital, where they swiftly took control of power-stations, tele-centres, waterworks, fire-stations and all important administrative and strategic points. Calm in the town was maintained as far as possible and there were neither exchanges of fire nor serious disturbances. A curfew was imposed. When the occupation had been carried out, the special commando of the Military Police went into action, and between 0400 hours and 0500 hours, between three and four hundred people were woken and arrested as suspected of subversive activities and preparing for insurrection. The traitors Janos Edner and Aranca Peterson, however, were not among these, because as a result of treachery, they were allowed to escape from the surrounded government office. On the morning of the thirteenth of December, when General Oswald was proclaimed Chief of State and head of the interim government in the new democratic republic, the Army was in control of both the capital and the other military areas, apart from the most eastern part of the Central Province. Complete calm reigned. In a radio message broadcast at ten o'clock in the morning, Doctor Tadeusz Haller, Minister of Foreign Affairs, Minister of War and Minister of Justice in the interim government, exhorted the people to remain calm and to return to their normal life in due order.

Developments in the third military area were also favourable. After motorised troops had by 0140 hours taken over administrative buildings and strategic centres of Marbella, along the coast—such as lighthouses, pilot-boat quays and so on—and in smaller towns of the South-West Province, Lieutenant-Colonel Orbal then rode at the head of the Third Motorised Infantry Regiment into Marbella. There was no fighting in its real sense except in the harbour area, where groups from the militia's Coastguard Force rebelled and offered armed resistance. These refractory units were rapidly put down with mortars and flame-throwers. But this exchange of fire caused some unrest in the town and among the relatively few tourists who were still in the area. (To spare overseas citizens as much as possible, no visas had been granted since the first of December—with reference to the impending referendum—and by the afternoon of the thirteenth of December the remaining foreigners were given the opportunity to leave the country by air or hovercraft.) Three of the patrol-boats which were lying in the harbour immediately went out to sea, after the crews had mutinied, and headed for Ludolfsport. Only a few arrests were necessary and in the morning, the troops had gained complete control not only over the town of Marbella, but also over the whole of the South-Western Province. During the morning, Lieutenant-Colonel Orbal's troops closed all the brothels, casinos and bars. But 'Operation Night-Exercise' was initiated in Marbella twenty minutes too early because of a misunderstanding at the military area General Staff Headquarters. This meant that the patrol-boats which fled out of the harbour could communicate by radio with treasonable cells in Ludolfsport, which was to have momentous consequences for developments there.

Colonel Orbal: Does it say that? Well I'm damned.

Major von Peters: Look here, Brown, are you insulting the presidium of this court martial to their very faces? Are you absolutely out of your mind?

Lieutenant Brown: I beg your pardon, sir, but ...

Major von Peters: No bloody buts here. I demand an apology.

Colonel Pigafetta: Allow me to point out that Lieutenant Brown can hardly be held responsible for the wording of a secret document from the National Historical Department of the General Staff.

Colonel Orbal: Ach, don't let's talk about this any more.

Lieutenant Brown: With all due respect to the presidium, I must submit that I am the injured party and with justification can request a correction.

Colonel Pigafetta: What do you say about that, von Peters? Who is to apologise to whom?

Major von Peters: What the hell do you mean, may I ask?

Colonel Pigafetta: You were Chief of Staff in the third military area at the time, weren't you? You were a major then and you're a major now. And Lieutenant-Colonel Orbal had indeed been promoted to Colonel Orbal, but during the whole period of the disturbances was Chief of Staff with General Winckelman. Wasn't he?

Major von Peters: Now, what the ...

Colonel Orbal: Adjournment for lunch. The session will start again in two hours' time.

*   *   *

Colonel Orbal: You shouldn't have said that, Pigafetta. Anyhow, not in the middle of a session.

Colonel Pigafetta: I won't accept unfounded insults and accusations against my officers.

Major von Peters: I only wanted to correct an error in the investigation material.

Colonel Pigafetta: Did you say an error?

Colonel Orbal: Don't start on that again now. There's a hell of a row going on, Pigafetta. Deafening.

Colonel Pigafetta: It's because the windows are open.

Colonel Orbal: What? Oh. Oh, yes. Call in the parties, Brown.

Lieutenant Brown: Captain Schmidt reports his absence for the day. The case for the armed forces will be put by the Assistant Prosecuting Officer, Mihail Bratianu.

Major von Peters: Excellent.

Lieutenant Bratianu: Colonel Orbal, Major von Peters, Colonel Pigafetta, Commander Kampenmann, Justice Haller! I request to be allowed to develop further the case for the prosecution.

Major von Peters: Granted.

Lieutenant Brown: May I point out that the presentation of Appendix V VI/1 had not yet been completed when the session was adjourned.

Lieutenant Bratianu: That summary, yes. I will not be needing that. You need not continue with the presentation.

Lieutenant Brown: I see.

Lieutenant Bratianu: In any case, in my view, that document lacks value as evidence in the case. I submit to this court martial that the document in question be excluded from the preliminary investigation and that the presentation of it be struck from the record.

Major von Peters: Damned intelligent and clever as Prosecuting Officer.

Colonel Orbal: What are you whispering about, Carl?

Major von Peters: That Bratianu's a good officer. What perception.

Colonel Orbal: Yes, of course. Yes, indeed. Where are those instructions? Oh, here they are.

Colonel Pigafetta: If your private discussion with von Peters is now over, Orbal, perhaps the presidium can now proceed to considering the Prosecuting Officer's request.

Colonel Orbal: What? Yes, of course. Granted. All right, Pigafetta?

Colonel Pigafetta: Certainly.

Colonel Orbal: And you, Carl?

Major von Peters: Granted.

Colonel Orbal: Kampenmann?

Commander Kampenmann: I reserve my decision.

Major von Peters: What now?

Colonel Orbal: Calm down, Carl. This extra-ordinary court martial has decided that Appendix number ... let's see ...

Lieutenant Bratianu: Number V VI/1, concerning the disturbances.

Colonel Orbal: Appendix V VI/1, concerning the disturbances, be removed from the preliminary investigation and its presentation be struck off the official record. Against this, Commander Kampenmann has reserved his decision.

Lieutenant Bratianu: I hereby call Corporal Erwin Velder as witness.

Major von Peters: Push him forward, Brown.

Commander Kampenmann: Do you know that the questioning of Velder must be carried out according to a new method, because of his physical and mental condition?

Lieutenant Bratianu: Yes, sir, I know of the accused's condition.

Commander Kampenmann: Good. Then you also know that there is no question of any cross-examination.

Major von Peters: You ought to have been a social worker, Kampenmann. Or joined the Women's Naval Auxiliary Service.

Lieutenant Bratianu: We have heard how Velder first deserted from the Army and then immediately entered into the most filthy and loathsome of all criminal activities, namely high treason. Before we go into this complex of offences, however, I request to be allowed to insert another charge into this section of the case for the prosecution.

Colonel Orbal: Of course, Bratianu. But what?

Lieutenant Bratianu: Velder's desertion occurred in a situation which could easily have developed into war. Although a state of war had not been declared, I consider it justified to extend the charge to include one of cowardice.

Major von Peters: Granted.

Lieutenant Bratianu: Turn the accused so that he can look me straight in the eye. That's right. Thank you. Corporal Velder, do you admit to cowardice in the face of the enemy?

Velder: No.

Lieutenant Bratianu: So you do not admit that you left your post at a critical stage because you were afraid? You do not admit your cowardice?

Velder: No.

Lieutenant Bratianu: It should be 'No, sir.' Have you forgotten that already? Look me in the eye!

Velder: Yes, sir.

Lieutenant Bratianu: You know perfectly well that you're not only a villain but also a cowardly villain, Velder. Do you admit it?

Commander Kampenmann: Lieutenant Bratianu, we have already seen far too many examples of the consequences of this kind of questioning.

Lieutenant Bratianu: I understand, sir. For that reason—I emphasise, only because of that reason—I will refrain from further questioning on this point and hand over this part of the case for this extra-ordinary court martial to consider, with the plea that against his own denial, the accused be found guilty of having shown cowardice in the face of the enemy.

Major von Peters: Yes, that'll probably be all right.

Lieutenant Bratianu: I return now to the accomplishment of Velder's high treason. In order not to give the accused the opportunity to sabotage the procedure of this court martial by malingering, I will allow him to take up his testimony in the same so-called narrative form as before. Captain Endicott, would you be so kind as to see to it that the accused speaks as clearly and concisely as possible.

Captain Endicott: I shall try to.

Lieutenant Bratianu: Thank you. And now, Velder, go on with your account of how you betrayed your friends, your superiors, your General and your country.

Colonel Orbal: That Endicott, what's he up to again now? Looks very peculiar.

Major von Peters: Fiddling about, as usual. He'd have made a good social worker, too. Or member of the Women's Auxiliary Air Force.

Lieutenant Bratianu: Begin, Velder.

Velder: We drove along the road towards Ludolfsport; the northern or old road which was one hundred and twenty kilometres long. When we'd passed the inn and the place where the road should have been barricaded, Janos Edner said that we should take the road past the ruined church, where I'd let the men bivouac, and fetch the trucks loaded with blockade materials. I did as he suggested. When we got there, the guards were indeed in their places. The rest of the men were asleep inside the ruin. When Edner saw their equipment, he changed his mind again. He then said that we should take both vehicles and men with us—none of the men seemed to suspect anything unusual and they hadn't attempted to use the radio equipment that had been left behind. I got the vehicles going again and ordered the men to embark. We took both the radio transmitters into our armoured car, drove back to the old road and continued eastwards with the whole convoy.

The only place where we saw any soldiers was in Brock, a village which lies forty kilometres west of Oswaldsburg. There was a road barrier there too, but the second-lieutenant in command thought that we were on our way to Ludolfsport with reinforcements and let us through without question. It was only twenty kilometres to the next village and in between the two communities ran the border between the Central and the Eastern Provinces. And the border between the first and second military areas too, for that matter. We could now hear quite a bit of radio traffic from the area ahead of us, but we couldn't really make out what was happening. Everyone seemed to be up and about and carts and cars had been overturned across the road. Quite a lot of people with white armbands were guarding the barriers and a number of them were armed, but not many. Janos Edner and I got down and talked to one who seemed to be a leader. He was a building worker in reality and he told us that the inhabitants of the village had been given the alarm just before two o'clock. There had been some fighting there with a small Army detachment, which had come to occupy the village, but the officer commanding it had been killed almost at once and then a number of the soldiers had changed sides and the others left. We also saw several soldiers with white armbands. I ordered my men out of the vehicles and lined them up without arms. They seemed quite bewildered. The man who was leader let them choose between going over to the People's Front, as he called it, or being taken prisoner. Six of them went over. The others were taken away, where to I don't know. Perhaps they were shot. There were already a number of dead, seven or eight, I think, lying on the ground.

Lieutenant Bratianu: See to it that the accused is not so long-winded, Captain Endicott. This court martial has other things to do besides listening to this swine.

Major von Peters: Quite right, Bratianu.

Velder: Aranca Peterson asked what had happened in Ludolfsport, and the leader replied that he didn't know, but that Stoloff, who was really a building expert, had taken over leadership there. He also said that the telephones were working and it was possible to get through. After some difficulties, Janos Edner managed to get Stoloff on the line. What they said I don't know, but the end of it was that we left all the arms behind, the trucks and material, the jeep and the other armoured car too, and drove on to Ludolfsport, a distance of about fifty or sixty kilometres still. That was myself, Janos Edner, Aranca Peterson, Danica Rodriguez, the nurse and the two kids. Danica Rodriguez drove, while Edner and I worked on the radio. Now and again on the way, we met carloads of armed civilians. They were wearing white armbands and were driving westwards. There weren't all that many, of course, but I must have seen between twenty and thirty carloads of volunteers like that. The children had grown frightened and were fretting and crying.

Lieutenant Bratianu: This is intolerable. There's a short official account of the tragedy in the second military area, Appendix V VI/7x. Read it out, Lieutenant Brown.

Lieutenant Brown: Appendix V VI/7x, compiled from a summary of events in the Eastern Province and other military areas on the night of the thirteenth of December, provided by the National Historical Department of the General Staff. Marked Secret according to paragraphs eight, eleven and twenty-two. The text is as follows:

The developments in Ludolfsport and the Eastern Province, which were to lead to a series of serious disturbances, were due to unfortunate circumstances. In Ludolfsport, considerable enlargement of the harbour facilities had been going on for several months and at the same time a whole new section of the town was being constructed. This work was being done by the same specially trained men who had earlier been responsible for all building activity in the country. Thus about two thousand five hundred of these building workers, most of them housed in the harbour areas, were to be found in the town.

A certain Boris Stoloff, a close co-operator with Joakim Ludolf, the enemy of the people, and much earlier seconded as organiser of the building industry, was also in Ludolfsport. At 0143 hours on the night of thirteenth of December, the aforementioned Stoloff received a radio-telegram which clarified the Army's and General Oswald's intentions to him and described the course of events in the South-Western Province. Stoloff was then in his work-room in the harbour area and within a few minutes was able to raise the alarm in the barracks where the workers were billeted, as well as to those working on the nightshift at the time. The crews of several ships in the harbour also joined the Red revolution. This hastily gathered up mob had no modern weapons at their disposal except those on the patrol-boats and at the coastguard stations, but on the other hand they had unlimited access to explosives, detonators and tools. The tele-centre, situated on the outskirts of the harbour area, was taken over by members of the Coastguard Service and when a few minutes later, regular troops reached the building, they were met with heavy fire and were forced to retreat. When at 0200 hours Colonel Milton Fox advanced into the town at the head of units from the Second Motorised Infantry Reginment, the regular troops were attacked from all quarters by hordes of rebellious workers, armed with bundles of explosives and even mines they had taken from the coastguard depôt in the harbour. The staff-car carrying Colonel Fox was blown up and not only the driver but the Chief of Staff was also killed. The colonel himself was wounded at the hands of the rebels, together with two other senior officers. He was taken to Boris Stoloff's office in the harbour, where he was later murdered. For two hours, there was confused street fighting. Robbed of their officers and inferior in numbers—many civilians and even women armed with axes and kitchen knives had now joined the murderous Red hordes—the loyal soldiers never succeeded in gaining control of the streets or of strategically important buildings. When the troops withdrew towards military headquarters and the barracks area south of the town, they found their retreat cut off and the roads partially blown up. During the early hours of the morning, the garrison was surrounded by hastily armed civilians.

Despite courageous resistance, the garrison area fell into rebel hands a few hours later. Similarly, events developed in other towns and villages within the second military area, where the soldiers who had been sent to protect the people were attacked and in many cases brutally murdered by guerillas and groups of gangsters. Between five and six in the morning on the thirteenth of December, the traitors Janos Edner and Aranca Peterson arrived at Ludolfsport, where they at once took the lead in the Red revolution. The following day, military stores were plundered.

Lieutenant Bratianu: Did you hear that, Velder?

Velder: Yes. Some of it is quite wrong. The soldiers left behind in the barracks didn't offer any resistance. Most of the ones left behind were members of the old militia. They took their own officers prisoner themselves and went over to the People's Front. Colonel Fox wasn't murdered. He was badly wounded and died of wounds in the hospital in Ludolfsport.

Lieutenant Bratianu: Hold your tongue, you monster! No more infamous lies! Stop trying to drag you superiors and dead comrades through the mud!

Colonel Orbal: Goodness, what a noise. Both out of doors and indoors. I think that'll do for today.

Lieutenant Bratianu: Yes, sir. The charges against Velder in points seventy-eight to eighty-two can now be considered gone into and the accused proved guilty. After one more brief questioning, I am prepared to commit the case to the court.

Major von Peters: Excellent, Bratianu.

Lieutenant Bratianu: As today's proceedings end with this committal of the case to the court, I cannot see any objection to a brief interrogation of Velder.

Colonel Orbal: No, just go ahead. But don't go on for too long.

Lieutenant Bratianu: Velder! So you admit to desertion and high treason.

Velder: Yes.

Lieutenant Bratianu: Answer in the regulation manner.

Velder: Yes, sir.

Lieutenant Bratianu: Do you also admit that your treachery and cowardice cost the lives of hundreds of your friends?

Velder: No, sir. What happened that night in Ludolfsport happened before we got there. It would have happened whether we'd gone there or not.

Lieutenant Bratianu: Don't argue with you superior.

Velder: No, sir.

Lieutenant Bratianu: Keep quiet until you are spoken to.

Colonel Orbal: Why does he swing his head about like that? Is he in pain?

Lieutenant Bratianu: Keep your head still, man. Do you regret your betrayal?

Velder: Yes.

Lieutenant Bratianu: It's still 'Yes, sir.'

Colonel Orbal: Heavens, how he yells!

Lieutenant Bratianu: You say yes, but I don't believe you. Turn towards the presidium of the court and say that you regret it.

Velder: I beg your pardon ...

Lieutenant Bratianu: Beg your pardon! How can you use such words? Your crimes are unpardonable. They cannot even be expiated with death. Say: I am a swine.

Colonel Orbal: What a row!

Lieutenant Bratianu: Answer, man!

Captain Endicott: The accused is unconscious.

Lieutenant Bratianu: Really? You're not being taken in, now?

Captain Endicott: No.

Lieutenant Bratianu: In that case I shall commit the case to court. Colonel Orbal! Major von Peters! Colonel Pigafetta! Commander Kampenmann! Justice Haller!

Major von Peters: Smart demeanour.

Colonel Orbal: That's good, Bratianu. The parties may leave. Push that creature away, Brown. And Endicott, if you must fiddle about with those hypodermic syringes, for God's sake do it somewhere else.

Major von Peters: Bit of luck Bratianu came in on it. Schmidt would have gone on nagging about this for three more days.

Commander Pigafetta: Interesting young man, that Bratianu.

Colonel Orbal: This session of this extra-ordinary court martial is adjourned until tomorrow at eleven o'clock.

Eleventh Day

Lieutenant Brown: Permanent members of the presidium present: Colonel Mateo Orbal, Army, also President of the Court Martial; Major Carl von Peters, Army, and Commander Arnold Kampenmann, Navy. Colonel Nicola Pigafetta and Justice Tadeusz Haller both report absence. Colonel Pigafetta is replaced by his personal substitute, Major Tetz Niblack, who consequently represents the Air Force. Officer presenting the case, Lieutenant Arie Brown. The prosecution is presented by the Prosecuting Officer, Captain Wilfred Schmidt, Navy, and the accused is assisted by Captain Roger Endicott, Air Force.

Colonel Orbal: What's wrong with Pigafetta?

Major Niblack: They say he's ill.

Colonel Orbal: Seriously?

Major Niblack: Not as far as I know. He was reckoning on taking his place in the presidium again by tomorrow.

Colonel Orbal: Oh, I see. Nothing serious.

Major von Peters: And Schmidt's back again. We've that pleasure yet again.

Commander Kampenmann: I'm afraid that you're rather alone in your penchant for Lieutenant Bratianu. I for one don't share it personally, anyhow.

Colonel Orbal: Nonsense. Bratianu's a first-rate young man. He'll go far.

Commander Kampenmann: I don't doubt that at all.

Colonel Orbal: Is there anything really wrong with Pigafetta? I mean, he's not seriously ill?

Major Niblack: No, not really.

Colonel Orbal: Perhaps he couldn't stand that windows business.

The draught, perhaps. Yes, I expect he couldn't stand that.

Major Niblack: Windows?

Colonel Orbal: We've got ventilation problems, you see.

Major Niblack: Oh, I heard something about it in the mess.

Colonel Orbal: I'm not really satisfied myself, either. It's a bit better, and the air does circulate, but there's such a bloody noise from outside. From your aeroplanes. That noise, we must get rid of it.

Major Niblack: It would seem a trifle difficult to eliminate that on an airfield.

Colonel Orbal: I've just had a couple of conversations on the matter, one with the Commanding Officer of the Engineers and the other with Major Carr of Stores. They've agreed on a compromise solution. We have a type of small portable fan, fan model eighteen for office tables, it says in the stores inventory. Major Carr promised to send over a dozen. Have they come, Brown?

Lieutenant Brown: Yes, sir.

Colonel Orbal: And have you got them fixed up?

Lieutenant Brown: Yes, sir.

Colonel Orbal: Well, let's have them on, then.

Lieutenant Brown: They're already working sir.

Colonel Orbal: Oh, are they? Carr said in a note he sent me this morning that these fans model eighteen don't solve the central problem, i.e. the circulation of the air. They are only able, as he so rightly pointed out, to circulate the air that's already in the room. But he had considerable expectations that they would make conditions more endurable, anyhow, giving an illusion of circulation of air, he wrote. We'll have to see. We must observe how they work.

Major von Peters: Call in the parties, now, Mateo.

Colonel Orbal: Time enough. What's the point, for that matter, of Schmidt and Endicott standing here babbling on, if the presidium is paralysed by lack of oxygen? I've also noticed that Velder smells bloody awful. Put him further to the left, Brown, not right in front of me.

Lieutenant Brown: Yes, sir.

Colonel Orbal: That's right. Well, now we can let the parties in.

Captain Schmidt: As the charges appertaining to Velder's desertion and high treason were clearly dealt with yesterday afternoon and have been handed over to the court for consideration, I request to be allowed to continue with the prosecution.

Major von Peters: What else could you do? Begin again from the beginning?

Captain Schmidt: I shall, therefore, go on to charges numbers eighty-three to and including one hundred and one, concerning rebel activities, terror, murder and accessory to murder, on nineteen different occasions. This complex includes the criminal activities committed by Velder during the time he collaborated with Janos Edner and Aranca Peterson. As the evidence mainly consists of the accused's own confession and statement, I request that Corporal Erwin Velder be called as witness.

Major von Peters: Yes, if that's necessary. Granted.

Captain Schmidt: Is Velder capable of continuing his story?

Captain Endicott: Yes. He's had several injections.

Captain Schmidt: Velder, describe you activities with the traitors Janos Edner and Aranca Peterson.

Velder: We got to Ludolfsport soon after five o'clock on the morning of December the thirteenth. There was a lot going on there, people with white armbands everywhere in the streets. They were both men and women. Only a few were in uniform and most of them weren't armed, either. We first stopped at a hotel in the middle of the town where the nurse and the children were accommodated. Then I went on with Janos Edner, Aranca Peterson and Danica Rodriguez to a building in the harbour area where Stoloff had set up his headquarters. Everything was humming there, people coming and going, and cars full of people, all sorts of people, leaving the harbour area at regular intervals. Stoloff was sitting in his shirtsleeves at a table on which there were three telephones and a radio-transmitter. On the wall in front of him hung two large maps, one of the whole island and one of the town of Ludolfsport. He gave us a short summary. Said that there seemed to be no doubt that the Army had acquired full control over the first and third m.litary areas, i.e. the Central and South-Western Provinces with Oswaldsburg and Marbella. On the other hand, the coup had failed completely in Ludolfsport, where the fighting was now over. The situation was more or less the same in the rest of the Eastern Province, with two exceptions. One was the lighthouse and pilot-boat quay on the point fifteen kilometres north of the town, which had been taken by a heavily armed Army unit, now ensconced on the point. And the other was the barracks and buildings of the military area's head-quarters ten kilometres south of Ludolfsport. The latter worried him less, he said, because by questioning prisoners he had found out that there were only a few soldiers left in the barracks and also that these troops were mostly units of the old militia, whom Colonel Fox had judged as less useful and reliable. He also told us that the majority of the regular units had been broken up in the street fighting and that about ten per cent of the soldiers had voluntarily gone over to our side. In that particular case, it was almost exclusively a matter of men who had been in the militia for a long time. What worried him most, he said, was the shortage of arms and means of transport. As people were armed, they were divided into groups and dispatched west along one of the three roads, that is, the big motor-way, the old road to Oswaldsburg—the one we'd come along—and the northern coastal road, which was however still cut off by the lighthouse and the pilot-boat station. The area south of the motorway —the autostrad divided the Eastern Province into a northern and southern part—consisted of flat land with scattered farms and a sparse network of small roads. Shortly before six, a message came through that the groups of armed citizens who had been sent for-ward along the motorway had met strong resistance from regular troops about five kilometres beyond the boundary of the Central Province. Those who tried to get along the old road were stopped at about the same line. A moment later the radio in Oswaldsburg broke silence with a message saying that Oswald had proclaimed himself Chief of State and head of the government with Haller as Ministers of Foreign Affairs, Justice and War, and that everyone was exhorted to obey the Army's orders. Stoloff really had done a lot. He'd also been in touch with Ludolf, who was expected on a special plane at Ludolfsport at about seven that morning. At about eight, a message came through that military area headquarters had fallen into our hands. At first, disturbances had broken out between different groups of soldiers in the barracks and then some of the troops had come over to us. The others capitulated. On the other hand, the point by the lighthouse was still held and the soldiers there could cover the northern coastal road. The Army units at the lighthouse kept up resistance for four days, until their ammunition and supplies ran out.

Major Niblack: This Stoloff, was he a Bolshevik?

Velder: Excuse me, what? Don't know. I mean I don't know what he was then. He was a building technologist. A powerful man with curly hair, not very tall. Aranca, Edner and Stoloff looked at the map together and calculated that Oswald had control over about sixty per cent of the island, while we still held thirty-five per cent of the area. Then, when the demarcation line was drawn, it turned out that those figures were a little more advantageous. We had in fact thirty-eight per cent against their sixty-two. There was a brief discussion on the prospects and then everyone agreed that the most important thing was to get people and barbed wire and other things that could be used as barricade material quickly to the line about five kilometres beyond the border of the province where the troops seemed to have set up their most eastern support-posts, their chain of outposts, as Stoloff called them. We also agreed that we had too few people and arms to risk an attack at once. Stoloff said that he had questioned Colonel Fox—he lived on for three or four days, although he was severely wounded—and other officers and thus had got a clear picture of the real strength of the Army in both military areas. He said he was convinced that Oswald would never dare make a serious advance towards Ludolfs-port until he had reinforcements. Aranca Peterson asked where those reinforcements were to come from. It was Janos Edner who answered her: 'There are bound to be far too many people who'd like to send regular troops as so-called volunteers to Oswald's assistance.' Then Stoloff said: 'We can get that kind of help, too. And we're going to need it.' That was the first discussion on that subject. In the morning, the Army's emergency depôts were found and opened. They turned out to contain ten times as many weapons and ammunition as had been thought. So now at least two-thirds of the people who wanted arms could have them. And Stoloff told us that stores of building materials were considerable. At about ten, Joakim Ludolf came, and then there was a council of war.

Captain Schmidt: We'll stop there for a moment, Velder.

Major Niblack: Why didn't the General put the Air Force in at once? When I was in Africa and South-East Asia, we nearly always used almost solely planes, both against guerillas and the civilian population. Not high explosives or atomic weapons. Gas and napalm. And rapid-firing weapons, of course, against built-up areas and crowds of civilians. It had a devastating effect on morale. If you can talk about morale in such circumstances, of course. Ha ha.

Commander Kampenmann: There were no effective planes at the time.

Major Niblack: Planes are always effective. In themselves, they have an effect on morale which is certainly not to be despised. A matter of environment, the feeling the person on the ground has of being controlled from a higher level, purely physically, I mean. I often think about, for instance, why we and many other countries use mounted police to control crowds. It's hardly just tradition.

Colonel Orbal: What?

Major Niblack: Good God, of course not! How many people today have ever heard of a troop of Cossacks? Not one in a thousand, I'm sure. And even fewer know enough about the phenomenon to feel traditional respect for a mounted authority. No, believe you me, it's something quite different. And yet a mounted policeman for instance in a crowd is very easy to render harmless if you know the trick. You just have to cut through his reins with an ordinary penknife. But how many people think of that? No, this really is quite a different phenomenon, as I said. In the same way, in Africa, I once scattered a whole column of infantry, well, Negroes or Arabs or some other sort of natives of course. Wogs, as we called them. Scattered them, made the unit ineffective, to put it briefly. The men just threw away their arms and ran. And what do you think I had? Well, a perfectly ordinary recce plane. Unarmed. Hardly even paraffin in the tank, either. That's where the psychological element comes in.

Major von Peters: This *is* meant to be a court martial. We're in session.

Major Niblack: Yes? Why do you say that? As if I didn't know. I've been court martialled myself once, as a matter of fact. Low flying over some kind of animal breeding station, a mink farm. Ten thousand of those mink died, just imagine, ten thousand. Had heart attacks or went mad with fright and bit each other to death.

Animals, of course, but exactly the same phenomenon, if you analyse it more closely.

Major von Peters: What were you going to say, Schmidt?

Major Niblack: Found not guilty, of course. Do you know what I did? Ha ha. Rang up that animal farm and asked if there were at least a couple of pelts left over for my wife. The idiots rang up my general and complained. He nearly died laughing. After that, it became quite a sport in the squadron. Frightening mink and foxes and musquash and God knows what else to death.

Colonel Orbal: What? What did you say? I don't understand a thing.

Captain Schmidt: Excuse me for interrupting. This so-called council of war that the accused mentioned is not accounted for or described in any other version except his own. Nevertheless it seems beyond all doubt that it actually took place and that it had the greatest significance for both what happened later and for Velder's future criminal activities.

Major von Peters: Just one moment. I'd like to answer that question that Niblack asked a little more thoroughly. We were very short of operationally effective planes at the time of the outbreak of the disturbances. But the General actually sent two of our recce planes over Ludolfsport on the thirteenth of December to see what the situation was.

Major Niblack: Yes. I thought so. You see, yet more evidence that as long as you've got planes, almost any kind of plane ... do you know, I've been involved in spreading terror and destruction with almost anything that can fly, from old air-buses of corrugated iron to small fire-protection planes which looked like farm wagons ...

Major von Peters: One moment. Both those planes were shot down. From the ground. Do you remember, Mateo?

Colonel Orbal: I certainly do.

Major von Peters: Then we didn't have any more planes. Perhaps you'd be so good as to keep your mouth shut now, Niblack. Go on, Schmidt.

Captain Schmidt: Velder.

Velder: I didn't hear.

Captain Schmidt: Velder, were you present at this meeting which you called a council of war, then?

Velder: Yes. In the afternoon, after Ludolf had come. We met at the harbour offices. First we'd listened to both Oswald and Haller speaking on the radio. They assured us that the situation was under control and complete calm reigned, but that the state of emergency would be continued until the Reds—that was us—had been smoked out of their holes in the Eastern Province. Edner and Stoloff had got some information from various individuals, some who had fled from Oswaldsburg and some who had left Marbella by sea. And what they said seemed to confirm what we were afraid of; the Army had the situation under control except at our end of the island. What did you want me to tell you about?

Captain Schmidt: The council of war.

Velder: Who was there? Janos Edner, Aranca Peterson, Joakim Ludolf, Stoloff and myself. And Dana. She served as a sort of secretary. And Gaspar Bartholic was there too. That was the first time I'd met him. He had known Edner and Ludolf for a long time, I think, but had lived in different places abroad. He'd come over with Ludolf, because of the war.

Major von Peters: I refuse to accept that expression.

Velder: Excuse me. What?

Captain Schmidt: I have made comprehensive efforts with Velder during the last few days. In a case such as this, one in which he thinks 'the war' but means 'the disturbances', it is pointless to try to correct him. When you've corrected him several times, he loses the thread and it is impossible to continue. So may I recommend the presidium to ignore such details.

Commander Kampenmann: Yes, that seems the only sensible thing to do.

Major von Peters: Do we really have to put up with anything just because that swine happens to be weak-minded?

Major Niblack: I must say I understand practically nothing at all of this. And I must say the accused looks absolutely damned awful. What's he been up to? But I like your tone, von Peters. Crude but heartfelt, as they say. Would you be so good as to keep your mouth shut, ha ha. That's what I like. It reminds me of...

Major von Peters: Dear Lord Jesus Christ in Heaven.

Major Niblack: Are you religious, von Peters? Most airmen are, if not before, anyhow they become so with the years. Perhaps a

166

matter of environment, too. Or logical evolution, just like what they call flying-phobia. It's said to be in everyone, professional airmen as well as ordinary passengers. Not so remarkable in itself, when you come to analyse it. For every take-off you get statistically closer to a certain moment: regardless of which moment it might be, it may be a question of one you wish to avoid. If you think of two statistical graphs, one representing one's own flying hours and the other setting out, shall we say, the unavoidable accident-frequency in graph form. Two parabolas which inexorably approach one another. Quite logical, isn't it? Have you anything similar at sea, Commander Kampenmann?

Commander Kampenmann: No.

Colonel Orbal: Seasickness, perhaps?

Commander Kampenmann: No, that's hardly the same thing.

Colonel Orbal: Makes me think of having a pee.

Major Niblack: I didn't understand that properly. What do you mean, sir? For instance that ...

Major von Peters: Go on, Velder. Talk, for Christ's sake. Anything's better than this.

Captain Schmidt: You mentioned Gaspar Bartholic, Velder?

Velder: Yes, he was there. He was considered a military expert.

Captain Schmidt: More of an expert in riots, civil war and terrorist activities, if you'll pardon the observation.

Velder: Yes. Bartholic knew a lot about such things. Janos Edner and Stoloff made summaries of the position. First Edner, who pointed out that the island was divided by a north-south line roughly halfway between Ludolfsport and Oswaldsburg. The two-thirds of the country west of this line were controlled by Oswald and Haller, the Army, in other words. The remaining third, east of the line, that is, was in our hands. He also said that for the moment neither party was sufficiently strong to go into attack and overwhelm the other. Within our area, there was no risk of new coups or attempts at take-over, but neither could one reckon with people in the Central and South-West Province being capable of carrying out any rising against the Army, as they lacked both arms and leaders. Then Stoloff described practical details of the situation, as he expressed it. The captured Army depôts had to some extent been very well stocked, he said. Amongst other things, they turned out to contain great quantities of ammunition and astonishingly enough—and fortunately—no less than four hundred thousand yards of barbed wire. Together with considerable stocks of cement, iron girders, scaffolding, machines and tools, which for other reasons had been stored in the area round Ludolfsport, the barbed wire suggested a swift way of achieving a fairly effective barricade along the boundary which we'd already begun to call the demarcation line. As far as other materials were concerned, there were relatively good supplies of hand-firearms, a number of machine-guns and grenade-throwers too, but no artillery, no fighter-planes and no tanks, which on the other hand, our opponents would also be short of. Means of transport were only just sufficient. On that score, however, Oswald was much better supplied. We, on the other hand, held the best harbour and the largest store of provisions. The mine-chain was intact and together with the topographical structure of the coastline, they formed a guarantee against surprise attack from the sea. Stoloff ended his summary by saying that for the moment we were inferior in materials, and that the difference in strength was about 1.5 to 1. We were also inferior when it came to military-trained personnel, but that shortage was more easily compensated and less significant, as Oswald had to use some of his soldiers to keep internal order. After that, Janos Edner brought out what turned out to be the really vital question, although I hadn't given it a thought before. I don't think anyone else had either. We'd had so much else to think about and everything had happened so quickly. Janos Edner asked: 'What shall we do?' The question went from one person to the next. Joakim Ludolf—who was very determined, in a way I'd never seen him before—said immediately: 'Fight.' Aranca Peterson: 'No. Anything, but not that. Not violence and war. If we're not going to be allowed to live in peace on this bit of our island, then it's better to give it all up and leave.' Janos Edner said that he was very uncertain, that he really thought the same as Aranca Peterson, but at the same time he refused to give up and capitulate to violence and treachery, 'for a couple of poor madmen who want to be dictators', was how he expressed it word for word. With that, the main members of the Council had expressed their opinions and the question was passed on to us others. Gaspar Bartholic said that he didn't think he had the right to influence the decision, but he was at the disposal of whichever line we others took. Stoloff glanced briefly at Ludolf and said: 'Fight.' Then it was my turn. I said something very ambiguous: 'I don't know. I can fight if you think it's necessary. But I don't want to.' That was absolutely true, in fact, just as I felt then. The last person to say anything was Danica Rodriguez. She sat for a long time, smoking and staring at the wall. Then she said: 'Might as well. Fight.'

Major Niblack: Funny council of war, I must say. What a bunch! Did you know these madmen, Colonel Orbal?

Colonel Orbal: What?

Commander Kampenmann: Go on, Velder.

Velder: Go on. Oh, yes. Well, the matter wasn't settled with that. Janos Edner asked if those who'd said 'Fight' meant that we should organise an army of our own and go into attack in order to restore the old order. Ludolf replied: 'Of course.' Stoloff said: 'Naturally, but first we'll have to think in terms of fighting on the defensive.' Dana put a counter-question: 'What alternative can you think of?' And Janos Edner replied: 'We could be content with defending the area that we have left.' Dana said at once: 'Peaceful co-existence with Oswald? That's no alternative. Only an unusually naïve way of committing suicide.' Then Gaspar Bartholic spoke too, and said: 'You're right, Miss Rodriguez. There's only the combination either–or. Friend Stoloff is right, too. We must first and foremost consolidate and build up our defences. Even attack and retake the lost provinces. Military offensives demand resources, planning and training, defence demands primarily just one thing—the will to defend.' After a while, Aranca Peterson sighed and said: 'The worst of it is that we're all right. If we want to stay here, we must obviously fight some kind of war. I want to stay here, but I don't want to fight, not even defend myself really, and yet I'll obviously be forced to.'

Captain Schmidt: Yes, Velder. Go on.

Velder: I remember that, that what Aranca said, especially well, because that's what I felt then. I was also worried about my children, my family. I missed them.

Major von Peters: I must say, Endicott, that even if Velder is weak-minded and one-eyed and mortally ill, he can't be allowed just to sit there and talk whatever rubbish he likes. Isn't there any possibility of getting him to stick to the point? I can't believe that I've gone through thirty years training as a soldier in order to sit here and listen to this sort of stuff.

Captain Schmidt: Anything like a decision seemed to be lacking at this meeting, a decision on a sort of over-all plan, didn't it, Velder?

Velder: Very true. Very true. The discussion on principles went on for a long time, but then a number of very practical important points were decided very rapidly. As I said, we controlled the whole of the Eastern Province, plus a roughly five kilometres wide strip of the Central Province. Now this area was divided into a northern and a southern sector, the autostrad from Ludolfsport to Oswaldsburg making a natural boundary. The northern sector was put under the command of Janos Edner and the southern under the command of Joakim Ludolf. As the autostrad reached the sea a few miles south of the town and then swung northwards along the coast, Ludolfsport came to lie in the northern sector, in Edner's area, that is. Gaspar Bartholic was made adviser or Chief-of-Staff to Edner, and Stoloff was given the same assignment with Ludolf. That Aranca Peterson was to be with Janos Edner was taken for granted, and Danica Rodriguez had worked with them since before the liberation. I didn't hesitate, either. I felt greater solidarity with Edner than with Ludolf then. And perhaps more than anything else, I had confidence in Janos. There was always something about Ludolf I didn't really understand. At the same time, the People's Front was officially proclaimed. As long as Oswald was in power and the threat of a Fascist dictatorship remained, all antagonisms and open differences of opinion were set aside. The war, if there was to be one, would naturally need a common strategic plan, but otherwise the sectors were to function as administratively independent parts of the country. The members of the new militia and people in the province in general would as far as possible have to decide for themselves which sector they wanted to serve, live or work in. The leaders of the two sectors had to decide for themselves to what extent they needed to acquire help from outside or purchase things from abroad. The People's Front in itself would function as a common political leadership. Existing material resources would be shared equally between the sectors. The common aim was at first to defend the Eastern Province and secondly to liberate the two other provinces from military dictatorship. The People's Front was declared to be the nation's official government and everyone under arms in both the northern and the southern sector was to be considered to belong to the same civil-military organisation, the government militia. All through this council of war—it went on until late into the evening— reports were coming in from different parts of the province. By the evening, Stoloff's experts had already succeeded in achieving an almost continuous barricade from north to south, in other words, from coast to coast. A thousand yards west of it, Oswald's men— some civilians, who were presumed to have been conscripted, as well as soldiers—were building a similar barricade. Hardly a single shot was fired along the border and in both west and east the situation appeared pretty calm. In less than twenty-four hours, the country had been cut into two in the middle, as if by a razor. I still remember a thought that struck me when I left Stoloff's room after the council of war. Twenty-four hours earlier, the thought of a military dictatorship would have seemed more alien than a trip to the moon. And now the nation had already fallen into three parts, under the leadership of three people, who in practice were all equipped with dictatorial powers. Edner, Ludolf and Oswald. And this wasn't just something I thought about just then. It was those three people who were to be known as 'The Three Generals'.

Major von Peters: I can't stand this another minute. Lunch break, now, please. If one can get any of Pigafetta's filthy swill down after listening to all this.

Colonel Orbal: Excellent idea. The session is adjourned for two hours.

* * *

Colonel Orbal: Well, what are we waiting for?

Major von Peters: Niblack, of course. He's probably still sitting in the mess talking a lot of balls. What does Pigafetta mean by landing us with that gas-bag?

Colonel Orbal: You shouldn't be so critical, Carl. I think Niblack is a sympathetic chap.

Major von Peters: Sympathetic?

Colonel Orbal: For an airman, of course. That business of those hens, or whatever they were, biting each other to death was quite a funny story. On the other hand, I don't notice those fans doing the slightest bit of good.

Major von Peters: I wish this circus were over so that we could go back to ordinary duty. Sitting here wasting day after day on a swine like Velder.

Colonel Orbal: Apropos Velder, yes. What was that thing he had round his neck? The thing that looks like a primus stove?

Commander Kampenmann: A specially constructed microphone, meant to strengthen his voice.

Colonel Orbal: Oh, Christ. Though you can hear him better. Couldn't they put in the same kind of thing on Bratianu, but to have the opposite effect. Voice-softener. Then he'd be perfect.

Major von Peters: Don't keep knocking Bratianu. Although Schmidt has systematically been holding him back, Bratianu has already saved us several days.

Colonel Orbal: I was only joking, Carl. Here's Niblack at last, anyhow. Call in the parties, Brown.

Captain Schmidt: After the division of the revolutionary Eastern Province into two sectors, Velder then took up his duties with the traitor Janos Edner, to whom he served approximately as adjutant. This relationship between them can be considered to have existed from the thirteenth of December to the fifteenth of March the following year. I presume that members of the presidium remember or are aware of the general political situation immediately after the division of the country.

Major Niblack: No, I've no idea whatsoever. I was in South Africa at the time. Interesting assignment, as a matter of fact.

Captain Schmidt: In that case I will refer to the summary in Appendix V VI/47. May I ask the officer presenting the case to read out the text.

Lieutenant Brown: Appendix V VI/47, concerning the disturbances in December and at the turn of year, compiled from accounts based on both home and foreign sources. The text is as follows:

After the murder of Colonel Fox and his officers, the Reds established a veritable régime of terror in Ludolfsport and the Eastern Province. Some diplomatic pressure and action from abroad was exerted to persuade General Oswald and the national government to recognise the demarcation line as a state boundary, which *de facto* would also have meant recognition of the sovereignty of the rebel Eastern Province. That the aim of this pressure was to bring on a weakening and collapse of the nation was without doubt. The Chief of State and the government also refused categorically to make any concessions. The apparent calm reigning along the demarcation line for the next few weeks was due to the military situation rather than to the political situation. The resources of the national Army, already limited before the take-over of power, had partly been used up during the rebellion in the Eastern Province, and General Oswald's staff considered it inadvisable to complete the mopping-up operations before reinforcements had been brought up to the demarcation line. By the third week in December, ten classes of men had been conscripted and an intensive training programme begun. At the same time, the government, through agreements with friendly nations, was assured of deliveries of arms, and many volunteers from these countries, among them a number of experienced and well-qualified officers, hastened to the assistance of the National Freedom Army. The revolutionaries, however, were not inactive either, and soon a steady stream of material and men was coming in from various socialist countries, who now saw their chance of sowing false doctrines and getting a foothold on our island. At this stage, the friendly democracies offered General Oswald an alliance agreement, according to which an expeditionary corps with the official title of Peace Corps would be sent to support the National Freedom Army. In return, General Oswald and the national government promised to allow the small islands off the coast to be used as air and naval bases for a period of fifty years. This agreement was ratified on the ninth of January and a fortnight later the first units of the Peace Corps landed in Marbella. Only a week later, an international non-intervention agreement was made according to which neither troops nor heavier war materials were to be put at the disposal of either party. Practically all nations concerned signed this agreement.

Captain Schmidt: Thank you, Brown. Velder had now established his high treason by joining the revolutionary movement in the Eastern Province. We shall now hear his own account of the events up to the fifteenth of March. Is the accused ready?

Captain Endicott: Yes. You can begin now, Velder.

Velder: The situation along the front was unchanged and completely calm all through December and most of January. Janos Edner set up his headquarters about thirteen kilometres east of the demarcation line, in a one-time manor house halfway between the autostrad and the northern road. At this place, the Army had earlier set up a secret commando centre with ten underground rooms, connected by a system of passages. They were built of logs and concrete and the ceiling lay about a foot below the surface of the earth. Gaspar Bartholic, Aranca Peterson, Danica Rodriguez, myself and a few others worked in this place during the following months. Janos and Aranca insisted on having the children and their nurse with them. At first we all lived together in the old farm buildings, but when Bartholic had nagged on about this every day for a week, Edner and his family moved down into the bunker and soon after that we all followed suit. Meanwhile a lot of things were happening; you could say activity was feverish. The line of defence was swiftly extended to a depth of five or six kilometres with a system of mines, trenches and anti-tank and barbed-wire obstacles. The plans were mostly drawn up by Edner, Bartholic and myself, as was the general plan for defence. During those first months the spirit and atmosphere were very good in the northern sector. Everyone was convinced of success, but no one was really clear about how that success was going to be achieved. Some wanted us to attack at once, and others thought that fighting wouldn't be necessary at all, but that everything would gradually be regulated by negotiations. Not until a long time later did we understand that we ought to have attacked at once, on the very first day.

Major Niblack: May I put a question in here? How did the rebels finance all this activity?

Captain Schmidt: Joakim Ludolf and Boris Stoloff had been more farsighted than anyone had imagined. Not only had they secretly shared out the gold reserves—which were quite considerable—between Ludolfsport and Oswaldsburg, but they had also made sure of comprehensive aid from outside.

Velder: When you think how ill-situated we were geographically; I mean, that the countries which might help us were so far away, then the aid deliveries started coming tremendously quickly. After only a few weeks, at least one ship a day was being unloaded in Ludolfsport. And by now the northern and southern sectors were operating so independently of each other that in fact we didn't even know that Ludolf and Stoloff had had a channel cleared through the minefield south-east of Ludolfsport and that the majority of their material was being unloaded there at night directly on to the shore. And it was by no means meagre quantities in question.

Major Niblack: I thought that this Stoloff who is often mentioned was a fortifications engineer. Is that correct?

Major von Peters: Yes, indeed.

Captain Schmidt: It was also the case that most of the very considerable deliveries Ludolf and Stoloff demanded and received from their so-called friends abroad consisted less of troops and offensive weapons than of technical experts, building materials, machines, provisions and defensive aids. Without being conscious of it themselves, Ludolf and Edner, and thus the planning for the southern and northern sectors respectively, obviously started out from wholly different tactical judgements. Let Velder continue, now, Captain Endicott.

Velder: Also, quite a lot of volunteers came over during those first months. A very peculiar mixture of people, idealists of many different kinds. And adventurers of course. Some of them were sent back by the control authority that Aranca Peterson had set up in Ludolfsport. But all the same, a number of agents and spies were of course smuggled in behind our lines. Of trained regular troops, we only got a few specially trained people who came directly under Gaspar Bartholic's command. Janos Edner was on the whole not very pleased with these additions to our personnel. Practically every man in the province had voluntarily joined the militia and he considered we had enough people under arms. In some ways he was right, too.

Colonel Orbal: Push the accused away a bit, Endicott. He stinks like an open grave.

Velder: Ludolf refused to have anything to do with these volunteers, except a few individuals who had special recommendations. On the other hand, he had women in the militia, amongst them Carla, my younger wife, who had managed to flee over the demarcation line. I didn't know that then. She was just one of many women on active service in the southern sector.

Colonel Orbal: That's quite correct. I saw some of them. Real Amazons. Looked hot stuff, too. Most of them were dead when we saw them. We—we just had the Women's Army Auxiliary. Society females. General Winckelman once really made a mess of things. He came into the tent in the middle of the night and saw one of them on the bed. A report-auxiliary, he thinks. So he just rips off her clothes and gets going, from behind first and then from in front, and in the middle of the third ...

Major von Peters: Cool off, Mateo. Not while the court is in session ...

Colonel Orbal: What's the matter with you? Court's in session—what sort of shit's that? We're all men here. Well, in the middle of the third Victoria-jerk, suddenly a signal rocket explodes outside and what does he see floating above the camp bed but his old woman. He'd gone into the wrong tent in the dark and she'd come out from town to screw his pay out of him. He was impotent as a eunuch for three weeks, or so he said. And that damn well doesn't surprise me.

Major Niblack: Very funny. I remember a similar episode in Angola ...

Commander Kampenmann: Perhaps we could go on now.

Captain Schmidt: The accused said something about what he called specially trained men who came directly under the command of Gaspar Bartholic. I would like him to describe more fully what these persons' special training consisted of and his own co-operation with them and with Bartholic.

Velder: Bartholic's men were sort of commandos, specially trained for swift raids into enemy territory. They operated in groups of four to ten men, and now and again we sent such patrols over to the other side of the demarcation line. I was the person in headquarters who knew the terrain best, so I used to help show them suitable look-out spots and terrain where the patrols could move forward without risking discovery. They mostly used rubber dinghies and outflanked the enemy via the sea. Their total strength consisted of about three hundred men. We hadn't much use for them, so they were fairly soon transferred over to the southern sector.

Captain Schmidt: I need hardly point out to the presidium that these 'special troops' in fact were professional terrorists, gangs of murderers trained in the art of killing. This is just to establish

176

Velder's rôle as organiser of this murderous terrorist activity. I can give you innumerable examples of this cruel and ruthless activity.

Major von Peters: To hell with that, Schmidt. We probably know more about that than you do.

Captain Endicott: I think it's necessary that the accused be given another injection now. I'll soon ...

Colonel Orbal: No, Endicott. Under no circumstances. You must carry out those unpleasantnesses before the beginning of the session or during the lunch break. You must see that ...

Velder: Optimism was, as I said, great. We knew that Oswald had got reinforcements, of course, but we didn't know how great they were or what they consisted of. Hundreds of people came over the demarcation line on to our side, but they seldom had much useful information. It seemed as though Oswald and Haller had succeeded in transforming the country on the other side into a police state, where everything was forbidden or barricaded off and where the individual knew nothing about what was happening. With us, almost everyone knew practically everything, and that was wrong too, of course. And the mood was positive and confident of victory, but far too many thought just like Aranca Peterson, that some sort of miracle would happen and we'd be victorious without having to fight, however that was going to happen. When we discovered that Ludolf and Stoloff were putting down mines and fortifying even the stretch facing the autostrad, that is, his own border against *us*, then we realised that we didn't know very much about the situation in the Eastern Province either. All through January, Oswald's Army did nothing. At regular intervals, sometimes almost every day, he and Haller showered us with hatred and threats over the radio and in leaflets and on their own television, which naturally we couldn't see even if we'd wanted to. In some way, we were broken by the calm and the waiting. I still don't know how it happened. A week or two after the signing of the international non-intervention agreement—it must have been pushed through by those who really wanted to break us, because Oswald didn't seem to be suffering from any shortage of supplies either then or later, as those who supported him circumvented the agreement or simply ignored it—well, a week or two after that, the seventh of February it must have been ... no, the eighth, that's it ... on the evening of the eighth, there was a conference at headquarters. Ours, that is, in the northern sector. Ludolf and Stoloff came in a caterpillar-track armoured car of a type we'd never seen before. And Ludolf was wearing a general's uniform, very simple and severe, of the overall type, but a general's uniform. The conference went on all night. Edner and Bartholic produced a plan we'd been working on for some time.

We said—I spoke too, in fact—that we were now as well equipped as we could be and this was the moment to strike. From this moment, the scales could not be reckoned to weigh in our favour and now the time factor was in Oswald's favour. Our plan of attack was carefully worked out; it entailed encircling the Army's western flank from the sea and then breaking through the front in the centre and driving a wedge in the direction of Oswaldsburg. Bartholic went through it all on the large map-table. We knew roughly how the Army was grouped, and the special commandos were to be sent in soon after midnight to destroy the communications network and try to liquidate staffs and centres of command. The small Air Force we had would have the same assignment, but that wasn't much to bank on. We were prepared to throw in everything we had at once. All on one card. Edner interrupted the discussions by pointing out that we could reckon on support from large groups of inhabitants in the occupied provinces. Aranca Peterson wasn't at this meeting, and as far as I remember, it was the only important meeting she'd voluntarily absented herself from during all the time I'd known her. She was so intensely opposed to the idea of us being the first to resort to force that she didn't even want to listen, but went to bed. Ludolf and Stoloff didn't say a word the whole time.

When Bartholic and Edner had finished, Ludolf said the plan was attractive but risky. So first of all, the militia in the northern sector should be used for the offensive. His own troops would develop a series of feint attacks in the south, but on the whole be held back to be able to cover the rear in case anything went wrong and Oswald succeeded in counter-attacking. Then he gave some advice, well, instructions on how the break-through place should be forced and promised some help with special materials. Stoloff said that Oswald was probably a military idiot but that Winckelman, Orbal and other old hands among the mercenaries shouldn't be under-estimated. It sounded just as if they had known everything beforehand, before they'd come, both what we would say and what they would answer. So it was decided that the attack was to be launched ten days later, at four o'clock in the morning on the eighteenth of February. Then we all shook hands and Ludolf and Stoloff went off in their armoured car. Well, you see, this really is only a summary; much more was said and prepared, but it was like that, largely speaking. But I remember that just before he put his cap on and left, Ludolf said as if in passing to Edner: 'Have you got plenty of drink?' Edner looked surprised and said he didn't know, but he'd look into the matter, and then Ludolf said: 'I've got everything you can think of for two years ahead—and two dozen full-size bottles of whisky.' Then he left. Everything was secret, of course. and we took all the following week working out the plans in detail. I hardly went out of the bunker once, but I heard that in Ludolfsport everything was ...

Colonel Orbal: What? What's happening now?

Major Niblack: Has he fallen asleep in the middle of a sentence?

Captain Endicott: Yes.

Major von Peters: Excellent. Let's stop now, then.

Colonel Orbal: Yes, of course. Don't forget to tell us that story from Angola, Niblack. This extra-ordinary court martial is adjourned until Monday the twelfth of April, at eleven o'clock.

Twelfth Day

Lieutenant Brown: Present Colonel Mateo Orbal, Army, also Presi-
dent of this Extra-ordinary Court Martial; Major Carl von Peters,
Army, Major Tetz Niblack, Air Force, and Commander Arnold
Kampenmann, Navy. The Prosecuting Officer is Captain Wilfred
Schmidt, Navy, and the accused is assisted by Captain Roger Endi-
cott, Air Force. Officer presenting the case Arie Brown, Air Force.
Colonel Pigafetta and Justice Haller have reported their absence.

Colonel Orbal: What's the situation, Niblack? Have you heard
anything new?

Major Niblack: An hour ago they said that the situation was unchanged.

Major von Peters: Will he die?

Major Niblack: None of us has really dared think about that.
But his condition seems to be serious.

Colonel Orbal: And you then, Brown? Have you heard anything
new?

Lieutenant Brown: Not directly, sir. An hour ago they were saying in the mess that the general's condition had improved slightly.

Major von Peters: Fifty per cent burns. He'll probably die.

Colonel Orbal: If Widder actually snuffs it now, will Pigafetta be
Commander-in-Chief of the Air Force?

Major Niblack: I imagine so.

Major von Peters: Christ!

Major Niblack: Colonel Pigafetta is already second-in-command
and undoubtedly the best qualified. But naturally the final decision
lies with the Chief of State.

Major von Peters: The department for unnecessary observations
has an unusual number of adherents in this place.

Colonel Orbal: I say, Niblack, you're an airman. What the hell was Widder doing in that crate?

Major Niblack: General Widder was ... is, I mean, naturally an experienced and skilful pilot and has always shown great interest in the technical and practical side of the service.

Colonel Orbal: Where was he thinking of going?

Major Niblack: Nowhere, I presume. It was just a routine flight.

Colonel Orbal: A routine flight? A general who suddenly flies off. No wonder things went askew.

Major von Peters: Funny business, making routine flights on a Sunday.

Major Niblack: Not in this case. General Widder made ... makes a habit of doing an inspection flight every Sunday at eleven o'clock. He always used to use the same plane.

Major von Peters: I wonder how the General reacted—the Chief of State, I mean.

Colonel Orbal: No doubt he wasn't pleased. He's always got on well with Widder.

Commander Kampenmann: I heard that the plane practically exploded in the air. Is that true?

Major Niblack: In any case, it stalled immediately after taking off and crash-landed on the airfield on the extension of the runway. If it caught fire before or after hitting the ground has not yet been established.

Major von Peters: Stalled, did it? Hmm.

Major Niblack: As I said, we don't know anything yet. A special accident enquiry has been ordered. That's what has prevented Pigafetta from coming here.

Colonel Orbal: Pigafetta doesn't usually make that kind of flight, does he?

Major Niblack: No, not often.

Colonel Orbal: I thought not. Well, we'd better get going now. Brown let the parties in.

Captain Schmidt: I request to be allowed to develop my case further on charges numbers eighty-three to and including one hundred and one, concerning rebel activities, terror, murder and accessory to murder. As the evidence for the prosecution is mainly based on the accused's own statements, I request that Erwin Velder be called as witness.

Major von Peters: Uhuh. Here we go again.

Colonel Orbal: Granted, Schmidt, granted.

Captain Endicott: From which point do you wish the accused to start? Mr Gerthoffer has once again examined the accused. He says that Velder is in a mental state in which he can virtually continue his simplified account of his impressions from the very words he had been about to say when he lost consciousness last Friday.

Major Niblack: Let him do that then. An interesting experiment.

Captain Endicott: Begin, Velder. I heard that in Ludolfsport everything was ...

Velder: Just as usual. Ships came and went in the harbour. People who came from there said that the town gave an almost peaceful impression. Along the demarcation line it was still calm and quiet. Our people and Oswald's people were patrolling the outpost lines. Between them lay a stretch of about a kilometre, a belt of no man's land which ran right across the island from north to south. We had no more meetings with Ludolf and Stoloff, but we spoke to them every day. Their own signalmen had installed a cable between the headquarters, just as if they couldn't trust us to manage that ourselves. As far as I heard, Ludolf seemed calm and satisfied. Janos Edner was also very confident in face of the attack, which he hoped would be a brief and bloody victory—that's how he expressed it several times. When this is out of the way, he said, both the Army and the militia would be disbanded and this time it would be for ever. Everyone at headquarters agreed with this except Gaspar Bartholic, who preferred to say nothing at all. Aranca Peterson, whose attitude was negative towards both attack and defence, put great energy into organising the medical corps, first-aid posts and hospitals. We were relatively well off for doctors, nurses and drugs, and I got the impression that she was doing a good job and ...

Major Niblack: Heavens above, it works just as he said it would. He began just where he stopped off last. I've found the place in the records now. Astonishing.

Velder: Excuse me? What did you say?

Commander Kampenmann: Niblack, we must ask you to try to the best of your ability to avoid interrupting Velder. It has the most

182

appalling consequences when you try to cross-examine him or cut in on him.

Major von Peters: Personally I still think that at least half of all this is pure bluff. I damned well think he's just sitting there mocking us behind that death-mask he has instead of a face. Just imagine, a filthy deserter and a corporal, who gets a free chance to let a colonel, two majors, two captains, a lieutenant and a commander in the Navy dance to his tune. It's damned grotesque.

Colonel Orbal: Let Velder go on now, Carl. Yes, yes, Endicott, get going and just mess about with him now. Don't bother about us.

Velder: And medical care we were indeed soon going to need. The only thing on our side which might be called warlike activity was that Bartholic and I sent patrols from the special units out every night to reconnoitre. They nearly always came back unscathed, but it wasn't long before I realised that their way of scouting was far less innocent than their reports made out. I'd known that for a long time, actually; their equipment of stilettos, gas-cartridges and piano-wires showed quite clearly what they were after. Ludolf was very interested in these special units all the time. He kept asking whether we were able to make the best use of them, and about five days before the attack, we let him take half of them over to the southern sector. On the fifteenth of February ...

Colonel Orbal: What's the matter now?

Captain Endicott: I don't know.

Commander Kampenmann: Is he crying?

Colonel Orbal: It looks bloody peculiar, anyhow.

Captain Endicott: That's right. Velder. Go on, now.

Velder: On the fifteenth of February in the morning, we had a long conversation on the situation and the prospects. We were still just as optimistic and believed in speedy success. On an international level, there was clearly optimism, too. The absence of military activity meant that diplomats generally regarded the crisis as over and the division of the country a fact. Janos Edner and Aranca Peterson were extremely annoyed that foreign newspapers and many others kept calling us either the 'socialist-liberal' or 'left-radical' régime. Danica Rodriguez, on the other hand, said that if they had to give us a label, then those two were the ones which lay nearest to hand. We were just going through the grouping of transport facilities and the transfer of ships—the outflanking manoeuvre was to be kept secret by the landing force being transported in small boats from the area around Ludolfsport—when the telephone rang. Gaspar Bartholic answered it and listened for a moment. I remember that he held up his right hand for us to keep quiet. Then he put his hand over the receiver and said perfectly calmly: 'There's an air-raid on Ludolfsport, between ten and fifteen planes bombing the harbour.' Immediately after that, the connection was broken. Then followed a whole series of raids on roads, transport depôts, and other targets in both the northern and southern sectors. They went on for about two hours. Eighteen planes were shot down from the ground and by a few fighter planes. That was quite a lot and we thought we knew that Oswald hadn't all that many left. And yet the attack was a surprise and the damage was quite great. When we did a survey, however, it was clear that we could still carry out the attack on the eighteenth as planned. Janos Edner made telephone contact with headquarters in the southern sector at about three o'clock in the afternoon. Ludolf just said: 'No damage.' After a while he added, as if explaining: 'We're not so vulnerable at ground level as you are.' An hour later, at exactly five minutes past four in the afternoon, artillery fire started. That was the real shock. We'd never very seriously reckoned with artillery barrages, and I still don't really understand where that fearful storm of shelling came from.

Major von Peters: It was bloody simple. It came from ninety-six field batteries, two hundred and eighty-eight pieces. It was all due to that non-intervention agreement. The signatory powers thought it sounded much too provocative and risky to the balance of power to give us planes. So we decided to hold the rabble down with artillery instead. The Chief of State decided to wait until we'd got enough pieces and the batteries were in place, but then, when it got started it was a really solid artillery barrage. The planes on the other hand, the few we had, were already used up on the first day.

Colonel Orbal: But it was tremendous how long the shelling went on. I remember that Winckelman was enraged that he wasn't allowed to advance and clear out the Reds at once.

Captain Schmidt: With the permission of the presidium, I request that the accused be allowed to continue his account.

Colonel Orbal: What? Yes, by all means.

Velder: We waited for the shelling to stop, but it never did. It went on hour after hour, right up until six o'clock the next morning. We thought that they'd attack then and the men in the forward lines got ready. It was deathly quiet for forty-five minutes. Then the guns began firing again. It seems incomprehensible, but it went on like that day after day.

Colonel Orbal: It's damned well not in the slightest incomprehensible. We fired off between ninety and a hundred and ten guns in slow salvoes for thirty-three hours fifteen minutes a day. The firing plan was to systematically shell quarter by quarter up to a depth of ten thousand yards behind the demarcation line. God knows how many barrels we wore out. But it was worth it. The finest concert I've ever heard. Wouldn't you agree, Carl?

Major von Peters: Yes, indeed. What's the matter with Velder now? Same old coma?

Captain Endicott: I request a brief pause to ...

Colonel Orbal: Yes, do as you like as long as you push the wretch out of the place first. We might as well go up and have a beer and sandwich and get an eyeful of Pigafetta's tarts. The session is adjourned for forty-five minutes.

* * *

Colonel Orbal: Fifty per cent burns. As I said, he might well make it.

Major von Peters: Doubt it. But it'd be a good thing if he survived.

Colonel Orbal: Of course. Let the parties in, Brown.

Captain Schmidt: The accused's condition is anything but satisfactory. It would be a good thing if we did not interrupt him, except when absolutely necessary. We'll try to continue, now, Endicott.

Major von Peters: All this experimental stuff is beginning to go too far. Schmidt, what about giving Velder a good beating just for a change? Then perhaps he'd tell us something we don't already know.

Captain Endicott: Start now, Velder.

Velder: By the end of the first day we knew we'd never be able to carry out the attack. Casualties were already great. The opportunity has gone for ever, Janos Edner said. But our disappointment was replaced by resolution to defend ourselves. In the headquarters bunker, we talked about giving up, but the people in the trenches talked about fighting to the last man. The strangest of all was Ludolf. Over the telephone, he said day after day: 'No serious damage. No, hardly any casualties.' And then he repeated: 'We're not so vulnerable at ground level as you are.' Anyhow, we did the best we could, digging in more and more. Working all round the clock, now on the defence plan. Stoloff sent us bits of advice from the southern sector. Sent over machines and special workers on a few occasions. The artillery fire went on for so long that people got used to it. That shows that people can get used to anything. People learnt to protect themselves too. Casualties got fewer quite quickly. Strangely enough, it wasn't long before they began to shell the area round headquarters. We soon realised that they had no imagination, but were just shelling according to geometrical tables. We learnt to evacuate like lightning. In that way, lots of people escaped death.

Captain Endicott: Go on, Velder.

Velder: The bunker was badly constructed. The Army had built it, of course, but we had reinforced it. Stoloff had also said that it should stand up to a direct hit. On the fourth of March, at nine in the evening, they began shelling the quarter where headquarters were situated. The first shell hit the section where Janos Edner and Aranca Peterson were living. The shell went straight through the casemate and exploded on the children's room. The kids and their nurse had just gone to bed. It must have been a howitzer.

Commander Kampenmann: What did you say, Velder?

Major von Peters: He said that the projectile must have come from a howitzer. A fully correct conclusion for once.

Velder: It was their own fault. The children should have been evacuated long before then. But no one wanted it, neither Janos nor Aranca nor the kids. Then we got three direct hits in the second section of the bunker. None of them came through. Janos Edner and Aranca Peterson always reacted strangely and often in exactly the same way, as if they were one and the same person. This time they said practically nothing. But I noticed that they looked at each other more often than usual. At a run-through a week later, that was on the eleventh of March, Aranca lost control. That was the only time I'd ever seen her do that. Our own artillery was in action then, actually. There wasn't much point to it, as we hadn't even a fifth of the guns Oswald had. The run-through was very dismal; the only positive thing was that reports on determination to defend and keenness to fight in the trenches were stronger than ever. I suppose that was lies. Aranca Peterson said: 'Keenness to fight, determination to defend ...' Janos Edner said: 'Yes, that's what we've got to fall back on. To be able to win.' That was when she lost control and shouted 'Win, win, win. And when we've won, yes, then we'll win, yes, then we'll win in a hundred years!' She half-shouted, half-sang it. Then after a while she calmed down. Edner looked at her. 'Don't you see that we have to?' And she said: 'Yes, I see that.' She was a remarkable person, Aranca Peterson. I remember looking at her and thinking that. Bartholic thought so too. He told me so a little later. Her children were dead and their idea was shot to hell and ...

Colonel Orbal: Fearfully boring and uninteresting, all this.

Captain Schmidt: It seems to be difficult today, but I'll do my best.

Velder: Every morning at the time when the shelling stopped, we went up to the front line. On the fourteenth of March, we were there as usual. At six o'clock the artillery fire stopped and the general alarm was sounded in the trenches. That's what had happened at exactly the same time for twenty-six consecutive days. The men went to their posts. They looked pretty apathetic.

Major von Peters: Well, go on, for Christ's sake.

Velder: Go on. The artillery fire never started again. At exactly half-past six the offensive began. First the barricade busters came ploughing through the minefields, then the tanks. Then the infantry in asbestos suits and with flame-throwers. They walked as if through a sea of floating fire. It looked slow. And inexorable. The crew of a machine-gun just near where I was standing were killed and Bartholic and I manned it for a quarter of an hour until we could get replacements. I was quite a good shot and I saw at least ten men fall.

Captain Schmidt: I must ask the presidium to take special note of what has just been said.

Velder: It was the first time I'd killed or seriously wounded anyone in the whole of my life. Very strange.

Captain Endicott: What do you mean, Velder? Very strange that ...

Velder: That I didn't react at all. Probably poisoned by militarism, as Edner said. We returned to headquarters, Bartholic and I. The atmosphere there was pure doomsday. Plans mostly functioned, the front held all day, but the casualties were alarming. They were above the calculated percentage, Bartholic said. Never forget the look Aranca Peterson gave him. Ludolf reported strong offensives along the whole of his section border too, but said the front line was intact and casualties few. During the night, the offensive weakened, but at about five the next morning, the fifteenth of March, they began again at full strength. By about ten, Oswald's units had driven a four kilometre long wedge into our positions just north of the motorway. After another hour, we got reports that the front had been broken through and we ordered what was left of the tactical reserve to seal the gap. Casualties were great now and all the first-aid posts overflowing. A little later Edner contacted Ludolf for the last time over the radio. Everything else had ceased to function by then. I'll try to recall ...

Captain Endicott: He can't go on much longer.

Captain Schmidt: We can refer to the section of our preliminary investigation records, number V VII/10A. If you please, Brown.

Lieutenant Brown: Number V VII/10A. Interrogation of Erwin Velder, number one hundred and sixty-seven. The text gives the radio conversation between Janos Edner and Joakim Ludolf, which took place at about eleven-twenty on the fifteenth of March.

Edner: Break-through on the front three kilometres north of the motorway.

Ludolf: How wide?

Edner: About eight hundred yards.

Ludolf: I see.

Edner: We're beaten. Do you understand? We're beaten.

Ludolf: You are perhaps, not us. They made a minor break-through at about nine this morning, but they've paid dearly for it. It's straightened out now.

Edner: We can't go on much longer now.

Ludolf: I see.

Edner: And you?

Ludolf: I'm going on. What are you thinking of doing?

Edner: Capitulating. It's pointless to allow people who've been lured here on false pretences to be slaughtered to no avail.

Ludolf: There's not much point in capitulating either.

Edner: I've no choice.

Ludolf: I see. When?

Edner: I must speak to Bartholic for a moment.

There's a pause mark here.

Edner: Within four hours. That's already too much. Several people are dying every minute here.

Ludolf: O.K. At three o'clock, then. Do this. Can you hear me?

Edner: Yes.

Ludolf: Let the units engaged at the front disengage themselves and retreat.

Edner: But your flank; we'll expose it.

Ludolf: Don't worry. It'll hold.

Edner: Hold?

Ludolf: Yes. Where are you thinking of going yourself?

Edner: Don't know.

Ludolf: You're welcome to come here. But ...

Edner: Yes?

Ludolf: Under my command. You'd keep your rank, of course.

Edner: I have no rank. Anyhow, that's pointless. I can't cope any longer.

Ludolf: Listen to me. We'll open a gap in the barrier into our lines at Point B3, kilometre marking 12 on the autostrad. That's by the crossroads where the old road turns south. It'll be opened fifteen minutes from ... now.

Edner: Yes?

Ludolf: Valuable materials and units and effective fighting men can retreat into the southern sector that way. Do you hear me? Valuable material and effective fighting men. Nothing else.

Edner: I hear you.

Ludolf: I want Bartholic's commandos especially. Every man-jack of them.

Edner: I see.

Ludolf: And others who can and will fight. Is the depôt at Ludolfsport intact?

Edner: As far as I know.

Ludolf: Give orders for it to be evacuated at once. I'll send as much transport as I can.

Edner: One moment—I'll tell Bartholic.

There is another pause mark here.

Edner: Yes, that's done.

Ludolf: One more thing. Get all the reserves available now to cover the gap.

Edner: Our reserves are largely already used up.

Ludolf: I neither can nor want to sacrifice people here. You'll have to pull the best units out of the front line, as soon as they've disengaged themselves. The gap and evacuation line must at all costs be held until the moment you give the cease fire order. Preferably half an hour longer. Those particular units need not be reached by the capitulation order. Jam their radio. Get them to dig in. And give the order at exactly 1600 hours. Wait a minute, Stoloff wants to say something.

Stoloff: General Edner? This is Colonel Stoloff. I advise you to get the demolition units working at once. Destroy all permanent constructions and all stores you can't evacuate in the southern sector. The harbour entrance must be mined and blocked and all ships that don't leave the harbour must be sunk. I myself have made preparations for this earlier on. Three minutes ago I sent group of sixty men over who'll see to the practical details. That's all. Good luck.

Ludolf: Anything else? Regards to Aranca and the others.

Edner: Wait a minute. Are you sure you're doing the right thing?

Ludolf: Yes. Good luck.

Edner: Same to you.

Ludolf: One more thing. Make sure he doesn't take you alive.

The conversation ended there.

Captain Schmidt: I am conscious of the fact that it is unorthodox to refer to the testimony of the accused in this form. But under the present circumstances, I consider it valid. Mr Gerthoffer has added a note to the interrogation record, in which he calls Velder's recall of the conversation 'a masterpiece of memorising'. He points out that Velder repeated the conversation at five separate interviews, spread over a period of three months, without once changing a single word. Striking evidence of the memory-stimulating effect of the surgical method, he writes.

Colonel Orbal: You know, Niblack, last night I was sitting thinking about something you said. When you asked von Peters whether he was religious. Well, that was amusing in itself. But then you said that most airmen were religious and it could be a matter of environment. Did you mean that you're nearer to God when you're flying?

Major Niblack: Did I really say that?

Major von Peters: Go on now, Schmidt. We haven't got the rest of our lives.

Captain Schmidt: What happened during the hours between eleven o'clock and five on the fifteenth of March is so well known that we can content ourselves with a brief recapitulation. There is such an account in the preliminary investigation, Appendix V VII/101x. If you please, Lieutenant Brown.

Lieutenant Brown: Appendix V VII/101x concerning the disturbances. Summary compiled by the National Historical Department of the General Staff. The text is as follows:

At midday on the fifteenth of March, combined assault infantry and tank units from the Peace Corps and the National Freedom Army north of the motorway crossed the demarcation line along its whole length and in two places broke through the rebel positions. In order to avoid disintegration, the revolutionary forces began to retreat. The retreat was slow at first and involved defensive fighting, but soon became more and more disorderly and finally grew into flight in certain places. At sixteen-thirty, when the rebel strength's tactical situation had become extremely precarious, their leader Janos Edner decided to give up.

Information about the capitulation was radioed uncoded. When, however, it was clear that the Reds in the southern part of the Eastern Province were not included in the capitulation, General Oswald ordered a continuation of the advance. At about 1800 hours in the afternoon, most of the rebels were fleeing wildly south, though a few groups remained in their positions and refused to give in. Soon after eight o'clock the following morning, the sixteenth of March, motorised units from the Peace Corps advanced into Ludolfsport, where all resistance had ceased. On the other hand, one rebel unit, which had clearly not heard the capitulation order, continued stubbornly to defend a position hastily constructed north of the motorway about fifteen kilometres south-west of Ludolfsport, until nine o'clock the next morning, when it was finally overcome. At this, all organised resistance in the northern part of the Eastern Province ceased. The enemies of the people Janos Edner and Aranca Peterson fled the country, leaving behind them widespread and frightening destruction. The harbour installations, warehouses and many buildings in Ludolfsport had been destroyed, as had the airfield and a large part of the road network. Several fanatical members of the Red militia had fled to the southern sector, to which a large amount of valuable materials had also been transferred.

Captain Schmidt: I do not think there is much more to add to this matter. We have here, however, also moved on to charge numbers one hundred and three and one hundred and four in the case against Velder, concerning sabotage and furthering escape from the country.

Commander Kampenmann: You skipped a charge, as far as I can see. Number one hundred and two.

Major von Peters: Must you interfere with everything, Kampenmann. We'll never get anywhere at this rate.

Captain Schmidt: Charge number one hundred and two is of a different nature. From the time point of view, I consider it an advantage at this point to abandon chronological order.

Commander Kampenmann: I see.

Colonel Orbal: Do you? If only I could say the same for myself.

Captain Schmidt: I will return to examining the witness. Is the accused ready, Captain Endicott?

Major von Peters: It's absolutely unbelievable how slow everything is. Well, Endicott, haven't you fiddled about enough? Can the swine speak or not?

Captain Endicott: We can go on now, sir.

Velder: We abandoned headquarters at about one, but it took us

192

almost three hours to get to Ludolfsport. There was terrible disorder everywhere. The roads were blocked with people and vehicles and in many places the roads had already been blown up. In Ludolfsport, total chaos reigned. Stoloff's demolition units from the southern sector had been at work for several hours and now they weren't only destroying stores and administrative buildings but also shops and ordinary houses. Many people were desperate and in some places people even offered resistance. Janos Edner was furious and ordered the marauders, as he called them, to stop at once, but the officer from the southern sector who was in charge of the demolition work—he was a foreigner, whom none of us had ever seen before—said that he was not under our command and he'd done everything strictly in accordance with his instructions. Then Aranca Peterson and Janos Edner tried to make contact with Ludolf, but it was no longer possible to establish any communications. Soon after three, the harbour-master came to see us. He was very nervous and said that the harbour was completely destroyed. Not even small boats could leave it any longer and anyhow there was nothing left afloat. He urged us to go on to the pilot-boat station fifteen miles north of the town at once, where one of the militia's patrol-boats was waiting to take us on board. The road there was still open, but if we stayed any longer in Ludolfsport, he couldn't guarantee our safety. Aranca Peterson said that for the moment there was hardly anything in the whole world that interested her less than her safety. At twenty past three, we all got away in an armoured car, and at ten to four we were at the pilot-boat station. The patrol-boat, which was roughly the size of a small torpedo boat, was ready; all we had to do was to remove the camouflage net and set off. At exactly four o'clock, Janos Edner sent out the capitulation order over the pilot-boat station's radio transmitter. He just said: 'To avoid further useless loss of life, I exhort the militia in the northern sector to cease fire. We have shown ourselves incapable of meeting our enemies with their own weapons, namely force and stupidity, and we have reason to be proud of that.' He was silent for a moment and then he said: 'Do what you wish.' At five past four, the patrol-boat moved away from the quay. On board, apart from the crew, were Janos, Aranca, Bartholic, Dana Rodriguez, myself, the harbour-master from Ludolfsport, the driver who had brought us and the staff of the lighthouse and pilot-boat station. The captain was scared of air attacks, but the only planes we saw were two Army helicopters cruising along the coast, recce planes, presumably.

Major von Peters: Well, why doesn't he go on? Pull yourself together, Mateo. Don't go off to sleep again.

Colonel Orbal: What's the matter? What?

Captain Endicott: The accused will continue in a moment. They say his memories are as if divided up into chapters, like in a book.

Major von Peters: Who is they?

Captain Endicott: Mr Gerthoffer.

Major von Peters: Funny how people never seem to learn to express themselves exactly.

Velder: As soon as we sailed, Bartholic went below deck, but the rest of us stayed in the stern looking at the island. I thought it was the last time I was going to see it. What the others thought, I don't know. But I remember their faces were absolutely expressionless. It was winter and a grey misty day. A giant plume of smoke hung over Ludolfsport from the houses and warehouses the demolition patrols had set fire to, and farther north the hangars and petrol and oil tanks on the airfield were burning. The smoke mixed with the clouds and lay like a thick bank of fog over the island. It was quite black, but flashes of light flared now and again, from new fires and explosions, I presume. Dana Rodriguez shivered and said: 'Our island.' Then she shrugged her shoulders and went below. Aranca Peterson said nothing and didn't move a muscle, but Janos Edner said: 'I still think we were right and we've proved it.' Then we were silent for a while. But we made a few more remarks. 'This must be regarded as the socialist-liberal-left-radical régime's collapse,' said Janos Edner. 'Are you thinking we shouldn't have left them in the lurch,' said Aranca. 'No,' said Edner. 'Why shouldn't we have done it?' 'They believed in us,' said Aranca. 'Probably. Now it's his bloody island, anyhow,' said Janos. 'And Ludolf's,' I said. The weather was bad and the waves kept coming in over the side, so soon after that I went into the wheelhouse, but Aranca Peterson and Janos Edner stayed in the stern until all that could be seen was a black bank of smoke above the horizon.

Major Niblack: That's all very poetic, but I don't see what it's got to do with the accused's crimes.

Commander Kampenmann: Furthering of escape. He helped those people get out of the country.

Captain Schmidt: Partly that. But this episode also shows some of the motives behind Velder's next step towards his downfall, what definitely carried him beyond reach of human kind. This is proved by the following. See to it that he continues, Captain Endicott.

Velder: Normally it would have taken us four hours to get to the nearest neutral harbour, which, by the way, lay in the old so-called mother country, but the weather was so bad that it took us five hours to get there. We asked for asylum and the police directed us to the quarantine station, where we were tied up. The authorities seemed embarrassed and bewildered and there was a lot of 'phoning back and forth. Finally they said that we were to stay in the quarantine station overnight and we would receive further orders the next day. Before we went on land, the captain of the patrol-boat gathered us together on the deck and said: 'I'm intending to go back to the island tonight. Anyone who wants to come with me to join General Ludolf may do so. But you've only got an hour left. We must get there before it's light.' Then we went on land. We were given hot coffee and shown quarters in the quarantine building. Janos Edner and Aranca Peterson said that they were not thinking of returning, because they doubted that Ludolf was acting in accordance with their ideas and principles. Danica Rodriguez said: 'No. I've had enough. It lasted six years, anyhow. And nothing's ever lasted that long for me before. And I think I know what's going to happen.' We talked about it with Bartholic, who said this: 'I've a feeling that I can be more use elsewhere. I'm sorry it didn't work out better, but I did my best.' Dana Rodriguez said: 'No one's blaming you.' Bartholic sat in silence for several minutes before answering: 'It was doomed from the start. To be honest, your ideas aren't worth fighting for.' Then Aranca Peterson said: 'Neither was it the idea that anyone should have to fight for them.' And that was the last thing I heard her say. 'And as you see, they play into the hands of the wrong parties all the time,' said Bartholic. I didn't even say goodbye, because I saw that both Janos and Aranca understood what I was going to do and I didn't bother about Bartholic. He could keep his anarchic syndicalism and his specialists. I went down to the quay and on board the patrol-boat and a quarter of an hour later, we cast off and went at slow speed out of the harbour and I don't think anyone noticed.

Captain Schmidt: With that we can consider charges numbers eighty-three to and including numbers one hundred and three and one hundred and four, concerning rebel activities, terror, murder and accessory to murder, organised sabotage and furthering of escape from the country to have been concluded. All of them have been admitted by the accused and corroborated further by his own testimony. As we still have part of the day left and the accused seems to have recovered somewhat, I suggest that we also deal with charge number ...

Colonel Orbal: What's that row? Is it an alarm clock, or what?

Major von Peters: Sounds like a telephone.

Major Niblack: It is a telephone, here on the shelf under the table—just a moment and I'll answer it.

Colonel Orbal: What sort of idiot is it 'phoning in the middle of a session?

Major Niblack: Hullo ... yes, Niblack here ... yes, sir ... yes, sir ... I see, sir ...

Velder: Excuse me? What did you say?

Major von Peters: Shut up, you.

Major Niblack: Gentlemen. That was Colonel Pigafetta 'phoning. General Widder died ten minutes ago at the military hospital in Oswaldsburg, without regaining consciousness.

Colonel Orbal: Oh, Christ!

Major von Peters: What did I tell you?

Colonel Orbal: What do we do about it then?

Major von Peters: We could have a minute's silence.

Colonel Orbal: Excellent idea. To honour the memory of our late Commander-in-Chief of the Air Force, General ... what was his first name, now?

Lieutenant Brown: Jan, sir.

Colonel Orbal: Oh, yes. To honour the memory of General Jan Widder, we will keep one minute's silence. Everyone stand to attention. You do the timing, Brown.

*　　*　　*

Colonel Orbal: For God's sake, Brown. Isn't the time up now?

Lieutenant Brown: Five seconds left, sir. Now.

Colonel Orbal: That's that. So Pigafetta's Commander-in-Chief of the Air Force now, is he?

Major von Peters: And a general. Christ!

Commander Kampenmann: With reference to what has happened, wouldn't it be appropriate to break off the session today.

Colonel Orbal: Exactly. Have you anything else to say, Schmidt?

Captain Schmidt: I request to be allowed to place this part of the case, which embraces charges eighty-three to and including one hundred and one, as well as one hundred and three and one hundred and four, before the court for consideration.

Major von Peters: Granted. The parties may leave.

Colonel Orbal: Bloody bad show, this business about Widder.

Major Niblack: I feel paralysed with grief and distress.

Colonel Orbal: What? Well, it's not much good moping now. That was a good story, Niblack, that one from Africa. Tried it out in the mess last night. Great success. But of course I'd forgotten what cunt was in Swahili.

Major Niblack: Kwahashu.

Colonel Orbal: That's it. Difficult word. Must write it down.

Major von Peters: Adjourn the session now, Mateo.

Colonel Orbal: Oh, yes. We'll be burying Widder tomorrow, I suppose, well, presumably. The session is adjourned until Wednesday at eleven o'clock.

Thirteenth Day

Lieutenant Brown: Those present, Colonel Mateo Orbal, Army, also Chairman of the Presidium of this Extra-ordinary Court Martial; Major Carl von Peters, Army, Commander Arnold Kampenmann, Navy. The Prosecuting Officer is Captain Wilfred Schmidt, Navy, and the accused is assisted by Captain Roger Endicott, Air Force. Officer presenting the case is Lieutenant Arie Brown, Air Force. Justice Tadeusz Haller reports his absence.

Colonel Orbal: Where's the representative of the Air Force then? Is neither Pigafetta nor that Niblack coming?

Lieutenant Brown: Colonel Pigafetta has not reported his absence. He has probably been delayed for a few minutes.

Colonel Orbal: And Haller's presumably boycotted the session completely. He's said to be occupied with important government matters. Oh, well, let's start, anyhow. Brown, call in ...

Commander Kampenmann: I'm afraid that won't do. We can do without Justice Haller, but all three branches of the armed forces must be represented on the presidium.

Major von Peters: That's correct, actually. It's down in the instructions. There, Mateo, paragraph eleven.

Colonel Orbal: Then we'll have to wait. Fearfully fancy uniform you were wearing at the funeral, Kampenmann.

Commander Kampenmann: Parade uniform was the order of the day. Nothing one could do about it.

Colonel Orbal: Looked like one of those chaps standing outside hotels summoning cars.

Major von Peters: I heard something sensational at HQ this morning. They say that the General's not thinking of appointing Pigafetta.

Colonel Orbal: Who the hell is he going to have then?

198

Major von Peters: Chief-of-Staff of the Air Force perhaps.

Colonel Orbal: Bloch? He's supposed to be a frightful dunderhead. Even for an airman.

Major von Peters: Well, I don't know. It's only a rumour.

Colonel Orbal: When's it being decided?

Major von Peters: Next meeting a week today.

Colonel Orbal: Pity Haller isn't here. He probably knows. Here's Pigafetta, anyhow.

Colonel Pigafetta: I apologise for being somewhat delayed, but the events of the last few days have left me up to my ears in work.

Colonel Orbal: I was thinking of saying a few words ... yes. As the senior officer present, I should like to convey our deep commiseration with the grief which has afflicted the Air Force. And the nation.

Colonel Pigafetta: Thank you. As you will understand, this has been a great blow, not least to myself personally.

Commander Kampenmann: How far have you got with the enquiry?

Colonel Pigafetta: The crash commission's work has been completed. Their report will be handed in this morning. But as is usual in cases like this, the direct cause of the accident is hard to establish.

Commander Kampenmann: They say that the plane exploded, or at least caught fire in the air.

Colonel Pigafetta: Nonsense. The general stalled immediately after taking off. Naturally the plane's tanks were full and the plane caught fire when it crash-landed on the airfield. When the rescue-team managed to get the general out of the plane, he was already seriously burnt. There are, unfortunately, many other examples of similar courses of events, from Air Forces in all countries.

Colonel Orbal: Damned fine speech you made yesterday, Pigafetta. Taut and gripping. The Chief of State thought so too.

Colonel Pigafetta: I hope you understand that I have been put in a very stressed position by being forced not only to act as Commander-in-Chief of the Air Force, but also having this court martial to think about.

Colonel Orbal: Of course. But it probably won't go on much longer. Perhaps we'd better get started, for that matter. Call in the parties, Brown.

Captain Schmidt: We have heard how the left-radical régime was dissolved and how the accused's co-operation with enemies of the people, Janos Edner and Aranca Peterson, came to an end.

Commander Kampenmann: Where did those people go to afterwards? That isn't clearly explained in the preliminary investigation.

Captain Schmidt: Danica Rodriguez is said to be in Africa and the last that was heard of Gaspar Bartholic was that he was in South America. What happened to the enemies of the people Janos Edner and Aranca Peterson, on the other hand, is now clear.

Commander Kampenmann: How did things go for them?

Captain Schmidt: Velder had nothing to do with the matter. But there is an extra appendix, V IX/13xxB, concerning the matter. It consists of a fragment of the unpublished and clearly also incomplete memoirs which Janos Edner and Aranca Peterson were working on. The document has been kept for the last year in the archives of the secret police, and is marked secret, third grade. It has nothing directly to do with the Velder case, except to the extent that it can be considered a passive indication that his connections with Janos Edner were really broken off on the night of the fifteenth of March and never taken up again. I do not consider it essential evidence in the case, but if anyone wishes it, then naturally it must be read out. Lieutenant Brown ...

Major von Peters: Kampenmann, what the hell use is this? Haven't we really had enough of this reading out aloud?

Commander Kampenmann: I consider the information valuable in order to have a clear picture, but if you don't ...

Captain Schmidt: Oh, the fragment is quite brief. The text is thought to have been written by Janos Edner no more than fourteen months ago. There is even a date on the first page. As far as I can make out, it's a kind of preface to those memoirs. If you please, Brown.

Lieutenant Brown: Appendix V IX/13xxB, concerning the circumstances and events after the break-through and victory of nationalism. Confiscated documentation, written by the traitor and enemy of the people Janos Edner. Marked secret according to paragraphs eight, nine, eleven and fourteen to twenty-two. The text is as follows:

The house we live in lies on a stony slope and outside it is the sea, which is blue in the summer and grey in the winter.

We had a little money placed abroad, not particularly much, but enough to buy this little white house and live in it, and we live in the only country which will give us a residence visa.

Outside the house is a veranda, and we usually sit there looking out over the sea, and below, a narrow stony path winds down to the gate and the road. During the first years, people used to stop at the gate and look at us and sometimes they took photographs, but I haven't seen anyone for a long time now.

They irritated me enormously, but now that they don't come any longer, I miss them.

At that time, I often imagined that someone I'd never seen before would open the gate and walk up the path, one hand in his coat pocket all the time, but now I've stopped expecting it. We had a revolver at home then, but Aranca threw it away over a year ago. She always disliked firearms.

Naturally, we're thinking of writing this account together, but I do the final draft, because I've always been the better writer of the two of us. I make no claim for its absolute accuracy in every detail, as there are things we've heard at second and third hand and certainly things we've never found out at all. Naturally, it isn't completely objective either. On the whole, I don't believe such a thing as true objectivity exists.

We've taken our time over it, but now we are going to start and we're sitting here looking out over the sea and now and again a fishing boat appears far away. So this is how it is to end, despite the fact that I always saw myself alone in a dark hotel room, where I was lying on my back in bed, smoking and watching the reflections of the street lights on the ceiling and listening to the sounds of an alien city. But naturally all that was much too romantic.

We're sitting here and when dusk falls we seldom bother to light the paraffin lamp. We're usually thinking about the same thing, but we never speak about it.

The text ends there.

Colonel Orbal: Quite incomprehensible, as usual.

Captain Schmidt: Well, as you see, it's just a fragment. However, it has been proved that Janos Edner wrote this fourteen months and three days ago, on the eleventh of February last year.

Commander Kampenmann: What happened then?

Captain Schmidt: Ten days later, that is on the twenty-third of February, the authorities in the country where they lived informed us that Janos Edner and Aranca Peterson had died. They were murdered by one or several unknown people, who made their way into the house through an open window and shot them dead with an automatic pistol. They had clearly been surprised in their sleep, for when the servants came next morning, both of them lay dead in bed. The assailants have not yet been found. The police down there presume that it was an ordinary bandit attack and that the murderers were after money. Both Janos Edner and Aranca Peterson were stateless, and the case attracted no special attention.

Commander Kampenmann: May I ask one more thing? How did that document come to be in the archives of the secret police?

Captain Schmidt: I really have no idea whatsoever.

Major von Peters: Have you any more speciality interests, Kampenmann? Or is this internal exchange between the representatives of the Navy now concluded, so that we might possibly go on to the actual matter in hand? This happens to be a court martial.

Captain Schmidt: I shall now take up charge number one hundred and two in the case against Erwin Velder. Within this complex of crimes, which includes points eighty-two to and including number one hundred and twenty-seven, this offence is to some extent unique. Nonetheless, it is, as are so many of Velder's crimes, of an unusually crude and unpleasant nature. The Ministry of Justice has laid special weight on insistence that this point is taken up for judgement and is thoroughly considered. The charge is one of rape.

Colonel Orbal: What? Rape?

Captain Schmidt: This crime was committed somewhat earlier than a number of others already dealt with. The event on which the charge is based occurred on the evening of the third of February at Janos Edner's so-called headquarters, where the accused was serving.

Colonel Orbal: Get to the point, now. Who was it he raped?

Captain Schmidt: The victim was one of Janos Edner's collaborators, or fellow-criminals I should say, the person who has been mentioned earlier on several occasions, Danica Rodriguez.

Colonel Orbal: God Almighty. The woman with a moustache.

Captain Schmidt: As the case for the prosecution and the evidence offered on this point is entirely based on the accused's own statement and his own account of the circumstances, I request to be allowed to call Corporal Erwin Velder as witness.

Colonel Orbal: Granted. See to it that that primus stove is working properly, Endicott, so that we can hear what he's saying. And Schmidt, don't let him get away with things like when he refused to describe the orgies with those two tarts he had living with him.

Captain Schmidt: Is the accused ready? Has he understood which section he is dealing with?

Captain Endicott: Yes, it should go well.

Colonel Orbal: Push him up to the rail then. That's it. Get going, now, Velder.

Captain Endicott: Velder, this is about what happened on the evening of the third of February.

Velder: Yes. About Dana. Oh, yes.

Colonel Orbal: Well, get weaving now.

Velder: Edner's headquarters were set up at that manor house by the fifteenth of December, and before the first of January, we had all moved down into the bunker. Colonel Fox had had the bunker built to use as an operations centre in case the bid for power failed in the Central Province and he'd been forced to send troops westwards to Oswaldsburg. At least that's what was said afterwards and we thought it seemed plausible.

Colonel Orbal: What's that got to do with it?

Major von Peters: One may well ask. Get this filth over and done with as soon as possible, Endicott. We haven't got the rest of our lives.

Velder: Excuse me? Yes, well, as I said, the bunker. It was there that Janos and Aranca's children were murdered ... and the nurse. Only a young girl. Her name was Irene Miller.

Colonel Orbal: What's all this nonsense? Miller? Did he rape her too?

Velder: The shell went through the concrete casemate and blew up the whole room. Everything was blown to bits. Everyone.

203

Major von Peters: Obviously a cartouche.

Colonel Orbal: For Christ's and all the bloody angels' sake, Endicott, get the man on the right track. He's going quite haywire.

Captain Endicott: I need a few minutes, I think, sir.

Colonel Orbal: Yes, yes, for God's sake.

* * *

Captain Endicott: It should be all right now, sir. If we avoid interrupting him.

Velder: The installation really only consisted of three bunkers connected by underground corridors. Five of the rooms we used as offices, communications centres, orderly rooms, operations department and so on. They made a group on their own. The second group was divided into two rooms where Janos Edner, Aranca Peterson, the children and their nurse lived. And in the third, Bartholic, Dana and I had our living quarters, a room each, all adjoining one another. We had electricity and water from our own power installations, which had also been put in before, by the Army.

Major von Peters: Extremely interesting.

Captain Endicott: Major von Peters, please ...

Major von Peters: Ach.

Velder: The position was that before that night when everything happened and which meant that the war started, I lived what you might call a very regular life. Sexually, too, of course.

Major von Peters: Why of course?

Colonel Orbal: Don't you see? With those two tarts. Go on, Velder.

Velder: Like so many other things, all that came to an end when I fetched Aranca and Janos from the government office that night. After that ... well, after that I didn't see my wives again and I had no contact with women. So we moved to headquarters on the fifteenth of December and we stayed there for three months. We worked together and I was constantly together with Dana Rodriguez in the daytime, and at night we slept in adjoining rooms. I can't deny that she soon began to make a tremendous impression on me. Why should I deny it, for that matter? She always wore khaki overalls and rubber boots and it was only too clear that she wore nothing underneath. At the beginning of January, I asked her if she'd like to sleep with me. She said: 'No.' Nothing else, just that. Then I went on asking her now and again, not every day, but perhaps every other. Every time she just said: 'No.' When I occasionally asked her why not, she said: 'Because I don't want to.' Each day that went by, she made a greater impression on me, but it didn't seem as if anyone else bothered with her. Edner had Aranca, and Bartholic went away now and again and arranged his life somewhere else, I think. I didn't understand Dana at all, although I thought I ought to have learnt a bit about women by then. But I did see that she wasn't sexually indifferent to me, nor uninterested in me. Sometimes I caught her looking at me and a few times her eyes were quite glazed, but still she said nothing but no. She didn't have anyone else either, I'm certain of that, as we only had a partition wall between us and I could hear most of what she was up to. Although I've never believed in force in connection with sex, she drove me absolutely crazy. It got worse every day and finally ...

Colonel Orbal: Yes, go on, for Christ's sake.

Velder: Go on. Go on. Well, finally I couldn't stand it any longer. It was on that evening of the third of February, late, because we'd been working for a long time on the plans for the offensive, but just as we were parting, she looked at me like that again. Bartholic had gone off somewhere, to Ludolfsport, I think. I got undressed and washed and was just going to get into bed and, well, then I heard her going into her room and then that she was having a shower—she'd been given that room because it had a bathroom. And that was when I couldn't stand it any longer, but just went out into the corridor and then into her room.

Colonel Orbal: Naked?

Velder: Oh, yes. The doors weren't locked. We never locked them. So when she'd dried herself and come out of the bathroom, there I was. She stared at me and said: 'Out.' She looked much nicer than I'd thought, even more exciting, if I can put it that way. I was absolutely beside myself. And she stared at me as if she, too, were crazy, as well as me. I took hold of her and laid her down on her back on the bed, but it didn't work. She was strong and lithe and fought like a madman, wriggling free and getting to her feet. She didn't scream, because she too knew that Bartholic was away and

205

no one could hear us. I didn't let her go and we fought, she trying to jab me with her knees and I hitting her, and then we both fell over, Dana underneath, and as we fell she hit her head so hard on the concrete floor that she lost consciousness. Almost, anyhow.

Colonel Orbal: And then you poked her, I suppose ...

Major von Peters: Quiet, Mateo. Did you complete the rape?

Velder: Yes. Oh, yes. But I couldn't have done it if she hadn't been almost unconscious ... and partly, well, so well prepared. Sexually, I mean. Just as it came for me she opened her eyes and then it began to come for her too, tremendously, too, and ... She raised her legs and I thought that she was at last giving in. But instead she caught me in a scissor-grip and took no notice of me being inside her and that she was in the middle of an orgasm ...

Major von Peters: But this is pure pornography.

Colonel Orbal: Is all this in the book?

Velder: It hurt and she tore herself free, got to her feet and kicked me three times as hard as she could. I was quite paralysed in the lower part of my body and lay curled up on all fours by the door. I almost thought she was going to kill me then, but she opened the door, placed a foot on my shoulder and hurled me out into the corridor. It took a long time before I could take myself back to my own room. I never got over those kicks, actually. When I met her the next day, she said: 'If there'd been any point in it, I'd have reported you for that business yesterday.' She meant it, too, and had it been before the war, I would have been deported, for sure.

Major von Peters: What are you scrabbling about for, Mateo?

Captain Schmidt: It starts on page four hundred and one, sir.

Colonel Orbal: Ah. Thanks, Schmidt.

Captain Schmidt: Well, with that ...

Velder: Dana meant everything, I think. Three days later she was away nearly all day. It was a Thursday, I remember. She seemed very systematic. When we were working in the map room that evening, Aranca asked her where she'd been and she said just like that, almost in passing: 'I went to Ludolfsport to get a scrape. Erwin was idiotic enough to rape me the other night. Pumped a whole year's need into me.'

Captain Schmidt: Let us swiftly conclude this unpleasant and shameful story. It is herewith proved conclusively that Velder was guilty of gross rape combined with ill-treatment, and under mitigating circumstances. I now hand this part of the case to the court for consideration.

Major von Peters: That was pretty hard to stomach. Let's have a lunch break now. Mateo, adjourn the session.

Colonel Orbal: What? What did you say? What's all the fuss about?

Major von Peters: We're having a break now. Adjourn the session.

Colonel Orbal: The session is adjourned for two hours.

*   *   *

Colonel Pigafetta: Very industrious of you, Orbal, to lug that volume of the preliminary investigation with you and study it in the mess during the lunch break.

Colonel Orbal: What? What's that?

Major von Peters: Call in the parties, Mateo.

Colonel Orbal: Oh, yes. Let them in. I must say that when you read the interrogations of Velder here in the book, you get a much clearer and more detailed picture of what happened than when he himself tries to tell it. Look at this, Carl. Read that bit.

Major von Peters: I'll read it later.

Captain Schmidt: I will now go on to the last part of the case for the prosecution in the case of the Armed Forces versus Erwin Velder. This section covers charges numbers one hundred and five to and including one hundred and twenty-seven, concerning murder, accessory to murder, accessory to mass-murder, preparation for genocide, subversive activities, armed rebellion, hounding of opponents, criminal promiscuity and communism. All these crimes were committed during the time when Velder acted as collaborator to enemy of the people, Joakim Ludolf. Does the accused admit that he is guilty of these offences?

Captain Endicott: Yes, the accused pleads guilty.

Captain Schmidt: The circumstances and events touched on in the case for the prosecution are based here, as on several previous points, mainly on the accused's own statements at interrogations. Therefore I request to be allowed to call as witness Erwin Velder.

Major von Peters: Granted.

Captain Schmidt: Before I allow the accused to begin his account of the events from the sixteenth of March onwards, I would like to refer to a summary which describes the political and military situation prevailing after the fifteenth of that month. Appendix V VIII/9. If you please, Lieutenant Brown.

Lieutenant Brown: Appendix V VIII/9, concerning the disturbances. Summary compiled by the National Historical Department of the General Staff. The text is as follows:

With the collapse of the left-radical rebel régime and the flight of enemies of the people, Janos Edner and Aranca Peterson from the country, the northern part of the Eastern Province was liberated from the terrorism that had reigned for three terrifying months. When the military mopping-up operations, which went on for three days, were over, the Chief of State and the government took all possible measures to return the liberated area to normal and honourable life. The glorious National Freedom Army had, as had the Peace Corps, been forced to sacrifice lives and valuable materials during this stage of the crusade, but calculations reveal that losses were limited to a third of those inflicted on the rebels. On the twentieth of March, General Oswald rode into Ludolfsport—later renamed Oswaldsport—where the victory was celebrated with a military parade of the combined branches of national defence. Destruction in the town as a result of rebel marauders' activities was very great. Large areas had been blown up or burnt down and lay in ruins, and in the harbour area the damage was so great that it was not possible for large ships to enter or be unloaded until four months later. Reconstruction was also extremely difficult, due to anarchic and communist saboteurs who had been infiltrated into the groups of workmen in the rehabilitation camps, who carried out most of the rebuilding. At the beginning of November, however, most of the harbour installations could once again be used, if only to a limited extent. Collaborators of the left-radical movement who fell into the hands of the troops were first placed into eight camps, dispersed in different parts of the country. Between three and four hundred people guilty of murder, looting and conspiracy against the nation's legal government were executed or given life sentences of hard labour, after being tried before military courts. Otherwise General

208

Oswald treated the rebels with great mildness. Many of them had undoubtedly been led astray by false and ruthless propaganda; to save these unfortunate people, within a few months the original camps were reorganised into regular retraining camps, where their readjustment to society was thoroughly attended to. In this way the increasing demand for labour in industry and construction ...

Captain Schmidt: You can stop there, Brown, and turn over three pages to section four.

Lieutenant Brown: Aha. The military situation then. The text is as follows:

After the capture of Oswaldsport (Ludolfsport) and victory in the north, the southern area of the Eastern Province and some of the small islands off the coast—constituting less than a sixth of the country's total area—still remained in the hands of the rebels. The leader of the rebel movement in this area was the enemy of the people, Joakim Ludolf, supported by his Bolshevik slavey Boris Stoloff. The topographical conditions in this section of the terrain, in the north bordered by the now destroyed and impassable autostrad between Oswaldsburg and Oswaldsport (Ludolfsport), in the west by a swift river about five kilometres west of the border between the Eastern and Central Province, and then in the south and west by the sea, proved to be advantageous to the rebels' purposes. The land consisted of a hilly plateau with an under-developed network of roads and a sparse scattering of farms and barns. The coasts were steep and inaccessible and easy to protect against any invasion attempt from the sea. The land border along the autostrad and southern part of the river (the old demarcation line) was strongly fortified and was defended with both desperation and complete ruthlessness by the Reds, who had entrenched themselves in the area. On the twenty-fifth of March, General Oswald decided to regroup the first and second army commands in face of the final mopping-up operation of the southern sector.

Captain Schmidt: That's enough, Brown. I will now go on to hearing Velder's own account of what happened after the fifteenth of March. Is the accused ready?

Captain Endicott: Yes, he's ready.

Major von Peters: Push the swine out then.

Colonel Orbal: No, for God's sake, Endicott, don't push him right under my nose. There, in front of Kampenmann, that's right, that's better.

Captain Schmidt: Velder, we now wish to hear what happened to you after you'd left the quarantine station and had gone aboard in patrol-boat number three on the night of the sixteenth of March.

Major von Peters: Can't you express yourself a little more carefully and exactly, Schmidt? It isn't 'aboard in patrol-boat', is it?

Commander Kampenmann: Yes, the expression is quite correct.

Major von Peters: Peculiar.

Velder: The weather was very bad during the night. Big waves. I was seasick and spewed ...

Colonel Orbal: Nothing but disgusting ...

Velder: ... but at about half-past four in the morning, we got into the lee of the bay south of Ludolfsport. A small pilot-boat or something similar met us and showed us the way through the channel in the minefield. When we got to the shore, there were high straight chalk cliffs there and the patrol-boat was hauled up into a hollow cliff, obviously a widened old cave, where there were already three similar boats. The men who met us didn't say much, but they seemed confident and efficient. They obviously belonged to the militia, as they were wearing similar khaki overalls to Ludolf's and Stoloff's, though with no rank badges. Everyone had red, five-pointed stars on their caps. That surprised me a little. Then I was taken in a small car—or sort of jeep with tracks, not unlike the armoured car Ludolf and Stoloff had come to headquarters in a month or so earlier. A woman, also in militia uniform and with a red star on her cap, was driving. Most of the way we went through tunnels, with short stretches above ground; it was still dark and I didn't see anything special. It took about half an hour to get to Ludolf's headquarters. Nothing was visible above ground. I was put in a lift and went down, quite far, it seemed. Then I was taken along a corridor and into what later turned out to be the operations centre of headquarters. General Ludolf and Colonel Stoloff ...

Major von Peters: Now, listen. There is a limit ...

Colonel Pigafetta: Stop taking exception to unimportant details, von Peters. Otherwise this'll never come to an end.

Major von Peters: Unimportant details. Calling that swine General and ...

Velder: They were in there and seemed to be in fine form, although neither of them could have slept for at least twenty-four hours.

Major von Peters: Good God, he's interrupting me again.

Colonel Orbal: Calm down, now, Carl. Don't take any notice of what these idiots say.

Colonel Pigafetta: I beg your pardon, what did you say?

Colonel Orbal: Nothing. Go on, now, Velder. Why isn't he saying anything?

Captain Endicott: The accused has come to a full stop, lost the thread, as you might say. One moment.

Colonel Orbal: God, how many times have I said it. Endicott, if you're going to mess about revoltingly like that, will you please at least push him outside.

Captain Endicott: Give me a hand, will you, Brown?

Colonel Orbal: Ten minutes break. That we have to damned well put up with these revolting things day after day.

Colonel Pigafetta: I'm no longer convinced of whom or what I find the most revolting in this place.

Colonel Orbal: The air, Pigafetta, the air. It's worse than everything else. In the winter we were so cold that our teeth chattered, and now we're being boiled alive. And hitherto there's been only three choices, to be blown away, deafened or suffocated. How do you endure it like this?

Colonel Pigafetta: This peculiar little propeller which blows air over my legs all the time, is that one of your ... improvements?

Colonel Orbal: Yes, it is. Though not especially successful, I must admit. I suggest that we move to another place. To Army Staff Headquarters, for instance.

Colonel Pigafetta: I won't agree to that.

Colonel Orbal: What? Why not? It's nothing to quibble about anyhow, is it?

Colonel Pigafetta: And I find it highly unnecessary and impractical to change locality now when the session is nearly over.

Commander Kampenmann: Yes, it does seem superfluous.

Major von Peters: How long does this wretched business have to go on, Schmidt?

Captain Schmidt: Not many more days. It depends on the accused's condition.

Colonel Orbal: Here's that carriage and pair coming back again. Come on, get a move on, now.

Captain Schmidt: We have heard how the accused visited the enemy of the people, Joakim Ludolf, and put himself at his disposal. What is of greatest importance is to clarify Velder's participation in four different stages in Ludolf's criminal attempts to acquire power. The first of these was what—still according to the accused's own testimony, almost the only evidence there is on this point—was called the 'general method'. Let him now continue, Endicott.

Velder: Ludolf was very taciturn. Generally speaking, he just bade me welcome. Stoloff on the other hand, talked quite a bit. He said that I knew more than almost anyone else about Oswald and his way of thinking and also that I had witnessed the collapse in the northern sector and seen practical results of the Fascists' tactics. Then he said that in future I would be a staff officer. Ludolf asked what had happened to Janos and Aranca and when I told him what I knew, he shrugged his shoulders and didn't say any more. What happened then?

Major von Peters: Are you asking me, you maniac?

Velder: Yes, Stoloff did a quick run-through of the situation. On the operations map, he showed that Army units were attacking along the old demarcation line—the western front, as he called it—and were trying to cross the river, and that at three or four places they were also attacking in the north, along the autostrad. But they were weaker units there. He judged the situation as favourable and said that the outer defence belt could not be forced with the methods the Army had used hitherto. The whole of the land border was well fortified and the mines were in three layers. He also considered it impossible that Oswald's units from the west would be able to cross the river and the ravine because the fortifications on our side were blasted into the mountain wall and could not be destroyed by artillery.

Major von Peters: Oh, Christ, letting him sit there talking about all that. As if I didn't remember that bloody river. Month after month ... oh, well, it doesn't matter.

Commander Kampenmann: I've studied all that. You landed into the same situation as Cadorna once did at Isonzo. You couldn't take the hills without crossing the river and you couldn't cross the river without controlling the hills.

Colonel Pigafetta: My dear Kampenmann, your officiousness is boundless. What do you know about Isonzo?

Commander Kampenmann: That it led to Caporetto.

Colonel Pigafetta: But do you by any chance remember who won the war?

Major von Peters: Pigafetta's right, but this is after all a court martial, not an academy for staff officers.

Colonel Pigafetta: Most of all, it's not a forum for amateur historians and café-strategists. Go on with the testimony.

Velder: Things went just as Stoloff had said. The Army attacked for ten days without making more than a few yards headway. Then Oswald saw that he must change tactics and the attacks stopped. From then on it was mostly shelling by artillery, but that didn't have much effect.

Captain Schmidt: Here I should like to steer the accused over into another track. What is meant by the 'general method'? To what extent did Velder participate in the carrying out of it and to what extent was he responsible for the consequences of it?

Captain Endicott: Velder, the general method ...

Velder: ... had two sides, an ideological one and a military one. The ideological side was based on application to Communist doctrines and thought. And giving every man and woman in the southern sector something which Ludolf called 'definite will to defend'. He himself had this quality and he'd clearly had it for a long time. As had Stoloff. To loathe the enemy to the extent that it seemed much better to die than to flee or give up. It was a dogma that was hammered in highly systematically, for a start. Then they stopped talking about it. I gradually realised that the majority of those in the southern sector had thought like that earlier, consciously or unconsciously, and that otherwise they wouldn't have been there. Everyone in the southern sector joined the militia, both men and women. Children and people who were so old that they were no use at anything had obviously been evacuated at a very early stage.

Quite a lot was also done to see that no more children were born. Abortions were done at first-aid stations, of course, and contraceptive pills were also dealt out to the women.

Captain Endicott: And the military side ...

Velder: ... consisted of a defence and fortification scheme which Stoloff had created. He saw to the military department and Ludolf to the psychological and ideological side, so to speak. When I saw what they'd achieved in three months, I couldn't believe it. When it came to the crunch, Stoloff did admit that some of the installations had been done long before under various pretexts and that they also could have been used for different civilian purposes. Well, what? Well, the general method started out from the theory that the whole of the southern sector was a permanent fortress. First there was the outer defence belt, minefields, trenches and bunkers, which lay inside each other along the whole of the northern border. The river in the west and the hills behind were a natural fortress in themselves. Not much work had been needed there. Along the coasts, the outer defence belt consisted of electric and magnetic mines, which to a great extent had been there before, and they'd mined the beaches as well. But that was just the beginning, if I may say so. Inside the outer defence belt, there were three chains of fortresses. The outer one was of thirty-two forts, connected to each other by underground passages. In the second, there were twenty forts or defence-units and in the third twelve. Many of them had several storeys. In the very centre was the headquarters itself. All this was only partly finished at the time, but the first chain, thirty-two concrete forts blasted into or dug out of the ground, were already complete, and they were working busily on the inner belts. The headquarters itself had been ready long before the war broke out. Stoloff had built it on three levels under the ground, as laboratories and storage space. But the thought had clearly been from the very beginning that it could easily be converted for military use. When I first saw it all on the map, I thought it looked like three necklaces of beads lying inside each other with a star in the middle.

Major von Peters: Nice necklaces, I must say.

Velder: It was a fortress, the whole thing. Like an anthill. The whole of the southern sector. Stoloff reckoned on having it all ready in six months and that happened, too. In August, all three fortified

214

lines were ready. There were huge stores too. They reckoned that provisions, fuel, ammunition and medical stores, even under bad conditions, would last for two years. That was how the general method ran. At first I thought it was awful. There was no land; nowhere where people could live as human beings. But soon I was caught up into the general atmosphere and spirit. I suppose I'd had it in me from the start. I suppose that was what had brought me there, of course. After I'd been there a week, I was made a staff officer. We had a lot of work to do, eighteen hours a day for the first months.

Captain Schmidt: That was what was called the 'general method' then?

Velder: Terrifying millstone ideologies.

Commander Kampenmann: What did you say, Velder?

Velder: 'Our island mustn't become an experimental field for terrifying millstone ideologies which grind people to dust beneath them.'

Colonel Orbal: What did he say? What's that peculiar talk?

Velder: Strategically it was like this: we were not going to do anything until the defence system was complete and intact. Only defend ourselves against attack. Keep casualties low. Then when the whole fortification system was ready, Plan A was to be set into action. We worked on it very carefully. That was when the raids began.

Major von Peters: That's enough for today.

Velder: Everything was like a dream. We were quite isolated, all of us in the southern sector. Communiqués were never sent out, and we had very few contacts with the outside world. It felt as if everyone had forgotten us. No one thought about it as war. Only us and Oswald of course. We hoped he'd underestimate us. We worked out three plans, Plan A, Plan B and Plan C. The last was an emergency plan and was Ludolf's idea. Sometimes I think that deep down inside, it was that one that he liked best.

Major von Peters: That's enough, I said. Can't you get the blighter to keep quiet, Endicott?

Colonel Orbal: If it's not one fault then it's another. Just like Pigafetta's air-conditioning.

Velder: So in August, on the third, we began ...

Major von Peters: Shut up, man. Push him out.

Colonel Orbal: The session is adjourned until tomorrow at eleven o'clock.

Fourteenth Day

Lieutenant Brown: Those present: Colonel Mateo Orbal, Army, also Chairman of the Presidium of this Extra-ordinary Court Martial. Colonel Nicola Pigafetta, Air Force, Major Carl von Peters, Army, and Commander Arnold Kampenmann, Navy. The Prosecuting Officer is Captain Wilfred Schmidt, Navy, and the accused is assisted by Captain Roger Endicott, Air Force. The officer presenting the case is Lieutenant Brown.

Colonel Pigafetta: First name and service, Brown.

Lieutenant Brown: The officer presenting the case is Lieutenant Arie Brown, Air Force. Justice Tadeusz Haller had reported his absence.

Colonel Orbal: I don't think Haller's going to come any more.

Colonel Pigafetta: No, I don't think he will.

Major von Peters: How do you know that?

Colonel Pigafetta: As you must know, Justice Haller fills a double rôle in this connection. He not only acts as an observer, but he's also chairman of what they call the Joint Commission from the Ministry of Justice and the Judicial Department of the General Staff, who are working out the formal verdicts and sentences in the case against Velder.

Commander Kampenmann: I had understood that decisions are to be announced almost immediately after the final summing-up.

Colonel Pigafetta: Yes, together with detailed argumentations. Bear in mind that it's a question of verdicts which will become precedents.

Commander Kampenmann: So the verdicts of this court martial will be settled virtually without our assistance.

Colonel Orbal: How you do complain and grub into everything, Kampenmann.

Colonel Pigafetta: The material collected will of course be placed before the presidium of this court martial. Then we have to state our opinion on verdicts and sentences.

Commander Kampenmann: I can't help thinking that the procedure seems somewhat simplified.

Major von Peters: Don't you see, Kampenmann, that otherwise we'd be sitting here raking about in all this muck for years.

Colonel Orbal: Exactly. Quite right. Quite right.

Commander Kampenmann: It worries me all the same. If the members of this Joint Commission are thinking along different lines from ours, then their work will be wasted. And Haller has only presented himself here on eight days out of the fourteen.

Colonel Pigafetta: Presented himself is probably not quite the right expression.

Major von Peters: Justice Haller is very close to the Chief of State.

Colonel Orbal: Haller isn't a man to talk out of turn with impunity, civilian though he may be. Do you remember how he ran the information services during the disturbances, Carl?

Major von Peters: He built the reputation up outwards. Both the nation's and the General's. Damnably well.

Commander Kampenmann: So he testified about ...

Colonel Orbal: That business, that's old hat, Kampenmann. The similarity between a priest and a pair of women's legs. Heard that in cadet school. Now let's start.

Commander Kampenmann: However strange it may seem, that wasn't quite what I was going to say.

Major von Peters: It doesn't matter. Call in the parties, Brown.

Captain Schmidt: I will now develop further charges numbers one hundred and five to and including one hundred and twenty-seven of the case for the prosecution, concerning murder, accessory to murder, accessory to mass-murder, preparation for genocide, subversive activities, Communism, hounding of opponents and criminal promiscuity. Request to call Corporal Erwin Velder as witness.

Major von Peters: Yes, yes, granted.

Captain Schmidt: I intend first to corroborate the accused's

218

participation in the so-called Plan A.

Captain Endicott: You can begin now, Velder.

Velder: On the third of August, Plan A was put into action. The defence system was complete then. The situation at the fronts had not changed, that is, not during the summer months. The Fascists launched two attacks at the beginning and end of May. During the first, they succeeded in breaking through the outer defence-belt in the far north-west and taking up positions along the river ravine on a stretch of about four kilometres, by taking it from the rear, from the east. But Ludolf and Stoloff did not seem in the slightest worried. We did indeed lose the corner in the north-west, an area of about twenty square kilometres, but the attack went on for eight days and the Army suffered many casualties in dead and wounded. Our losses were comparatively small, both in manpower and materials. The next offensive, the one at the end of the month, went on for six days without them achieving anything except insignificant breaks in the outer defence belt. After that, all activity ceased completely—well, shelling went on of course, and there were one or two air raids, but they did no great damage. We found out through foreign sources and our own agents that Oswald's protectors did not dare use atomic weapons—they were afraid of international complications—and his military advisers considered it better to starve us out by a blockade, until we were so weakened that the so-called bridgehead could be forced or until it capitulated. Meanwhile Oswald was receiving constant reinforcements, but this had to be done discreetly, as the people who were sending arms and men had also signed the non-intervention agreement.

Major von Peters: Balderdash, pure and simple. I refuse to listen to this.

Captain Schmidt: We have a summary in Volume Nine which could be considered to present a correct picture of the situation, Appendix V IX/16. May I ask you to read it, Lieutenant Brown.

Lieutenant Brown: Appendix V IX/16, concerning the disturbances, summary compiled by the National Historical Department of the General Staff. The text is as follows:

After local punitive expeditions at the beginning and end of May, General Oswald decided to stop all further military mopping-up operations. During the course of the summer, attempts were made to return refractory elements in the Eastern Province's southern areas to order, amongst other things by offering an amnesty to those who had not been guilty of murder or other serious crimes. Since bandit attacks had begun in August, however, it was clear that the rebels, who had received powerful support from international Bolshevism, would only be brought to their senses by force. As humanitarian reasons excluded the use of atomic weapons, the now strongly fortified rebel forts would have to be routed out by conventional means. The General and his closest collaborators in the Peace Corps and the National Freedom Army, however, hesitated for a long time before resorting to offensive weapons.

Captain Schmidt: Thank you, that's enough. Let the accused continue.

Velder: We were geographically ill-placed for the countries which wished to send us aid, and from the month of May onwards, we were cut off from practically all deliveries from outside. Then the powers that were protecting Oswald began to blockade our coasts with warships, for the maintenance of peace, as they put it. General Ludolf and Colonel Stoloff, however, seemed to have foreseen this and nothing in the original plans was changed.

Captain Schmidt: Try to link him to Plan A, if you can.

Captain Endicott: I'll try to.

Major von Peters: If you gentlemen didn't mess about so damned much, this business would be cleared up in half the time.

Velder: Oh, yes, Plan A. This was implemented on the third of August as a logical preparation for Plan B. All the time we had been training people who were going to launch night-attacks, some against enemy position, but most of all against various vital points in the area behind the front. At first, the core of these troops was made up of the people Bartholic had left behind him. The commando units were built up round these men, shock-patrols, as they were called ...

Major von Peters: Assassins would be a better description ...

Velder: ... but we trained, as I said, many more, and it soon became evident that our own people were better than Bartholic's. They operated in groups, five men in each, and they had very light and efficient equipment. On the night of the fourth of August, we sent out the first wave of shock-patrols, over a hundred groups. The results went far beyond our expectations. The Fascists were quite unprepared and nearly all the patrols came back without a scratch.

Major von Peters: If he says Fascists again, I'll shoot him.

Colonel Pigafetta: That expression really is very irritating.

Velder: Then we went on striking, sometimes night after night, sometimes with longer or shorter intervals. The plans were very thorough, based on variation in everything, time, place, strength and methods. These attacks continued during the whole of August and September. Guarding on the other side was naturally improved very swiftly and our casualties grew greater. But all this had been foreseen, and in October we allowed shock-patrol activities to ebb away, also according to plan.

Captain Schmidt: That was Plan A, then. I must now attempt to put a few direct questions to the accused.

Major von Peters: About time, too.

Captain Schmidt: Velder, did you participate in the planning of these raids?

Velder: Yes.

Captain Schmidt: Were you also aware of the fact that these activities involved innumerable people being murdered, not just soldiers, but also civilians? That women, too, and even children were killed and maimed by bomb attacks and arson?

Velder: Oh, yes. We discussed the matter at headquarters. The aim in sending out shock-patrols was to spread fear and uncertainty. I remember there was a memorandum in which we stated that it was unfortunate that innocents were sacrificed, but that no such obstacles were to hinder the patrols from carrying out their assignments. On the other hand, the attacks were never directly against truly civilian targets. The doctrine of terror, it was said, could not be used to its full extent in the ways in which it had been in other countries and in other people's struggle for freedom, because in our case it was a matter of liberating our comrades in the area occupied by the Fascists. I myself had signed this memo together with Ludolf and Stoloff. The reason for allowing the raids to culminate and then successively cease was to get the enemy to believe that the threat had been averted and in that way lull them into a false sense of security.

Captain Schmidt: That should corroborate sufficiently the accused's participation in and responsibility for the crimes contained in the concept Plan A. From the régime of terror that the enemy of the people, Joakim Ludolf set up in the southern sector, only a few documents have survived and most of these are rather uninteresting. To illuminate the atmosphere and to show what dreadful doctrines applied, I shall, however, refer to one of these confiscated documents, Appendix V IX/31. If you please, Lieutenant Brown.

Lieutenant Brown: Appendix V IX/31, concerning the disturbances. Order of the day issued on the seventeenth of March by the enemy of the people, Joakim Ludolf. The text is as follows:

Comrades. Through this extreme right-wing coup we have been forced into civil war. Paul Oswald and Tadeusz Haller have oppressed the people in the Central and South-Western Provinces by force. They have also allowed foreign troops to invade the country. Our comrades in the northern sector have been defeated. The reasons for this were vacillation, obscure aims and poor preparations. Nothing similar will happen to us. The prerequisites are as follows. Peaceful co-existence with adherents to a capitalist-Fascist military dictatorship is unthinkable. Our earlier system has shown itself to be untenable. So a return to the old order is meaningless. Socialism is the people's only road to salvation.

To bring about Socialism peacefully is impossible. So with all our strength and means, we must fight the Fascists and the foreign invaders. We are materially and numerically inferior to our opponents. Our situation is thus serious, but by no means hopeless. The enemy has not succeeded in breaking through our positions anywhere. Our supplies are considerable, our arms first-class and our belief in victory unassailable. But establishing socialism will demand great sacrifices. It is incumbent upon every man and woman in the southern sector to prepare themselves for the moment when the situation demands their total commitment. Ludolf. General. Leader of the Socialist Government Militia.

Major von Peters: Singularly enlightening.

Captain Schmidt: Is the accused ready to continue?

Captain Endicott: He's ready.

Velder: Organisationally, the militia in the southern sector was based on the following principle: we at headquarters supervised the whole system, of course, but each and every one of the sixty-four forts in the three inner fortification chains was in itself a closed self-sufficient unit, under the command of one commandant. The personnel in each fort were practically never moved, except a tactical reserve which was used to relieve units in the outer defence belt. Ludolf and Stoloff said that in this way we could be sure that there was no one outside headquarters who knew enough about the defence arrangements to be of any use, should it so happen that that person fell into the hands of the enemy. We virtually ignored the possibility of spies. All those suspected of unreliability had been eliminated at an earlier stage. We ourselves seldom moved outside headquarters—control was exercised by means of a communications network which was very well developed. One thing happened to me personally which showed how isolated the different units were from each other. On the twenty-second of September ...

Major von Peters: Must we plod through all this?

Captain Schmidt: The episode Velder mentions is evidence for one of the charges.

Velder: On the afternoon of the twenty-second of September, I had to go to support-post thirty-five, which lay on the coast about fifteen kilometres due south of the central fortress, that is, headquarters. I went there with a new militia officer, by the way. Individual people still occasionally came over from the occupied areas. They were always put through a very thorough test before they were enrolled.

Captain Schmidt: It's worth inserting here that if they did not pass this test, they were—as Velder so eloquently put it—eliminated.

Colonel Orbal: Oh, Christ! So that's what happened to those we sent over.

Captain Schmidt: Go on, Velder.

Velder: There, at support-post thirty-five, in the first fortification line, which lay on the coast about fifteen kilometres south of the central fort, that is, headquarters ...

Major von Peters: He's already said that.

Captain Endicott: One moment, Velder, you're already at support-post thirty-five.

Velder: Yes, and suddenly I was standing face to face with my younger wife, Carla. Neither of us had known that the other was in the southern sector, although she'd been there for nine months and

I over six months. We were both very surprised. She was in militia uniform, of course, and was serving as a signaller. She said she'd fled from Oswaldsburg on the very first day of the military revolt, then made her way into the southern sector and at once joined General Ludolf. She'd been at support-post thirty-five ever since, since they'd begun to build the fort. It was all very confusing and embarrassing. Carla told me that Doris had stayed behind in Oswaldsburg with two of the children. Doris was the older of my wives. Carla had taken her own girl with her and had had her evacuated abroad before the turn of the year. She herself was living with a militiaman now, who was stationed at the same fort, the commandant, by the way. They'd signed a marriage contract six months earlier, which you could still do in the southern sector. She went on to say that she hadn't really believed that I'd betrayed the cause and stayed in the Army, but that she'd presumed that I'd fled the country, and in any case she'd considered she had the right to regard me as dead. I really had no answer to such reasoning. In reality then, she had remarried and the situation was, as I said, difficult. Carla was very beautiful too, and now more so than ever, I thought. I wanted her and she said that naturally we could go down to her quarters, but that she was on duty and so it could only be a matter of a short while, and she didn't think much of that. Carla was in fact the more erotic of my wives. Doris, on the other hand, was the more sexual.

Colonel Orbal: I didn't understand that at all? What on earth does he mean? Are you sitting there joking, man?

Velder: The end of it all was that I made a special pass out for her so that she could be taken through the various connecting passes to headquarters when she went off duty, which was at nine o'clock that night. The man she lived with fortunately did not react negatively to the situation, which I'd been afraid of, and he, too, signed her pass. Well, perhaps that was also because I was a lieutenant-colonel on the staff then.

Major von Peters: God, the things one has to listen to ...

Velder: Though she was in fact my wife. It was a peculiar situation. I went back to headquarters. I'd reckoned that it'd take her an hour to get there, with all the barriers she would have to get through, so at ten o'clock, I went into my room and got into bed. Five minutes later, she did indeed open the door and come in. As I'd expected, Carla was reliable. She undressed at once, taking off her uniform and rubber boots ... well, everything, and then got into bed with me without saying a word. Though she undressed slowly; she was always slow when it came to making love, both in her movements and with her hands. Carla was extremely lovely. Slim, she had the most supple and beautiful body I've ever seen, and stimulating, exciting in some way, dark and incomprehensible, and the hair between her legs and in her groin was absolutely black. And she had a kind of deep, thoughtful seriousness, in love as in everything else. It was an hour before she said anything and then she said exactly this: 'I'm so glad. Not because we're lying here making love, for it's become so complicated, but because you really came over to us. Can you forgive me for doubting you?' Carla was very erotic, as I said, and it was three hours before she was sufficiently helpless to want to be ... well, fucked, quite simply. She could balance both herself and the person she was with, me, that is, on the edge of this apparent calm for hours. She had certain characteristics, sexual ones I mean, in her way of using her lips and tongue and hands ...

Captain Schmidt: Stop there, Velder. That's enough. The preliminary investigation contains an account many pages long of this intercourse. It begins on page four hundred and sixty-one in Volume Nine.

Major von Peters: Why did you point out that particular detail, Schmidt? And in that tone of voice?

Colonel Orbal: Exactly, Captain Schmidt. Watch your step.

Captain Schmidt: I beg your pardon, sir.

Major von Peters: Don't let it happen again.

Colonel Orbal: Exactly. Which page did he say, Carl? Oh, yes, note it down.

Captain Schmidt: Would you try to lift the accused's thoughts, so to speak, a little further in time, Captain Endicott?

Colonel Pigafetta: I should like to put a question to the Prosecuting Officer. What in heaven's name is this episode supposed to prove?

Captain Schmidt: In the case for the prosecution, the testimony in question has been registered as evidence in charge number one hundred and thirteen, concerning criminal promiscuity.

Commander Kampenmann: It seems somewhat incomprehensible to me, or somewhat doubtful.

Major von Peters: Doubtful? That these filthy wretches practised intercourse any old how, just like rabbits, and clearly in the most perverted forms! You surprise me, Kampenmann.

Velder: Carla had extended leave and was free until eleven o'clock the next morning, so she got up at a quarter to ten. She stood for a moment looking down at her own body—there weren't any mirrors—and ran her hands over her loins and breasts, fingering her large nipples. Then she said: 'Funny. You had two wives, Erwin. Now I've got two husbands. I never thought that would happen.' Then she quickly pulled on her pants and bra and khaki overalls and socks and boots and left. That was the last time I ever saw her. Later, however, I got a telling-off from Ludolf and Stoloff, because I'd brought her there. Ludolf went so far as to say we really ought to transfer her to headquarters or have her shot. He seemed quite serious when he said it.

Commander Kampenmann: What happened to this woman?

Captain Schmidt: Carla Velder was executed for murder on the twenty-second of May the following year. Seven months to a day later, that is.

Major von Peters: Murder? Of whom?

Captain Schmidt: A warrant officer in the Peace Corps. She killed him with his own bayonet.

Major von Peters: Delightful young lady.

Colonel Pigafetta: May I suggest we take our lunch break.

Major von Peters: Adjourn the session, Mateo.

Colonel Orbal: What? What did you say? What's the fuss, Carl?

Major von Peters: The interim Commander-in-Chief of the Air Force has requested a lunch break.

Colonel Orbal: Oh, yes. The session is adjourned for two hours.

* * *

Colonel Pigafetta: Not that I'm especially interested, but I happened to think about a small point over lunch. At an earlier stage in the session, Velder refused to say a word about his relations with this woman and now he's described exactly the same thing so extremely thoroughly and copiously that it seems to have given the President of the court martial an hour's reading. A trifle puzzling, isn't it?

Major von Peters: I don't think so at all. The man's quite simply mental.

Lieutenant Brown: I think I can explain that, sir. In the previous case, it was a matter of home circumstances during Velder's so-called marriage. They haven't managed to persuade him that those particular events were criminal, and as a result he had decided that what happened within the walls of his own home was his private life, which he considers inviolable. In the latter case, on the other hand, he has been made to realise that he was guilty of criminal promiscuity because he had a relationship with another man's wife.

Major von Peters: As I said, the man's stark staring mad.

Colonel Pigafetta: Oh, yes. Uhuh. Shrewd explanation, Brown. Almost too shrewd.

Colonel Orbal: Do you call that an explanation. Everything gets more and more incomprehensible. Who smells of garlic, by the way?

Major von Peters: No, now let's get going.

Colonel Orbal: Yes, perhaps that's best. Before we all go mad. Call in the parties, Brown.

Captain Schmidt: I now intend to demonstrate the accused's responsibility for and participation in the so-called Plan B. This is, considering the damage done, the most serious crime Velder has been involved in. Before the accused's testimony continues, I shall refer to the concentrated account of the military situation which is described in Appendix V X/3x. I request that the officer presenting the case read this.

Lieutenant Brown: Appendix V X/3x, concerning the disturbances. Summary of the outline compiled at the National Historical Department of the General Staff. The document is stamped Secret, Grade Three. That is, paragraphs ...

Major von Peters: Yes, yes. We know. That's all of them except the obscenity paragraph.

Lieutenant Brown: The text is as follows: The situation in the country during the first half of November did not seem to give cause for special alarm. A sixth of the area of the country, that is, the southern sector of the Eastern Province, was in fact still controlled by the Reds, but the area was cut off from all connections with the outer world, and the preparations for the final clearing operations were almost complete. The planning of these operations was not done by General Oswald's staff, but as a result of international pressure, had been entrusted to the Peace Corps. Despite their experience of other centres of unrest, they did not have sufficient knowledge of either the special geographical difficulties or the desperation and ruthlessness which to a greater and greater extent had come to set their stamp on the rebels and their activities. When the deep harbour in Oswaldsport (Ludolfsport) was again in use at the beginning of November, the Peace Corps leaders decided to bring in the exchange-troops (in reality reinforcements) which were considered necessary for the final clearing operations, through this harbour. These troops, who consisted of specially trained storm-troopers with heavy equipment, arrived at Oswaldsport (Ludolfsport) late in the evening of the eighteenth of November, on board two large transports. Only one of these was able to dock at the quay, which to some extent delayed and complicated disembarkation, which could not start until shortly before midnight. As recently as a month before, in a memorandum through the General Staff, the Chief-of-State had warned the leaders of the Peace Corps against allowing transport ships to dock at Oswaldsport (Ludolfsport), and instead had suggested Marbella as being safer. However, this warning was ignored by the Peace Corps leaders.

It was pointed out that no activity from the rebels' side had occurred for several months, that conditions in the harbour were considerably better in Oswaldsport than in Marbella and that landing the storm-troopers and their equipment on the east coast, i.e. in the immediate proximity of the section of land where they would shortly be sent into action, achieved a much-needed off-loading from the two still usable roads which led to the western part of the Eastern Province. These advantages were considered sufficiently worthy of consideration that General Oswald's memorandum was not awarded appropriate significance, just as little as the fact that the Reds' forward posts were only six to seven kilometres south of the harbour in Oswaldsport (Ludolfsport). To protect disembarkation as much as possible, General Oswald gave orders to cover the north-eastern part of the southern sector with a blanket of artillery fire, but the unsuitable weather conditions made the regrouping of the guns very much more difficult.

Colonel Pigafetta: That is undoubtedly the right paper to be marked secret. Our allies in the pact would certainly not appreciate that type of honest history writing.

Major von Peters: Christ, no.

Commander Kampenmann: If we're to be absolutely honest, that much talked-of memorandum—which incidentally came from Naval Command—was really a warning against a certain danger from mines outside the harbour. And the harbour entrance was swept, as far as I know, very thoroughly before the troop transports came in.

Major von Peters: Now listen, Kampenmann, that was almost the most bloody awful remark I've ever heard.

Colonel Orbal: Quite wrong, Kampenmann, quite wrong.

Colonel Pigafetta: There are limits even to honesty, commander.

Major von Peters: And to cheek, Kampenmann.

Colonel Orbal: Yes, watch your step.

Colonel Pigafetta: If nothing else, you should consider the sensitivity our friends usually show in matters like this.

Commander Kampenmann: Naturally. I apologise.

Colonel Pigafetta: I don't think there's any need for us to go any further into the subject. Perhaps the Prosecuting Officer would continue to develop his case.

Captain Schmidt: Velder. The matter in hand is the so-called Plan B. Describe briefly what you know about it and your own part in its conception and execution.

Captain Endicott: All you've got to do is to start where we said, Velder. Plan B, it was.

Velder: We'd been very successful in two things. An external intelligence service which was small in so far as it occupied very few people, but which never offered anything but essential information. And then we'd been able to break down a lot of their codes. We knew about these troop transports to Ludolfsport two days before-hand. That knowledge was decisive for setting Plan B into action. Those three plans, A, B and C had been worked out more or less parallel at headquarters. Plan B was incomparably the most important. The basic features of it had been sketched out by Ludolf and Stoloff, then we completed it as best we could. When I heard it mentioned for the first time, Ludolf gave me a very concise description. He said: 'Plan A is a preparatory stage, Plan C is what remains when everything else has failed.' I was the one who came up with the logical question: 'But what about Plan B?' Ludolf was silent for a long time, and then he said: 'Plan B is a constructive and perfectly feasible offensive operation. If it is carried out correctly and at the right moment, it will lead Socialism to victory within three or four days. The only thing that can crack it is something utterly unexpected. Provided, as I said, we don't choose the wrong moment.' That conversation must have been held sometime in early April. Then followed two months' planning, and that in its turn we'd completed by the sixteenth of June. On that day we had a thorough run-through of Plan B at headquarters. Only three people were present, Ludolf, Stoloff and myself. The principles were as follows: At a certain given moment, we were to throw all our resources into a combined counter-action, which included two major offensives in different directions, plus two minor offensives which were mainly intended as diversions. General Ludolf ...

Colonel Orbal: What's gone wrong now?

Major von Peters: He's probably been choked by calling that filthy bandit general. The word itself got stuck in his throat, so to speak.

Captain Endicott: I think there's some technical fault in the voice-strengthener.

Major von Peters: Practically the only words I've heard you say during these sessions, Endicott, have been 'think' and 'try' and 'perhaps' and 'I don't know'.

Captain Endicott: With all due respect, sir ...

Colonel Pigafetta: Don't stand there arguing, Endicott. Get that apparatus repaired instead. Our own electrical engineers made it. Brown'll help you dismantle it.

Lieutenant Brown: Yes, sir.

Colonel Pigafetta: That's it. Send the thing down to the lab. Get it off, now.

Captain Endicott: Yes, sir.

Colonel Orbal: What shall we do now, then? Go up and have a beer?

Captain Schmidt: I suggest we diverge from the routine again, as we did once before. Namely, that we let Lieutenant Brown read the next part of Velder's testimony directly out of the record of the preliminary investigation. You'll find the document on page seventy-six in the first part of Volume Ten.

Colonel Pigafetta: Excellent. That'll save us time.

Lieutenant Brown: Document V X/5B. Interrogation of Erwin Velder. Interrogation number one thousand one hundred and two. The text repeats what was said by the enemies of the people, Joakim Ludolf, Boris Stoloff and Erwin Velder at a run-through of what was called Plan B, on the sixteenth of June. The text is as follows:

The discussion was largely held between Joakim Ludolf and Boris Stoloff, who—according to the witness—had obviously often discussed the plan between them.

Ludolf confirmed conclusively that the combined counter-action would embrace two major offensives, one in a north-westerly and the other in a north-easterly direction, simultaneously with minor amphibious units outflanking the enemy in the south and east and setting up two bridgeheads; one in a small fishing village on the south coast thirty kilometres east of the river-mouth, which coincided with what was then the front line. The other amphibious force would take by surprise the lighthouse and the pilot-station fifteen kilometres north of Oswaldsport (Ludolfsport) and establish themselves on the point where these installations were situated. After that came the following conversation (wording should be considered approximate):

Ludolf: Have we got enough boats for the amphibious operations and are they all fully seaworthy?

Velder: Yes. They're also well protected in the cliff cave. (The witness indicates here that he was responsible for this special transport detail.)

Ludolf: How long will it be before the militia has received the necessary training for carrying out a major offensive operation?

Stoloff: From that point of view, we should be able to start within a few weeks. But the most important prerequisite is still that we must be able to protect ourselves against air attack while the offensive is on.

Ludolf: So you're saying that we must wait for bad weather.

Stoloff: Yes. As far as I can make out, the best time would be some time during late autumn, in October or November, when the mists come. Whatever happens, we must attack before winter.

Velder: Before that, the harbour in Ludolfsport will have been rebuilt to an extent that they can begin to use it.

Stoloff: All the better for us. I would say that the more people Oswald concentrates in Ludolfsport, the greater are our chances of gaining a swift and decisive victory.

Velder: Yes, we'll have them like kittens in a sack.

Captain Schmidt: I should like to draw the presidium's attention to that last remark.

Lieutenant Brown: Stoloff went on to give an account of the supplies situation. 'Plan B,' he said, amongst other things, 'must for different reasons be implemented before the turn of the year. Firstly, a winter in our present positions would make large inroads into our fuel stores and power reserves. Secondly, the militia's winter equipment is so deficient that even a moderately low temperature would make any extensive operations on the ground impossible. Thirdly, we must remember that by a certain time, by October for instance, the militia will have reached the peak of its offensive strength. After that, we cannot reckon on getting any stronger, while on the other hand, Oswald will receive new additions in men and material.'

Joakim Ludolf then summarized the actual strength situation, which in his opinion was about one to three in Oswald's favour, in men and arms and materials. Most questionable he considered inferiority in the air, which could only be made up for by special circumstances.

Finally it was decided that the militia's qualitative peak, with reference to training and arms as well as psychic resources, would be reached before the fifteenth of October.

Colonel Pigafetta: Well, Endicott, how did it go?

Captain Endicott: The assemblage is all right, sir. There'd been a short-circuit in one of the batteries, that's all.

Major von Peters: Can we hear what the wretch says now?

Captain Endicott: Yes, the strengthener should work.

Major von Peters: Get weaving, then, Velder. I've no desire to sit here all evening.

Velder: On the fifteenth of November, the intelligence service reported that the transports of Peace Corps reinforcements could be reckoned on coming into Ludolfsport in the afternoon or the evening of the eighteenth. We also knew that the troops on board consisted of heavily equipped storm-troopers, who were to be sent directly to the north-eastern section of the front, which was already our weakest point. On the evening of the fifteenth, we had a decisive meeting in the operations centre at headquarters. On that occasion, the executive commanders who were to lead the four different offensives were also present. We stood in front of the big wall-map all the time. I had stared at this map so often and for so long that I dreamt about it for years afterwards. Schematically, it looked like this: the island like a rectangle lying on its side, one hundred and forty kilometres long and with one short side about fifty kilometres long—in fact the island was sixty-three kilometres at its widest and forty-six at its narrowest. I saw it divided up into six roughly equal rectangular fields, of which one, the farthest down in the right hand corner, belonged to us.

Major von Peters: Thank you, we know what the map looked like.

Velder: Uhuh. Uhuh. At that meeting on the evening of the fifteenth and during the night into the sixteenth, we decided that Plan B should be put into action, beginning at one o'clock in the morning of the nineteenth. It was the decision we'd talked about for so long and we all had a feeling of great relief, I think. This was also an opportunity which was unlikely to arise again. From many points of view, the situation was by and large the most favourable we could hope for. It had been raining without ceasing for almost two weeks, the fields were waterlogged and the roads difficult to pass. The nights were long and misty and during the last few days, one rain area after another had driven in from the north, alternating with fog banks. The temperature had varied between forty and fifty degrees centigrade, exactly what our militia could manage with their light equipment. It was normal weather for the time of year and we did not reckon on any surprises. It had been possible for years to predict the weather on the island with almost a hundred per cent certainty. Planning was what Ludolf called flexible. We would have to strike before the fresh storm-troopers had had time to get into their positions, but if the ships were delayed, the offensive was to be held back until they'd got into harbour and the troops had begun disembarking. Otherwise Oswald's new reinforcements could only too easily be transferred to another point along the coast.

Colonel Orbal: I say, Pigafetta, that man Niblack, wasn't he runner-up in the golf championship a couple of years ago?

Colonel Pigafetta: Yes, that's right.

Colonel Orbal: Yes, I thought I'd seen the man before. Oh, excuse the interruption. Just carry on.

Velder: General Ludolf, Colonel Stoloff and I were jointly responsible for Plan B. Everything had been ready for a long time and now we'd decided on the day. At midnight exactly, the two diversionary forces were to be shipped out, and for that purpose all available patrol-ships and motor-boats we had were needed. It was to take them exactly an hour to reach their respective targets, the lighthouse on the north-eastern point and that fishing village ...

Commander Kampenmann: Melora, wasn't it?

Captain Endicott: Yes, that's it. The place was called Melora.

Velder: To that fishing village on the south coast, then. At the same time, the first strike-force was to break through the autostrad line and advance north of the town, just north of the airfield. With that, both main communication lines, the old road and the northern coast road, were cut off, and Ludolfsport surrounded. At best, the first units would reach the coast between four and five o'clock in the morning.

At the same moment as the first groups reached the sea north of Ludolfsport, the second strike-force was to launch the main offensive. The grouping area for the second strike-force lay up in the north-west corner of our territory. The second strike-force's assignment was to break through the actual angle between the northern and western fronts, and advance into the area which Oswald had taken in May and which was still insufficiently fortified. Then the militia were to cross the river and the motorway and advance into the village of Brock, which lay on the old road between Oswaldsburg and Ludolfsport, only four kilometres from the capital. When Brock had been captured and the main road between Oswaldsburg and the eastern parts of the country cut off, fast motorised units would then continue the attack due north over the plain and cut off the northern coast road, too. With that, the part of the country controlled by the Fascists would be cut into two. Ludolfsport was surrounded from the land side and the road to Oswaldsburg would lie open. It was essential for the fulfilment of this plan that the enemy was kept in ignorance all the time of what our next step was to be. We reckoned with Oswald first thinking that the diversions against the point and the fishing village were attacks against primary targets. Not until the enemy began regrouping to meet these threats would the second strike-force start the offensive against Brock. Of all forces at our disposal, thirty per cent were left behind to hold the old positions. Five per cent were used for the two amphibious operations against the lighthouse and the fishing village.

Twenty-five per cent were used in the first strike-force, which was to fight its way to the east coast and cut off Ludolfsport. The remaining forty per cent were sent into the main thrust towards Brock. Practically all our wheeled vehicles, mostly small tracked armoured cars, were divided between the two strike-forces. The most important things—apart from determination to win, of course—were mobility and speed and the militia's light equipment and arms. The Fascists were to be made to believe as long as possible that it was the old raid-system according to Plan A which had begun to be used again, but on a larger scale.

Colonel Orbal: Fearfully boring all this. One knows already what happened.

Velder: Our greatest problem was the Air Force.

Colonel Pigafetta: I can quite believe that.

Velder: We had no Air Force, except a few hydroplanes in the cliff cave, and the only airfield in the southern sector had been destroyed by bombing and shelling. As far as we knew, there were three fully equipped airfields in Oswald's area. The best one lay just west of Oswaldsburg, the two others immediately north of Ludolfsport and Marbella. Stoloff had spent a lot of time on this question, and he came to the conclusion that if the first strike-force fulfilled its tasks according to plan, then the airfield in Ludolfsport would be in our hands well before dawn, i.e. seven o'clock in the morning. But the worst threat, of course, came from Oswaldsburg, where the majority of the Fascists' Air Force was concentrated. However, for a long time Stoloff had been infiltrating specialists among the workers in the retraining camps round Oswaldsburg and he'd also smuggled in a number of people into the town itself. We had a lot of comrades there too, of course, and among them there were some who were prepared to be activists. The specialists I mentioned were almost all ex-building workers, people who already knew the art of handling explosives and who had then been given a special training as saboteurs.

From these, a number of sabotage groups were crystallized out, and they were given orders to go into action ten minutes before the raiding units reached the fishing village, Melora, it's name was, by the way, and the lighthouse on the north-eastern point. The saboteurs would make a co-ordinated attack on the airfield, beginning at ten to one. We couldn't do much about the airfield at Marbella. Our party hadn't all that number of adherents in that area and also we knew that the airfield was well protected.

Major von Peters: Haven't we had enough now?

Velder: Otherwise we relied on the weather. The new military reserve airfields weren't usable as they had no concrete runways and the markings were washed out by the rain. And anyhow, as usual at this time of year, it was so misty and cloud levels were so low that it would be impossible to operate with aeroplanes. And anyhow, Oswald hadn't that many. The situation hitherto had not been very inviting for air warfare, as Stoloff expressed it. Neither did we believe that Oswald's protector among the imperialistic powers would dare to start raids from aircraft carriers, for fear of the international row that would start. The aeroplanes ...

Colonel Pigafetta: It is possible that I may be thought excessively sensitive, but is there really no means whatsoever of persuading the accused to avoid that word. I would be grateful if that were possible, Endicott.

Velder: On the sixteenth, we received information which seemed to improve our starting position. A well-known foreign commentator had been to Oswaldsburg and had also visited the fronts. He had obviously been allowed to meet some prisoners, too. He had written an article which was published all over the world and which ...

Captain Schmidt: The document is contained in the preliminary investigation. Appendix V X/49xx. If you please, Lieutenant Brown.

Velder: ... explained that we ...

Captain Endicott: Ssh, Velder.

Colonel Orbal: What on earth are you doing, Endicott?

Major von Peters: Captain Endicott thinks that perhaps he might try to get that monstrous swine to shut up.

Colonel Orbal: It sounded as if he were enticing a cat.

Lieutenant Brown: Appendix V X/49xx, concerning the disturbances. Extract from an article published in the international press about the tenth of November. The text is as follows:

There is no question or likelihood of it being a game between the great powers. The remainder of the communist guerillas, after their severe defeats of the spring, have entrenched themselves in the south-western part of the island. This is an inaccessible and barren area, apparently thoroughly fortified. The guerillas' supplies have, however, been used up at approximately the same rate as their hopes have faded. Their strength has now run out and their courage definitely ebbed away.

Since the signing of the non-intervention pact, their distance from the Communist part of the world has become immeasurable and their isolation complete. With good reason, one expects that the guerillas will admit that the battle is lost and will capitulate within a few weeks. In all probability, this is also what will happen.

The moment of defeat is not difficult to predict either. The rebels, who are led by a certain Joakim Ludolf, will have to surrender before the winter, as their chances of surviving the cold season at all are almost non-existent.

During my visit to Oswaldsburg, I was given the opportunity of speaking to Major-General Henry Winckelman, who is Commander-in-Chief of the National Freedom Army—this army and the Peace Corps, are of course, under the direct command of the Chief of State, General Oswald.

Major-General Winckelman considered that a forceful offensive operation would enable them to clear the rebel area in less than twenty-four hours, which does not seem unlikely. That this has not already happened is obviously due to the Chief of State's unwillingness to use any more force than the situation demands. The war, so loudly shouted about in certain quarters, is no war. And the 'Communist minority' which some sources continue to pity, consists largely of starving groups of bandits. A member of the government, Tadeusz Haller, said in a public statement a few days ago 'that it is only general lack of will to work and fear of punishment that has hitherto stopped the rebels from creeping out of their holes.'

Even if it appears believable that individual fanatical idealists are to be found in the Ludolfian free companies, I am convinced that Mr Haller is largely right. International Communism's attempts to gain a foothold in this part of the free world have failed hideously. And with these words, this subject would seem to have been exhausted.

Colonel Orbal: Good statement, though of course Winckelman knew that it'd take weeks to smoke that mob out of their holes. We'd analysed that on the staff.

Major von Peters: Now, that's enough for today, I think.

Colonel Orbal: Good God, is that the time? The session is adjourned until eleven o'clock tomorrow.

Fifteenth Day

Lieutenant Brown: Those present: Colonel Mateo Orbal, Army, also chairman of the Presidium of this Extra-ordinary Court Martial, Colonel Nicola Pigafetta, Air Force, Major Carl von Peters, Army, and Commander Arnold Kampenmann, Navy. The Prosecuting Officers are Captain Wilfred Schmidt, Navy, and Lieutenant Mihail Bratianu, Army. The accused is assisted by Captain Roger Endicott, Air Force. Justice Tadeusz Haller has reported his absence.

Colonel Orbal: Oh, Pigafetta's here, is he? I can't see him.

Major von Peters: What do you mean, Brown? Is Colonel Pigafetta here or isn't he? Perhaps he's sent his astral body?

Colonel Orbal: Hardly.

Lieutenant Brown: The colonel has been delayed for a few minutes, sir.

Colonel Orbal: Hoho, yes, yes. And a week today he'll be a general.

Major von Peters: I'm not so sure about that.

Colonel Orbal: It seems quite absurd that the Chief of State should appoint such an unbelievable ass as Bloch as Commander-in-Chief of the Air Force.

Major von Peters: Want to bet me?

Colonel Orbal: Keep your money, Carl. Well, Kampenmann, how are you today?

Commander Kampenman: Very well indeed, thank you.

Major von Peters: Couldn't you lure the Commander-in-Chief of the Navy on board one of your old tubs and blow it up? Then you'd be an admiral.

Commander Kampenmann: I don't understand what you mean.

Major von Peters: What a bloody lot of fun you lot must have in

239

the ship's mess or whatever it's called.

Commander Kampenmann: The gunroom.

Colonel Orbal: Talking of gunrooms, I knew a ballet dancer in Marbella some years ago. Her name was Florinda. Happened to think of her when I was reading that interrogation of Velder. The bastard maintains he had a hard-on for seven hours before he poked that Clara or whatever her name was. Although she rocked him and sucked him alternately. Liar. I don't believe a word of it.

Major von Peters: What's that got to do with the ballet dancer?

Colonel Orbal: Well, with her I got a priapism, you know, an erection that doesn't stop. Fucked her all night and most of ... well, of the following day. Then I was forced to fly home. Sat like a bloody candelebra on the plane, about to crack the roof. Well, then I got back to the old woman, and it went over.

Commander Kampenmann: Excuse me, but what has that got to do with the gunroom?

Colonel Orbal: With what? Oh, yes. Well, that's not easy to answer. Next time, anyway, this Florinda ran away as fast as she could as soon as she saw me. After that experience, so to speak.

Major von Peters: Lay off, now, Mateo. Here comes Pigafetta.

Colonel Pigafetta: I regret this delay.

Major von Peters: So do we. Call in the parties, Brown.

Captain Schmidt: We are still occupied with the last complex of charges.

Major von Peters: Nice to see you, Bratianu.

Lieutenant Bratianu: Thank you, sir.

Major von Peters: Are you Prosecuting Officer today?

Lieutenant Bratianu: I don't think so, sir. But the case will shortly be completed and we are preparing the final summing-up.

Captain Schmidt: I request to be allowed to return to questioning the accused. Concerning his contribution to the so-called Plan B.

Colonel Orbal: Oh, yes. Push the wretch over then.

Velder: The eighteenth of November was a Monday. At about eight in the evening, one of our observation posts on the islands reported that the transport ships were just running into Ludolfsport. With that the matter was clear. At half-past eight, General Ludolf gave orders that Plan B should be implemented. Then it was just a matter of waiting. We couldn't do anything else; every man and woman in the militia was in place.

Commander Kampenmann: Were there women on operations too?

Colonel Orbal: Must you be so damned inquisitive, Kampenmann?

Captain Schmidt: As far as is known, there were women personnel in both the offensive forces and in the amphibious units.

Major von Peters: It should be 'in the so-called offensive forces and the so-called amphibious units'.

Captain Schmidt: Naturally, sir. I apologise. Let the accused continue.

Velder: Everything had been so well prepared that we hadn't a thing to do. But we stayed in the operations centre. We were to stay there for four days, as a matter of fact, keeping ourselves awake with pills. General Ludolf and Colonel Stoloff played chess while we were waiting. They were skilful players, both of them. Shortly before midnight, it came to a draw and they shook hands. I remember that Ludolf said: 'Have I ever succeeded in beating you with a Sicilian?' Stoloff said: 'No. Now it's time to start work.' The diversionary forces got away just when they should have, at exactly midnight. Then we heard nothing from them for almost an hour. All the time, we were receiving decoded signals from the enemy's side, as our people had more or less cracked their codes completely by then. Everything seemed calm, only routine type radio-traffic coming over. It was quite quiet in the operations room. At regular intervals, our woman orderly came in with strips of text from the code technologists and signallers who were working in the bunker alongside.

Colonel Orbal: Woman orderly, indeed. Whom you all slept with in turns, I suppose.

Velder: I don't think so. She was over sixty.

Colonel Orbal: Ugh! What a piggy-wig.

Colonel Pigafetta: Sorry, what did you say, Orbal?

Colonel Orbal: Nothing. Just an old expression; used it when I was a child.

Commander Kampenmann: The accused is answering questions again now.

Captain Endicott: Velder has recouped astonishingly during these last two days. He seems to have an unusually strong physique.

Velder: At eight minutes to one, the first sign that anything was happening came through. It was a brief report stating that suspicious boats had been spotted off the coast just east of Melora and they were being shelled by artillery. It sounded extremely negative, but neither Ludolf nor Stoloff said a word. I remember that Ludolf was standing in front of the operations map with his hands in his pockets, sucking on his pipe. Tobacco supplies were running out by then, by the way, for the general usually smoked cigarettes.

Lieutenant Bratianu: Don't presume to call that swine general ever again!

Captain Schmidt: As long as I am present, I am the one who supervises the questioning.

Major von Peters: Perhaps so, but Bratianu is right.

Captain Schmidt: Go on, Velder.

Velder: In actual fact, the southern diversionary force had already got itself into great difficulties at Melora. Just east of the fishing village, there was a battery of field artillery which we hadn't reckoned on. The boats were spotted and three of them were sunk by artillery fire. The rest turned back to sea again and the flotilla commander was forced to land the militia force five kilometres west of Melora. The bridgehead wasn't established until half-past two, under fire from that battery. They didn't succeed in taking Melora, and the advance was soon stopped by reinforcements from the north. At ten o'clock the next morning, the bridgehead collapsed and only an eighth of the force managed to evacuate and retreat to the southern sector. This looked like a bad start, but the diversion towards Melora had fulfilled its function, all the same. The Fascists had brought troops from the north and that made the second offensive force's task easier. After that first message, reports came in thick and fast, the code technologists hardly having time to decode them. The second message that we picked up implied progress, as from that we could see that the sabotage groups on the airfield in Oswaldsburg had blown up the runways and set fire to three large hangars before they had been wiped out. As far as we could make out, every single one of the saboteurs was killed.

Captain Schmidt: Four men and a woman were taken prisoner.

They were executed the next day.

Major von Peters: Is it really the Prosecuting Officer's task to give the accused complementary information?

Captain Schmidt: The interjection was intended as information for the presidium.

Colonel Pigafetta: In that case, it was superfluous. I signed the death sentences myself. It was one of my first duties. The swine were shot here, down in the basement. They weren't so big-mouthed by then.

Captain Schmidt: I beg your pardon. Go on, Velder.

Velder: Part of the finesse of Plan B was that it was totally unconventional. There was, for instance, no tactical reserve. If any of the operations failed, there was nothing we could do about it. All instructions had been issued and could not be complemented. So we could really only sit and wait and see how things went, and for that we at first had to turn to what we could intercept from the enemy's radio communications. Our own units kept radio silence and had orders to use couriers and dogs until the signallers had had time to put up telephone lines. So several hours went by before the picture of what had happened began to clear. Meanwhile, we were waiting in front of that map. We said very little to each other.

Captain Schmidt: Can you try to get the accused to give a more lucid account of what happened, Endicott?

Colonel Orbal: This is all just damned tittle-tattle. What are you doing?

Velder: The raid on Melora failed, but things went much better on the point in the north-west. The boats got to the beach without being discovered, the lighthouse and the pilot-boat station were taken without noticeable difficulties and the Army units' positions on the point were taken from the rear. Resistance was insignificant. By two o'clock, the whole point was in our hands.

Major von Peters: There was only one infantry company up there.

Velder: The first offensive force set off at exactly one o'clock and broke through the autostrad line along a five-hundred-yard stretch within less than half an hour. The force was grouped in wedges and by two o'clock, motorised militia units had advanced through the gap. The ground was so waterlogged that some of the vehicles got stuck in the mud, but the light tracked armoured cars went ahead.

243

In actual fact, they advanced over twenty kilometres in two hours. Soon after three, the northern road was cut off and at a quarter past four ... no, it was exactly twenty-three minutes past four when the orderly came in with a telex strip. General Ludolf read it. Then he took his pipe out of his mouth and said quite calmly: 'They've reached the beach one kilometre north of the airfield.' That meant that Ludolfsport was cut off. Five minutes later, the second offensive force set off. The whole operation was in action. By five o'clock, when the second force had already driven a five-hundred-yard wedge into the Army's positions in the angle between the northern and western fronts, there was still nothing to indicate that the Fascists understood what was happening. As far as I could make out later, the confusion was almost total. When the first militia units reached the sea north of Ludolfsport and blocked the coast road, the Peace Corps troops stationed at the airfield were moving north to attack the bridgehead at the lighthouse. So they were heading in a direction away from the real offensive. When they tried to turn back later, the convoy fell into disorder and soon after that, they broke out from the bridgehead and attacked the convoy in the rear. The result was that the airfield was left undefended and was taken by our troops almost without any fighting, planes and all. At eight o'clock in the morning, the seconds offensive force had broken through too, and crossed the river and the autostrad. The covering troops began to dig themselves in and set up posts west of the river, and before they'd even made any contact with the enemy, the main militia force had begun to advance through the terrain towards the north-west, to take Brock and cut off the road between Oswaldsburg and the Eastern Province. In Ludolfsport, everything was going according to our calculations. The operation there ...

Captain Schmidt: One moment, Endicott. Can you let the accused rest for a while. There is now a full account of what happened in and around Ludolfsport. It has been compiled with material from a number of sources, of which the most important is the testimony of a certain Alaric Scott. This Scott was a sergeant belonging to a Peace Corps unit stationed in the harbour area of Ludolfsport. Amongst other things, he was partially responsible for the disembarkation and unloading of the transport ships. In connection with the events we are now touching on, he deserted to the Communists.

He was later taken prisoner and was executed more than three years ago. Before that, he gave his testimony, which was marked Top Secret and was only released for the first time a few months ago, because of the Velder investigation. It is to be found in the preliminary investigation as Appendix V X/41. I will now hand over to the officer presenting the case.

Lieutenant Brown: Appendix V X/41, concerning the disturbances. Testimony of Sergeant Alaric Scott, alien citizen. The document is marked Secret to the Third Degree. The text is as follows:

Shortly before eight o'clock in the evening, the first transport ship was towed into the deep harbour, where it was tied up at eleven o'clock. Meanwhile, the other ship anchored in the outer harbour basin, as it proved impossible to have both ships at the quay at the same time. I was at this time, and during most of the night, in the control-tower of the harbour authority's office building. At about half-past eleven, the officer in command of the troops on the ships, a Colonel Joao Zarco, came into the control-tower with his adjutant. There he had a long conversation with the commandant of the town. This conversation was carried out with the help of an interpreter. Colonel Zarco demanded that the disembarkation should be started immediately, partly with gangways and partly with barges from the anchored ship. The commandant of the town—a major in the National Freedom Army—protested that the vehicles that were to take the troops to their posts had still not been brought up and that from every point of view it would be better to wait until daylight. After a brief discussion, they telephoned headquarters in the first military area, where the officer on duty replied that Major-General Winckelman had retired and was not to be disturbed, and that the Chief-of-Staff, Lieutenant-Colonel Orbal was in Oswaldsburg. The duty-officer referred us to General Oswald's headquarters, which were situated in Marbella. A major who was clearly guard-officer at headquarters said that the decision should be made by the officer in command of the Peace Corps, whose headquarters were in Oswaldsburg. Colonel Zarco rang there, too, but the general in command of the Corps was at a function at his embassy. However, the Chief-of-Staff was woken up, and he at once referred us to Naval Command. This had been set up adjoining Army Headquarters in Marbella, so we rang there again. The major who had previously referred us to the officer in command of the Peace Corps turned out to be the officer on duty for Naval Command too. After a while, he managed to connect us to a naval commander, who considered the affair of a local character which should be settled by the harbour authorities in Oswaldsport (Ludolfsport). The commandant of the town summoned the harbour-master, who was in the next room. After a brief discussion, they told Colonel Zarco that he could start bringing the troops on land at once, but in that case they would have to bivouac on the quay until eight o'clock, when they could start marching to the collecting-place. The trucks which were to take them to their posts were expected at the collecting-place shortly after nine. To this, Colonel Zarco replied that anything was better than having the troops left on board the ships. It was now half-past twelve at night. The disembarkation of the troops began at once, but it was rather slow, especially when it came to the ship lying at anchor, from which the soldiers had to get into barges first and then be brought to the quay by tugboats.

Soon after one o'clock, we got a telephone message that one of the rebel patrols had made an attack on the lighthouse on the north-west point. Such raids had not happened for over a month. A moment later, we heard that it was no longer possible to make contact with either the tugboats, the lighthouse staff or the Army post up there and that the defence force at the airfield had been roused and given orders to go north to restore order. Only a quarter of an hour later, a very unclear report came in to say that other rebel patrols had started a series of attacks on Army front line positions by the motorway, fifteen kilometres south-west of the town. The town commandant put this report aside and said that there was no reason to make Colonel Zarco even more anxious than he had already seemed earlier. After yet another half an hour, a regimental officer at the front line reported that there was rebel activity in a limited sector and that a few patrols may have penetrated the front and continued in the direction of Oswaldsport (Ludolfsport). The commandant then regrouped a number of local guard forces towards the south to capture any guerilla units trying to make their way towards the town. At the same time, he informed the head of the riot-police and the gendarmerie. A number of motor-cycle police were also sent to the southern outskirts to stop any possible attempts at sabotage.

The police force in Oswaldsport (Ludolfsport) was relatively speaking smaller than in other parts of the country. Many of the inhabitants were adherents to the Oswald régime and were strongly anti-Communist. This was said to be due to the fact that large numbers of civilian buildings had been destroyed by the demolition commandos on the rebels' retreat from the northern sector eight months beforehand. Meanwhile, disembarkation continued in good order, but rather slowly, and there were no signs to indicate that anything special was going on. The harbour-master went home to bed, but the commandant and his two officers stayed behind, together with the communications officer from the staff of the military area, Second-Lieutenant de Wilde, who was lying asleep on a sofa in the next room all the time.

At three o'clock, I drove round the harbour area in a patrol jeep with three men from the guard. Disembarkation was continuing normally, and the soldiers who had already landed were lying curled up asleep in their coats on the quay or in the warehouses round about. It was raw and cold and very misty. I also made a tour of the town. The streets were empty—there was a curfew on, of course—and everything was calm and quiet. On the northern outskirts, I noticed that most of the defence posts were not manned, presumably because the men had been sent south. We parked the jeep for a few moments on the hill by the road out to the northern coast road. The town lay below us, dark and silent in the mist, and all we could hear were faint sounds from the harbour area. When I got back to the control-tower, it was ten past four. The commandant seemed tired and sleepy and the other two officers were playing cards in a corner of the room.

At about half-past five, the telephone rang. I picked up the receiver and a voice shouted: 'This is Lieutenant Olson, the rebel patrols are just ...' Then the conversation was cut off. I didn't know any Lieutenant Olson and neither did anyone else. Not until afterwards did I realise that it must have been the duty-officer at the airfield. The commandant thought for a few minutes, then he rang up the tele-centre, who said that there'd just been a total break in communications—except in the actual town area. The commandant began to get worried, but nothing happened except that tele-communications were still broken off. There was a radio-centre one floor up in the harbour office building, but we heard nothing from those manning it. At twenty minutes past five, a dispatch soldier from one of the patrol boats came running in with a message which was not at all clear, but which said that the rebels had tried to break out and that the general alarm had been sounded.

The commandant went into the room next door and woke up Second-Lieutenant de Wilde, who at first tried to contact the military area staff on the Army's own telephone network. After a quarter of an hour or so, he realised that he couldn't and he set off for the radio-centre. The door to it was locked and Second-Lieutenant de Wilde called three men from the guard, who blew it open. Inside the radio-centre, one of the radio men was lying dead on the floor. The other was standing with his back to the entrance, doing something to the installations. He turned round and shot Second-Lieutenant de Wilde in the stomach and was himself shot dead by the guards immediately afterwards. Second-Lieutenant de Wilde died half an hour later. The whole of the radio-centre was out of action. The shots were heard up in the control-tower, and the commander ran downstairs one floor. It was six o'clock now and beginning to get light outside. The mist was thicker than ever. The commandant seemed quite bewildered and I can quite see why. It wasn't easy to grasp how it all connected up. After a while, he realised that one of the radio men had been a Communist fifth columnist, and that he'd first killed his colleague and then put the installations out of action. Yet another quarter of an hour went by before the commandant gave orders to the tele-centre to sound the alarm.

I don't know exactly what the time was by then, but only twenty minutes later a fierce exchange of shots began along the ridge above the town. This was government militia attacking and beginning to clear the lines of defence posts from the north. The confusion was clearly very great up there. The only sensible report that came in during the next half hour was this: 'They're coming from the north, attacking us in the rear with flame-throwers and automatic weapons. Send reinforcements at once.' Colonel Zarco came rushing up to the control-tower with a couple of officers, who obviously belonged to his staff. He ranted and raved and wanted to know what was going on. The commandant at long last replied that the town was being attacked by rebel patrols and that all communications inland were broken off. Colonel Zarco turned scarlet in the face with rage and left the room without saying a word. He came back twenty minutes later with signallers from his own force. They had portable radio equipment with them and lots of other stuff. Half an hour later, the radio installations were partially in action again. It was quite light now and very misty. The sound of shooting came nearer and nearer and it was clear that the rebel advance was continuing. In many places in the centre of the town, the gendarmes and police began to build barricades across the street with overturned cars, furniture and other lumber. The disorder grew worse and worse. The only instruction we received was a categorical message from General Oswald that not a square yard of ground was to be surrendered.

A short while later, the military area staff at last reported that reinforcements would soon be arriving and that road communications were to be cleared at once. Everything seemed to be vague and worrying. It was raw and cold out, but the mist was beginning to lift a little. The next time Colonel Zarco came back, he was absolutely beside himself with rage. By then he'd surveyed the situation and knew more about it than the commandant did. 'You've lured us into a deathtrap,' he cried. 'The town's in the middle of the front line! And you're retreating all along it!' The commandant, who had gradually become very worried indeed, said that Colonel Zarco's own troops must be thrown into the fighting. Then Colonel Zarco said: 'Two-thirds of my men are still on the transport ships, trapped like rats in a sealed tin. The ones who have disembarked are exhausted after a crossing in very bad weather. And many of them haven't been issued with their equipment. My officers don't know anything about the situation here, there's no transport, no maps, nothing. But we'll fight to the last man all the same.'

The situation was quite hopeless. Of the storm-troopers who had landed, most of them were sitting or lying on their packs. They understood nothing of what was happening, and neither did their officers. The last active attempt made was that two tugs tried to tow one of the transports out into open water after severing the anchor chains. At almost exactly the same moment, two batteries of field artillery the militia had captured began to shell the harbour from the hills west of the town. The transport ship in the outer harbour was hit almost at once and began to burn. That wasn't surprising, as the harbour lay quite open and any gunner could score with almost every shot. It was about as difficult as hitting a barn with a rifle at a distance of fifty yars.

At eleven o'clock, Colonel Zarco came into the control-tower for the last time. By then one of the transport ships had keeled over at the quay and the other was drifting round the outer harbour basin on fire. He was very formal and said icily that the situation was hopeless and that he had decided that he would rather allow his men to capitulate than to see them slaughtered to no purpose. He then made radio contact with Army Headquarters and requested permission to capitulate. At headquarters, this request clearly hit them like a bomb. They still didn't seem to have realised what was happening and repeated again and again that Zarco should counter-attack with units from the National Freedom Army. Finally the Chief of State himself came to the microphone and said that not even a square yard was to be lost. Five minutes later, all resistance ceased and the militia stormed the harbour area. Colonel Zarco was killed by machine-gun fire from an armoured car ten steps from the harbour office building. Most of the troops on the quay and in the warehouses did not even have time to give themselves up. Some tried to entrench and offer resistance, but everything was too late. Thousands of gallons of oil and petrol, which had poured out of the transport ships, caught fire and washed over the men swimming in the harbour basin. The militia took practically no prisoners.

Major von Peters: Schmidt, what the hell do you mean by forcing us to listen to this kind of endless harangue?

Captain Schmidt: The case for the prosecution intends to demonstrate the results of the evil deeds the accused planned and co-operated in executing. The massacre in Oswaldsport is in my view the most serious and terrible of Velder's crimes, although he himself sat secure and safe in a bunker many miles away while it was all happening.

Colonel Orbal: What did this sergeant, Scott or whatever his name is, do?

Captain Schmidt: Alaric Scott, who had for many years been infected by Communist ideas, disarmed the officers in the harbour office building and hung a red flag out of the window.

Colonel Orbal: Where did he get that from?

Captain Schmidt: I'm afraid I don't know.

Colonel Orbal: Well, it doesn't really matter, but I just wondered. Peculiar.

Colonel Pigafetta: Just as well to have a lunch break, then you can think about the matter in peace and quiet, Orbal.

Colonel Orbal: Excellent idea. The session is adjourned for two hours.

* * *

Colonel Orbal: Dreadful food you give us, Pigafetta. Greens with everything. It's not good. Builds up gases. I was farting half the night. No, give me a beefsteak and beer ...

Major von Peters: Let the parties in now, Brown.

Captain Schmidt: I intend to allow the accused to continue his testimony.

Major von Peters: Yes, but just see to it that he's brief about it.

Captain Endicott: He is prepared.

Velder: The first attack force, then, captured Ludolfsport at eleven o'clock, several hours earlier than had been calculated. At five o'clock in the afternoon, the second offensive force captured Brock and cut off the main road between Oswaldsburg and Ludolfsport at a point only forty kilometres east of the capital. From the radio traffic we heard, we realised that the enemy had been taken completely by surprise.

Colonel Orbal: Yes, it came as a damned shock, I must admit. Our headquarters were only a little way away from there. General Winckelman was absolutely flummoxed. I remember he said to me: 'Everything's going straight to hell.' Our forces were more or less intact, but the tactical situation was shot to bloody pieces. But I said: 'It's just a matter of holding on, Henry.' And he said: 'Mateo, you're wonderful.' Yes, that's what he said. But I'm not supposed to be sitting here telling this story. Go on, Velder.

Velder: In the afternoon, Ludolf issued a communiqué, the only one he wrote throughout the war.

Captain Schmidt: Appendix V X/101x. If you please, Brown.

Lieutenant Brown: Appendix V X/101x, concerning the disturb-

251

ances. The communiqué issued by the enemy of the people, Joakim Ludolf, on 19th November at 1000 hours. The text is as follows:

The Socialist Government Militia this morning went into attack along the whole of the front line. Ludolfsport was surrounded during the morning and soon after ten o'clock three brigades of the Socialist Government Militia advanced into the town, which was rapidly cleared of Fascist troops. A large prey fell into the hands of the victors. Later in the day, militia units that had broken through into the Central Province liberated the important village of Brock. The advance continues.

Velder: Yes, that's how it was worded. From seven o'clock in the evening onwards, we had firm signal-communications with both the offensive forces and a complete picture of the situation. Everything was going exactly according to plan. When the position at Brock had been consolidated and built out, some of the motorised units continued northwards. They set off at about ten in the evening and between them and the sea, the north coast, that is, there was no more than twenty kilometres of largely undefended plain. The intention was that from now onwards Brock would constitute the central point for operations and that the offensive should be developed from there in four different directions, first and foremost to the north, as I said. Other militiamen were advancing to the south-west to cut off the autostrad, at the same time as some units were advancing westwards, along the old road to Oswaldsburg. In the fourth direction, the old road to the Eastern Province's northern sector, we put in the comparatively weakest groups. They were stopped soon after midnight too, by the river, where the Fascists had blown up the bridge and dug themselves in along the banks. Then soon after one o'clock ...

Captain Schmidt: Yes, just go on.

Velder: Soon after one o'clock, a message came from the militia forces on their way northwards from Brock. The officer in command there said that the advance had been delayed by the rain turning to snow and both men and equipment were beginning to suffer from the wet and cold. Half an hour later, the pilot-boat station on the north-eastern point reported sleet and rain and that the temperature had dropped to thirteen degrees. I was the one who received that message. I read it out and when I'd finished, the others stared questioningly at me. It didn't match up with the weather forecasts at all. Stoloff at once set people to work investigating the matter. Gradually we got a vague statement from the meteorologists that a current of cold air had suddenly changed direction and was pressing an area of rain and snow southwards. The change of temperature was probably temporary, they said, and anyhow there was no risk of the weather clearing. There was a strange atmosphere in the operations centre that night. Every hour that went by was decisive, and yet I personally felt quite relaxed, and Ludolf and Stoloff seemed much the same. Not even this question of the weather worried us seriously. At nine in the morning, two important things happened practically simultaneously. First, the Fascists' resistance collapsed totally in the area south and south-west of Ludolfsport. Five kilometres of the autostrad line, that is the stretch between the original break-through position and the sea, were taken and the troops there capitulated. A minute later, a radio message came through from the forward northern groups of the second attack force. 'Have reached the sea. Northern coast road cut off.' This meant that we'd cut Oswald's Army and all the Fascist-occupied part of the country into two. I remember that I lost control and began walking up and down like a madman saying: 'Now we've got them. Now they're in the clamp.' Ludolf took his pipe out of his mouth and said calmly: 'Yes. It looks like it.' Stoloff poked his ear with his pen, which he always did when he was thinking. 'Yes,' he said, 'it really does look like it.' That was all that was said just then. But what we didn't know was ...

Colonel Orbal: I've been listening to all this. It was a tricky morning, I must admit. At ten o'clock, General Oswald personally came to headquarters in Marbella, although it was such bloody awful weather. Both he and General Winckelman were fearfully pessimistic; the western flank in a state of dissolution and a whole Army division cut off and no one knowing a thing. In Oswaldsburg and in other places, the police had become quite hysterical and were shooting people out of hand. They probably thought that every single person was a Bolshevik and was going to desert. But in actual fact things weren't so bad. Just hold on. I said so, too. I threw in reserves to form a front between Oswaldsburg and Brock and held back the élite units as barricade battalions, that old system, you know. If the forward line retreated, then they were shot by their own people from behind. So it paid to make a stand. But the Chief of State wasn't very happy that morning. I remember him standing in front of the map and talking to himself, as he usually did. 'The bastard,' he kept saying, over and over again. I suppose he meant Ludolf.

Major von Peters: Don't sit there chattering, Mateo. Let Velder go on instead. What was it you didn't know?

Velder: We didn't know that the temperature had fallen to below thirty degrees and that snow-storms were raging all along the north coast. The roads and the fields were already impassable. This message came at midday, on the twentieth. Ludolf stared at the telex strip for a whole minute at least. Then he handed it to Stoloff and said one single word. 'Unique.' And it was true, too. We had studied the meteorological statistics of the last fifty years and nothing like it had ever happened during that time.

Colonel Orbal: What the matter with him? Is he crying?

Captain Endicott: I don't think so, sir.

Colonel Pigafetta: Some kind of emotion, clearly.

Colonel Orbal: Looks funny.

Major von Peters: Don't stand there staring, Endicott. Get the man going.

Captain Endicott: Get on with your account, Velder.

Velder: There's nothing else to say. That was the end. Of everything. The snow came down all day, the temperature just fell. Everything went all to hell. First the engines froze up, and then the men. They had no winter equipment. And winter came two months too early. It snowed for three days. Everything seized up; the whole operation was paralysed. Then came the air-raids from bases in Marbella and simultaneously the counter-attack started.

There was nothing wrong with the other side's winter equipment. Men and women on the northern coastal road froze to death at their posts, to no purpose, as on the forth day the Fascists retook the road along the shore and opened communications between the Central and Eastern Provinces. The rest of the second offensive force was stuck in Brock and the area round about. Oswald sent in reserves all the time from the west and as I said, their equipment was better suited to the conditions. The militia south of Brock began to be pushed back from the autostrad. On the night of the fourth day, Stoloff said: 'Gentlemen, Plan B has failed. The time has come to abandon it.' We'd been awake all the time, more or less, keeping upright on pills, like most of the militia in general. I remember that I was in a strange condition, feeling as if I were neither awake nor asleep. There was only one thing left to do; let the second offensive force withdraw from Brock while a retreat route was still passable. This was so obvious that the question didn't even warrant discussion. The fourth was a difficult day, with clear cold air and a good view. The Fascists began to use their Air Force seriously and their artillery hammered us continuously. During the night, militia from Brock retreated and evacuated the area west of the river and north of the autostrad. We managed to hold the retreat route open and disengage some of the units involved in the fighting, but the price was high. Everyone and everything north of Brock was lost. In the last stages, we put in demolition units. All Brock was razed to the ground and all buildings within the area over which we had had control were destroyed. Many prisoners were shot, and other people too, for that matter.

Captain Schmidt: Were you also involved in giving those orders?

Velder: Oh, yes. We often discussed at length whether it hadn't been a foolish thing to do. It created antagonism to us in fact, even among people who were really sympathisers, or at least neutral. But there was no place for neutrals any longer. We didn't need to discuss the retreat from Brock, as I said. But General Ludolf and Colonel Stoloff held different opinions on what we should do about Ludolfsport. Stoloff considered that the most rational thing to do was to withdraw the militia from there, although we had full control of the town and the surrounding area. He said that our powers of resistance would be greater if we returned to the old positions and concentrated all our militia units on the fortress and the outer defence belt. Ludolf, however, wanted the town held, and that's what happened. He had no special motivation. We got a harbour, of course, but now we lacked the means of getting it working, and the blockade also meant that it wasn't any use to us. By this time, the airfield had been made useless by artillery fire and attacks from the air. We did make some use of the four or five serviceable planes we captured there, however. Before they were shot down, they relieved militia groups in Brock and covered some of their retreat. As soon as it was decided that we were to hold the captured area,

Stoloff left headquarters and set off for Ludolfsport to plan its defence and start new fortifications. Then Ludolf and I composed an order of the day, which was sent out that same evening.

Captain Schmidt: A copy of this order has been found and kept. Appendix V XI/15.

Lieutenant Brown: Appendix V XI/15, concerning the disturbances. Order of the day issued on the evening of the twenty-fifth of November by the enemy of the people, Joakim Ludolf. The text is as follows:

The attempt to crush the Fascist régime has failed. The reasons for this are circumstances which lie outside both our own and the enemy's control. During the first stage of the offensive, the Socialist Government Militia liberated Ludolfsport and the surrounding area and all of the east coast, including the lighthouse and the pilot-boat station on the north-eastern point. The town of Ludolfsport and its surroundings will be held and thus included in the fortification system of the southern sector. The village of Brock and parts of the Central Province were also taken. These areas have now been evacuated. The Socialist Government Militia's losses in dead, wounded and missing constitute twelve per cent of its total strength. Losses were overwhelmingly in the groups operating in the Central Province and round the village of Melora in the South-Western Province. These losses cannot for the time being be replaced. Large quantities of materials were lost during the fighting in the Central Province, but more than double this quantity was captured at Ludolfsport. Fascist losses in men are three times as great as our own. No one can be blamed for the fact that a decisive victory was not achieved. During the fighting, every man and woman in the southern sector did his or her best. Ludolf. General. Leader of the Socialist Government Militia.

Velder: When the order had been issued, we talked together for a while. I was very tired and the thought of how extremely close we'd been to victory ground round and round in my head. I remember talking and talking, going through the operation on the map. Ludolf was watching without moving a muscle. Finally he said: 'Yes, it was close.' Then we separated—for the first time for more than five days. Although none of us said so, we knew that our chance had gone for ever. Plan B could be filed away and would never have a successor. The cold wave only lasted for a week, anyhow. Then the temperature rose to fifty degrees, which was normal for the time of year, and the snow vanished. We suffered much from the thawing snow and Stoloff found it difficult to carry out the fortifications round Ludolfsport. He himself always regarded them as provisional anyhow. He used mostly captured Fascists on the work and most of them were killed by their own people in the air-raids.

Captain Schmidt: Were you involved in making that decision, too? To use people, whose liberty you had unlawfully taken, as slave workers?

Velder: Yes. We regarded them as prisoners-of-war.

Commander Kampennmann: What happened then?

Velder: The fighting had given us a pretty good idea of Oswald's dispositions. We knew it would be some time before he took the offensive. Naturally we predicted that he would first strengthen his positions all along the front. He had been considerably shaken and was taking no risks. The only thing we could do was to wait and make ourselves even more inaccessible than we already were. Absurdly enough, the winter was very mild. That was lucky for us, as although our stores were large, they were by no means inexhaustible. We were very isolated during January and February, first and foremost from the outside, as most of our agents had been killed during mopping-up operations by the Army and the police in Oswaldsburg and Marbella in December. From the little we could find out, it was clear that Oswald was stocking up, that large reinforcements were coming in to Marbella, despite the non-intervention agreement. But we were also isolated from each other. Every fort, or defence unit as we called them, lived its own life. This was good from some points of view, for solidarity, for instance, and it was easy to limit epidemics. We avoided deficiency diseases, thanks to our medical stores which were very comprehensive and well run. But everything became abstract in some way, almost ghost-like, to use a silly expression. Our whole existence was hardly an existence at all.

Captain Schmidt: Well, now, only one matter remains to be dealt with, namely the accused's participation in the so-called Plan C. Before Velder's testimony, I will refer to a brief summary of military developments and activities up to the end of March and the beginning of April. Appendix V XII/10. If you wouldn't mind reading it, Lieutenant Brown.

Lieutenant Brown: Appendix V XII/10, concerning the disturbances. Compiled from summaries put together by the National Historical Department of the General Staff. Marked Secret according to paragraphs eight and eighteen. The text is as follows:

After the rebels' desperate sortie at the end of November, which amongst other things gave the terrorists control over the town of Oswaldsport (Ludolfsport) and all of the east coast, General Oswald ordered his Army Staff to plan a mopping-up operation, which in one blow would liberate the country from the Red hydra. On the third of January, it was decided that this operation would come under the personal command of the Chief of State and that it should be started on the twentieth of March. The timing was chosen with consideration of weather conditions; it was reckoned that the spring, with its warm and dry weather, would create favourable circumstances for an operation on a large scale. During January and February, both the National Freedom Army and the Peace Corps were replenished with materials and especially trained storm-troopers. Apart from artillery, the first phase of the action included the largest concentration of air power that had hitherto been used against the guerillas. At 0500 hours on the twentieth of March, the rebels' positions were assailed with rockets and artillery fire, while simultaneously large parts of the southern sector were attacked with napalm bombs.

Captain Schmidt: Thank you, that's enough. We will now return to the accused's part in the so-called Plan C.

Velder: On the morning of the twentieth of March, the Fascists' offensive began. For us, it came as almost a relief. We had been waiting for so long and we no longer had any expectations that anything would change for the better. So it felt in some way as if ... yes, it was liberating when the reports of the first air-raids began to come in. A fortnight earlier, Stoloff had presented a surprising alternative. We had just carried out a thorough check on stores and concluded that it would take Oswald another eight months to starve us out, when Stoloff suddenly looked up from his statistics and said: 'What if we should capitulate.' Ludolf asked: 'When?' And Stoloff said: 'Now, immediately. It would be the most astonishing thing to happen to Oswald in the circumstances. We three and many others would naturally be shot—but he can hardly kill everyone. Then he'd have a considerable Communist minority round his neck. If, on the other hand, he is allowed to complete this mopping-up operation, then it's true he'll lose a lot of men, but on the other hand he'll be in the same favourable position as Franco was after the Spanish Civil War. All useful forces had been killed or had given of their best during the fighting, and it'll be years before the country will have an active Socialist opposition.' Ludolf thought for a moment before he replied: 'It wouldn't work. They'd never accept it.' I asked: 'Who wouldn't accept it?' He looked up at me in surprise and said: 'Everyone here in the southern sector. The party members. The militia. They'd probably remove us the moment we attempted to betray the idea.' And Stoloff said: 'It wouldn't be betraying the idea, but the other way round, but that would be difficult to explain off the cuff. Consequently you're right. Naturally, we'll fight.'

Captain Schmidt: I would like to ask a question here. You used the words party members. A political party existed in the southern sector, then?

Velder: Oh, yes. We all joined. Stoloff functioned as party leader. Well, later on it struck me that this discussion on the possibility of capitulation had nothing to do with the question of saving human lives. It was more a matter of how one could do the greatest possible damage to the enemy.

Captain Schmidt: Let us return to Plan C.

Velder: Plan C had always been Ludolf's baby. It was well prepared from the very beginning. But Plan C did not come into action when the offensive started. The offensive, yes. We at once noticed that Oswald wasn't leaving anything to chance this time. He had six or seven times as many men as we did and was superior in nearly everything, anyhow when it came to materials. On the afternoon of the twenty-first, many observation posts in the outer defence belt reported 'that it looked as if everything was on fire, even concrete blocks and the ground itself,' and in some places we were already having trouble with the ventilation. The storm-troopers attacked systematically, but were in no great hurry. It took them a week to drive the militia out of Ludolfsport and the coastal strip in the east, which we'd taken four months earlier. On the thirtieth, the eleventh day, that is, we had to abandon the outer defence belt completely and withdraw all living personnel to the forts in the fortified lines. The line along the river might possibly have been held for a few days, but we judged that pointless. Then the Fascists worked their way forward to the first fortification chain, but the first permanent support-post did not fall until the seventeenth day, that is, on the fifth of April. That was fort forty-six, up in the north-west, quite near the coast. Stoloff had always considered our weakest point was just there. During the next eight days, they took ten more forts, all in the first fortified chain and most of them along the east coast, where according to the old pattern they took the defence line from the north. Stoloff's support-posts were so constructed that it didn't make any difference from which direction they were attacked. The moment a fort fell, all the connecting passages leading to and from it were automatically blown up. And in the operations centre, we removed a numbered red metal disc from the map. In principle, survivors were to retreat to the nearest intact fort before the stores were destroyed and the tunnels blown up. By the eighteenth of April, they had taken twenty-two support-posts, still in the outer defence belt. But it was slow and the price they paid was high.

Colonel Orbal: Yes, I'll say it was. The whole of that damned bit of country was like an anthill, a conglomeration of caves and mine-workings and underground passages and buried warrens on several levels. And everything you touched exploded. We practically had to dig the rabble out, just like you dig moles out of a lawn.

Commander Kampenmann: A kind of *défense à outrance*, in other words. Reminds me of Iwo Jima. There, thirty-five thousand Japs had ...

Colonel Pigafetta: It would be extremly kind of you if you would hold your lectures on military history somewhere else, Kampenmann. My time is in fact extremely valuable, although no one seems to realise it.

Major von Peters: Bravo, sir. Go on, Velder.

Velder: On the thirty-fourth day, they took support-post twenty-eight in the second fortified chain and the day after that support-post nine, which was in the inner fortification chain. Support-post nine lay less than ten thousand yards west of the central fortress, in other words, headquarters, and there were no permanent defence installations in between. Well, passive ones, of course. This constituted a break-through and technically speaking we were defeated at that moment, despite the fact that the militia still held thirty-two forts out of sixty-five. Things had moved a little more quickly for the Fascists at the end, and a day or two went by before we found out why. Their artillery had begun to use gas shells.

Colonel Orbal: Yes, that was stroke of genius, that was. General Winckelman's idea. And the Air Force were chucking down napalm at the same time. Then it was just a matter of holding out. Well, go on.

Velder: When we discovered what it was all about, we rapidly fixed up relatively serviceable filters, and there were plenty of gas masks. Though it was worse with napalm, really—that stole our oxygen out of the air. On the thirty-fifth day, communications between the defence units began to break up. We could only reach the forts in the west and south-west by radio. On the surface of the ground, everything was on fire. Thirty-two support-posts were still intact, the central fortress plus eleven in the third and innermost chain, fourteen in the second, and six which were still holding on in the first line. Funny.

Major von Peters: Funny? What the hell does he mean?

Velder: I happened to think about number sixty-five still holding on after thirty-five days. Sixty-five lay to the south in the first line. That's where Carla, my younger wife, was. She had taken part in the raid on Melora in November, but was one of those who had come back unscathed. I'd found that out, actually. I thought of writing a letter to her, but I never did.

Major von Peters: What on earth has that got to do with Plan C? You really must pull yourself together, Schmidt, and bring the accused to order.

Velder: At that moment, on the thirty-fifth day, that is the twenty-third of April, General Ludolf brought Plan C into action. It had been sketched out by him and worked on technically by myself and Colonel Stoloff. Briefly, it meant that all openings, tunnels and connecting passages were to be blown up and blocked, and that all communications between the remaining forts were to cease. The militia received just one single order: 'Resistance by all means in all situations.' Originally the words 'to the last man' had been included, but Ludolf struck them out, thinking they were silly and unnecessary. At half-past eleven on the night of the twenty-fourth of March, everything was cut off. After that I don't know what happened outside the central fortress.

Major von Peters: We know. It's enough for a long time.

Captain Schmidt: This so-called Plan C, worked out by Velder on orders from the enemy of the people, Joakim Ludolf, as we all know, led to the murder of thousands of people.

Colonel Orbal: Yes, I'll say it did. They fought like crazy rats. Not least the women, and they're said to have been most dangerous on their backs. Anyone stupid enough to undress and go to bed didn't live for long. Sooner or later one falls asleep.

Captain Schmidt: I consider the accused's participation in this so-called Plan C now proven. With that, the case against Erwin Velder is now complete and I request a break for half an hour before the final summing-up, which from our side, anyhow, will be extremely brief. Then I shall be prepared to hand over the case as a whole for consideration by this extra-ordinary court martial.

Colonel Orbal: Oh, so you've finished now. Good.

Commander Kampenmann: What happened after the twenty-third of April, Velder? How and when were you taken prisoner?

Major von Peters: For Christ's sake, Kampenmann. Haven't you had enough? It's almost over now.

Lieutenant Bratianu: I protest. The question is irrelevant. It has nothing to do with the case. The case for the prosecution is not concerned with crimes that Corporal Velder committed after the twenty-third of April.

Commander Kampenmann: I asked the accused a question and am waiting for it to be answered.

Colonal Orbal: But in heaven's name, Kampenmann, why?

Major von Peters: You've done nothing but interfere and be awkward all through the session, Kampenmann. You and Schmidt have lengthened the whole thing with your dilly-dallying and pointless comments.

Lieutenant Bratianu: I adhere to my protest.

Commander Kampenmann: One moment, gentlemen. I have asked the accused a question and as I said, I am waiting for it to be answered. To you, Lieutenant Bratianu, I would first like to say that if you had read the court martial regulations—which you previously made a great show of being an expert on—then you would also realise that you are in rough waters with your protests. You are right to protest to the presidium over the questions put by the representative of the defence, in this case Captain Endicott. What the presidium asks is a matter with which you have no right to interfere. Secondly, you have no right to speak at all as long as the Prosecuting Officer, in this case Captain Schmidt, has not handed over to you. In quite general terms, I should like to point out, still strictly according to the regulations, that neither the President nor the other members of the court, and naturally least of all the parties has the right to object to the formulation of any question which a representative of the defence forces, in this case myself, wishes to ask.

Colonel Orbal: Oh, God, now you've got him worked up, Carl. Now it'll never come to an end.

Colonel Pigafetta: Although I am reluctant to admit it, you are in fact right, Kampenmann. I have also read the regulations.

Commander Kampenmann: May I now have an answer to my question? Velder, what happened as far as you were concerned from and including the night of the twenty-third of April to and including the evening of the eighth of May, when according to information, you were taken to the military hospital?

Velder: As I said, we were quite isolated. So I only know what happened in the central fortress. There we did the only thing we could do, and that was to wait. All defence measures had already been taken. From certain points of view, the central fortress was more difficult to hold than some of the other forts, as in its capacity as headquarters, it was not just constructed as a defence post. On the other hand, the units there were especially well trained. During the first week, the silence was the most remarkable thing. Then we heard the fighting coming closer, like distant thunder. We also began to feel the vibrations in the ground. Explosions of different kinds, of course. That was the situation on the forty-third day. We celebrated the first of May then, for the second year running.

Major von Peters: Is there no limit to this madness? Celebrated the first of May?

Velder: Yes. Stoloff made a statement. On the third of May, we made contact with the enemy for the first time. The day after that, the Fascists blasted their way into the western sector. They were thrown back, but the next day we had to leave the western section, which was devastated. We were having great difficulties with ventilation. Despite all the filters and complicated air-spaces, the fans sucked in quantities of smoke and gas. During the following days, the sixth and seventh of May, the attacks were reinforced. The storm-troopers blasted their way in bit by bit, then attacked through the breaks with flame-throwers and grenades. By the morning of the eighth, only one of our three lighting systems was working and we realised our prospects of surviving that day, which was the fiftieth, were not particularly great. Everything went quite quickly at the end. At nine o'clock, it seemed as if most of the militia in our sector had been killed. Ludolf, Stoloff, myself and an orderly were in the operations room, which was the best protected. We were armed with machine-pistols and Stoloff was just hooking hand-grenades into his belt. Ludolf and I were standing about five yards away from him, near the map wall. I know I looked at the clock and saw that it was ten minutes past nine. There was an awful lot of smoke in the room and it was hard to breathe. At that moment a grenade exploded, presumably in the air space above us, however it had got through to there. I can't have lost consciousness at once, because I know I saw Stoloff fall.

Commander Kampenmann: Yes, go on.

Velder: When I came round, it was quite light in the bunker. Later I realised that it was daylight seeping in through the roof, and that the floors above had been blown away. Stoloff was dead. He had had his head practically torn off by a stick of explosive and his body was lying on the concrete floor about five yards away from me. Several soldiers in gas masks and asbestos suits were in there too. The wound in my neck was hurting badly and I lay still. But I think I saw Ludolf moving. After a few minutes, I realised that the soldiers were waiting for something and after a short while a tall officer in Army uniform did indeed come into the room. He looked at me and the general and said: 'These two are alive. Get them up.' Now I remember too that it was quiet everywhere, so all resistance in the central fortress must have ceased. The next time I woke up,

I was lying on a blanket on the ground, alongside some kind of tracked jeep. That was the first time for a long time that I had had fresh air in my lungs and I came to quite quickly. Ludolf was standing by the jeep in his dirty khaki uniform, his hands on his hips. Three storm-infantrymen in Peace Corps uniform were standing with their machine-guns cocked. Someone had put a dressing on the wound on my neck. After perhaps a quarter of an hour, that tall officer came back. He was a captain and had a narrow black moustache. I don't know what his name was.

Major von Peters: Captain da Zara.

Colonel Orbal: That's right, da Zara.

Velder: He was very friendly and had an elegant manner. He helped me to my feet and into the back seat of the jeep. 'I'll take these two gentlemen to headquarters,' he said. Ludolf was made to sit beside me in the back seat. The officer sat beside the driver. A soldier was standing on the back bumper, as guard, I presume. We drove along a twisting uneven road which had apparently been cleared through the minefield. Far away, we could hear occasional explosions, so I presume that some support-posts were still holding. It took two hours to get to the old road between Ludolfsport and Oswaldsburg. It was hot and I looked at my watch, which was still going, strangely enough, and I saw that it was two o'clock. No one in the jeep said a word. At about three we passed Brock. They had repaired the road but the village lay in complete ruins. Ludolf looked about him indifferently. Then we swung southwards, crossed the autostrad and continued along the main road to Marbella. In some way, it was as if the country had changed character and you didn't recognise where you were. There weren't many soldiers on the road, but we met a number of police patrols and lots of gendarmes cycling in pairs. We drove past a lot of low grey metal barracks, which looked like some kind of emergency housing, and smoke-blackened workshops. Near Marbella, we passed a large area which appeared to consist of marked-out allotments. It was a fine day, as I said, and lots of people were standing there, poking about in their potato patches, or whatever they were. Ludolf looked at me at that moment and frowned slightly. I remember exactly what he looked like, red-eyed, deathly pale, with lumps of pus on his eyelashes. Like myself, he found it difficult to see and was peering in the light. We never got to Marbella, because the jeep swung down a side-road to the right just outside the town and ten minutes later we reached headquarters. It was a row of low grey ...

Major von Peters: Yes, yes, yes. Even Kampenmann knows what headquarters looked like.

Velder: The officer showed us into a bare room where there was nothing but a table and two chairs. He was still very friendly. Then he left, leaving two guards on the door. We sat on the chairs and said nothing. A quarter of an hour later, the officer came back. He looked in a troubled way from one to the other of us, then turned to Ludolf and said courteously: 'You're to be executed shortly. Do you want to express a last wish?' Ludolf said at once: 'I want to see Oswald.' The officer was somewhat taken aback and said: 'The Chief of State? General Oswald? That's out of the question, of course.' Ludolf said: 'A little whisky, please.' The officer said: 'Unfortunately spirits have been strictly forbidden in the country for over a year.' Ludolf shrugged his shoulders and said: 'Then give me a cigarette.' The officer said: 'Of course.' He took out his case at once and politely offered it. Then he lit the cigarette. Ludolf puffed at it twice, looked at the cigarette and then threw it away. I know why. We'd quite simply got used to not smoking and found it unpleasant. The officer was sitting perched on the edge of the table, swinging one leg back and forth, as if he were troubled and didn't know what to say, or as if he were waiting for someone. He was wearing shiny black leather boots. After a while, the door opened and a soldier in linen uniform and low black shoes came in. He pointed at me with his pistol and said: 'Follow me.' I glanced at Ludolf, but he was looking in another direction at that moment. The guard walked behind me, across a yard and into another building. It appeared to be a back way. There was a corridor with several doors. He opened one of them and pushed me inside. Then he followed me in and stood with his back to the door, his pistol cocked.

Commander Kampenmann: Well? What happened?

Velder: Oswald was in there. The room was obviously his private office and was very large. The steel blinds were down so it was rather murky. Oswald was wearing a general's uniform, but he'd unbuttoned his shirt and loosened his tie. His boots were standing by

266

the door and he was padding back and forth in his stockinged feet. His false teeth were in a glass on the desk. When I came in, he stopped and looked at me. 'Good-day, Erwin,' he said. 'Hi,' I said. 'Where's Edner and what's he thinking of doing?' he said. 'I don't know,' I said. 'You're lying,' he said. 'Of course you know.' I said: 'No, I don't.' Then he gave me a long look and said: 'That's a pity, Erwin. Otherwise I'd have been able to offer you a swift and relatively painless end. Like this. Look.' He went over to the window and beckoned me to follow. Then he manipulated the blinds a little so that you could see through the slats. They had led Ludolf out into the yard in front of the building and placed him against a heap of sandbags only ten or fifteen yards from the window. He was standing quite still, looking tired more than anything else. The tall officer set up the execution squad and ordered them to fire. The salvo struck low and it almost looked as if Ludolf were still alive when the officer bent over him and shot him through the head with his pistol. Oswald took two steps into the room and stood there with his head lowered, as he usually did when there was something special occupying his thoughts. I heard him say to himself: 'That's one of them. But the other bastard's alive. What the hell is he thinking of doing?' He repeated the last sentence several times. Then he made an impatient gesture towards me and said to the guard: 'Take him away.' I was very weak by then, from loss of blood, I imagine, and they took me straight to the military hospital.

Major von Peters: Are you satisfied now, Kampenmann? Do you think the Chief of State will be pleased to hear that you've let a murderer and deserter stand and shout out all those lies about him?

Colonel Orbal: Ach, do we have to have that summing-up today? It'll soon be dark.

Colonel Pigafetta: They say it'll soon be got through. And I also heard from Justice Haller that the Chief of State is expecting it to be done today.

Colonel Orbal: O.K. Let's go up and have a beer, shall we? The session is adjourned for thirty minutes.

*   *   *

Colonel Orbal: And Pigafetta's late as usual. Peculiar person.

Commander Kampenmann: By the way, how long did the remaining forts hold out?

Major von Peters: We blew the last one up on the seventeenth of May, if I remember rightly. Anyhow, why did you insist on hearing all that about Ludolf's execution?

Commander Kampenmann: I didn't in fact know about it.

Colonel Orbal: You're so fearfully inquisitive, Kampenmann. That's dangerous. And you're soft. That's dangerous, too. Watch yourself.

Major von Peters: Here's Pigafetta. And he's got Haller with him.

Tadeusz Haller: I'm sorry I haven't been able to come until now. But I hear that the session has advanced swiftly. The Chief of State seemed quite satisfied when I spoke to him.

Colonel Orbal: Though it'll be late today. And the air in here is worse than ever.

Tadeusz Haller: It shouldn't need to be lengthy. I've spoken to the parties and instructed them to make their final summings-up as lucid as possible.

Major von Peters: Good. Call in the parties, Brown.

Lieutenant Brown: Is this extra-ordinary court martial prepared to proceed to the parties' final summing-up in the case of the Armed Forces versus Erwin Velder?

Colonel Orbal: Of course, Brown. Why do you ask that?

Captain Schmidt: I request to be allowed to hand over to the Assistant Prosecuting Officer, Lieutenant Mihail Bratianu.

Major von Peters: Oh, so you're doing the final summing-up, Bratianu. Excellent. Go ahead.

Lieutenant Bratianu: Would you mind pushing the accused forward, Captain Endicott. And turn him so that I can look him straight in the eye. That's right. Thank you.

Colonel Orbal: Just don't go on for too long, Bratianu.

Lieutenant Bratianu: I shall be quite brief, sir. Mr President, members of the presidium, honoured court martial! To use a mild expression, I should like to say that the person we see before us is the most odious criminal that has ever been before any court in this country. There is nothing to say in his defence. For even if a perverted régime created the circumstances which facilitated and occasionally directly invited criminal activities, Erwin Velder is in himself a monster of depravity and distorted thinking. In the preliminary investigation, and during the proceedings of this extraordinary court martial, it has been described in detail how during the last decade of his life, the accused sank deeper and deeper into the slough of immorality and crime. As we see him now before us here—scarcely human—through his own person he constitutes a living proof not only of his own guilt but also of how far an individual can sink into the slough I have just mentioned. Erwin Velder's crimes are so terrible that they cannot be expiated, anyhow not by death, nor by any other form of punishment that I know of. That Velder might be made into an object for correction to some extent, I find absolutely out of the question. But undeniably there is a possibility, and even a person of such deficient moral quality as he could have been channelled into another way of life—if from the beginning of his criminal activities he had become the object of social care. It is from this aspect that the verdicts against Velder are of interest. By their precedential character, they will form the basis for legislation which is not only intended to protect and help our nation and to maintain its dignity and independence, but will also in future offer us the opportunity at an early stage, perhaps as early as during youth, to correct people with criminal tendencies. Therefore in the name of this court martial and of the whole nation, I demand that for every one of the one hundred and twenty-eight crimes he has been accused of, Velder shall be considered liable for irrevocable punishment. The accused has beyond all doubt been proved guilty not only of the one hundred and twenty-six crimes he has pleaded guilty to, but also in both cases in which even before this court martial he has been presumptuous enough to deny criminality, namely the question of bigamy and cowardice in face of the enemy.

The sentences pronounced and the verdicts cited are thus of vital interest to the future of the nation. On the other hand, the accused personally is of no interest whatsoever. Nevertheless, the question must be asked, *pro forma*: What shall the armed forces and the nation do with Erwin Velder?

Nowadays we have the advantage of living in a well-ordered country in which the security and welfare of our citizens rest on the three fundamental concepts of religion, morality and dignity. Another corner-stone in this our society, created by the Chief of State, General Paul Oswald, is humanity and respect for human rights. Despite the fact that Velder as a being has long stood below that of swine, despite his horrible crimes and animal behaviour patterns, we should in accordance with our accepted norms treat him with a certain leniency. For that is what our way of life teaches us. Therefore I submit quite simply that Corporal Erwin Velder be stripped of his national citizenship and his military rank, be dismissed from the Army and declared to have forfeited any right to his military distinctions. And that after that he be executed.

Lieutenant Brown: We have heard the final summing-up from the Prosecuting Officer. I now hand over to the Defending Officer.

Captain Endicott: Honoured presidium. In my capacity as the Defending Officer of Velder, I consider it my duty to request a lenient sentence.

Colonel Orbal: What? Is that all?

Captain Endicott: Yes, sir.

Major von Peters: Bravo, Endicott. That was the best thing you've done during this whole session.

Colonel Orbal: Uhuh, then that would be all for today.

Tadeusz Haller: For technical reasons, I find it appropriate that the session is adjourned until next Tuesday. Then the work of the Joint Commission will be completed, which gives this court martial the opportunity of pronouncing judgement and then closing the case.

Colonel Orbal: Oh, yes. That gives us a long weekend, too. The session is adjourned until Tuesday the twentieth of April at eleven o'clock.

270

Sixteenth Day

Lieutenant Brown: Those present: Colonel Mateo Orbal, Army, also Chairman of the Presidium of this Extra-ordinary Court Martial; Major Carl von Peters, Army, and Commander Arnold Kampenmann, Navy. The officer presenting the case is Lieutenant Arie Brown, Air Force. Colonel Nicola Pigafetta has reported that he will be a few minutes late and Justice Tadeusz Haller is on his way here from the Ministry of Justice. The accused has been told to wait in the hall with Roger ... I beg your pardon, Captain Roger Endicott, Air Force, and Captain Wilfred Schmidt, Navy.

Major von Peters: Pigafetta must be pretty long in the face today. It's been widely rumoured that Bloch's appointment is fixed and down on paper.

Colonel Orbal: Yes, I heard that too. Doesn't make much difference. Numbskull or numbskull.

Major von Peters: It must make a difference to Pigafetta. Here's Haller, anyhow.

Colonel Orbal: What's that colossal tome?

Tadeusz Haller: The fruits of the labours of this extra-ordinary court martial, gentlemen. Verdicts and sentences in the case against Velder.

Colonel Orbal: For God's sake, you're not going to make us read all that, are you?

Major von Peters: Or have Brown read it out? I won't agree to that.

Tadeusz Haller: Oh, that probably won't be necessary. Here is a stencilled summary of the actual judgements. It should suffice as a basis for discussion at the internal deliberations. Would you please hand these round, Lieutenant Brown.

Major von Peters: Ah, look, here's Pigafetta. Good morning, Commander-in-Chief of the Air Force. How are you today?

Colonel Pigafetta: Excellent, thank you. I apologise for the delay.

Tadeusz Haller: Is everyone here? Then perhaps we can take a look at this for a few minutes. Before the private deliberations begin, I must return to the chancery.

Colonel Pigafetta: I didn't see Lieutenant Bratianu in the hall. Isn't he going to be present when judgement is pronounced?

Major von Peters: No, we'll have to make do with Schmidt. Bratianu has had a posting.

Colonel Pigafetta: Where to?

Major von Peters: I don't know. Why are you so interested in Bratianu all of a sudden?

Colonel Pigafetta: Oh, no special reason. I just wondered.

Colonel Orbal: This looks good. Nicely and neatly set out.

Tadeusz Haller: Well, as you can see from the summary you have before you, the Joint Commission from the Ministry of Justice and the Judicial Department of the General Staff recommend the following: first are ten different crimes, namely high treason, desertion, cowardice in face of the enemy, participation in rebellion, murder, accessory to murder, terrorism, sabotage, mass murder and subversive activities. For these Velder is sentenced, according to military law, in each case to execution by firing-squad, with no right of appeal elsewhere. For four of these crimes, which may become subject to civilian court proceedings as well, he is sentenced to death by hanging, with the right to appeal to the High Court. In that event, the judgement is confirmed even where he has the opportunity of appealing for mercy from the Chief of State.

Colonel Orbal: I'm afraid I'm not really with you yet.

Tadeusz Haller: That doesn't really matter. Let us continue.

Colonel Orbal: Not so much hurry. If he's first shot and then hanged, how the hell can he then ...

Colonel Pigafetta: We can talk about that later, Orbal.

Colonel Orbal: What a scramble!

Tadeusz Haller: Thirty-four crimes ranged under twelve different headings are referred to in the category of disciplinary offences and may be subject to court martial proceedings. Here terms of imprisonment of varying lengths are recommended. The shortest is fourteen days for indiscretion on duty and the longest five years for dereliction of duty. You will see the detailed summary on page two.

Colonel Pigafetta: Yes, that's fine.

Tadeusz Haller: Then we have thirty-two more crimes gathered under ten different headings, which may be subject to both military and civil judgement. These concern, for instance, fornication, drunkenness, theft, carelessness and abuse of rank. Imprisonment is also recommended here, imprisonment in military or civil prison, i.e. hard labour. The length of sentence in the different cases varies from one week to six months. Right?

Colonel Pigafetta: Yes, go on.

Tadeusz Haller: In the next group, ten specified crimes of the blasphemy and atheism type should also incur imprisonment, the Commission thinks. The shortest sentence is a month's imprisonment for blasphemy and the longest three years for spreading heresy. The corresponding sentences apply to military administration of law, though here too the court martial shall sentence to imprisonment instead of hard labour. Generally, of course, criminals sentenced to longer terms of imprisonment are handed over to civil authorities, at which military imprisonment is changed to civil.

Colonel Pigafetta: We understand.

Colonel Orbal: Do we?

Tadeusz Haller: Further, it is suggested that Velder is sentenced to life imprisonment for illegal intelligence activities, ten years for bigamy, and ten years for Communism, and eight years for furthering the flight from the country of enemies of the people. Shorter sentences are recommended for a number of other charges, for instance, three months for criminal promiscuity and fourteen days for incitement. As you will see on page three, sexual offences are set up in a number of different special cases. There, three months is meted out for oral intercourse, four months for fornication in a public place and so on.

Major von Peters: Why do you keep looking at your watch, Pigafetta?

Colonel Orbal: Perhaps it's stopped.

Tadeusz Haller: To summarise, it can be said that Velder has been found guilty of one hundred and twenty-seven of the prosecution's one hundred and twenty-eight charges. The case was extended

273

by one charge during the session, by Lieutenant Bratianu. On one charge, he has been found not guilty. That is charge number one hundred and two, that of rape. The case for the prosecution here has not been approved and has been struck from the record.

Commander Kampenmann: Why?

Tadeusz Haller: Velder was at that particular moment still a corporal in the National Freedom Army and the person he is said to have raped belonged to the revolutionary guerilla forces. Field service conditions prevailed, and a soldier cannot possibly be blamed for taking similar measures, especially when the same action at a later stage of the disturbances is in fact recommended as a military means of correction of Communist guerilla members of the female sex. Yes, that's what it says.

Colonel Orbal: My God, how confusing it all seems.

Tadeusz Haller: Not at all. Naturally, I suggest that the presidium follows the recommendations of the Joint Commission. The statement can be put like this:

This extra-ordinary court martial hereby sentences Corporal Erwin Velder to death. Further, the same Velder forfeits his rank and his national citizenship. He is dismissed from the armed forces and forfeits his right to decorations.

Sentence: The accused has been found guilty of the crimes he has been accused of, except charge number one hundred and two, concerning rape. The sentence will be carried out within twenty-four hours by firing squad, without military honours. Here is the draft.

Colonel Orbal: Uhuh. That's good.

Tadeusz Haller: Unfortunately I must return at once to the Ministry. Good-day, gentlemen.

Colonel Orbal: He was in a hell of a hurry.

Lieutenant Brown: Can the internal part of the proceedings now be considered concluded?

Major von Peters: Yes, there's nothing much to discuss. You can call in ...

Commander Kampenmann: One moment. I consider that a good deal can and should be discussed. I consider all this doubtful, the whole proceedings, and not least the sentences that have been suggested. We mustn't forget that in matters of verdicts and sentences this concerns recommendations which we are quite within our rights

274

to change or reject. Anyhow it is our duty to study the material with the greatest care.

Colonel Orbal: But, my dear Kampenmann ...

Commander Kampenmann: A number of points are, in my view, utterly absurd. Look at this, for instance. Velder is sentenced to imprisonment because he has had intimate relations with his own wife, but is found not guilty when he knocks a woman unconscious and rapes her. A number of offences should fall under statute of limitation. I'm not at all certain that Velder should be executed at all. At this stage, the man is an invalid and practically a mental case. And also his defence has been appallingly carried out. That summing-up yesterday was scandalous and ...

Colonel Pigafetta: Captain Endicott dealt with it strictly according to his instructions.

Commander Kampenmann: Under any circumstances, I wish to have time to ...

Major von Peters: Put a stop to this now, Mateo.

Colonel Orbal: One moment, Kampenmann, don't overdo it now. Let's vote on the matter. Personally I'm inclined to accept these recommendations without any more talk, to confirm the sentences, or whatever it's called. What do you say, Carl?

Major von Peters: Yes, naturally.

Colonel Orbal: And you, Pigafetta?

Colonel Pigafetta: As the Chairman of the Presidium has the casting vote in the event of equal numbers, it doesn't really matter what I say. I abstain.

Colonel Orbal: And Kampenmann reserves judgement?

Commander Kampenmann: Yes, unquestionably. And ...

Major von Peters: That makes two votes to one and one abstention. The matter's clear.

Commander Kampenmann: I demand that my reservation is put on record.

Colonel Orbal: That can probably be done. What's all that noise, anyhow? What kind of idiot is it ringing in the middle of a session?

Colonel Pigafetta: One moment, it's probably for me ... Yes, this is Colonel Pigafetta ... yes ... I see ... excellent, Niblack ... I'm sorry, gentlemen, it was an urgent matter.

Major von Peters: Huh.

Lieutenant Brown: Is the extra-ordinary court martial prepared to proceed to the open section of the session?

Colonel Orbal: Oh, yes. Call in the parties.

Lieutenant Brown: Will the parties please take their places.

Colonel Orbal: Dreadfully close and awful day. It's thundering too.

Major von Peters: Is that meant to be the general public? What the hell do your men mean by blundering in in that way, Pigafetta, with their arms, too?

Colonel Pigafetta: That isn't thunder you can hear, Orbal. That's the Air Force bombing the Chief of State's palace. Three minutes early, incidentally.

Colonel Orbal: What? What?

Major von Peters: What the hell's going on, anyhow? Has General Winckelman ...

Colonel Pigafetta: General Winckelman was arrested ten minutes ago. The government buildings are surrounded and all Army units have orders to stay in their positions.

Colonel Orbal: Have you gone out of your mind, Pigafetta? Take this madman pointing that thing at me away.

Colonel Pigafetta: Until further notice, you are under arrest, gentlemen. Endicott, take care of Colonel Orbal and Major von Peters. Brown, get the rest of the guard to clear the place. That's it. Kampenmann and Schmidt, would you mind staying in your places. Answer the 'phone, Brown.

Lieutenant Brown: Yes, sir. This is Lieutenant Brown ... yes ... the colonel is here ... one moment ...

Colonel Pigafetta: Oh, yes. Really ... excellent ... I'll be there in about fifteen minutes.

Commander Kampenmann: What really has happened?

Colonel Pigafetta: General Oswald is in all probability dead. That was Justice Haller on the 'phone. He sent his regards, by the way.

Commander Kampenmann: Then you and Haller ...

Colonel Pigafetta: Yes. We must have order in the country. Justice Haller has taken over the post as Prime Minister. He's forming a government this afternoon.

Commander Kampenmann: And the new Chief of State is called General Pigafetta then?

Colonel Pigafetta: I am not vain. For you two, the situation at the moment is just a trifle sensitive, if I may put it that way. Negotiations are now in progress with the Commander-in-Chief of the Navy, who is at the chancery. Presumably they will come to some agreement. As you will understand, I have no wish to sink the only frigates and minesweepers we possess. But until agreement with the admiral is clear, I must ask you to stay here in this room.

Commander Kampenmann: I understand.

Colonel Pigafetta: Excellent. Otherwise I agree with you entirely on your protests against the treatment of Velder. At least, on some points.

Lieutenant Brown: Excuse me, sir. What shall I do with the accused.

Colonel Pigafetta: Take him down into the basement and shoot him.

Velder: Thank you, sir.

Colonel Pigafetta: I must leave now, gentlemen. Naturally, there's a guard in the hall and the telephone is connected to the exchange at Air Force Staff Headquarters. But we must hope that you won't have to stay here for more than half an hour or so. Good-day to you.

*   *   *

Commander Kampenmann: Did he really say thank you?

Captain Schmidt: I think so. Of course, he hears very badly. Perhaps he heard his name mentioned, but misunderstood what he said.

Commander Kampenmann: Why did you let Bratianu do the final summing-up?

Captain Schmidt: To some extent to protect my ... well, let's say that my view of the case was to some extent changed during the course of the session.

Commander Kampenmann: How did you come to be in the forces at all?

Captain Schmidt: Well, my father was a naval officer ... it just happened, really. And you?

Commander Kampenmann: I don't know, really. Perhaps because I like the sea. On the other hand, there are merchant ships.

Captain Schmidt: The tape-recorder is still switched on.

Commander Kampenmann: Better switch it off.